The Jasmine Garden

To Odette,

Best Wishes always;
June, 2006

Soraya Erian

For Mohammed

The Jasmine Garden

a novel by
Soraya Erian

Borealis Press
Ottawa, Canada
2005

Canada

*The Publishers gratefully acknowledge the financial assistance of the
Government of Canada through the Book Publishing Industry Development
Program (BPIDP) for our publishing activities.*

National Library of Canada Cataloguing in Publication Data

Erian, Soraya, 1936-
    The jasmine garden / Soraya Erian.

ISBN 0-88887-301-8

I. Title.

PS8559.R53J38 2005   C811'.54   C2005-904525-6

Paintings by Soraya Erian.
Cover design by Bull's Eye Design, Ottawa.

Printed and bound in Canada on acid free paper.

Memory is the servant of imagination,
which decks itself in a silken garb and seduces the mind
to believe in a past that never was.

Contents

Chapter One
Jasmine

White jasmine[1] hung like pearls from tendrils of green leaves, its buds hidden, waiting to burst into petals. The climber would offer its flowers to the morning air until October, sometimes as late as November. Nadia stepped out onto her porch into the sunlight: seven in the morning and the buds enveloped her with their haunting fragrance. The vine spread out on her left around their bedroom window, a few of its white flowers more delicate than the luscious gardenia forming a carpet on the ground. Their fragrance reminded her of the In Love essence Yasser bought her in England on their way to Canada, and evoked her persistent dream.

She is wearing a necklace of these flowers in her search dream. They are filling her with a sultry wildness that matches the tempestuousness of the Mediterranean Sea. Mist fills the air. Yasser's taking her for a walk . . . in Alexandria? Ras-El-Bar? They are standing on high rocks. Under their feet, slippery weeds. Yasser slips. Salt spray is splashing her, hitting the air, filling it with mist, she is saying, "The waves are too high!" but before she utters a sound, water covers her ankles. "Yasser!" her voice rolls out, "Yasser! Where are you?" Distant echoes of screams are muffled in mist, she submerged in a water vortex. She is reaching out to the father of her sons: "Yasser!" Big fish swim between them, their eyes dark olives swishing in brine. Yasser floats past her in a shoal of cat fish as large as whales. Her fingers touch his hair. It's sea-weed. He doesn't swim, dear God, "Yasser!" salt water chokes her. Bubbles

---

1 The glossary at the end of the novel provides a chapter by chapter explanation/definition of the flora and fauna of Egypt, Arabic words and phrases, places and their location in the country, references to contemporary and ancient Egyptian names, legends and myths.

1

burst from her mouth. He is floating, she swirling, her eyes dim in opaque water. She has to take him out to shore. Home! She battles waves, gets entangled in her own hair, swallows salt water, pushes away algae, but algae is in her hair, algae is her hair, it is floating before her blurry eyes, she cannot see him. Bubbles push out of her mouth. He and she are going home. She wriggles, among fish, and plants. Their young sons are alone on shore. "Yasser, stretch your arm to me, let me know you're there . . . !"

Nadia had this dream a few years after she and Yasser were married, the earliest search dream she could remember in a long string of others which had begun after she had given birth to her second son, Samy, in Toronto. Twenty-one years ago, and the disturbing dream remained with her. She hurried down the garden steps onto the dusty path to the front entrance and up the stairs to her mailbox. Empty.

Before she left Toronto for Cairo in July, her younger son, Samy, teased her, "Mother and jasmine, they're inseparable! You're going to Egypt, Mother, to grow jasmine, and you're leaving your gardenias behind. Who's going to look after them?" Half in earnest, half in fun, he was volunteering to water her plants: Samy, shoulders curved, carrying an invisible sky, eyes tinged with mockery.

No letters from Yasser, nothing from her older son, Amir. After months of waiting, she had forgotten to check the mailbox. Yasser had not arrived at the Delta Barrage six months ago as he had promised her, nor had he answered her letters. Under the acacia in the back garden, chickens pecked at her feet; this meant their tray was empty. She sprinkled a handful of seeds on the ground, in their metal-mesh coop, filled their tray, picked up the hose and replenished their water trough. "Don't forget to feed the chickens, Nadia. Make sure their coop is full of seed," Yasser had told her when he helped her open the house a year ago. Rearing chickens was Yasser's way of resurrecting his parents' domicile which had housed chicken, turkeys, pigeons and, in the early morning, the aroma of fresh pita bread his mother baked in her earthen oven.

I've fed your chickens, Yasser, watered the trees, nurtured the vine, bought your favourite Egyptian cotton bed-sheets which iron like cool silk. Remember Luxor, our bodies between silken sheets at the Hilton, how many years ago, fifteen? The months are passing, the palms are heavy with dates, now a bright red, and you're still in Toronto. A year ago in September, she and he were walking in this garden, red light falling on palms fringing the white stone fence. Dusk. The wiry eighty-six-year-old owner—in white *gallabiah* striped with threads shining silvery in the afternoon sun, toes curled in the wet soil, hair a fragile sheen—was hosing down the plants and telling them of his grandfather's purchase of the land. Nadia fell in love with the old man, his reverence for the soil, his lingering touch on tree and shrub, his gentleness with his senile wife whom he bathed and fed, his impish smile, his land. His garden enveloped them with its soft greenery and red dates. "Come," he was saying in a conspiring voice, "Come over here, I have something to show you," his veined hand beckoning them to the edge of the property. The autumn sun hung low, its crimson circled with faint purple peering from behind the palms. "This is where I have spent my evenings, eighty-six years of them," he said, fingers trembling towards the darkening palms. He and his home were wrapped in watermelon gauze against the dusk sky. She could not wait for the dates to turn a sugary brown, their dark sweetness gliding on her tongue. Yellow guava smooth, mango trees still green, prickly cactus, and Yasser reaching for a pear, peeling it with his pen-knife, slicing its white flesh, giving it to Nadia. "Sweeter than ripe mango," he had said. By agreeing to buy this house, he was renewing his promise of love to her.

He had not come. He had said he would be in Egypt in March; it was August. This was to have been their home for three years. He had to get here before the first year and its summer were over. Nadia's hands swept twigs under trees, piled dried leaves into mounds, her fingers moving fast, digging deep into the soil, lingering in the soft mud to destroy each second of time, lest she notice its slouchiness. Cramming chores into the day, she worked hard so she could meet the setting sun with equanimity. Yasser, you and I decided to come here to make a fresh start, to search for our roots, remember? She could hear him say, "Of course I do. Have I ever let you down? I'll be there." His sense of time was fluid, not sharp-edged like hers, each moment a tip of shattered glass.

One hour north of Cairo, where her mother and relatives lived, her sun-drenched Delta home stood: square, with large windows, open shutters, its balconies sitting on the ground as she had imagined it in Canada. Its white walls imitated light when the closed shutters kept out the noon heat. In her first few months in this garden, she had become attached to her baby chickens, white, dappled-grey, their canary yellow feet imprinting three-way designs in the dust. And when her gardener, Nessim—his *gallabiah* tied around his waist, the lower edge of his white *serwal* underclothing down to his ankles— came with his sharpened knife and chased one of the chickens to the white fence then slaughtered it, Nadia had cried and rushed indoors to avoid the stench of blood that had spurted over his *serwal* and bare toes. Three months had passed before she could overcome her sense of dread at the ritual, but she had accepted the cycle of hatching, feeding, growing, the killing, and had become accustomed to Nessim bringing her poultry into the kitchen, slicing its throat and siphoning its blood into the sink. He had reminded her that everything moved in cycles, the small overcome by the big and powerful, as long as the killing was necessary and no violence or waste practised, it was all right. She had learned to spare a moth and not cringe at the slaughter of chickens. Yet she could not handle the knife, nor stand where Nessim performed his act, her brand of cowardice, for had she accepted the ritual she would have performed it herself, but her excuse was, the hand that feeds should not be the one that executes. Yasser had not cringed from the slaughter, for soon after they emigrated to Canada, he had helped one of his friends chase a lamb on a farm, kill and barbeque it on a spit, and when she had cried at the spectacle, his answer was, "Everything in nature feeds on the weaker; even plants are parasites! It's a cycle. Why do you want to disrupt it?"—his way of accepting. She missed his easy comfort with life's stark moments, his minutes vivid shots or points in time, he would say, giving life meaning, *her* seconds racing meteors shooting into a violet sky. He teased her, for what he called her "cringing from life's necessities!" and Samy, now twenty-two, cajoled her, "Mother, you're most at ease when you're splashing colour on canvas, not in the dark alleys of humanity!" Yet Samy liked her paintings because they burst with life; she knew he liked motion and her paintings vibrated with tension.

Yet she could not paint the slaughtered chickens nor the lambs swaying from wire hooks in butchers' shops, their blood dripping onto the ground, nor did she dare portray them in colour. She had created joy and sorrow on people's faces, in watercolours that illumined paper. Human suffering, confusion, joy she was good at: night blues, olive greens, mauves, but she could not record the bloodied flesh of animals, nor the twisted necks of chickens. In Toronto, Yasser bought meat wrapped in cellophane, and now, she suspected, he would not be able to slaughter a lamb. She could not decide whether this change was for the better or was a form of hypocrisy they practised to cushion themselves against life's shadows. She watched her chickens drink, fourteen pairs of golden feet and white feathers, a few speckled beige and brown. She would watercolour their fluidity under the shade of palm, but she could not bring herself to paint them hanging from a branch, their blood dripping on mud, while her gardener cleaned their feathers.

For eleven months here by the Nile, she had waited for Yasser. Sometimes he telephoned her; more often not. Her oldest son, Amir, wrote her: "Father's in a grey cloud; no one can talk to him. He's lost without you." She knew that whenever Amir referred to his father, he exaggerated a little, yet he was attentive and observant, and so far Yasser had not confirmed his date of arrival, for when he was preoccupied he tended to smudge out time. Her haunting dream about her search for their home was recurring at the Delta Barrage where she felt she was waiting for Yasser so she could begin to live. The dates were a deep crimson, almost ripe, something Yasser had wanted to enjoy. Nessim, their gardener, would be in, when the heat had subsided at five or six in the afternoon, a wicker basket tied to his waist, and he would climb the palm bark barefoot—his toes like spider's legs, heels maps of earth-tested soles—and collect the fruit: crimson, crisp, great for jam, the kind Nadia's mother made, each date filled with an almond, dipped in sugar and simmered into a bright, red glaze. "Remember to roast the almonds so they stay crisp!" her mother had coached her, her voice ringing with the joy of creation. Sealed jars would keep the fruit for Yasser and their sons. Samy would finish a small jar at one sitting, as he did chocolate-covered strawberries in Canada. Smiling, he would slip one glazed date after another into his mouth, crunch the almond and, between jokes to Amir, would relish each bite until he emptied the jar. She missed his hilarity. Amir ate frugally, maintaining a slim build, reflecting his adherence to all things organic. She would save most of the jars for them, but she would set some aside for Esmat, her housekeeper, to distribute to their neighbours at the Delta Barrage, and to take home to her four children.

The sun at the tops of trees spilled shadows over the grass, dark phantoms released onto the ground. Nadia unwound the garden hose to water the snapdragons, fruit and tropical trees, then she wound her shoulder-length brown hair to the back of her head and wrapped it in a kerchief to protect her from the sun. Dry heat spread a glow through her body. She sprinkled the leaves before the burning haze of noon oppressed them, their water drops falling on dusty paths, keeping the earth compact until Nessim came to water them in the late afternoon. A warm earth-smell rose from the ground, and the cool water comforted her toes.

Jasmine was her idea, the chickens Yasser's. She had Nessim plant the bushes in the fall, and now the climbers by their bedroom window filled their room at night with a fragrance that reminded her of Yasser's absence from their king-sized bed. A chasm had opened at her feet, a sense of loss dogged her, and earth under her toes cracked a little. She was afraid of taking another step for fear of falling into the split, for everything around her was static and within her was an alien silence, ahead a cracking earth.

"It would be too peaceful here without the squawking of chickens!" Yasser had joked.

In Toronto, when snow piled up on the window sill, he left his radio on to insulate him from the silence outdoors. There, the absence of dogs howling, cats crying, a rooster celebrating dawn, had nudged him closer to a precipice of longing for the land he had left behind; being far from Egypt was his own choice, yet it filled him with restlessness, a loneliness like a suffocating guilt. Nadia loved Canada's copious elms, birch, oak, and maple trees, their rustle soft in the breeze. You heard the wind swish the leaves, and unless you lived in the heart of Toronto, you did not hear the blare of car horns. Silence pushed her deeper into her work; solitude vivified colours, sharpened sounds, made her world spin in a dance whose rhythms energized her. Here at the Delta Barrage, Yasser loved to listen to the chickens pecking, roosters crowing at dawn, dogs and wolves howling at night, to merge him with his native soil. As she watered the jasmine branches, she was careful not to splash the white flowers so at noon they would release their full-bodied fragrance.

She was wearing jasmine many years ago on the Cornice road at the old harbour in Alexandria. The flowers' full fragrance, heavy and somnolent, wrapped her and Yasser with its promise of love in the black night. Winds high and salty on the open sea; fishing boats diamond-dotted; water lapping stones in the harbour, its pavement low—two feet above sea level—allowing waves to splash over surrounding walls, this

stretch of the Alexandria Cornice overlooking the sea elevated
four storeys high. Several strings of fresh flowers circled her
neck where Yasser had placed them after hailing a vendor from
their taxi window at a stop in mid-traffic at the Metro
Cinema, downtown Alexandria. He had bent and kissed her
neck, signalling their night of love. She nineteen, Yasser twenty-
four, married, before they had emigrated to Canada.

Jasmine pinned to the silk dress of her late maternal
grandmother, the woman Nadia resembled: medium height,
round breasts, delicate features, slanted almond eyes, hair
gathered at the nape of her neck in a fine sequined net. The
difference between them was Nadia's unruly hair, its loose
strands bunching around her face and frazzled into a mop on
her forehead. Yasser once said, "You are a musician on the
walls of ancient temples, and when you have this contemplative
look, you're . . . the Sphinx of Egypt!" Female-human-animal,
astride time and space? Hardly, for she was not conscious of
her own existence. Her wild hair resembled that of the Sphinx,
perhaps, but that was easy, for it was naturally wavy as was the
hair of so many people in the region. Yet, the Sphinx is so
much in control of Her destiny, Her face peaceful, unhurried,
in tune with the unravelling sands of time, in command.
Nadia could not identify with these qualities.

Scents accentuated by salt spray, vibrant colours surfacing
through the years, and now Nadia did not feel any different,
except for a nagging solitude that plagued her, its cloud threatening to break into a storm. On her first visit to the Delta
Barrage, this house had evoked memories of her grandparents'
home with its white walls and large windows, but her grandparents' villa had been the biggest in El Mansoura, with six
servants, gardener, a driver. Yet its opulence had not impressed
Nadia, for what had lingered in her mind was the fragrance of
its white flowers growing in her grandmother's balcony and
garden. She remembered her grandmother by the scent of the
jasmine flower she wore on her lapel, and by the others she
placed into the small crystal vases around her home. One fresh

flower stood on her night table. By comparison, Nadia's home was peasant-like, with bare walls, rooms scantily furnished, flowers in earthen pots; still, jasmine had remained her link with her grandmother in time.

"Your grandfather was an artist and writer," her mother had told her a couple of months ago, "you take after him." But Nadia had known her grandfather as a famous oculist. Her mother said, "He used to climb up the steps of my mother's carriage on her evening promenades and recite his poems to her. That's how they met. While my father hung on to the steps of the carriage, my mother, sitting by her governess, pretended she did not like nor encourage his serenade." A daring adventure, Nadia thought, ninety years ago at El Mansoura, when a girl acknowledging a man's attentions would have been labelled forward and outlandish. In Nadia's mind, her family tree grew heavy with crimson hibiscus against olive green, a violet sky and turquoise river. Colours invaded her; they drowned her. She would paint her ancestors on canvas, weave them into tapestries and they would be trees, each species representing a character. Birds. Animals. Masks. Her moments would take shape and transform into concrete figures. Twenty-five years in Canada, now here at the shoulder of the Nile—not in Heliopolis a north-east suburb of Cairo where her mother and cousins lived, but close to the Delta Barrage—her work would come to life, near where a few of her relatives had died. Her mother had said, "You come all the way to Egypt and choose to live far away. I thought you would stay here with me in the dry heat of Heliopolis, and I would see you every day."

Nadia did not explain to her mother that she wanted to absorb the earth and sky, sense leaves soft and shiny, taste solitude under acacia, and water-paint by the lapping waters of the Nile. This small dam in the Delta Barrage, with its ten sluices holding back water in the narrow stream, was different from the monstrous one astride the wide river at Aswan. Months ago, she and Yasser were standing on the huge granite structure overlooking the deep roar of the High Aswan Dam, and an engineer was shouting against the froth, saying enough water was being held back behind the gates to flood the whole land of Egypt. Water in a mist splashing down the chasm at their feet, and behind them cracking walls, one gate at a time closed for restoration, Yasser questioning the engineer, discussing fissures, she thinking of waters rolling over the soil: Egypt, the black land, as it used to be? The engineer was telling them of the flooded expanse of Lake Nasser—named after Egypt's President, Gamal Abd El Nasser, who authorized the building of the dam—its waters seeping underground, covering farmlands in Nubia. She dare not paint its rising anger drowning the land, or her cataclysm on canvas would be a way of courting it.

Water spurted from her hose and glistened on the *guava* fruit. Nadia drenched the leaves of the tree knowing that the moisture beads would soon evaporate. Without the Aswan Dam, there would not have been enough water or electricity; at least, this is what Russian advisors had said to Gamal Abd El Nasser. Egyptian engineers had believed otherwise: that smaller dams at intervals in the river would have been sufficient power, but Nasser had sold out to the risky Russian vision. Nadia turned off the hose and swept under the acacia trees, filled her basket with dead leaves and carried it to the back of the garden. Nessim would pick it up and deliver it to the garbage collector, who daily emptied their baskets over the mound of garbage on his open cart. His donkey ambled to the next stop down the road, man and animal enduring the fierce heat—the man mahogany, his donkey a warm brown—kin relatives to the wood cart on their pilgrimage to the disposal site. A wide brush dipped in water and a little colour would capture their earth-brown softness. She wiped her feet on the straw mat outside the entrance to her house. Last week, Yasser had called her to say he hoped he would be at the Delta in two weeks' time.

She entered the kitchen and took a deep breath; nothing would taste better than a cup of tea. At the counter under the window, she looked out at the white fence crowned with riotous cyclamen bougainvillea. Years back, not in sunlight but in dark, she was returning home in Toronto at five in a blizzard and was worrying about her sons—Amir and Samy— coming home from school in the snow. A young mother, she had worked, cleaned, given of her energy, thinking: somewhere in the future lay a prize she would earn. She awoke before sunrise and returned home after dark, no time to sip coffee in the sun, and by her side, Yasser silent, an ocean forming between them, and outside their home, snow piled up on their window sills creating soft insulation against the whispers of their hearts.

***

At his cramped desk in his Toronto home, Yasser shuffled his mail: bills, cheques, letters. Paper spilled out of his filing cabinet and waited for his spurt of energy before he left Canada. He could not wait to be in Egypt's sun to relax his muscles, to sleep on the warm sand. The years were telling on his aching back and strained breathing. He missed Nadia's hair, its scent of herbal greenery, garden of rosemary and thyme. In her absence, his work felt onerous, the paper-work draining. Before they left for Egypt, she had existed in an inner chamber of her mind, in a room where she wrote and painted, and he had had no time to share her work. In his childhood, he had spent time in his uncle's car lot, under the greasy metal of broken cars, choking on exhaust fumes. Now he regarded words on paper as unreal by comparison to concrete and bricks. Aswan, the wide part of the Nile gliding in the sun, yellow sands rolling to the horizon, a dry heat, and the bones of his body surrendering their hurry, that's what he needed. He would take Nadia to the old Aswan Cataract Hotel, to a suite overlooking the Nile, but he would need to book it early.

"Nadia," he told her aloud, "you should see Samy taking care of your plants. Your gardenia leaves are a deep green." And, "I don't visit anyone; I go through the motions of work."

He had no urge to visit his relatives in Egypt. After his father's death, he had inherited the burden of heading the family, its individuals strangers to him, especially the younger ones. His four brothers with numerous children, his cousins, aunts, uncles, waited for him to solve their problems of land ownership and settle their marital squabbles. They assumed that he and Nadia were doubt-free and led lives woven with golden threads. But he worked more hours a day than all his siblings combined. He lived a tense life, had no male relatives to spend his off-work hours with at a trick-track table, inhaling tobacco smoke from a bubbly hooka at a café. His fingers moved the paper; no time to deal with details. He had to make arrangements for his trip, the stop-over in Scandinavia, then to Italy to buy Nadia designer clothes and perfume. He needed to get out of the rain. Selim—his friend from Cairo University days—would be waiting for him at Cairo Airport.

Yasser reached the bottom of the file and, without opening the letters, swept them into the garbage. After his return, he'd find some excuse for not responding. He stretched out on the sofa. All he wanted was to be on the aeroplane, in a first class armchair, a bottle of chilled champagne, stack of international papers, bunch of attractive hostesses. His life was work; he had not had time to glance at a beautiful woman.

***

Nadia looked up at her housekeeper, Esmat, who entered the kitchen with her bundle of work clothes. Thirty-two years old, two hundred pounds strong, with high blood pressure and five children. The father thought nothing of sleeping all day and spending his evenings in cafès playing backgammon with his friends. Esmat set her bundle down on the floor. She would not work in the only good *gallabiah* she had, of black cotton, ankle-length, blue sequined chest, the one piece of luxury she wore on the streets as if to say, "This beauty is the work of my hands," her dimpled fingers flashing her single gold ring.

She straightened her back and said, "The sun is too strong."
Nadia handed the woman a glass of water. Esmat sat on
the floor, set her back against the wall, stretched her legs and
sipped the cold water. Nadia did not bother her with words,
for this is when Esmat put her family's problems behind her, a
truce of silence the two observed before their day began.
Esmat wore deep kohl around the large almonds staring out of
an oval face, frizzy hair tucked under a black kerchief with
coloured sequins. Her lively cats' eyes moved with the stealth
of a jungle leopard, and her perfume clung to her like oil
squeezed from gardenias. She had bought the scent in the
inner streets of Khan-El-Khalili—Cairo's ancient bazaar—
from an admirer who had given her twice the quantity she had
paid for, and she had splashed it, rubbing it into her face, fore-
arms, into the cleft between her breasts, knowing she would
receive more for nothing, if she gave the man a raindrop of a
hope that he would enjoy her aromatic flesh. Had she gone to
school, she would have distinguished herself, but she was illiterate. She picked up the grocery lists Nadia wrote and guessed
a few words, but when Nadia offered to teach her, the woman
said she had little time. "At least my children will know how."
She spent her spare time plucking her eyebrows to a thin
arched line which she accentuated with a black liner, her face
and body clear of hair with the aid of the elastic *halawa*—
boiled sugar, lemon and water—she had learned to make in
her village. She coddled her flesh with creams and yogurt, her
smoothness testifying to a longing that did not revolve around
her old, ailing husband, but manifested itself in her untamed
eyes, alive and eager for the attention she gleaned from men in
her alley. Esmat did not talk of lovers, but when a man called
her on the phone she would, with dancing eyes, explain to
Nadia that her brother-in-law wanted her to look after his
daughters and she would leave early to fulfill her pressing duty.
Her children attended a government school and did well,
except that her seventeen-year-old son gambled away what little money he made running errands for old people.

Esmat stood up and straightened her back as though aligning the different battle zones in her body, her limbs a burden she carried without complaint as if her hefty body were rubber, ready to sway with the uneven road and bounce back like a new ball. She gathered the floor brushes from the cupboard and moved away, knowing that when Nadia sat by the kitchen window sipping her tea with milk—an unheard-of drink to replace the traditional boiled brew which Esmat drank with plenty of sugar—she would be thinking of her paintings and writings, the papers she would send abroad to some man to publish. Esmat did not think the man was Nadia's husband, Mr. Yasser, who was in another country and whose absence saddened Nadia. Perhaps because Nadia wrote in a foreign tongue, Esmat regarded her as translator, not of words or numbers, but of life's problems. Esmat opened the bedroom shutters and beat the wooden slats with a cloth; she could not keep thoughts of her husband out of her mind. Her father had sold her to the thirty-six-year-old man when she was fourteen. The plantations outside this window reminded her of her pregnancies, a time when her twenty-year-old cousin had had her while she was expecting her second daughter at the village, his furtive hand under her *gallabiah*, his fingers on her thighs, wind-blown reeds on her hair-free pubic triangle, her own hands busy above the plant emptying brown pods overflowing with soft, white cotton, their meetings in the barn at night on the hay while her mother and neighbours performed their evening prayers, the few moments of pleasure Esmat had known.

One night, when her mother's voice surfaced near the barn where they were wrapped in lust, Esmat withdrew from her lover, pulled down her *gallabiah*—which she kept on for such emergencies—buried the throbbing young man under hay, emerged into her mother's arms, grabbed and whisked her off from the open barn door. Her mother wanted her to check the chickens and collect the eggs. Esmat took the straw tray from her mother's hands, refused to answer her questions, complained how a pregnant woman had no time to rest her weary body, but her knees shook and her belly fluttered. Her mother had not suspected the warm young flesh lying muffled under the hay, since having fun with a man—in a barn during evening prayers while one was pregnant and one's husband worked in another city—was the farthest thought from the pious woman's mind.

Esmat was not going to forget those days. She suffered no guilt, no regrets, but felt, serve them right for selling her to a man as old as her father. This is why, she suspected, her second daughter Rasha, now fourteen and lusty, hankered after the men.

***

For many years, her mother's image haunted Magda, daughter of a prominent general in the Egyptian Army. She remembered lying under olive and mulberry trees, her hair spread over her mother's lap—a still picture printed in her mind. At her villa in Mariout—south west of Alexandria— Magda remembered her father's rotund sisters, water-buffaloes tanning on the grass in the park, their wicker baskets full of traditional sun-dried fish, bread and onions to celebrate Sham-El-Nessim, the first day of spring. Hunched on a wool carpet at the edge of this group, her mother reclined, thin, alien, her clothes flowing, her hair coifed, a classical hat shading her powdered face, Magda's clear image of her mother and the only one. In Magda's memory were other still-shots, like the day she was eight and left her father's apartment to walk into the night through the dim streets, through cars' headlights, surrounded by peoples' legs, tripping on the pavement, talking to herself, excited about going to see her estranged mother, even though she did not know where. She had fallen asleep on the pavement, awoke among strange uniformed men, and her father had picked her up at what she later understood to be the police station. Enjoying major prestige in the army, her father exercised his clout at the police station in a silent and authorial demeanour, but at home, her father's face bulged above hers as he beat her. Thereafter photographs of her mother had disappeared from their house, and her father claimed he did not know where they had gone. He had frowned when she mentioned her mother, and the flush on his forehead spread over his cheeks and throat as though he were choking.

Magda needed a lover to wipe out these images, to enfold her in a world of fantasy horses, tents and deserts, to electrify her body in a night of ecstasy. On one of her outings with her friends—Soheir and Selim—she would meet him. Now, she knew the ones who grabbed her body to satisfy their lust.

***

Oil paint kit, easel and canvas under her arm, Nadia walked towards the Nile at the Delta Barrage, through a short-cut in fallow ground between her property and the neighbours'. In fifteen minutes she could see the silt-laden green of the river. Some steps down the slope, she set up her easel on the river bank where she had a view of the dam, its wall of yellowing stone bearing testimony to its ancient years. Ten open sluices and two small falls poured their foam into the river, and she could see the checked-back water rippling at the top of the dam wall and beyond it. A peasant woman washed her clothes in the river, but when she lifted her head and saw Nadia, she stared at the easel as at an intrusion, returned to her chores swaying her body as she beat her clothes into the lapping water. Nadia applied her turquoise wash and painted the curved body, but she felt like an imposter, even though she was born on this soil, not at El Khanatir by this dam, but close by. Nadia's father had come from a village on the outskirts of Cairo, had travelled through Europe, America and the Far East, and on his return from one of his trips had told her, "Places do not differ. Once surface differences are assimilated, all places are the same. Contentment is function of self, not of space." When he visited her in Toronto, he remarked, "Canada is a wonderful place, but it is far from Egypt." He had not adjusted to the empty space his only child had left behind. What she remembered was his tactile sense of place, his affinity with his native land which his extensive travels had augmented. Now he rested at his burial site in the ochre desert. Unlike her, he had not lived many years outside his birth-place; she saw him as part of the sand he loved at Ras El Bar, lying stretched in front of the straw cabin they rented.

Despite her shame at intruding on the peasant woman's privacy, Nadia's hands moved fast, filling in earthy ochres and deep olives. She curved the back in black and created semi-circles for the hips. Women married young and wore black in public. Yasser liked Nadia in black, but the the fitted dinner dresses she wore in Canada were different from the loose, long, black *gallabiahs* and veils women wore here as protection from men's eyes. In Canada, black hinted sexuality, or expressed mourning; here, it was meant to hide attraction and suggest piety. The woman piled her washed clothes in an orange dish, lifted it to her head, set off on her path. Nadia relaxed her tension on the brush and applied the aqua of the river; today, it was smooth. Noon would soon be here, and she would have to wind up her work for the day. Rippling river water would indicate a balmy evening, but the river was still. Even with a kerchief on her hair under a leafy eucalyptus, Nadia felt the white heat press down on her. She was unlike the women of the area who did their chores at mid-noon. They wet their faces in the river or poured water on their kerchiefs to cool their hair. Nadia used this trick when she remembered to carry a small water bottle; today she had forgotten.

Easel and equipment in hand, she wound her way under the outspread banyan trees, between their aerial roots descending from thick branches, dipping into the soil where they re-rooted and sprang back into new bark. Smaller roots hung in air, yearning to reach the ground, sweeping across her face when she passed under their harbouring green. She was satisfied with her morning's work, but had she been able to stay longer, she would have put in the natural hues. Tomorrow, she would return to this spot to create the spreading, self-starting roots of the banyan. Perhaps Yasser was hesitant to come to the Delta because it was too quiet; or he might have come sooner had they bought a house in Cairo, or in Ismailia where his family lived.

When she entered the dark interior of her home, she found Esmat had finished her cleaning and closed the shutters. Nadia's body relaxed in the balmy feel of the hall. This is what she liked about a stone house in Egypt's summer: the moment she entered it, the atmosphere was cool and soothing, not the air-conditioning in Canada which froze her body and stifled her breath. Today they had not done any cooking, since Nadia was invited for lunch at the Mansours' house next door. Esmat stood in the hallway with a wet handkerchief around her forehead, her eyes red, kohl streaming down her face; Nadia sat down on the nearest chair.

Esmat blurted, "Madam, it's my daughter, Rasha, she's done it! She's gone! I don't know where, but she's run away." She sat down on the floor with Roda, her youngest, by her side. "Rasha has disappeared with that scum Nouri. I knew he was going to heap disaster on our heads. Heaven help me, I wish I'd stayed home. I thought my kids were old enough to manage." She rocked, her head in her hands. "She's gone, with that scum," she sobbed. Roda sat beside her mother, an alert nine-year-old not wanting to disturb. She whispered: "When my older sister found out Rasha had run away, she sent me here and I got a ride in our neighbour's taxi."

Nadia asked, "What are you going to do, Esmat? Roda, what did your father do when he found out?"

"He's not home," wailed Esmat, pressing the layers of flesh at her waist and bending forward until her elbows rested on her knees. "He's in Alexandria. God knows where he is." As an afterthought, "May Allah have mercy upon us, I have to find her before he returns, or he'll kill her."

Nadia went to her bedroom closet, took some pound notes from her purse and returned. "Here, Esmat, take these, you will need them." Esmat wiped her face, took the bills, folded and slipped them into her brassiere. Then, to keep them close to her skin, she gave the bills a sharp pat. "May Allah bless you in your children. May He never let you see a black day." She wrapped her head and shoulders with her black veil, picked up her change of clothes, took Roda by the hand. "Peace be with you Madam," she said and left the house, her head bent against the sun. At the living room window, Nadia watched the child and mother recede, a small green climber holding on to a spreading dark tree.

Nadia showered, slipped into a white *gallabiah* and gold sandals, then waited at her doorway for the Mansour car and driver. When he arrived, the driver opened the back door of the black Cadillac, and she slipped into its grey-velvet interior. They wound through the few kilometres that separated the two properties to the large house on top of the hill overlooking the Nile above the dam site. A symbol of authority, the government house for the director of the dam had a high stone wall which hid it from the road with a wrought-iron gate, at which stood a servant in white garb. They passed through the open front gate, wound around the grass and came to a stop at the entrance. Yasser should have been here by now, Nadia thought. The iron-trellis door, with the opaque glass, swung open and Mahmoud—in white *gallabiah*—ushered her into the living room. His wife, Amina, white veil wrapped around her face and draped over her shoulders, blue cotton dress reaching the floor, stood up from a gold damask chair and kissed Nadia on both cheeks. "Madam Nadia, welcome to our home,"and she repeated her kisses on both of Nadia's cheeks.

They sat at the table piled high with delicacies which the Mansours expected Nadia to sample, but all she wanted was cool yogurt. She filled her plate with salad and olives and chatted about her garden. She took her time chewing.

"Madam Nadia, please try our pan-fried veal, it is specially cut for us by our butcher," Amina urged, her cheeks full, her robust figure hidden under the folds of her veil.

"Yes, Madam Amina, I'll be ready in a minute." Nadia lingered at the table taking her time and making the proper motions.

They discussed the Delta Dam which was being refurbished under Mr. Mahmoud's authority. He explained, "We're reinforcing the walls and keeping the gates in perfect condition. Our dam is one of the oldest in the country. If need be, we can manage without the one in Aswan." He sipped his Turkish coffee with relish, for here in his home, he could count on the best being served, and he the sole provider. He licked his lips with satisfaction.

He said, "We're enlarging our services, and we need someone like you who knows English to look after the tourists," his smile revealed coffee and tobacco-stained teeth.

Amina turned to Nadia. "To be honest with you, Madame Nadia, I think you're perfect for the job. This work will fill your time when your husband is away."

Now that Yasser's absence was duly recorded, Nadia responded with, "I'm overwhelmed by your kindness. This job is wonderful, but I have so much to do at home right now." An irrelevant answer, she thought. They were extending to her a courtesy any returned compatriot would have welcomed, and with her refusal she had transgressed the unwritten code of her people. Amir's words rang in her head. "Mother, when are you going to do what you want?" Her first-born son, observant, detached, self-contained. Soon the Mansours forgot the subject, but Nadia remained uncomfortable and was relieved to step out into the late afternoon sun and walk home. She had refused their car and chauffeur even though she knew her refusal would embarrass, if not offend them.

Her feet set a quick pace on the pebble road. She wanted to fly in the sky, dive into the river, anything to be free of the claustrophobia in their house. The Mansours' walls had been closing in on her, holding her captive in an alien culture. Sand swept into her sandals and lodged between her toes. She accelerated her steps; she had to stay alert, be ready. She knew she could not slip back into a past she had left behind her decades ago; she had to run, to stay alive, to tear away the stifling bondage of a life she had not lived even before she had left Egypt. Exhilarated by the breeze, she kept on running, relieved the afternoon sun hid behind cypress branches. She did not know to whom she was going, yet running was a compulsion that had to lead to some kind of rest.

***

Chapter Two

Dolphin

Yasser pushed his luggage through the crowded passageway into the humming hall in Cairo Airport and merged with a sea of swarming humanity: bodies, waving hands, voices, people jammed together, luggage. The man in front of him in the line shouted and waved to a porter yards away; the woman behind him chided her daughter for leaving their suitcases unattended. Yasser's heart pounded. Whenever he stepped down on Egyptian soil, his fatigue surfaced and his raw nerves got mangled by the exaggerated auditory stimulus. He had been rushing to get here, first the eight-hour trip over the Atlantic, second changing planes at Amsterdam to Italy, then surging into this crowd, when all he wanted was to be in the Delta Barrage showered and rested.

Irritable and exposed, he was a tree pulled out of its soil, roots flung in air, like the trees he saw when hiking in Toronto's ravines. Without Nadia, their home had felt cold and bare. In the past five or six years, his sense of being uprooted had nagged him on his business trips, but in recent months it had tracked him everywhere and now in this congested din it suffocated him. He had tried to convince Samy to accompany him to Egypt, but his younger son wanted to go later with his brother. Yasser missed Samy; his older son, Amir, he did not understand. Not that he had not tried, but something in his older son had maintained its distance. Fathers, he supposed, slaved at their jobs to put their sons through medical school and all they earned was rejection. Amir's watchful eyes peered over his father's shoulder, checking him, always checking, displeasure shining through his well-guarded eyes. What did he see to be displeased about?

Around Yasser, travellers' shouts echoed from the alabaster floors and ceramic counters, no carpets, insufficient sound acoustics to soften the mayhem. Even here, in this new hall of the airport, Yasser could not avoid the long lines of travellers. Six lines of passengers started from the customs officers' cubicles and wound their way back into the passageway along the long corridor from which they had arrived. More people waited here than he had seen at Heathrow or Kennedy airports: Turbans, American Bermuda shorts, French designer clothes. "Watch your step," "Take this luggage," "Where's my passport?" words bouncing, arms and legs hitting his back and calves, feet stumbling over his baggage, children screaming. In this packed humanity, perfume congealed with perspiration irked him, but at least the new air-conditioning system kept the hall cool. He inched his way up the Customs line; he would go see Nadia at the Delta Barrage before he phoned his family in Ismailia, but all he could summon in his mind's eye was Luxor by the Nile and iced beer overflowing glasses, the gold liquid glistening in the noon sun, those dark, turbaned waiters, like garden snakes harmless, stealthy, punctilious, attentive.

When he managed to work his way through customs and reach the corridor into the outer hall of the airport, Yasser was overcome by the crowds pushing against the rope barrier, their arms waving in air, their noise triggering an onslaught on his defenceless ears. Voices shouted, "Mohammed, *Alf hamdoullah alla el salama!*" "Welcome, welcome home!" Just about everyone in Egypt was a Mohammed-Something, for the Prophet's name was a blessing to the people bearing it; from a symbol of grace it had become an identity stamp. "There they are, just behind that woman over there": screams of recognition, arms waving, fingers pointing , but none for him. Noise drilled his nerve-ends. By contrast, Toronto was a cotton-wrapped cocoon. Outside the Airport Building, he set his luggage down and combed the crowds for Selim with whom he had kept up a business exchange since their university days and whom he had visited in Cairo every two or three years.

Across the street, in the middle of a line of navy and white taxis, Selim leaned over the front fender of one, spotted Yasser, ran into the traffic shouting and waving his arms. Cars swerved around him, Selim the aggressor, cars the defendants. Yasser pulled his friend up onto the pavement and heaved a sigh. They hugged and kissed.

"Welcome to Cairo, dear friend. I'm sorry my car isn't running, but I have a taxi. Here, give me your suitcases." On previous trips, Yasser had not seen Selim's car, but his friend always referred to it as to a concrete reality. Perhaps he owned one he kept in the garage under his apartment building to use on rare occasions, as one would place a pair of new shoes in a box to await the special day which does not arrive. Though shorter and heavier than Yasser, Selim carried both suitcases and wobbled across the street to the taxi, then handed them to the driver, who threw them onto a metal rack on the roof-top, no rope to prevent them from jostling and crashing to the ground. Yasser had thought Toronto was fast-moving, but now he noted it could not compare with this rush. The driver was in the taxi and the engine gurgling; Yasser jumped into the moving smoke-filled vehicle, and in a hurry slammed the door shut. The lock was broken and the handle landed on his lap. Selim laughed at Yasser's consternation. The driver got into a rage about people who accosted his car as though it were a ton of bricks, no care for its condition, just crash and destroy other people's cars. He stopped the car, went in search of the out-door handle, risked being run over by the traffic, but he could not find it. Upon climbing back into his seat, the driver fumed, so Yasser, mindful of the extra danger the man's fury would cost them, offered to pay for the handle. In a greater huff, the driver, shouted, "What money? Which handle? *Ya Ragel haram aleak!* God forgive you, man, I am not a beggar. I don't *want* your money! Why don't you watch what you're doing? Bang! Bang! The door is ruined," he punched his fist in the air and hunched his back to express his grief. Yasser had no idea his thrust on the door was that heavy, since he used more energy to close the door of his Volvo in Canada. Now he realized that the taxi door was an old tin plate hanging onto its hinges with rusted wire and sensed the man's anguish over the demise of the only vehicle he had called his own. Yasser had forgotten how to dodge cars and avoid danger on the road; he had to remind himself that his suitcases would survive the trip, that everything was possible in this his native land of wonders. He shivered. Cabs overburdened with luggage, people dangling out of windows, lorries, donkey-carts choked the road. The dissonance of hooting horns reached the sky but, farther at the edge of the desert, baby eucalyptus trees fringed the Airport Road, sending their elongated shadows swaying over the naked sand stretched to the horizon.

Selim nodded to Yasser in approval of his appearance and of some other quality Yasser could not fathom. Selim harboured an admiration for Yasser climbing the executive ladder to the top of an architectural firm in Canada, an impressive feat for an immigrant; but then, things had always been easy for Yasser; he had the charm and the wit. Selim remembered the days when they frequented the Faculty of Arts Cafeteria at Cairo University in Giza—since there were no females in Engineering—to watch the girls come and go pretending not to notice the men, but even then Yasser had been the focus of their yearning eyes. The Arts cafeteria was worth the visit when women were models not the veiled shrouds they are today. The Engineering students had fought for the few straw chairs in the sun outside the cafeteria and had haunted the area by ordering a Coca-Cola, lingering there when they had no lectures and sometimes when they did. He said, "My God, man, you're younger than ever, not a white hair on your head! And how do you stay so slim?" He grinned, patted Yasser's arm. "It's obvious you don't live in *our* world. Look at me, half bald and greying!" He slid his fingers along his shiny forehead back to the bald spot at the top of his skull, then fumbled with the rough hair at the nape of his neck.

Yasser recognized Selim's familiar opening gambit and

suspected his friend would have liked to live elsewhere had he worked at fulfilling his dream. Selim dallied with an emigration fantasy, like a dripping faucet in the back of his head, but he had not initiated a break and had allowed the drops to keep on niggling his inner ear reproaching him for his failure to realize his dream. He was rounder at the waist and balding, yet alert and full of energy. Yasser felt years older than his friend, although he knew he appeared younger, because he was thinner and had healthier hair. Their taxi lurched into the crowd and Yasser's worry about his luggage was replaced by his fear for their own and other people's lives, but heads and limbs dissolved from in front of their taxi unharmed. Then their cab bumped into the car ahead. Cigarette burning its filter between his lips, their driver shot out of his car, exchanged vociferous words with the other driver, took out his note-pad and pencil, scribbled a few words, shoved the pad and pencil back into his trouser pocket, disengaged the front fender with the help of a couple of bystanders, climbed back in, manoeuvred the wheel, and roared off as though his vehicle were the latest in technological prowess. He swerved his car to the left, saluted his helpers and drove into the crowd, spinning his driving-wheel right and left to protect his car against the surge of humans. His radio switched onto high-pitch, a singer mourning her lost lover. If not national marches, Yasser thought, then eerie songs of unrequited love. Where had he heard that a people's entertainment ran in inverse direction from their reality, so if their songs were saturated with yearning, they were love-starved. The driver's left elbow rested on the open window, and his fingers drummed a beat on the roof of his car, as though the singer's voice, car horns, screeching of wheels were insufficient to pump his adrenalin. Yasser's apprehensive face drew a choking laugh from Selim. "Relax man, this is Cairo! Do you think we can afford to drive in lanes? It would take us a century to get anywhere!" He offered Yasser a cigarette and when his friend refused it, Selim lit it, settled back on the dusty leather cushions, curled the smoke up in circles which overpowered the smell of car exhaust, human breath and dust.

Yasser was thinking of the accident. "The police did not come to check the collision," he mumbled more to himself than to his friend. Selim chuckled. "How can a police car reach the scene of an accident? He cannot make it in eight hours even if he wanted to break through this mess, which he doesn't! The drivers have to settle among themselves. It depends if the one at fault is honest or if it's the month of Ramadan. Otherwise the victim is out of luck." Selim enjoyed making rousing statements to watch his Canadian friend's face, for Yasser cherished the memory of Cairo more than twenty years ago which, in his mind, had merged with North American memories. He had acquired foreign ways, was nervous on crowded streets, bought expensive clothes without haggling over the price. He had lost the traits that made Egyptians flexible lovers of life. He had become brittle. Yet these changes had not diminished his attraction; on the contrary, his experience had given him polish, a sense of being above crowds. Dynamism, that's what! Perhaps it's his face, lean, almost stern, long full nose, a masculine ruggedness difficult to match, and most of all, his hair, wavy, dark, not frayed with lacklustre ends, no shining spot on *his* skull!

Yasser studied the locked traffic and—for the first time in many years—wished he had not given up smoking. The way was long; it would take them forever to get there. They had to cross the Nile River to the island—El Gizereh—and then work their way through car-clogged streets to Selim's apartment overlooking the Nile. Cranky cars wedged in between Mercedes, Jaguars, beaten-up trucks, donkey-drawn carts choked the main artery of the city as pedestrians cut in through the congestion. Yasser glanced at his watch: two p.m. Stores were barred with iron doors and locks. Siesta time. People leaving downtown joined the slow procession home from the small side-roads, choking the flow of cars. He rolled down the glass. Black exhaust from the bus ahead hit his face.

He rolled the glass back up again. Young men hung in a cluster at the bus door, their toes tucked among others' on the lowest step, their fingers embracing the side of the vehicle or clutching window sills. *Gallabiahs* and feet—like tattered clothes hanging from dried tree branches—dangled over the back of the dusty roof. He glanced sideways at Selim reclining on the gouged leather as though he were lying on velvet at home: the man managed to relax in this hooting, exhaust-ridden chaos.

Selim extinguished a shrivelled cigarette in the ashtray by his side. "Imagine," he said, "this rush happens three times a day. The new bridge was clogged since its first week. By the time a road is built, we need a couple more. Yet people are busy producing more children; it's our national pastime!" He shrugged. "We used to hang on to buses, like these boys! Remember the day I slipped and almost got run over by a taxi?" He chuckled. "I've considered this my second life ever since!" He turned to Yasser. "Listen, as soon as we get to my apartment, take a shower and rest, then we'll go to the Nile Hilton for a beer." He grinned to see his friend sit upright, his hand clutching the door as though ready to jump out, or holding it firm to prevent it from hurtling away.

In the apartment, Yasser found salads and cheeses on platters in the dining room. "There's iced beer in the fridge," Selim offered. But Yasser was too tired; he went to his assigned small room, threw himself on the bed and let himself be lulled by the hum of traffic. On the seventh floor, street sounds were a soft clash of cymbals in his ears, and a cool breeze from the Nile blew in through the open window. White sheers flapped, enfolding him in a sound sleep.

***

"Where is she going? Home? Nadia's on the road again. She's walking down a windy dust-path, running. Her sleeping brain tells her she has her young sons with her. She's holding each by the hand. The street is empty. Why is she on this dusty road? Neither

she nor the boys have any clothes other than the ones on their backs. Noon becomes afternoon, then night. Wind pierces their ears. No money, no clothes. How are they going to live through the gathering storm? Someone is bound to show up; she has to go on. Why is she so far from home? Her two sons are with her, running on the desolate street, zigzagging against wind. She is pulling them along. Her sons are young, the younger one hobbling along to keep up with them.

Their faces are frozen. They are running on a dusty road. In the distance, a brick house is hurtling towards them and others follow in a stream of swaying houses passing them in a maelstrom on the street. Her eyes pan over them. A woman in her forties, hair dishevelled by wind, torn blouse and skirt, is standing on her moving porch, beckoning them to the door of her small house. They are spending the night there.

The woman's son, in his early twenties, takes them down a dark stairway to a room full of old suitcases. He is not paying attention to them. His mother is handing him bread and vegetables which he piles into an old cloth bag. The two are opening boxes, taking out sweaters, old skirts, packing them in a suitcase. Nadia is not sure how she would carry the suitcase and take her children with her, but her older son would help.

They are on the road wandering through streets, darkly lit, cold, empty. Sometimes a man or a woman offers them bread, allows them to sit in a warm café, but they continue walking. They are not hungry. They are nowhere. No money. She is lonely. For short periods she wonders why she has been so foolish to set out on the road leaving her home behind; but only for a few moments. She has to.

Her boys are dragging their feet; they need to rest. The road is empty, no trees. Small, dark, brick houses are surfacing from a watery mirage. Her loneliness on the road urges her back to the woman and her son. He is at the door waiting for them in pyjama pants, no shirt. They are following him down the stairs of his home to the basement. As he turns to leave the room, Nadia touches his shoulder, and he gathers her to his bare skin, holds her close as though he has noticed her before. His muscles firm, their embrace complete, his hands searching, a rigorous lover, unassuming, gentle.

Nadia wakes up, but she is still with the young lover, he within her soul. She is desolate, but determined to continue. Where is she heading? She rose from her bed and shook her head free of the troubling dream. Light through the slats of closed shutters streaked the walls of her room, leaving sofa, chair and dresser in darkness. She needed warmth. Barefoot, she went to the shutters and pushed them open. Morning sun flooded the room, but her dream lingered on. She went to the kitchen, made tea, sat by the window, looked out at her guava trees. The man in the dream was with her. How did she get to take this strange trip with her sons so young? How young, she did not know because in her dream their ages were hazy. Amir reached her waist, Samy was several inches shorter. She had lost twenty years of their lives. In her dream she did not know their names. She was wandering in Canada, somewhere, on a country road, or in an undeveloped area. Why was she searching? And what for? Where were Yasser and her boys when she was with the man in the basement?

Searching. Always searching. On roads, strange or familiar, looking.

On his return from one of his trips to Europe, her father—a dedicated world traveller—had said, "People leave their homes and seek new lands to discover different versions of themselves. They want to get away from what they know. If they travel far enough, they will find nothing new and end up uncovering their own persistent patterns of behaviour." That was many years ago, but she had not accepted his words—yet what did her dream mean? How long does one take to discover a home in a corner of the globe? Was it possible to be landing between mirages of homes, each one a bit more alien, a bit more forlorn? She did not like the feeling of having left something good behind, in her dream, or in Canada, she did not know which, as though she had given up a part of her body. She had left her home and did not know how she was going to find it. She did not have a home, her sons were not known to her—worse, she did not have a partner the way a decent woman should, and this was of her own doing.

She did not like the feeling of having left something good behind. The dream hovered over her like a bat trapped in an abandoned attic.

***

On the airy roof of the Nile Hilton, Yasser relaxed in a cushioned straw chair by a potted tree, its branches surrounding him; Selim reclined on a sofa on the other side of their table, the balcony fence behind him, and beyond which it, the babbling waters of the Nile. From Toronto, Yasser had called his brother in Ismailia, and Ali had talked about the large piece of land their father had owned until the 1967 war, when it was seized by the government to station its forces. The family needed a lot of cash to work through the bureaucracy and reclaim the property. "Ten thousand American dollars to bribe the officials," Ali had said. This would work out to at least twenty thousand by the time the transaction was over, thought Yasser. The family must think him a running river of dollars. They had no idea how hard he worked for the cash, and how much it cost him to purchase American dollars with Canadian money. Of course all he had to say was "No," but he couldn't. He felt the weight of his responsibility, although he no longer lived on this land, or *because* he didn't. His mother had piled this guilt on him by asking him to rescue the land before their rights to it had disappeared into some government officials' coffers, as, in his opinion, it was bound to do. What did his family want of him, his life?

Yasser focused on the small bulbs on the tree branches above his head, making the balcony feel like a *felucca* flying in the dark. The cool sky a midnight velvet studded with diamonds, and a breeze soothing him into illusory calm. Eleven o'clock, too late for him to be heading out, too early for Selim, but Yasser knew he had to adjust to their hectic hours. The Stella beer light and frothy, cold breeze from the Nile refreshing. His breathing settled down. Selim was on his favourite topic, ". . . the washroom on the aeroplane is where we landed. A few men in the business class, most of them drinking or sleeping, so what do I do? *I* go in; *she* follows, I squeeze her against the door! As we are in the middle of it, we hit turbulence! Just my rotten luck! Try to do it while the plane is jittering!" His laughter spurted out in waves. Selim was on one of his imaginary trips, so Yasser's mind skipped back to their student days when they went at night with girls in cars into the desert, no headlights for fear of what the girls' brothers might do if they discovered their sisters' escapades: fumbling in the dark, wind shifting on the desert floor, camels with dreamy riders bouncing by in the dusk.

But Selim had switched to another topic. "The Minister of Trade wants to see you. He'll make you a good offer. You should stay here and serve your country for two or three years. Our country needs people like you. The Foreign Trade department invites advisors to Egypt to help us set up computerized offices, to suggest new ways of marketing, to supervise engineering projects, and here you are with the required training, a native of our country, fluent in languages, just the one for the job!" He slurped foam off his beer and burped with undisguised satisfaction. If he could get Yasser to accept this job, they would have two years of uninterrupted fun.

Yasser nodded. "Fine," he said. He would let his life free to dream a little. When else? It would cost him less to live in Egypt, so he could give his brothers the money, but he would let them do the running around in government offices.

Selim smiled. "I'll set up the meeting with Mr. Abdullah," then leaning across the table in a confidential tone, "by the way, two women are joining us here tonight: my girlfriend, Soheir, and her friend, Magda." He stretched back on the sofa cushion and closed his eyes. This was news to Yasser. They were on their second beers when the women arrived. The first, middle height, full body, a smiling face, hair in short fluffy curls, and behind her a tall, dark woman in a black dress cut low over her breasts, exposing her long neck within her smooth, flowing hair. Selim introduced the shorter woman as Soheir, and she introduced her friend as Magda. Yasser was not prepared for Magda's eyes, heavily made up with kohl and aqua eye-shadow, her pupils floating in a sea of green. Under tree lights, her shoulder-length straight hair a reddish-green, big, dark dolphin breaking the waters of the Mediterranean, smooth and shiny. His heart tripped. He held out a chair for her then sank back into his own. He was not going to have more drinks.

But somewhere in the distance he heard sirens sing. They were lying on rock, half-women, half-birds, fluttering over sea-foam. Where had he been, asleep? All his life was work. He had not taken time to live. Magda's lips half open, a splash in his ears, seagulls roaming, boats sailing far from shore. As a child, his father had forbidden him to go near the sea. "Its currents will pull you in," he had said. His first brother, three years older than he, also named Yasser, had drowned off the beach in Ismailia. Yasser had disobeyed his father and gone to the beach, lay on his stomach in the sand and allowed the waves to break over his back. He had found large shells. One day, his truant cousin joined him, and they stretched in the shallow foaming water and held shells to their ears. His cousin had said, "Each shell has a spirit. If you hold it to your ear, you will hear the sea-spirit roar." Yasser had strained but had heard the waves breaking over him. Later in his bed, when he held the shell to his ear, he thought he heard waves swishing, and before he drifted to sleep he heard sirens sing. From then on, whenever he was stifled at home during his summer holidays, he went to the beach, where he courted girls from a distance, for sand and unbending social customs formed an invisible barrier between them. But he had kept the shell for later, in bed, when he heard sirens calling.

Selim ordered a bottle of whisky. He had been with Soheir for ten years, longer than with any woman. He was forty-six, she thirty-four. Time to think of marriage, but God forbid she should want children. He would have to make a prenuptial agreement with her before he committed to anything.

Across from Yasser, Magda sat upright, head erect as if she were expecting news from the wind. Everything about her was dark, except the opening of her dress revealing a swan's neck and a wide cleft between her melon breasts. Her lashes heavy, her eyes a jungle of green; aggressively feminine. Her vibrant invitation was not unwelcome. Yasser felt satisfied to command the attention of a woman younger than himself, thirty something, but he wasn't going to worry about her age, whether she was interested, or was out for an evening of fun. Cool air soothed him. In this balcony, well above the congestion on the street below, sounds from the road were pleasingly sensual, stirring the fires of youth in his soul. Fun to have her make the overtures. He sank into her eyes, not caring if it were morning or night, right or just fun. And sirens on the seashore whispered sweet nothings in his ear. Her lips slipped off the rim of glass leaving a crimson stain she massaged off with her glossy fingertips. She said, "Our luxury boats go up to Aswan. If you want to see Abu Simbel, you can take a plane from Cairo there and back to Aswan in one day, then return by boat to Cairo. You need ten days for the trip. The food, boats, drinks, everything makes you feel as Antony did when he went up the Nile to meet Cleopatra." She shrugged and her strap slipped off her shoulder. Her eyes held his as her enamelled finger-nails stroked the tip of her glass.

He said, "Great! When does the next boat leave?" and laughed, but he wondered about her aggression, her stilted talk about the archetypal Egyptian love story. Cleopatra was Ptolemaic, of Greek origin, not a descendant of ancient Egyptian kings and queens. He pushed the thought aside.

She said, "Every day, several times a day," her eyes holding his. She leaned over the table and touched her cigarette to the glowing match he held for her. Her crimson nails were long; he disliked long nails and hated crimson, but these nails stirred him. The back of her hand shone with musky oil. Her fingers caressed him without touching his skin. He ignored his earlier resolution and poured himself a fresh whisky and replenished hers. He wanted to head off to the boat, to jump into the waves.

Let's splash in foam, let's jump and rock on waves.

***

Nadia had accepted her neighbours'—the Mansours'— invitation to their son's engagement party. Betrothals were second in importance to weddings and a refusal to attend would be seen as an insult, a gesture of ill will towards the young couple. She knew that the women at the party would be veiled, so she dressed in long sleeves and ankle-length skirt.

At the Mansour residence, she stepped into a room full of dark-suited men. Where were the women, the music? And why had she agreed to attend without Yasser? Then, Mahmoud ushered her into an inner hall, full of women. At first glance, she could not spot the bride among the veiled heads, but soon the frilly peach veil declared itself among the white or grey ones worn by other women. Amina introduced Nadia around the circle of guests—nuns with rouged faces and heavy jewellery filched from their mothers' closets. Amina intoned, "Madam so-and-so, married to Professor So-and-So." Nadia knew that everyone in Egypt, including the butcher or baker, was Professor, a form of respect. After a few minutes of hand-shaking, Amina led Nadia to a chair closest to the bride. Having pegged Nadia as someone not-from-us but decent nonetheless, the women resumed their exuberant exchange.

The bride was regal in an armchair with thick hand-rests, her embroidered peach dress of rich satin clinging to her skin from neck to thighs, the rest of her skirt spread in voluminous folds on the floor, her jewelled shoes peeking from below the hem. A frilly peach veil reached her shoulders and gathered around her face, bunching in white-and-peach sequined flowers to the side of her left brow. Crimson lipstick. Pencilled

eyebrows; dark lashes, a ton of mascara. Fresh rouge; finger-
nails matching her lips, but not the dress. The ladies came and
went. They asked who had designed the dress and the bride re-
told her story: her mother was the seamstress and she, the
bride, had chosen the design and helped sew it. Modest, she
exhibited the resourcefulness expected of a wife-to-be. Amina
regaled Nadia with pertinent details: the groom, a first cousin
of the bride, had been promised to her since infancy, a union
much wished for by the affluent families.

One by one the veiled women got up to belly-dance. A
small girl ran and closed the door. Their place a sanctum, the
women gyrated to the tunes of Abd-El-Halim Hafez, their
inhibitions dissolving with the singer's fantasy; their long belts
hugging their thighs, they shimmied and jiggled. One came to
Nadia and pulled her out of her chair, but Nadia did not know
how to belly-dance and a knock on the door saved her.
Mahmoud stood outside, beckoned her, and took her to
where the men were gathered. Did this mean they classified
her as a foreigner for whom Egyptian social niceties were
relaxed? Did they not equate her with their women? Was it a
compliment, or an insult? Had Yasser been here, she would
have been spared such embarrassment. Customs had changed
since their time, when men and women mixed at parties, and
women took pride in their hairdos and clothes.

Mahmoud offered her a chair beside the groom. One by
one, the men got up and offered the young man praise, then
told their ribald jokes about women's beauty and men's viril-
ity. A few glances at Nadia assured them she was not perturbed
by their brand of humour, so they laughed at their own jokes.
Their tales centred around the groom's sexual prowess, his
ability to rise to the occasion, and foretold the stallion's
inevitable demise as he surrenders to the harness. The young
man sat in magnificent self-assurance, for these scenes depicting man's struggle to maintain his freedom in the face of
oncoming dominance of the woman were not in *his* cards. He
had been in love with his cousin since early puberty. She was

sweet, never a sour note to dull his ardour. She was not like the others. How would his pent-up love—he was not allowed to visit her without the presence of her family—ever come to a stop, or be fulfilled? He had harboured the desire of oceans to drown them in turbulent ecstasy. These older men's nihilism would not encroach upon his heart, for his passion would not abate. Thin, scrawny and famished, he sat shrivelled in his dark blue suit, his brown eyes shiny marbles behind his glasses. He would have to endure the next six months before the wedding, but perhaps now his intentions were public, he could be alone with his fiancée. Or would her age—nineteen, not the legal age of twenty-one—render her unapproachable? Tomorrow would tell. He was twenty-two, had waited all those long years. He would have to live the hours, the moments, in a virginal freeze until he and she were together alone.

***

At the Nile Hilton, Selim said, "Let's go to the disco." He beckoned the waiter for the bill. Lights above Selim's head swayed in the breeze; things were going his way. Yasser had agreed to see the Minister of Trade who, Selim felt certain, would offer him the senior trade job. Ahead was a year, perhaps two, of excitement.

"Sure," Yasser answered. He had not been near a disco in years and considered rock music more appropriate for his sons, but all he was aware of was his floating on waves watching Magda, and sirens fluttering his heart-beats. In a few minutes the four were huddled in the back seat of a taxi, Magda's thigh pressed against his, her eyes focused ahead. Yasser could not keep his mind off her body, how smooth her skin, how ample her breasts; he tucked Nadia's face in a blur at the back of his mind. They had agreed to be apart for a while and he had been faithful to her, but in this warm weather, whisky floating in his head, lights rising from the river, his thoughts alive with images, what harm was there?

God knows he had earned his night after a lot of hard work. In the dark taxi, no one spoke.

The disco walls shimmered with myriad reflections of a silver ball turning above the dancers' heads, the changing colours placing couples on a roller coaster of emotion. The four wedged their way between the clustered bodies to a table near the bar, and on the other side of the room musicians with electronic guitars and xylophones blared their music as though playing in open air at the pyramids. The four sank into large leather chairs; Soheir and Selim joked then danced, Selim in a casual beige summer suit and Soheir in a silk violet dress, multiple gold chains wound around her neck. Magda's hand touched Yasser's, its softness teasing his skin and, without speaking, she pulled him to the dance floor between the jostling bodies. He followed her, drunk with music, his mind tripping. Whisky uplifted him as his eyes were fixed on the pupils swimming in aqua blue. He was suspended with her above the animation, turning on a stage of light, even though the fast beat of rock kept their bodies apart. Her face, a magnet, led him through gyrations he had not done before, this dark lady with long hair, sea-flowing eyes beckoning him through waves of time, and he would not stop. And when he did, he did not know whether he had been drinking or floating. Someone pulled his sleeve, and as he followed out of the room all he knew were the curves of her body.

A few yards down the grassy slope off the Cornice, the Nile beckoned them, its stars dancing on the water's surface. Magda's fingers roamed in and out of his and their chests touched as they stood under palm. No one was there, only a few flashing car lights. Selim hailed a cab, the four climbed in, reached his apartment, and without exchanging words, Yasser and Magda knew they were spending the night together. Pulled-back curtains in the small bedroom beamed silvery moonlight on the white sheets. She slipped out of her dress, lay down, spread her hair out in light, her body in darkness, an urgent call in her eyes. His hands fumbled at his zipper, out of his clothes onto her body, a tide thrusting him, his hands thrashing to settle in the hollow of her back, down her thighs; he was drowning in a sea so strong that when he circled her back to undo her bras, his fingers could not pull it apart. She laughed, undid her underwear and released her curves to his ravenous hunger. He lunged into a wave, slid on a surfboard that would not come to a stop. Dimly, he knew she shared his frenzy. Her teeth dipped into his lips; her fingers tugged at his hair; her strands brushed his forehead, their legs battled for domination, they plunged into oblivion, as light receded from the window and night covered them.

***

"What happened?" Nadia asked her housekeeper, Esmat, as she handed her a glass of cold water. At ten in the evening, the woman showed up, set her bundle down, lowered her body to the floor. She did not wear kohl.

"Nothing, nothing at all." She set her empty glass by her side and tightened her kerchief around her head, a sign she had a headache. "The whole day, I and my neighbour's husband searched for my daughter, Rasha, but we couldn't find her. The grocer told us Rasha had come in at noon with Nouri—that good-for-nothing *säälook*, that riffraff who has been running after her for months—bought sweets and left. The grocer thought she was going home," Esmat intoned, sobbing. "This is all we know. One kid said Nouri had gone home to his village. If he has, then we need a car to look for them." Her sobs wrenched a stomach that had ballooned out over the years to contain what life had meted out to her. Dark stains circled her eyes. Nadia knew that in Esmat's neighbourhood, a girl leaving home with a man who was not her fiancé would be an outcast for life, unless she were returned immediately to her mother's safety. The girl's purity was essential for a future marriage. Nadia looked into her kitchen cupboard for aspirin, handed Esmat two pills and another glass of water.

"I'll come, Esmat," Nadia offered. "I'll search with you, but we need a car."

Nadia's mother would have been horrified to know her daughter was joining her maid on a wild goose chase for a house-keeper's missing daughter, yet Nadia had an inner urge to go.

Pressing her temples with her dimpled fingers, Esmat said, "Nessim's brother drives a taxi; he'll take us. I saw Nessim in the garden when I came in." Out of the window, a figure in white sat erect on the dark bench under the cypress. "Nessim," Nadia called, and the white *gallabiah* approached. At her back, Esmat whispered, "He knows about Rasha. I hope he keeps his mouth shut. If I don't find that girl before her father returns, he'll kill her!"

Nadia bent out the window and asked Nessim to reserve his brother with the taxi for eight o'clock in the morning. He nodded and dissolved into the dark. The two women washed and went to bed early.

***

Monir, professor of Archeology at Cairo University, tourist guide in his spare time, took time off teaching to spend a day with his son, Kareem. The father spread a carpet on the sand where he and Kareem could get a clear view of the Giza Pyramids. Rugged in their solitude, the three triangles stood apart and commanded the elevation that overlooked the low-lying valley in which a trickle of Nile water meandered through stones and dry branches. At one time, this stream had been deep enough for Pharaohs to bring their cargos in by boat from Aswan. Monir motioned Kareem to take his place on the carpet, then he lay down by his son's side. Kareem's toes stuck out of the carpet onto the sand inches farther than his father's. Monir's friends had sons taller and more robust than they. He wondered if chemical fertilizers imported from America and used all over Egypt's land had created the difference between generations.

Today, instead of teaching and taking his load of tourists on their scheduled itinerary, Monir had come to the pyramids to be with Kareem, a student at Alexandria University. Despite their heavy schedules, father and son made time to spend together and this had been their way since Monir's wife had died when Kareem was eight. Side by side, their heads propped up on their arms, they contemplated the pyramids. A white cotton sheet, stretched between four poles, flapped above them, shielding them from the sun.

Monir mused, "It must have taken faith to have these pyramids completed, but I doubt that the Pharaohs misused their subjects and enslaved them as some history books state."

Kareem stared into space. He knew his father's diatribes which had nothing to do with current problems but had a lot to do with many millennia ago. His father could not see the Egypt of today, tottering on the brink of collapse, swayed by political forces from without and pushed by religious ones from within. His father's interest in things past had become his way of escaping the present after Kareem's mother had died, and he continued to bury himself in ancient Egyptian lore to forget his loneliness, when he would have been better off with a new wife. He was saying, "I don't think you've heard a word I've said, Kareem."

"Of course I have, Father! You're trying to convince me that some belief of the ancients in an after-life inspired the pyramids. So what? These stone structures are no longer part of our lives. They don't fill hungry stomachs. They don't provide jobs. Our people are poor. The pyramids don't prove we have know-how today. Look at us, for heaven's sake; we import all our technology from the West and even some of our food!"

Monir could not see how his son espoused values so different from his own, but then, Kareem had opted for engineering, not archaeology. Monir got up, unpacked lunch, handed Kareem his feta cheese and cucumber sandwich.

"All I can see from where I sit," Kareem continued with rising vehemence, "are not the pyramids, but the restless energy simmering in our nation. If you look down there in the distance, Father, you will see the pollution, the thousands of bodies jostling on the streets, the poor and hungry, mothers begging with their children. I and my generation want to know how are we going to find jobs, get married and have children when incomes are not enough for us to lead meagre lives?" Kareem took vengeful bites off his sandwich. Camels passed by father and son, carrying their loads of human cargo.

Kareem was half angry at himself. His father had the right analysis of things Egyptian, but his generation had been able to survive, not so his own. Even if he and his friends had money for rent, which they did not, they could not find vacant apartments. The few available places were out of their financial reach. You had to be the son of a General or a Minister to have the contacts and money, otherwise, no chance. Marry it, was the password among his friends, but rich girls married richer men. If the men worked hard until the age of thirty-five, how would they get married? As things stood, most young women took up the veil, looked like scare-crows, and those who did not, hid behind unseemly clothes. Parties were a nightmare with men and women segregated. His life was arid like the parched sand surrounding him.

Monir watched his son take large mouthfuls and chew on them with fury, and he acknowledged to himself that times have changed even though the underlying truths have not. If things were tougher today, the basic qualities of his people were the same. Kareem would discover this later.

He said, "My point is, if our ancestors had faith and know-how, how come we don't have any today?"

"Of course we do! But how can we use this know-how when so many of us are jammed together in such overcrowded spaces? The uneducated are multiplying like flies! Do you realize that every nine months Egypt's population increases by more than a million?"

A camel—carrying a blond woman wearing sun-glasses, straw hat and hugging a water bottle—came up to Kareem and stood there chewing wildly on a bunch of shrivelled straw.

***

Chapter Three
Gazelle

Sun spread warmth through Yasser's body as he reached his arm out for Magda, but the bed-sheets were empty. From the window, sounds of cars and trucks fought each other, but his room was high enough that the sounds were a hum of energy. His body tingled with the memory of the woman in moonlight: black velvet adorned with hard diamond, sensual and demanding. He jumped out of bed to find her. She was not in the kitchen nor in the living room, neither was Soheir; but stretched on the sofa with multiple cushions behind his back and a newspaper in his hands Selim—reading glasses hanging low over his wide nose—was mumbling about an item in the news. He lowered the paper, took a sip of tea from the glass on the side table and raised his brows in mock concern. *"Ahlan wa sahlan!* So you're up? Can't you take an innocent night of fun without sleeping till the afternoon? What happened to you, have you become soft with luxury in Canada?"

There he was again, thought Yasser, like his own relatives, thinking life in North America was a dark sleep, lightened by shiny dollars pouring down from above.

It was noon. Yasser smiled. "Where's Magda?"

"She left early with Soheir. *They* have to earn a living and must be on time for the tourist buses."

Yasser brewed his black tea in the kitchen, stirred in one spoon of sugar—instead of the five he took before he emigrated to Canada—and carried his steaming glass into the living room. "And you, why aren't *you* at work?" he asked.

"I've taken the day off. I told you last night, but I suppose you didn't hear me, since you had so much on your hands or should I say, *'Alla atraff assabaak'*, on your finger tips. We have

45

an appointment at three with Mr. Abdullah, about a position for you in the Trade Office."

Selim contemplated the candidate he had nominated for the task of making an arms deal with the Americans, a feat requiring fluency in English and Arabic, the ability to catch nuances of words, the art of deciphering body language, and the seductive looks that would win newcomers. The candidate had to have energy, courage, resourcefulness, who other than Yasser? The deal was risky, that much Selim knew from his previous negotiations with the Americans, who did not hand over weapons without demanding a foothold in the country. But Yasser had a way of mitigating problems before they arose; his self-command worked wonders in achieving goals.

A meeting with the Minister of Trade, Yasser thought as he showered, another deadline, the last thing he needed. He had come here for a rest, and for an escape from his self-induced labour. As the oldest child in a large family, he had been expected by his father and uncles to be an example to his siblings and cousins. But his two brothers had taken seven years each to complete their four-year university degrees at *his* expense, and that had been all right because they were the *young ones*. He had sent money to his father for his brothers' education, but they had shown no appreciation, and now lived with their wives and children oblivious of their responsibility for their parents' possessions. When Yasser had called his younger brother, Ali, in Ismailia, Ali had reminded him that their father's thirty *fedans* were as good as lost, because the family had no papers with which to reclaim the land from the government. In 1967, Israeli army officials had seized their thirty *fedans* on a hill overlooking the Mediterranean Sea, an ideal spot for controlling the port. Then when the Egyptians had reclaimed Sinai, Ali had had no papers from their late father to re-acquire the land from government officials because in their town, heritage matters were handled by elders who made vocal decisions to younger generations, a custom which had been as good as gold before 1967 but was now useless. First the Egyptian troops had used their land as a base for a year, then the Israelis took it over and camped on it for twelve years; now it was back in Egyptian hands for the last fifteen years and Ali expected Yasser to resolve the problem. Papers were somewhere in a government office, Ali had mumbled.

"Great," Yasser had answered, "so why didn't *you* go get them? Are you waiting for me to come all the way from Canada to Egypt to get the papers from some lazy desk clerk?" Money was the problem, money to bribe the officials to get action started on their file, Ali had complained, and their conversation had ended there.

Yasser scrubbed his arms with *loofa* and soap, watched the dark suds drip from his limbs—amazing how much soot one acquired from limited exposure to the streets—and remembered how hard he had worked in Canada to send his brothers money for his parents' medical and living expenses, then for their funerals, but when his brothers had started their jobs, each had concentrated on his own family's expenses. Yasser was the compulsive one. His body was tired, like an over-wound clock, his nerves jittery, his body needed to let off steam, now was the time to live a little before he reached his fifth decade.

He stepped out of the shower and walked into his room. How different was his upbringing from that of his oldest son, Amir, whom he supported throughout his undergraduate university and was now helping until he graduated from Medical School. Amir had no idea how the yolk of family had weighed his father down; worse, Amir was hostile, as though he found everything Yasser did an irritant. A twinge of guilt reminded Yasser of the night Amir was conceived. Yasser tugged at his shirt in the mirror and gave his stomach a critical look. That night he had had a few drinks, his condom had sprung a leak, and he had discovered it when he awoke, but Nadia had been fast asleep. He had convinced himself it was Nadia's safe period, rolled over and slept. He had not wanted his early years with her complicated with children. This son of his was

an accident. How else could he, Yasser, define Amir's concep-
tion? A mistake. Amir may have sensed his father's denial, or
as a child may have heard Yasser saying this to Nadia late at
night. Amir had mentioned to him that medical research
showed the foetus sensed the parents' feelings during concep-
tion and the mother's emotional state during pregnancy. Yasser
was not sure these ideas were tenable and didn't feel comfortable when Amir informed him of them. Perhaps his son was
sending him a specific message. Did a foetus sense the angst of
the parents who conceived it? Does stress during mating affect
a foetus's growth, or the way he feels about himself or his parents? This was too bizarre! Nadia had not conceded their son
was a mistake, because she had wanted him. Was he, Yasser,
the odd one? Amir may be aware of his father's feelings, or perhaps Yasser's guilt had brought on these thoughts, but once his
son was born, Yasser had put his denial behind him. His sons
were not going to bear the financial burdens he carried, and
this is why they will not realize what it was to keep on working without taking time off until one reached old age; he had
made sure they would not know. He would be leaving them
enough resources so they can exercise choice.

He sat on the bed and flipped through the morning paper
Selim had given him. On the front page were photographs of
the new American delegates shaking hands with Egyptian personnel, but before he had read their names, his mind had
dovetailed to Magda, oval face on silvery pillow, dark hair an
open fan of eagle's feathers.

***

Nessim and his brother arrived with the taxi at eight in
the morning to pick up Nadia and Esmat. The women
climbed into the back seat, and Nessim sat in the front beside
his brother to assume leadership of the group. He held his thin
shoulders back, puffed his emaciated chest to demonstrate his
determination to hunt down the culprit who had besmirched
Esmat's daughter. A peacock with upright feathers, Nadia

thought, so if she were to paint his sculpted face and his wiry body, she would use whites, ochres, browns, shades of silver for his clothes, skin and hair, a touch of verdant green for the vest, a splash of bluish-green for the background to emulate his outstretched feathers. Inflated with his own importance, Nessim intimated he would strike with venom, quite a different persona from that of the passive gardener who floated in bare feet around their garden at the Delta, comfortable with the wet soil, his white turban crowning his bent head as it bobbed up and down in the sun.

The day was hot, but a slight breeze came in through Nadia's window. At her side, Esmat was an untidy bundle of dark clothes, her face flushed, her kohl dark. Nadia turned to the window on her right to avoid the tension of oncoming cars, for the way this driver manoeuvred the taxi was bound to land them in a ditch. He over-sped, stayed in the middle of the road, swerved to the left, then when an oncoming vehicle appeared in front of his windshield, he swung his car to the right missing the other by inches, returned to the left and continued driving at high speed. In England, Nadia supposed, he would have driven on the right of the road.

This hunt for Esmat's daughter would help Nadia forget the seconds, or this is what she thought when she left her home. Time had hung heavy in her garden at the Delta Barrage, under the sycamores, in the middle of pecking chickens, by the Nile, as she painted the peasant washing her clothes in the river. This trip would slice through her conundrum. Perhaps when their journey was over, she would find a message from Yasser in the mail-box. Like granite statues, three brown camels stood glued to their spot on the sand. What did *they* wait for? A shady spot to mate? They had limitless patience standing there staring out on the monotonous ochre of their lives. A few olive-green shrubs in sand, and across the desert a clump of palms tall and unbending in their solitude, their willowy branches swaying with dates. In a month, the fruit would be crimson, then the dates would mellow into a dark brown, soft and sweet, and the clusters of fig-bushes—their round purple fruits visible under green leaves—would spread out in the sand a few feet from the road. Bedouins do not worry about others picking their fruit, for each family knows its cluster of figs or palm trees, looks after them, then wanders away. Bedouins return to nurture their plants and to pick their ripened fruit. For them, the desert is a detailed map in a city dweller's hands: they recognize their own plots without placing stones for landmarks.

Their taxi came to a stop, and the driver announced a short break at a shelter of palm branches attached to a shack no bigger than a tent for two. A bedouin man and a dark-veiled woman in a bright orange *gallabiah* sat straight-backed on their straw chairs, awaiting news from nowhere, their eyes staring into an infinity of sand. For them, there were no hours or seconds, only space and fluidity. Esmat led Nadia by the arm to a straw chair, set her apart from the others, for her mistress was not going to have tea in the company of men below her social level. Nadia knew enough not to resist; she would have confused the men and enraged Esmat, who lowered her body on the straw mat at Nadia's feet and tucked her legs under her torso in lotus fashion. Breeze swished the sand. Nadia ordered tea. The brick-red brew arrived in steaming, hot glasses, the only drink that quenches thirst in the heat. They sipped. In the desert, there is no need for words. The bedouin and his wife sat erect under their straw hut, no possessions, no way of travel except by camel, no home but their shack, no vegetation other than fig bushes, watermelons and dates. Bread, cheese, condiments they bought or bartered from nearby villages when they went for their flour or took from taxi drivers in exchange for tea and snacks. The driver gave them a carton of matches and a sack of flour. Perhaps he had a running account with them. No fixed price, just what he thought he owed them. Nadia gave them money.

Women gave birth here in the middle of nowhere without access to flowing water. They squatted on a mat, a pail of well-water at their side. No neon lights, no hard stretchers, no metal stirrups to fasten their feet high in a V shape; no strangers under the glare of floodlights staring into their open bodies twisting with pain; the dignity of the bedouin women's lives, the peace, the quiet of it. Nadia would have liked her own life to have had an open fluidity, her dream, a mirage wavering on sand.

***

Alone in her apartment in Douki, Magda recalled Yasser, her lover of one night at Selim's place. She saw him as a desert chieftain, tall, well-built yet slim, wavy hair salt-sea waves on her lips, his body new fallen rain, chest aromatic with musky herbs engendering waves of comfort in caves of sea-green moss and underwater flowers. This was Yasser in their night-dream. Her cheek on his chest, his hair a reality under her skin, his arms around her, fingers wandering over her back-bone and settling into the enclave of her buttocks.

***

The driver entered the taxi, a signal for the group to continue their journey. When Nadia asked for a washroom, the bedouin woman motioned her to a spot under a palm tree. Nadia trudged to a place behind bushes with a hole in the ground and was embarrassed to walk back to the car, but no one seemed either aware of her actions, or interested. Perhaps if she were to spend time in the desert this crouching would become natural to her.

***

And if Yasser were married, thought Magda, as Soheir insisted on telling her, that would make no difference. It would not change his flavoured skin sun-soaked in warmth, nor erase their full-bodied love-making in moonlight, eclipse her first glimpse of him on the terrace at the Nile Hilton, his eyes forging steel barbs into her heart. Since she was fourteen,

Magda had yearned for a man like Yasser. She had hungered for a love to erase her mother's shadow and do away with her father's oppressive power.

***

Noon sun pressed down on sand as Nadia and her group resumed their trip. This was going to be the rough part, Nadia thought, and placed her shawl between the frame and the top of the rolled-up window pane. In her mind, the desert sun transformed into the white light that shone on snow at night. It was years ago, she recalled, when she and Yasser had had an argument in the car on their way home from a late movie, and she had jumped out of the still-running car and opted to walk home. She had had no boots on. He had driven beside her to coax her into the car, but even though she was freezing, she would not give in. He had given up and driven away. Only then did she realize it was Sunday, and buses ran sporadically. A dense snow had piled up. Around her, white cottony wildness, no glassed-in room at the station, so that by the time the bus had arrived, she had been blinded by snow, her toes curled inwards to stone. She had climbed into the vehicle, eyes filled with the cold fluff, tears frozen. By the window, she sat deaf to the steady stream of words coming from the bus driver. Yasser had gone and left her in the storm, but upon arriving home, she had found out that he had been following her bus. Why did she put herself in situations of exile? In Canada snow, here sand, two isolators, not picture-beauty worlds, but clear canvases that allow her eye to search, discover and create whatever meaning it finds, looking for the subject of its perfection, a singular image to lift itself above others and illuminate time.

Their taxi stopped at a small village marked by a sprinkling of cypress trees. The sun was at a slant, and light from the window brought in a subdued warmth. Nadia guessed it would be about five. She must have dozed. Light greyish-brown huts made of hardened Nile sediment—their roofs interlaced with yellow palm branches—lined both sides of the road. Their taxi raised a cloud of dust as children in *gallabiahs* gathered to watch it go by. Esmat gave the driver directions she had taken from people in her neighbourhood, but he had to stop to ask store owners for instructions. Two men on the side-road, who appeared to know everyone in the village, gave him a description of the street where Nouri lived. At a distance from them, a young man ran ahead in the direction the men gave, then disappeared. The taxi passed by low mud houses and small stores with smaller windows, dusty pavements loaded with vegetable baskets and over-ripe bananas, then it took the wrong side street and had to turn back. When they stopped at a yellow one-storey house with small windows fringed by palms bearing orange-red dates, Esmat stormed out of the taxi and rushed to the slightly open door; she pushed it and disappeared indoors. Soon, her angry voice bellowed above that of a crying girl. Nadia relaxed; Esmat had found her daughter.

The driver and Nessim entered the house as Esmat emerged from it dragging her girl by the arm and thrusting her beside Nadia in the back seat. The tall girl, in a lime shiny dress, frizzy hair highlighted with peroxide, wailed about her mother's unceremonious behaviour and repeated she had to go back to the house to gather her belongings. Stone-faced, the two men emerged from the open door of the house, marched back to the taxi and took their places in the front seats. Esmat bent over the back of the front seat, prodded Nessim's shoulder and bellowed, "The coward took off before we arrived! He was alerted by the young man who ran ahead of us. What scum! Nessim, you would have given him a good beating, wouldn't you?" She poked his shoulder for a response. Nessim nodded his acceptance of his potent role.

Wedged between her mother and Nadia, Rasha quivered, tears streaking her mascara in blue and black streams. She was afraid of the men in her mother's company. Esmat hit her daughter on the shoulder and side and kept hitting her until Nadia intervened. Children peered in at the window to find

out why this indignity was being showered upon their beautiful bride from Cairo; they gathered close and pressed their
noses to the windows. Esmat asked the driver to start the car.
The kids ran alongside the vehicle until it passed out of sight.
Nadia had expected the episode to have taken longer, that the
men would have pursued Nouri, but no one seemed interested. She was glad it was over and suspected it would be close
to ten before they got to the Delta Barrage. Nadia remembered her hunger. She asked the driver, "Is there a clean place
close by to buy sandwiches?"

Pointing to a corner in the road, Esmat shouted, "Stop,
Stop! There he goes. Good-for-nothing scum. There is Nouri.
Over there. He saw us and ran behind that house."

The car swerved to the right and around the corner into a
muddy side-street. Stepping on the gas, the driver set off after
the two young men, one in *gallabiah*, the other in dark
trousers and white shirt. The young men headed off to the
green fields at the end of the road then, like twin-ghosts, white
gallabiah and dark trousers slipped sideways into the plantation. Corn shoots rustled back into place.

Their car ground to a halt. Selim and his brother jumped
out and dived into the corn. This happened before Nadia had
the time to see the spot where the men had entered the field.
She restrained Rasha from throwing her body against the door
as Esmat hurled threats out of the window at the culprits. For
a while, the women heard shouts but saw nothing. Rasha
wailed. Then the men emerged from the green shoots carrying
the young man in the white shirt, one holding him up by his
arms, the other by his feet; they swayed him, right and left, as
though to toss him back into the plantation. Nessim's digni-
fied face reflected the prize catch of the day, his brother's
muscled fore-arms rose to the challenge as he checked to make
sure they had a large audience before they tossed their cargo
up and down then threw him on the ground and beat and
punched him black and blue. Other young men arrived to
deliver the victim from his pursuers' hands, but they received

their share of punches, until the rescuers dragged the young man away, his clothes tattered, his body limp. Nessim and his brother slapped their hands as though to brush off dirt and clean them of contact with their victim. They had enacted their job on his body, strutted back to the taxi, climbed in, checked to see if their audience was there, headed out of the village in a triumphal cloud of dust. Hunger pangs now forgotten, Nadia's fatigue set in. Rasha whimpered in the corner. The car sped into the darkening horizon. Barring a punctured tire, a common occurrence on these dusty roads, they would get there without further delay. The day's search behind her, Nadia wondered why she had agreed to join this cruel caper. What if the men had injured or killed the culprit? Yet they seemed satisfied with the lesson they had taught Nouri's circle, that they would not tolerate indignity on their women. They had vindicated the girl's honour and proven her family to be respectable. Rasha slept from exhaustion.

Like disembodied souls, faces of the village kids reminded Nadia of the skimpy children at Luxor, years ago, before she and Yasser had bought their Delta house. Both had felt guilty, about what? Yasser had handed the oldest boy a few *piastres*, then on impulse gave him a pound note. The boy threw the pound on the sand and headed the group into a run. The kids were frightened, as Nadia's mother explained later; not being used to receiving so much money from strangers, they thought they were being bribed to do something awful. Guilt money, it never works, thought Nadia.

***

In her veranda overlooking the desert in Heliopolis, a suburb of Cairo, Nadia's mother sat on a straw chair and embroidered the infant dress she had promised her church group for their charity fair. On the day Nadia, her only child, was born in Heliopolis, *Khamseen* winds had raged through the desert and dropped their load of sand over the city. Her husband was on a trip to Italy as she lay on her bed thinking how he would discover she had given birth two weeks before her expected date. Unlike other men who had to have sons, her husband had been happy to see his girl. They had named her Nadia, because her name derived from *nada*, or dew, something the mother loved to see on leaves in March when things were dry; her baby was the fresh dew on her hitherto childless life. Now, after decades in Canada, Nadia was back in Egypt and had visited her mother a few times, promised to come and stay with her in Heliopolis for longer. Would she fulfill her promise?

Soon after her daughter married Yasser, a Moslem not a Coptic Orthodox Christian like themselves, the couple had left for Canada. This was the loneliest day in the mother's life, when she had to cope with the derision of Copts and face up to her only child opting to live ten thousand miles away. But she should have expected that of a daughter who, when eight, had wandered away on the beach at Ras-El-Bar and was lost for hours. Neighbours and friends combed the bay for her and found her in a wooded area, tired, her feet blistered by the scalding sand, happy to be alone. She was searching for a nook in a big tree she had spotted weeks before, when she and her father had gone for a walk. The nook was on the upper branches of the tree, and her father had not allowed her to climb. This same Nadia had elected to marry a man who wanted to live abroad. Now, back in Egypt, she was in a house two hours away from Heliopolis. The faraway and the strange, Nadia, never the known and tried, her mother thought, not satisfied to stay with your family, the way your father and grandparents did. A pilgrim in a desert, wanderer set to capture dreams, to thrive on images of your mind! Is this why you are so dear to me, because unlike other young ones in our family, you have to *make* your world, not receive it? And I, a wanderer in my mind, reach out through you to limitless skies, which I only dream about.

Nadia's mother pulled on the green thread to round off the leaf in the multi-coloured smock. She imagined an orphan's tiny face, round, dark skinned, peering out of the wool dress. She had not seen her own grandsons so young. The smock was vibrant with colour. Since her childhood, Nadia had liked colours and had drawn houses, not in the Egyptian style of flat roofs, but in European style, with sloping red tiles, useful because there they had a lot of rain. This had puzzled her teachers. They had demanded she be realistic and copy what she saw, but Nadia continued to create red brick houses, with slanted roofs, windows with curtains held back by cords on both sides, chimneys letting out smoke in the manner of books imported from Europe, where they used wood for fuel in their harsh winters. Her father had bought her these books on his travels. Nadia had not drawn whitewashed houses with flat tops, vines on verandas, home-raised pigeons flying from roof tops, building their nests in the vine, classical Egyptian buildings and beautiful enough. Nadia's hearths had bristled with lit logs, something most Egyptian children did not know existed. Nadia was destined to live abroad and had sensed it as a child.

She had not come home this March to celebrate her birthday. Perhaps she would drop in for a chat and tea between her wanderings, before her time in Egypt was over.

***

Yasser opened his suitcase on the bed and piled his clothes into it. After his interview with Mr. Abdullah, he would leave Cairo; to stay in Selim's apartment would be to increase his chances of seeing Magda, but one night's deception was duplicity enough. In a couple of weeks, he would have a job in Cairo, if only for a few months, and Nadia would be with him. The James and Sons company he worked for in Toronto for the last fifteen years was a source of stress for him. As Senior Design Architect, he liked the work but felt he should have become Vice President of Production after Michael's retirement. Management had quoted seniority as the reason when they had promoted Hicks, a man with no inkling of

·design nor interest in schooling himself. He must have joined the firm through a family connection when such was qualification enough. Maybe he, Yasser, would get the position after Hicks, but this was too long a wait. He needed time away from his office. In a year or so, he would return, then he would have time to work on his promotion. He might or might not become Vice President, but he would not go beyond that. Had to think about his next move: either break through the invisible veil that held him back from his rightful place in the company, or accept his treatment, the trademark of his generation of so-called new Canadians. Perhaps he would leave the company and start his own business: Amin and Associates. Sounded good. Did he have the energy to put this scheme through, and would Samy join him, or was his son sold on his bio-engineering experiments with the University of Western Ontario? Amin and Son Limited. He could train Samy in the business in no time, and his son's knowledge of computers would be an asset. His older son, Amir, was out of the question; he would be an MD soon and, in any case, this son and he could not see eye to eye.

You're a snail who has overstayed his days in the shell, Yasser told himself. Time to get out and plunge into the deep. But for now, rest. He would check his ideas with Nadia, for she was clear-headed and he missed her.

***

When their taxi swerved off the road, Nadia awoke with a start. Through the open window, the sky was navy with silver stars; a breeze blew in, but rather than feel refreshed, she was warm and uncomfortable. What had she been doing running away like this? What was she searching for? What a mad caper with people whose ways she did not know, in parts of Egypt she had not been, in the company of those to whose social level she did not belong. At least the venture had ended well. Rasha was safe and Esmat's family honour vindicated. When they came to a stop outside her house, Nadia and

Nessim stepped out, and the taxi sped with Esmat, Rasha and the driver to Cairo. As she turned the lights on in the hall-way, she remembered the mailbox.

She ran out, opened it, found the telegram. Tearing off the seal, she ran back into the hall-way. From Cairo. Yasser was arriving tonight, at midnight. He had arranged for his transportation and would be seeing her at their home in the Delta Barrage.

Tonight, at midnight. In one hour and a half, so suddenly.

***

Monir, with tourists close on his heals, stopped half-way up the steep incline inside the Cheops pyramid at Giza, in the small passageway leading to the Pharaoh's burial chamber. Today, the passageway seemed darker than usual. He made this ascent every week, but perhaps for the first time he stopped to catch his breath. The wood planks under his feet were old and dusty; they wavered and creaked. They led upwards into unrelieved blackness. The tourists behind him shifted their feet, eager to get to the chamber, but the sloping ceiling over their crouching bodies was low and inhibited their speedy progress. His back ached from his bent posture. It must have been a feat for ancient Egyptians to have used a series of reflective surfaces, starting from the sunny outdoors and placed at right angles from each other, to reflect the sun's rays all the way up through the dim corridors to the inner chamber of the tomb.

Wavering light from his torch was helpless against the overwhelming confinement of the interior of the pyramid. Today, he regretted that these marvellous structures had been extracted from their protective sand cover. If tombs, even temples, in Upper Egypt had remained under warm sand, they might have been protected from humidity and pollution; they would have remained unblemished, just as they were on the day his ancestors had left them. Pharaoh's bodies would have lain in their shrouds untouched and they would have continued to bless the land. Yet early thieves had broken in and stolen some of the treasures, and he could not imagine how he could have lived his life without seeing these ancient artifacts. But he had a sense of trespassing on sacred soil and felt that uncovering a corpse from its place óf rest was sacrilege.

Nothing had shocked Monir more than the recent story in the national newspaper, *Al Ahram*, about Lord Carnarvon's theft of ancient treasures from the tomb of Tutankhamun at the time of discovery. All these years he, Monir, had suspected just that: that Howard Carter and his financier, Lord Carnarvon, had taken priceless treasures of gold and jewel-encrusted statues out of the tomb, but Monir had had no proof for his suspicions. A week ago, he had read an article which reported that upon Lord Carnarvon's death, his nephew had stumbled upon an inner chamber in his uncle's house which he had accidentally accessed by pressing a button behind a portrait, thus opening a section of the wall and revealing a hidden door leading into a room where lay the choicest treasures of King Tutankhamun's tomb! Just as Monir had suspected, and the nephew could have helped himself to the best pieces before he acknowledged them to the authorities. No one knew what had happened to those precious objects, thousands of them. Monir had not read a list of the stolen artifacts either in Egyptian or British newspapers. Had these treasures landed in the British Museum, or like so many others, had they been re-plundered by relatives? Had Egyptian personnel shared in the take? How many more pieces lay squandered in museums and in private collections all over the world? Worse still, why had not his own people built a new museum to house the thousands of pieces which lay cluttered in the basement of the old, sloppily renovated Cairo Museum?

Someone tripped on his heels. He pressed on, climbed the dusty wood gingerly as though side-stepping his ancestor's ribs. The way was narrow and dark. They would soon reach the highest point that turned to the right and down a few steps to the inner chamber. Dampish dust closed in on him. Fascinated by the idea of an inner chamber where Pharaoh had lain in splendour for thousands of years, tens of tourists pushed behind him. Some believed that the pyramid shape itself emanated mystical waves of longevity. Monir had read about this pyramid craze that had swept the marketing business in America. He had wondered how the triangular shape, devoid of its spiritual trappings and bodies of ancient beings, away from the soil that had harboured years of ancient history, could be regarded as a mystical presence. Surely the miracle was in the spirit, in the souls of people who lived there, in the bodies buried in the living soil, as well as in the geometric design.

Apart from archaeologists who came here knowing what to expect, few tourists believed the chamber was vacant, that like any deserted or plundered tomb it was devoid of the spirit that had filled it. Every group he had brought in to explore the pyramid had insisted on climbing the height of the structure, on going down the few steps at the end of the trip and entering the chamber. There, they found a dusty place, dark, except for the small flashlights held up by the guides. Tourists rushed to the *mastaba*, the granite rectangle that had housed Pharaoh's sarcophagus, and leaned over the elevated cold structure to find it empty. Careful not to be contaminated by the dust of the departed, they did not touch the cold granite; they peered into the hollow tomb to catch a lingering essence of death, an imprint of the visage or one of its forgotten fingerprints, but they walked away disappointed. Monir sensed the group's rising expectation behind him, their restless feet shuffling, and he cringed from their inevitable deflation. Outdoors he had warned them the chamber was empty, but that had been in broad sunlight and they had forgotten, or perhaps they had hoped he would somehow be wrong, that they would discover something, anything, that would give them a key to the interminable mysteries of the grave. The body-full Pharaonic grave.

***

The Minister of Trade offered Yasser the position of Consultant for Foreign Contracts, one year renewable. Later in the evening, Yasser and Selim elbowed their way through the crowds in Liberty Square, but as Yasser pushed through the throng all he wanted was to be at the Delta Barrage. He had decided to stay in Egypt for at least one year, and Nadia would be happy with his decision. He had asked for a leave of absence from his job in Canada, and with recent financial restraints in the firm, he was confident his request would be approved. He hoped young Tufford would not fill his space too well. Yasser had hired him, so the guy would not dare do anything stealthy in his absence.

Selim offered to take him to Le Meridien Hotel on the Nile to meet the two women, but Yasser answered, "Not tonight, Selim, I want to go home. Nadia's expecting me." And he added, "About yesterday: Magda's fine, but I want to be with my wife. Last night was a mistake." Referring to Magda out loud made Yasser uncomfortable. She was the wild cat prowling the jungle of his dreams, but talking about her made her real. He must have been out of his mind to go to bed with her.

Selim had seen Nadia decades ago on their wedding day and could not remember her. He knew her to be attractive in a wild sort of way, for Yasser admired shapely women, but Yasser had lived with her for twenty-four years and owed himself, if not her, a little romance on the side.

Yasser caught the eleven o'clock bus to the Delta Barrage. Two days and a night to change from a Western consciousness to a Mid-Eastern one. He took pride in adapting to change, but this time there was a hitch, his slip with Magda. He had been unprepared for the sudden shock of recognition she had triggered in him. Perhaps he had been tired, his reflexes swift, his controls eroded. He settled back against the cushions to lessen the effect of the bumps on the road. Nadia. By now she would be relaxed, immersed in her work. When she painted, she had this look as though she had come in from a faraway trip and could not focus on people or things close to her. Her work was a mystery rite of which he knew little. She liked to have him beside her, but she could also adapt to solitude. Why spend hours on work she did not put up for sale? She had said she would take time to market it, but whenever she had the choice of doing that or painting, she painted. Still, he wished he had a passion such as hers. She would be thrilled with his new job, would want to know about their boys, and their news was good: Amir on his way to becoming an MD, Samy due for promotion at the computer company. Yasser was tired. The bus bumped to a stop. Midnight. He had arrived at the Delta Barrage. He took a taxi home.

His finger pressed the bell and when Nadia opened the door, he threw himself into her arms as into safe refuge. In white silk housecoat, her hair shiny, eyes a peaceful stream. He held her, afraid he would sink, his body complete. He was home; he knew where he was and why and suddenly felt a drowning fatigue. He went out on the porch to get his luggage and could barely lift it to bring it into the hall. Staggering in, he set it down by the sofa.

As he followed Nadia out into the balcony, he smelled the jasmine. Their climber had been a shrub the last time he was here, but now it was reaching the ceiling in full bloom. He stretched his body on the sofa and she sat by his side on a straw chair. Nadia's hand lay on his. She did not ask questions. His limbs' trembling subsided and a drowsiness overtook him.

She sat in the night's breeze, listening to him breathe.

***

Chapter Four

Lotus

The *Lotus* lay at the dock's side in the shade of the Cairo Nile Hilton Hotel; on its upper deck Nadia and Yasser bent over the rails to watch passengers board. In light winter clothes, foreigners and Egyptians crowded the plank connecting the river's bank to the boat, their laughter rising to the upper deck of the ship of their dreams. Seven in the morning and the sun was still behind the high-rise of the hotel, the December day warm and breezy, the leaves of the poinsettia trees—a shiny silver in the early sunrise—rustling in the breeze along the Cornice pavement. Despite the winter's chill, Nadia was glad they were going on the trip at this time of year, since the sand in Upper Egypt would be a pleasant warmth, instead of the hot, dry glare they would encounter in April.

Yasser watched the passengers jostle on the plank and focused his attention on a tall woman—in black sweater and pants with imitation leopard-skin scarf—her large gold earrings hanging low within her swaying black hair. In front of her, a shorter woman in purple, decked in layers of gold necklaces and long earrings, was talking to the balding man ahead of her. Untidy, in a T-shirt barely covering his belly, the man's hair flew sideways like wisps of a fan torn by the wind. He could have been the mad scientist in films, except that his stomach signalled he was more entranced by pleasures of the flesh. Nadia wondered why this ill-assorted group was the centre of Yasser's attention. She studied the hand-painted lotus flowers on the walls of the Nile Hilton Hotel, their brilliant white against the vibrant turquoise background, their colours a synthetic brightness contrasting the soft blue of the sky. The sun would peek out from behind the high-rise and warm the upper deck. Yasser had agreed to set aside time to sail with her to Luxor and Aswan, and from there to fly to Abu Simbel, then back to Cairo. The trio he watched was making slow progress, the line ahead of them jammed with passengers clogged at the entrance of the boat.

Nadia asked, "Anyone you know?"

"Yes, that's Selim over there, the friend who helped me get my job."

She remembered the name and guessed the shorter woman behind Selim was his wife, and perhaps the other one was her friend or relative. The two women wore elaborate sweaters and tight pants, their jewellery outdone by high heals, on which they balanced, holding their heads high as though posing for a cinematographer's lens, their hairstyles immaculate, sprayed into starched wings, holding out against the sway of the morning breeze.

"You didn't tell me we were having company," she chided Yasser.

"I didn't know Selim was coming," he retorted.

"We don't have to be with them, do we? When we get to Luxor, we can go to a different hotel," Nadia suggested.

"I'm not sure we can: it's a package deal," he answered.

Yasser was under siege; he had made the mistake of reserving his tickets through Selim, who had booked them through Soheir. He hoped the man would show some decency by remaining with the two women on the lower deck. Yasser counted the seconds. Above the entrance to the Captain's cabin, the arm of the clock ticked through fifteen minutes and the trio did not appear on the upper deck. Perhaps Selim had more sense than Yasser credited him with, but why had Selim not warned him that he and the women were travelling on the same boat? Perhaps this was Selim's way of blackmailing him into participating in an arms deal he had refused to handle. A half-hour later, the boat pushed through the Nile, and the trio had not made an appearance.

Nadia and Yasser bent over the rails to watch the boat's hull slice the water. On their right, concrete buildings towered above the Cornice Road running alongside the river, and Cairo's First Radio Station commanded a rounded edge jutting into the Nile. Nadia took in the details: palm trees, red, white and orange flowers, and on their left El Gizereh—a small island in the river—its edges dotted with waterside cafés, their verandas displaying pottery with cyclamen bougainvillea, snapdragon and rose of Sharon, and on both sides, acacia shrubs and high-rise buildings receded to uncover long stretches of greenery. The boat moved in a dream-like smoothness, and the cool air refreshed them even as the sun, now high, filled them with its sedate heat. They pulled their collars up to protect their necks against the river's keen breeze.

Nadia twined her arm through Yasser's. This was the trip she had planned for through many winters in Canada. They discussed their sons' visit to Egypt over New Year's, and Yasser said: "We have to take them everywhere, because we don't know when they'll be back."

Nadia reflected, "They should take this trip on the Nile."

Amir was one year from completing his medical school and Laura, his biologist girlfriend—who had completed her studies—was quiet and thoughtful like him. Samy had a grant to create biological programs on the computer. Both sons were searching for ways to prolong life, but for Nadia they were not far from the youngsters who had played hockey on snowy streets at night in Canada, for whom she had waited at the living-room window peering out at the white fluff until their woollen hats had bobbed up and down the corner of their street. She leaned her head on Yasser's shoulder. This year she would surround him with the caring she had not given him while their sons were young, and he would learn to share with her the vitality he reserved for his work. No evenings waiting for his return home, no silences keeping them apart, each in a corner of the sofa, twin rocks guarding an alien shore.

Now, together and alone, she would not be asking too much to re-create the space where she had met him decades ago, full of energy and laughter.

***

Yasser checked the clock in their cabin radio: two in the morning. The motion of the boat disturbed him, and he had gotten into the habit of not sleeping until dawn. Nadia's eyes were closed, but he did not know if she were sleeping or thinking, so he stroked her hair and found comfort in the feather-like movements. He did not want to disturb her but needed to touch her. His fingers wavered over her nightgown as he whispered, "Nadia." She stirred and lay on her back, her body open for him like a smooth plant stretching out to the sun, her way of welcoming his touch. He stroked her shoulders, breasts, thighs, down to her knees: the gentlest body he had known. Her breathing accelerated and her hand slipped over his back-bone tracing each disk. She liked resting her fingertips in the hollow nooks of his body, her favourite above his collar-bone. He ran his fingers through her hair, kissed her eye-lids, circled her nipples, her stomach, then his fingers came to rest on her thighs, and his desires crowded in upon him. He kissed her lips and was comforted by her slumberous response. She was half awake, in a land between feeling and memory, and this is how he liked to have her, because this was his Nadia, the woman in a land of dreams moving to his touch, relaying to him memories of a limbo where each found the other's forgotten part and quickened it to life.

She unbuttoned his pyjamas, breathed warmth on his skin, until he was transported to a sky with stars where the boat's motion edged him closer to a star-burst of constellations. But the moon out of the window irked him. Magda: what a fool he'd been. He changed his position and gave his back to the bright glass and Nadia adjusted herself to face him. He touched her hair lying on his thighs and knew he would never sense such light in the arms of another. She shifted and led him into her, each facing the other, her eyes on the shiny water out the window. In moments of love, she liked to see the sky, the earth, and at this instant, Yasser knew he loved her, the mother of his boys, the gentle companion of his heart, and he could never love another. He held her to him, shoulder to shoulder, face to face, her legs wound around his back, he riding high and higher into his energy, higher and forever, she urging him on, clasping him as though his body had melded with hers. Her face—clear in silvery light, like the most peaceful stream he had ever seen—soothed him. His only love. He ran his fingers through her tangled hair—a herbal garden—and rested her head on his shoulder as her lips fastened on his neck. He bent his head on her shoulder. They sat holding each other. When his skin lost its love-warmth, he stirred, put his clothes on and she did too, then they lay close together. But he could not sleep and this was not like him. Love with Nadia meant his tensions were released, his heart peaceful, and he could rest; but not tonight. He moved away from her and lay on the edge of the bed facing the moon. What did Selim mean by showing up with Magda and Soheir? He, Yasser, had told him he wanted to take this trip alone with Nadia. Luckily, they had not met the trio on deck; Selim might have enough tact to keep their paths separate, but the man was unpredictable and thrived on practical jokes. Yasser felt a foreigner to these tactics and hoped that the day's sun would wipe away his frustrations. He was not sure that one evening's fling was worth the guilt he was suffering, the anxiety he harboured about Nadia finding out. But he had sullied the one woman who meant something to him, and he had given his body to another. Duplicity was a fecund pool of dirt: you plunged into its murky waters in a dormant ravine and you wallowed in it. After twenty-five years of marriage, he had cheated on his wife. Since he was twenty-four, an architect on his first job, he had been faithful to her, and now his niggling regret triggered a deeper sense of loss. He could not rid himself of this mounting dread; his heart thumped pushing his nerves to an unsettling disquietude. He knew he had to escape this accelerating gloom yet guessed that guilt about a one-night fling did not trigger such tremors; in fact, the seeds of fear had been plaguing him in Toronto for a number of years, now they were full blown.

Sure, he missed his son, Samy, the fullness of his presence, but there was something else he missed: his own youth? His native country? His status as leader of the family? His stature at work? Was he grieving his estrangement from his native soil? Not so simple. He had misplaced something. Guilt filled him, but he was not sure that Magda was the reason. She might be the trigger or the symptom, but not the reason. A *self*-pity? Had he spent his youth running after unreal goals? Had he *lived*? Was his son Samy right when he said, "You think you've been around, Father, but really, you've had a pretty safe life. Have you known any woman other than Mother? Have you changed jobs? If not, then you haven't experienced a serious division in your life, so how can you understand my conflicts?"

Had Yasser made the wrong decision to live in a country that was not his by birth, and was he reaping the razor edge of loneliness and uncertainty about this decision? But engaging in deception in middle age? How would he face Amir if his son knew what he had done? Amir had implied earlier that Yasser was not treating Nadia fairly, but what did *he* know about it?

Yasser was tired; he needed rest. He fell asleep at five when he had heard a rooster crow on shore. Its crowing was loud and close, no noise impeding its sound ringing in the sky at dawn.

***

From her bench on the lower deck, Magda was alert to Yasser's presence on board the boat. In Cairo, she had known that his wife would be with him, but Magda had not resisted the temptation of showing up to see them. She had thought it would be easy to stay close to Soheir and to observe the couple from afar, but her friend was busy with Selim. Yasser's wife—medium height, shapely body, light make-up, shaggy hair bunched around her oval face—was dressed as though she were lounging at home in pants and shirt, yet something about the woman's eyes commanded. The man beside Magda on the bench gave her a jaded smile, and she turned away. If she frowned, she would be acknowledging his grin, and he would take it as flirtatious feminine wile. The strangeness of men! She had spent her days in the company of such loners; Yasser was not one of them, yet he would not have made love to her the way he had that night if he were satisfied with his marriage: his wild fingers exploring her curves as if he could not get enough of her. What a change from Ezzat, her ex-husband, his hands rough, hurried, his alcohol breath overpowering, his belch of garlic-drenched food. The memory of him made her shrivel. The balding man beside her on the bench edged in closer; she moved away. It seemed no one befriended her for herself, only for her skin.

When Ezzat first saw her, he had played up to her at the disco club, the night she had waited for Soheir and Selim who were one hour late; he had smiled at her, run his eyes over her body as though lapping her skin with his tongue—Ezzat, the violent ape she had married in secret and up to now, months after their separation and divorce, her father did not know. He had thought she was having an affair and that had seemed all right, and this in a country where pre-marital sex was taboo, for to him casual sex was better than his daughter marrying a man he had not chosen. Her father would have killed them had he guessed they were married without his knowledge, or worse, his blessing. What had helped her were her father's absences from Cairo on army missions to unspecified locations in the desert. There had been something about Ezzat's obsessed face, its piercing eyes, which held her captive, and it seemed then that she could not get away from him, even when she knew he was kilometres below her social level, a roughly

shod man of peasant background with little refinement or
education. As in a bad dream, Ezzat had attacked her in bed
and bruised her, and even when he was not angry his actions
were heavy, his fingers searing her skin, his skin temperature
so high he seemed to burn with rage, perhaps, as she thought
then, about something she had said or done. Now she knew it
was his frenzied rage, with her, with people who, like her, had
come from wealthy or prestigious families. She had stopped
going near him before they went to bed and had waited in the
bathroom or kitchen until he had fallen into a drunken sleep,
then she had crawled into her small spot in the bed. But in the
night, he would awaken and help himself to her body, and she
had not had a soul to turn to. Her father believed she was
alone in her apartment in Douki; of course, he wanted her to
be alone, so he could coerce her to do what he believed was
right for her, his only child. What her father offered her was
his power: over her life and over the lives of everyone she
knew, but not the love she needed. Never the love. Perhaps in
retrospect, this is what drew her to Ezzat; she would have done
anything to get away from her father's shadow and feel life for
herself, and Ezzat had enveloped her with his energy which, at
the time, seemed to have been a blind love. Perhaps he did
love her, but his love was like a snake's stranglehold around her
throat. After their divorce, Ezzat followed her everywhere;
inside dark doors of buildings his shadow frightened her. She
thought she saw him on streets at night but knew he dare not
touch her, for he was a soldier and her father a General in the
army. Still, she did not like him dogging her footsteps.

Now she waited to have a few moments alone with Yasser.
One week ago was her thirty-third birthday, and here she was
waiting for a married man to come and see her, the one whose
child she wanted. A girl, she wanted a girl. She would hold her
to her breast and shield her from loneliness. She needed
Yasser's child, but this dream was hopeless, unless he decided
to leave his wife, since he was this kind of man; yet he had not
spoken of his wife. Magda would not hesitate to go with him

to Canada, better there than here, her freedom curtailed by her father. She could not wait to get off the boat at Luxor, where she would wander into bazaars, instead of sit here bound to the lower deck like a thief in the night.

***

The following morning, Yasser and Nadia were late for brunch. As they climbed the stairs, Yasser scanned the deck for the trio, but they were not there. People came and went, talking in whispers as though afraid to disturb the hush of sunrise. The land on Nadia's right lay in verdant squares: wide stretches of greenery spotted with mud houses, one storey high with flat roofs, date palms near the entrances and straw matting set up as tents around the houses. A *sakhia* with a water buffalo circled in the distance, filling each of its pails with water from a stream and pouring it into a small irrigation canal. A dark-veiled woman in the field carried her drinking water in an earthen pot zeer high on her head, one arm supporting it, the other holding a child. Farther still, the ochre desert—like a papyrus parchment—stretched towards the horizon. This full-bodied scenery could flatten into a field or desert when painted, but Nadia would pry the sand open on canvas and make it whisper its own solitude, apply swirls of white or whitish ochre sparkling on sand, set off circles of colour to the horizon, take life from its brilliant gold and make it blaze in the sky. She would try quick water-colour brush strokes when she returned to the Delta.

Peasants here reminded her of Eskimos in Canada. The land is their mother; they protect her from the ravages of the elements and from the destruction of humans; they take from her only what they can use and in return give her all they have: their lives. As they plant and care for vegetation, they know they are passing the unspoiled soil on to their children, for the earth is greater than they and the sand in the desert precious. The view before her was the one she wished her sons to see, but they might not have enough time for the boat trip, instead, they might opt for the plane from Cairo to Luxor then to Aswan and Abu Simbel, the standard tourist fare, missing the boat journey up the Nile. Samy would summarize the ancient sites with, "This is great, Mom," then turn his attention to Yasser to discuss technical objectives; Amir would study the stone temples as a visitor might when coming to terms with someone else's culture, dutifully and with care. On Nadia's left in the distance, the green ended as though someone had drawn a straight line at the edge of the ochre sand, creating the contrast between green fields and yellow sand she had dreamed of, the river a turquoise-brown carrying rich booty at its bottom, and on its banks, willows drooping as if they had all the time in the world to dip for a reflection. She filled her memory with the hues. Land lay as in an aerial view of a map designed to enhance colour. The dry air contained none of the tell-tale moisture that had crept into Cairo's atmosphere of late. What a difference between this land and the city's streets tottering with their cargoes, cars, shops, humans and stifling smog. Two lands, not the same country.

Until her gaze fell on the border of the river awash with the brown soot from the boats. The water's undulations moved towards the bank, oiling it, delivering slimy weed and algae, the jasmine garden of her Canadian dreams mocking her. She was seized with panic, but what about or whom? Yasser? He appeared to be forcing himself to have fun. In bed he lay restless, could not sleep as she had hoped he would, and although their embraces were warm, his mind was far away. His silence irritated her. Why did she have to take the first step to break it? But she was wasting her time on this boat having these negative thoughts; this was a time for beginnings. Joining him at the buffet, she helped herself to grapes, figs, juice and selected items from the platters of eggs, *feta* cheese, fava beans, olives, a variety of breads and jams. Later in her cabin, she would sketch this display before its harmony of line and colour dissipated from her mind. When Selim joined them, the three took their plates and sat on a bench by the rails. Yasser made the introductions.

Selim said, "Your husband has been impressing the Minister of Trade with the deals he has proposed to make with the Americans." Nadia smiled, hiding her disinterest. Between gulps of cheese and bread, Selim's jaw moved with vigour; he continued, "Mr. Abdullah is thinking of creating a new position—Director of Business Projects in Cairo—with the view of promoting Yasser to this level. It's two years, renewable. What do you think?" As he gobbled his food, Selim's throat made thankful noises for the pleasing flavours passing through it. Everything he did was tactile, for to him people were his world of fun and sharing his pleasures with them his greatest reward. Rather than her first impression of him as a mad scientist, he now appeared to qualify as a blustery buffoon in a cartoon series. When Nadia turned from him to Yasser, she glimpsed a startled look on her husband's face as though a grandfather-whale was heaving its body towards the boat.

She murmured, "It all depends on Yasser's business in Canada. What do *you* think, Yasser?"

Selim's two female companions approached them, and Selim held out his arms and pulled the women in. "Here Soheir, here, let me introduce you. These are my friends: Yasser Amin and his wife, Nadia. Soheir, my fiancée, Magda, her friend."

Yasser could have pounded Selim's face to pulp. While Soheir talked to Nadia, Magda's eyes lingered on his, filling him with a swift anger for having placed himself in such a trap. Invisible steel bars closed in on him. Selim went to the buffet. Yasser stood by Magda but did not speak. Returning with a plate of ripe cherries, Selim passed it around and said, "Yasser, what are you and your wife planning to do in Luxor? This package deal is dull. Why don't you join us on a horse-and-buggy ride through the old quarter? We'll have local food, iced Stella beer, and we'll see Luxor at night."

Nadia turned to Yasser, but before he could say a word, Selim placed a hand on his arm. "We'll have a great time at the bazaar. That settles it! We'll see you at the hotel foyer at nine."

In Selim's mind, Yasser's fling with Magda had not amounted to much. A one-night stand in a marriage that had lasted as long as theirs was no big deal. Why not forget that night and let things proceed? Yet, as he joined arms with Soheir and Magda and sauntered down the stairs to the lower deck, he was uneasy about Yasser's strangled look. Selim hoped he had not antagonized the friend whom he needed for the new arms deal with the Americans.

Magda had wanted to study Nadia up close, even to see her with Yasser, perhaps to reassure herself that things were not right between them. But Yasser's face turned to stone, and she realized that his wife had an aura that she could not explain away. Magda felt sick.

Nadia watched the flush on Yasser's cheeks spread over his face. He could have refused the offer Selim had made to him, when he had the chance. "Selim doesn't think we need time for ourselves," Yasser mumbled and shrugged, knowing that it was a poor attempt at explaining Selim's arrogance. As Yasser watched Magda go down the stairs, he froze. Her helpless demeanour combined with a seductive tremor, sullen and aggressive, soft, dark hair, tight-fitting pants were an obsessive trap. A moment ago when he had looked into her eyes, he was back in Selim's apartment on the bed in silvery light, all boorish instinct to attack. He must have lost all sense of decency. He shook himself free of his fantasy and turned to Nadia, but her eyes avoided his. He put his arm around her and rubbed his hair against hers, "Want to take a drink and go for a dip in the whirlpool? I'm going to the cabin to change; do you want to join me?"

Nadia contemplated her fruit plate: "You go ahead, I'll catch up with you when I'm finished." She noted his high-pitched voice, his jerky movements. He had agreed to join these people in Luxor even when he *knew* she didn't want to be with them.

***

That afternoon, Yasser's restlessness grew as he and Nadia mingled with foreigners and Egyptians on the upper deck. They had joined the English-speaking group to practise the skit they would present at dinner. Prizes from The Boutique would be awarded the best group presentation. Mercifully, Selim and his companions had signed up with the Italian group.

This morning had been bad enough. Across the pool from Yasser, Magda had stretched on a long chair in her cinnamon bikini with strawberry designs clustered on her breasts and pelvis, and he had reclined on his deck chair with his back to her but had not been able to keep his mind off her dark skin. By his side, Nadia lay on a towel on the deck-floor reading, her tanned body in a white, two-piece bathing suit. Most men might wish to exchange places with him, but he felt caged; he had to break through the invisible bars that held him. Which bars? No one, not even his autocratic father, had placed restrictions on his actions. He had been his own navigator since he was seventeen, when he had left his family in Ismailia and gone to Cairo to attend university. He had financed his way through college and was responsible to none. His decisions had been his own: his choice of wife, job, emigration. But now he had this nagging regret; in Toronto, he had pushed it aside, yet like ice-water under a bridge, it was breaking through and threatening more eruptions. No one had warned him of such anxiety at his age. This evening, he would wear a rented costume for the dumb show he had agreed to join: the English-speaking group would be presenting a skit on the crowning of Pharaoh. He hated masked parties, the noise of people making-believe, yet he had gone along with it for Nadia's sake, no, for his own sake, to put his own turbulence to sleep. People in his group would be dressed as Pharaoh and courtiers; he would be Vizier, Nadia the Scribe.

***

That evening on the upper deck, tables for dinner and show were set in a square by the boat's railings surrounding the dance floor. Yasser sat with his group at the edge of a long table on one side of the square, the other groups sat on the other sides. His purple costume and headdress encrusted with coloured stones represented a wheat harvest. He knew he looked ridiculous in his yellow and purple gear, light purple top, long toga in a darker shade, a ceremonial crosier, and he had agreed to go ahead with this charade to assuage his guilt. Worse, as he was selecting his outfit in The Boutique, Magda had come in and helped him pick out the rings of fake amber and emerald to match his necklaces, and she had laughed at his discomfort when she piled up the jewellery on the counter. The beard was her idea.

Across the table from him, Nadia—in flesh-toned top, green cloth around her waist, parchment in one hand and a peacock feather in the other—smiled as she talked to the courtier sitting on her right, the guide conducting their tours in Luxor. She had a quiet way of conversing as though she were researching material for an article and found the experience easy, her thoughts flowing like a stream or, more like it, *she* was the flowing stream. But he was uncomfortable around these people and their outrageous gear. While the world was full of hunger and homelessness, this lot indulged in wasteful and perverse practices. Pharaoh in a high chair headed their table, a golden crown on his head, white tunic flowing to the floor, pompous demeanour, happy to hold the highest power in the crowd. On his right his Queen, in gold and white, his traditional adjunct. Priests with beards, in serpentine headgear, surrounded the King and Queen, a still-shot of incongruous colours, cheap jewellery, cloying perfumes and human sweat. Yasser suspected the men wanted to step back into a time-cocoon, where they could be aggressive and uncaring about everything except their own pleasures. Their wives, most over forty or fifty, relaxed in a harem-like setting happy to be enjoying the role. When our neighbours and friends are not looking, thought Yasser, let's slip into a barbaric routine and become a little depraved. But why was *he* angry? He himself wasn't a paragon of honour. What irked him, perhaps, was having to see Ancient Egypt in a frivolous light. No. What maddened him was his taking part in the ritual, and this other thing within him that yearned for disguise. Lights swayed above his head and on the dark waters below. In one corner of the deck, a band of six musicians played plaintive tunes, an odd blend of Pharaonic themes and Arabic drum beats. Players sipped their iced ouzo then set their glasses down under their chairs. In starched tuxedos, waiters held platters above the masqueraders' heads then, with flourish, reached over and placed them on the tables. The platters spilled over with mounds of saltwater fish and shrimp; salad had the aroma of onion and mint; white wine dripped from chilled bottles. The formality of the waiters' clothes clashed with their sloppy service, and with the cheap glitter of costumes around the tables.

Yasser drank, but the liquid did not soften his anxiety at being with Nadia and Magda on the same deck. But soon, the cool air soothed him, the alcohol infiltrated his fears, and the night wooed him into a youthful brashness. Such headiness rising with the spirited music made the ceremony advance in slow motion while he, the breathless photographer, was on fast forward. He walked away from the noise on deck and glanced down at the water. The Maitre d' bleated through the microphone, "Ladies and Gentlemen, here comes the majestic ceremony of the crowning of Ramses II. Make way for the royal procession at the shrine of Amun in Al Karnak Temple. First," with histrionic musical accompaniment and rising voice, "the musicians, dancers, courtiers, and on his royal throne, Pharaoh, Ramses II!"

Yasser bent his head as he joined in the procession. An announcer went to the Maitre d', took the microphone and recounted the plot of the skit. One of the courtiers slipped and fell; another came in while getting dressed; female dancers wore see-through tops and heavier skirts. Yasser watched courtiers dance with members of the audience, but he did not participate. Pharaoh nodded in his sleep and slipped off his throne onto the floor causing confusion for the dancers. Nadia, as Scribe, reminded Pharaoh he was on display, but he kept on nodding and sliding off his throne. People's laughter rose. When Pharaoh had been restored to his throne, he slumped and snored and had to be carried out on a stretcher as the crowd cheered the finale.

***

Monir sat at the corner of the table with his Italian tourists and wished Kareem, his son, were by his side. Instead of feeling free of responsibility, Monir sensed the vacuum in his life. He must be careful not to impinge on Kareem's life, though he missed him on a day like this, in the middle of people who were on the boat for reasons other than the enjoyment of the heart of Egypt, as he liked to think of his birthplace, Luxor. Although he knew it was good thing to have foreigners enjoy the skits and come to Egypt, he was frustrated when people who did not know much about ancient times re-enacted its history half drunk and off cue. They replaced meaning with mimicry, spirituality with materialism. Their jokes were demeaning. He despised the Egyptian officials who had sanctioned such clowning based on a superficial knowledge of the country's history, all for the sake of encouraging tourism.

When he took tourists to the pyramids of Giza, he was irked by the same feeling. Most held the view that through extreme forms of slavery ancient Egyptians had built the pyramids of Giza. Tourists did not notice the Egyptian builders climbing many storeys of scaffolding on a building site while carrying cement and other heavy materials on their heads and shoulders. Even in an age of technology, the Egyptian worker used his body as a winch to carry materials up many floors of buildings. No one today held a whip to these people. It could be argued, of course, that the workers were hungry and did not need a whip to take the job, but Monir knew they were proud of their work. Their group chants synchronized their actions, and their choral tunes harmonized their uplifted shovels. In other countries, cranes did this work, so visitors would see this co-ordinated group effort as a form of slavery. Not so in Egypt. Egyptian workers took pride in their wiry limbs, in their lasting endurance, and whenever Monir watched a man go up a wood scaffold carrying his load of cement or limestone, he recognized in him the qualities his ancestors had when they hauled granite slabs up ramps to build Cheops Pyramid on the Giza Plateau. Yet, he was thankful that tourists, for whatever reason, enjoyed Egypt; he had to stop ruminating and talk to the woman, the Scribe, next to him at the table. He looked forward to setting foot on the rolling sands of Upper Egypt and visiting his parents' home in Luxor.

***

Yasser walked to the empty deck at the rear of the boat and bent over the rails to watch the frothing water. A glance behind him discovered Nadia in the middle of their group laughing with the courtier; Yasser picked up an ouzo from a waiter and gulped it down without worrying about its potency. Even though alcohol was not served in street cafés, it existed in abundance everywhere tourists went—in expensive hotels, on tours like this—a double standard that had remained the custom since Yasser's university days. Now, he noticed that strictures on alcohol were mandated in smaller hotels, for only a few places had cocktail hours. He bent over the rails under the lights and gazed at the rushing water. His father—dead for five years—would have been scandalized had he suspected his son had betrayed his wife. His father had married twice, but his first wife had not been to his liking, because she was the family's choice for him when he was eighteen, and he had separated from her, then married Yasser's mother and had had four children with her. But he had not been undecided between the two women. The first wife he supported but did not see; the second one he lived with. Once, while on a visit to Ismailia, Yasser had jokingly suggested that it might be time for him, Yasser, to take a second wife, as his father had done.

"You don't joke about such matters," his father had reprimanded him in outraged voice, "Your wife is a good woman. No self-respecting man would repeat the mistakes of his father and grandfather." And that had been the only time his father had chided him.

The announcer at Yasser's back introduced the Italian group skit. An electric shock ran through him as he scanned the heads of the players for Magda. Wailing women in black with ashes on their heads thrust their hands skywards in weepy supplication to the heavens; court jesters wobbled in huge pants stuffed with straw; scribes followed them drinking beer; dancers, mostly middle-aged women in see-through tops, paraded their breasts and their husbands were too drunk to mind, but even had they been sober they would not have cared, for they had watched their women bare their sagging breasts on the shores of the Greek islands. Yasser knew these types, for he had seen them in Europe. The music and dancing were funereal, the action of masqueraders a soundless track of slow-motion. The boat with the dead Pharaoh lying in state in his gold mask swayed sideways above the courtiers' heads and threatened to spill its sleeping figure on the floor. Then she came, Pharaoh's wife, in a flowing white tunic, straight hair, bangs on her forehead, and the golden crown of Upper Egypt on her head, face white except for eyes darkened with eye-liner. And Magda suited her part. Her eyes shone bright green encircled with silver eye-shadow. She rippled past him without a glance. What would he have done had Samy fallen for a woman like her? The thought sent warm blood coursing through Yasser's head: an unreasonable fear. Samy was only twenty-two and had never been interested in women of Magda's type. But what if he were?

Priests followed, then Selim as High Priest in navy
tunic—a star motif on his headdress and silver necklace spread
fan-like on his chest, his back straight, his chest puffed out—
strutted out in his finery. The group came to a standstill in
front of Yasser. Carriers of Pharaoh's boat lowered it to the
floor and covered it with a sheet, then the High Priest began
the ceremony of mummification. He placed his hand under
the linen and fumbled to prepare the body for the removal of
entrails. Singers' voices screeched in mournful song, dancers
moved in forced propriety, and courtiers lifted their arms in
exaggerated supplication to the God Ra. Eyes downcast, the
Queen stood in submissive mourning. One by one the entrails
of the dead Pharaoh appeared. Selim, as High Priest, pulled
out the heart: his hands waved an eggplant in air; then the
liver, a wilted beetroot; intestines, a long leather snake. Music
rose in crescendo as he groped and pulled out a carrot,
searched again and came out with two eggs. Laughter greeted
his discoveries; viewers clapped and whistled. He bowed low,
then glanced around him, and kept on bowing in a circle like
a trainer at a circus. The Italian group had won the crowd's
enthusiasm.

Yasser's eyes fastened on Magda. Her curves showed
through the transparent gauze, her eyes were ancient Egyptian
in their exaggerated guise. He followed her movements until
her back disappeared behind Pharaoh's shrine. Yasser was
betraying himself. Drinking alcohol was an act of betrayal. As
far as he knew, no one in his family, other than his father, had
tasted it. In this, the family had followed its strict religious
beliefs. His father had had a lot of alcohol in his youth but had
spurned the habit in his mature years. In Ismailia, his father
had introduced Yasser to his old cronies as "my oldest son, the
architect." His son's university training had meant a lot to
him, having not had a chance to complete his own schooling,
and having had to work to support his mother and brothers
after his father's death. He had been married at the age of
twenty. After Yasser's father died, the family, the hundred or so

of them whom Yasser knew, regarded him as its head. This meant that whether at home or abroad Yasser had moral obligations to fulfill, but he wanted none of them, steel bars holding him in. The skits scattered people away from the formal table arrangement, and masqueraders walked, drinks in hand, talking in clusters on the deck. Nadia was with the courtier.

Yasser was not sure whether he had moved towards Magda or she had sought him out. They were standing in the middle of the Italian group near the rails. He offered her a sip of his drink and stood close, so his chest almost touched her nipples through the gauze. A thick gold chain hugged her neck. His eyes held hers.

"You're enjoying yourself." She smiled.

He countered, lamely, "It's good to see you."

Heavy lashes hid her eyes as she glanced downwards, "There's a small house outside Luxor, on the river," she whispered. "It has a veranda, just like this house over there." She pointed to a spot illumined by the boat's headlights. "I know the owner; he'll let me have it whenever I want." He watched her lips, nodded, then corrected himself, "But I don't think that's possible." He turned to go away. Nadia was dancing. He swivelled back, held Magda by the waist and led her to the packed floor. Her body pressed against his, his hand slid down her back, he drank cool springs from her eyes, blessed the crowds that pushed them close together and hid them from view. Her defiant posture trapped him with its sullenness. She was cancelling the codes that separated them, pushing him to break the chains that fastened him to his goals. He was a runaway. He recalled an oil painting he had seen at The National Gallery of Canada, of a horse in full harness, running away in a meadow at top speed, having broken away from the carriage to which he had been harnessed. The title of the painting was "The Runaway", and the horse's eyes he would always remember, fiery with unbridled exhilaration at his newly acquired freedom, his nostrils flaring his muscles stretched and taut.

He, Yasser, would scale fences, break open steel doors, float over the floor with Magda, feel his body awaken to her touch. Now he was dancing the night into oblivion. His eyes assured her that the jostling, the costumes, the swaying lights, the easy-to-get-at drinks had re-created the bounding Yasser who had been her lover that first night in Cairo.

Lights dimmed on deck as the dancers met in unabashed disguise.

***

As Nadia danced with the masked courtier—the guide whose name she had not caught in the din—her eyes combed the deck for Yasser. He had walked away, or gone down to the lower deck. She could not distinguish the bodies congested on the dance floor. The coloured bulbs swaying above their heads were dimmed, and people had turned into shadows moving in glittering guise. He would be on the lower deck in conversation with Selim; after this dance, she would go find him.

The courtier she danced with was reassuring, his wise-cracks on the skits perceptive. But then, a lot of tourists appeared to like the masquerade. Dancing with him, she felt protected on this garish ship of dreams.

***

Yasser led Magda to the front deck: deserted, cold. They huddled behind the captain's room. In the dark, his lips found hers, then he ceased to take note of his actions. His body quivered, he floundered between her lips, cold wind struck his back. Thrusting himself on her breasts and pelvis, he dug in as into rough terrain. They were spinning in a vortex. Her tongue roamed his lips, a voyager in search of forbidden fruit. Her fingers massaged his back, laughter drenched her eyes, her shiny, deep pupils sparkled like stalactites in a cave. He explored their hidden life, heady music compelling him to dive, sink in, push into the darkest cove. His hand moved under her top, but hers pushed him back.

"In Luxor," she said, "when we see each other at the house." Wrapping her shawl around her body, she disappeared around the dark corner of the wall. Yasser pressed his back against the cold cabin wall. His head throbbed. The boat tilted. Cold wind shrivelled his body.

Below him, water foamed against the silver prow of the boat.

***

Nadia pushed the cabin door open and found their room empty. Yasser was not on deck; he must be with Selim at the bar. She turned to go back but felt tired. By the time she had showered he would be in. When she came out of the stall, she found him sitting on the side of their bed.

"You're okay?" she stroked his back. His muscles tensed. "What's the matter? Where were you?" He lay down on the bed and muttered, "I'm cold; I feel cold."

"Take a shower; it'll warm you." He did not move. She brought his pyjamas to bed, helped him into them and covered him.

A night of make-believe to help people forget they're alive, she thought. She should have stayed closer to Yasser. She stroked his damp hair then turned the sheets down on her side of the bed and sank into it, placing her hand on his arm.

***

Chapter Five

Genie

From a small, rectangular opening in the ceiling, light funnelled down on the altar in the dark interior of Edfu Temple. Tourists were scattered in the Temple and behind them, Nadia observed the faces and silhouettes turned up to the guide on the platform in the sanctuary. When he shifted his position, his head and shirt entered the beam of light cutting him diagonally, illuminating his face and shoulders, leaving his lower body in darkness. His voice reached her in stray sentences: "Every day the sun shines on the altar for a few minutes at ten in the morning."

In the darkness, inaudible Time spoke to her through the hieroglyphics engraved in stone. Outdoors, the structure maintained its perfect shape; indoors, it was touched by the passage of time and the shadow of silence. The smell of dust filled the air with its tangible immediacy. ". . . ancients built this Temple knowing that at ten in the morning a ray of light would come in, through the small opening you see up there, in time for their daily service to Khepera." His finger pointed to the open spot in the ceiling where the ray entered, and his voice trailed off into space. Nadia's mind re-enacted the ancient rituals of priests leading their congregation in musical procession, their voices rising under the high ceiling within the hand-carved walls inlaid with gold, reflecting the torch lights, the eyes of gods and goddesses in the reliefs made of jewels, hand-woven carpets on the granite floors, choral music and dance filling space, the gold-shine paying homage to the gods, since no other metal would have done justice to infinity. Now no gold, precious jewels or carpets, yet the place reflected the ancients' reverence for deity, a far cry from the clowning mimicry of the previous night's party-makers on board the

Lotus. What was sacred to some was mimicry to others yet, she thought here in the awesome dark, Time whispers its own story to the reverential observer.

"This groove collected blood from sacrificial lambs." The guide's skinny fingers traced the ridge of the square altar. "You see, they believed that the sacrifice of an animal and their own physical labour building the temple were the purifying experiences. They saw sacrifice as the soul's cleansing journey to a new life. Rebirth was their shared destiny. No soul ever died; it travelled through the ocean at night to re-emerge with the rising sun, which was, of course, Khepera."

Not a silhouette moved. If caught by a photographer's lens, the scene before Nadia would have surfaced on paper as interspersed human shadows, stilled in an alert somnolence, a ray of light piercing the dark, highlighting the guide's black head. Upturned faces focused on the ray of light spotlighting the guide and altar. " . . . today the sacrifice of an animal is practised by Muslims at Ramadan. They slaughter lambs for their feasts and distribute the meat to the poor, and Christians observe this ritual at Easter time."

Accustomed to the dark, Nadia wandered away from the group. Intact wall carvings surrounded her, and the spirit of place spoke to her through ancient stone. One relief showed Pharaoh in a triumphant battle over his dark-skinned enemies, he gigantic in size, his Queen much smaller, seated at his left foot, his opponents in shrunken forms grovelling on the floor on his right. In another, triumphant Pharaoh exhibited a stalwart erection to symbolize his might over his small enemies grovelling at his feet. In yet another relief, the Queen sat by Pharaoh and protected him with an arm wound around his shoulder. Though she was of lesser status, the Queen was nurturer and supporter of Pharaoh, the heart of his kingdom. The roster of the revered in ancient Egypt included goddesses like Hathor, Nut, Isis, especially Isis, spirit of life's continuity, because of her endless search for her husband's, Osiris's, scattered limbs. Nut—the most elegant—was sky goddess, contrary to other mythologies where the sky deity was male. In Arabic, the word sky is female, an important detail, thought Nadia, since the sky is the home of spiritual beings. Nut was a prominent figure in this divine roster, unlike in other religious hierarchies where males dominate the tip of the apex. Nadia liked the long, yearning figure of Nut stretched across the top of reliefs, her elongated body—asexual, emphasizing her spiritual yearnings—hugging the horizon, her arms drooping earthwards on one side of the relief, her legs on the other side, embracing all of nature. As goddess of the sky, she was in contact with earth.

Hathor embodied Earth. As female divine cow, Hathor attracted Nadia for the opposite reason: her well-shaped breasts, her two horns rising in semi-circles from the top of her head, hands raised in supplication, she embodied fertility and all things physical. Some day Nadia would visit Hathor's temple in Abu Simbel, and Hatshepsut's in Deir-el-Bahri. Hatshepsut, the only Egyptian queen to rule over ancient Egypt, Nadia revered the most for—unlike the popular Queen Cleopatra who betrayed Egypt—Hatshepsut was the country's saviour. She had raised her people's spiritual awareness. On the walls of her temple, she appeared in men's apparel and false ceremonial beard of kingship, for she knew she could not assume full control over her kingdom if she were to appear in woman's garb. Nadia wondered if it was a coincidence that the 1997 terrorist attack against foreigners in Luxor had been launched from the confines of Hatshepsut's Temple. Did contemporary men regard it as a fort from which to launch their attack on their so-called enemies? As Queen, she was one of the most influential and powerful of Pharaohs. Cleopatra—the one most often talked about in Western books because of her romances with Caesar and Antony—was not Egyptian born; a Ptolemaic, of Greek parentage, she lived in Egypt and ruled it, but was not indigenous to it. She had espoused the Egyptian way but had not become a part of it.

Sun-drenched, Nadia stood in the doorway leading out into the hall of colonnades. In an expanse of bright floor, lined with the shadows of high pillars, the guide stood in sun, his smooth dark hair shiny, a few grey hairs at the temple, his white shirt a contrast to his tanned skin and charcoal pants; he exuded energy, his wiry body nervous, compelling: a genie released from an ancient bottle. He was saying, ". . . these columns at one time had an elaborate ceiling. People worshipped here, but priests prayed in the sanctuary where we were a minute ago." Behind his brown-rimmed glasses, his eyes were dark marbles of light. Tall and slim, almost undernourished, with the face of a man familiar with the pages of books, his nose thin, eyes alert, tapered fingers sketching reliefs in air, blue veins on the back of his hand, he led the group to another colonnade. Nadia came up to him. "You said these temples were inlaid with gold and jewels. Where did the ancients get their materials?" He answered, "Gold was plentiful in Egypt and in the Persian Gulf. The lapis stone was Egyptian and can be still found here." He paused, then continued, "They used jewels for eyes, because for them eyes were the gateway to the soul."

He contemplated her as though recognizing her from a previous time. She kept pace with him. "I like the fact that the ancient three-fold division of temples survives in Christian Churches." His eyes touched her, tracing her eyes, forehead and hair as though aligning her features for a photograph. He said, "I'm taking a handful of interested people through Al Karnak Temple tonight. Would you like to join us?" She nodded. He asked her to meet the group in the hotel foyer at seven, excused himself and rejoined the rest of the group.

The moment he was gone, Nadia realized he was the courtier with whom she had danced the previous night on the *Lotus*. Energetic eyes. But the false wig and beard he wore in the evening's guise had made him seem heavier, and this is why she had not recognized him. Staying in step with the group, Nadia passed through the outer hall—no colonnades and open to the sky—into a courtyard, through the gate to the dusty road. Glaring heat pressed down on them as they scrambled into the air-conditioned bus. Nadia lingered behind. For here she had sensed the strong presence of those who had built the place and prayed in it, a spiritual home, alive and comforting. She would bring Amir to this place, because he would know what she meant by the lingering spirit in the abodes of Pharaohs. She would have liked to spend more time here, but as soon as the tourists resumed their seats she climbed onto the bus, and as it moved away she watched the preserved stone walls recede out of the back window until they were overtaken by ochre sands and sporadic palms. The group was scheduled for dinner at a restaurant in the desert on the outskirts of the city; she would have preferred to have returned to the hotel, but the restaurant was far out of town. Yasser had missed this trip. Although he did not care for sight-seeing, he would have enjoyed Edfu Temple, if only as an enduring feat of architecture, but instead he had opted to go sailing on the Nile. Perhaps he found that more relaxing.

***

Muffled sounds of horse's hooves hit the dusty road. The cabby handled his horse from a high seat in front of the leather screen separating him from his customers. Reclining on the back seat, Yasser and Magda followed the twisting road from the sides of their carriage. In a cluster so thick that nothing penetrated their ancient darkness, large acacias fringed the way. A deepening blue sky, softened rose tinge of a disappearing sun, the ground an uneven sequence of bumps, the road a silvery grey thread winding ahead between the trees. Dust from the swaying wheels of the *huntour* clouded the air. Under the blanket covering their legs up to their waists, Magda rested her open bottle of Scotch. Even so late at night in the carriage, she had to be furtive with alcohol, for liquor was taboo in public. She wrapped the bottle in her scarf, took a mouthful, passed it on to Yasser. His arm pulled her closer and her curves settled into the side of his body. Cool air fanned their faces and released them from the heat of the day's sun. Yasser had

wanted to go sailing, but the outing had been cancelled when
the oarsman had not shown up, and the local organizer had
not wanted to hire someone from another agency. That had
left time on his hands and, as he walked out of the hotel sauna,
he had bumped into Magda. What had made him so cowardly
when he faced her? Instantly, he had signed out of his familiar
terrain. Now, her hand on his hair was an errant butterfly in
the breeze, her lips a flutter on his ear, "You'll like it there, the
view from the veranda is magical," her breath heat-waves on
his neck, her fingers electric shocks in his hair.

Within him were yearnings, a wildness he had not known
since childhood. Sirens' voices far from shore, water lapping at
the foot of the hill, but after he had had her, what then? What
if Nadia discovered his sailing trip had not happened? He had
to invent an explanation. To want something that was not his,
to be anxious about a future he did not know, to have to lie
like a teenager, how could he be in such uncertainty? At a
bend in the road, their carriage lurched sideways throwing
Magda over him. She pulled the blanket up to their chins until
her fingers found his zipper. Her curves fit into the spaces of
his body. She undid his trousers, covered his lips with hers, her
tongue seeking refuge in his mouth. She did not worry about
the driver, for he was in his own world behind the leather
screen that separated him and them, a leather tent above his
head harbouring him as he tugged at his horse. Together, man
and animal, oblivious of their surroundings, clattered along
the road in a hypnotic rhythm, and found their way in the
dark as by a mystical compass.

Yasser threw his head back on the leather cushions, fastened his eyes on the grey road slipping by as Magda dipped
her head under the blanket and her lips found his penis. The
lurching motion of the carriage added urgency to her actions
and to his response. Her tongue lapped him and he was exhilarated when she pulled the blanket down so he could see her
actions and his responding body. The cool air rushing his skin,
her lips moist, the burning whisky, in this instant all he knew

were his aching nerves. He was excited by his own rising aggression and by the suddenness of her desire.

She covered him, withdrew, lay back whispering about waiting till they got there. He reached for her, but she pushed him back. He wanted to roll her in the dust, but he had a sip of whisky instead, and it seemed like endless time before he saw the low building where their carriage came to a stop. Each step closer to the building thrust him deeper into his vortex. The house smelled of dust; it was tight and damp. Magda threw the front windows open and fresh air burst in. The Nile muttered in the distance. He went up to her. Everything was dark. Crickets spilled out some unknown doom. But from the underground, danger's steel magnet drew him on. He had not felt so fraught with tumultuous feelings since his university days, when he had watched the bouncing girls whom he was forbidden to touch. He drew her to him; she laughed and moved away, picking up her food parcels, liquor bottles, and stepping outdoors to the veranda. Beyond the rails, the small hill was covered with wild mint and shrubs bearing orange blossoms sloping down to the river's edge.

He spotted a metal couch with a quilt near the wall of the veranda and rolled it out under the vine trellis. The watching face of the moon shone between the leaves. She unpacked lamb from the foil, took out a bottle of *ouzo*, Arabic bread, green onions, placed the food on a tray, which he carried to the couch. They kicked off their shoes, climbed in, pulled the damp quilt over them, placed the tray on their laps, her laughter ringing in the silence, an echo of a sensual goddess in revelry. Peal after peal. While holding bread and lamb in one hand, she put her other hand under Yasser's shirt, freeing him of tension, as though the dark water, the scent of flowers, sound of crickets were there for *him*. Watching each other, they sliced lamb and filled pocket bread, garnished it with onions and ate. They diluted the *ouzo* with water and drank. Her nipples were hard under her cotton blouse. The moon shone down on them through the vine leaves and the river rippled far below the hill. He gulped bread with lamb as though someone threatened to snatch them from him. Years ago, he, his siblings and cousins had to wait until the men in the family—fathers and uncles—had eaten. But the men had lingered at their coffee. When the children were allowed at the table, Yasser took all the food he could get and swallowed it before his younger brothers could snatch it from his plate. That was then; now, he dreaded something, some interruption he could not spell out. Perhaps he feared himself, for his head might veto what his body demanded.

He watched Magda, handed her the bread and onion, dipped his fingers in *ouzo* and in mock ceremony bathed her eye-lids and cheeks. He wet her lips with the concentrated drink from the bottle. They had to throw the tray with the remainder of the food off the couch and send glasses tumbling onto the floor. She burst into laughter. Yasser's tongue sank between her lips, he traced her neck and lapped fresh water after weeks of travel in the dust. He rolled with her under the quilt and commanded her twisting body with his own. Her eyes teased him; he sought to close them with his tongue. The more he gained mastery over her, the higher his energy became. He quelled her thirst with *ouzo*, tasted her breasts, her abdomen, seeking every part of her. When he entered her, he pressed her down onto the couch, she kept moaning, and he kept pressing. He wanted to annihilate her. But when they were quiet, he lay over her with a sense of defeat. Instead of peace, he felt dread. What was he doing?

Magda shook herself free, pulled him off the couch, wrapped the quilt around their bodies, led him in bare feet through the mint shoots down the incline. Not heeding prickly weeds, they reached the lapping water where she spread the quilt on the ground, made him lie down, threw herself over him and moved slowly. Her shadow above him blocked the moon's halo.

She hung over him, a bat with wings hovering in cold space where the water's voice was time-keeper. The shadow of her head eclipsed the light above, and he knew the pain of darkness.

***

A bright sun on a bowl of fruit: mangoes, papayas, seedless green grapes, navel oranges. Nadia selected an orange, peeled it and gave it to Yasser. As he munched it, he fixed his eyes on the river. They were on a tenth floor balcony at the Luxor Hilton Hotel, the place they had dreamed of in Canada, but Nadia knew that Yasser was not with her. Since they had arrived at the hotel two days ago, they had avoided Selim and for this she was thankful; yet she had been to Edfu Temple with tourists and guide, and Yasser had stayed at the hotel, then gone sailing. His eyes concentrated on a barge overburdened with cargo. Nadia asked him if he was going to join her in the afternoon on the guided tour to Karnak Temple, and without lifting his eyes, he said, "I'd like to, but Selim insists we have to discuss a proposal from the Minister of Trade."

"You can talk to him when we come back."

"He says it's urgent." Yasser studied the barge as if he were deciphering a message in the wood. The rowers' chant rose and fell with the beat of their oars.

"What's the matter with you? You're so pensive. Aren't you enjoying yourself?"

"Nothing," he said, "I'm all right." Then, "I feel my life isn't mine. I want to do something . . . useful." Although he looked in her direction, his eyes were not focused on her. He seemed to be running pursued by shadows, but instead of arriving at a resting place, he had stumbled into a cave of underground figures to which Nadia could not find an entrance. "I thought you liked being here."

"I do. But right now, I feel . . . empty." Hardly a compliment to her. He picked up his coffee cup and drained it. She was on a rocking ocean and he in some mountain tunnel. They had come to Luxor to share their solitudes, but he was turning inwards and away from her. At his side, she was the inconspicuous, small queen on mosaic temple walls, but, unlike those queens, she had no hold on her husband's reality. Yasser's need for compelling action did not merge with her path on sand, her journey inside stone walls carved with thousands of years of history. She placed her hand on his arm, but he did not turn to her. Moments ago, the veranda had seemed to her to be bathed in light; now Yasser's pain had spilled into it. She could have spent her life here near the river's rocky borders, where the Valley of Kings contained secrets in its numerous tombs, but Yasser was far away, alien to the terrain, his hair a dark sculpture against the sand of distant hills.

She said, "I won't be back from Al Karnak Temple before ten or eleven." Her voice was receding, even from her.

***

While taking his siesta at the Luxor Hilton, Monir recalled the day's events. Soon after he arrived in Luxor, he had visited his parents on the outskirts of the city, in their two-bedroom apartment, a small veranda overlooking the desert: tiny place in comparison to his childhood home. His father thin, his limbs emaciated in his grey trousers, shoulders bent in a white shirt; he would have been shocked to see Monir in a red or pink shirt, for to the old man, all cars were black and all shirts white. Although his limbs had become frail, almost breakable, his mind had remained alert and healthy. Monir's mother, energetic, hopeful, wore her hair in her signature braid down her back. Neat in her long cotton dress, her back erect, face washed and powdered, she loved baking her bread and serving it hot to her men, though now she used a small electric pan to make a few loaves, not the oven she used when Monir was a child. He remembered the aroma of her bread baking in the mud oven, a mixture of baking crust and animal fat. Earthy. When you ate it you felt your taste buds awaken. A slice of feta cheese and green onion with the bread made a more satisfying meal than *kebab-halla*. Meat could not measure up to her crusty whole-wheat loaf, puffed into a circle like a blown up balloon. She had insisted on using her mud oven long after his father had bought her an electric stove and dishwasher in their rebuilt kitchen, for she disliked new appliances, and the new oven baked food without an aroma to fill her home with its warm comfort. She had asked his father to return the appliances to the merchant, but he had refused, believing she would come around to the new ways. She had not. Instead, she continued baking in her mud oven in the garden, squatting down to place her long bake-sheets with the round dough on the oven shelves. With a poker, she had stoked the plant cakes she used for fuel. Nothing tasted better than her bread. From the mud oven to the electric frying pan. The pan did the job, but the bread did not have the same aroma. She was still washing her dishes by hand.

When their salutes were over, his father had talked to him about the subject Monir dreaded most, the unrest between Copts and Muslims in Luxor. "They have burned our church." His father's voice was a reminder that no matter how much Monir immersed himself in the history of his country, he could not avoid witnessing the tension between its two religious groups. "One of the choristers lives close by it, and he can see the church from his bedroom. He caught the smoke early and called the fire crew. People gathered and put out the fire with pails and hoses, but by then many of our icons were destroyed." His father wiped the corner of his eye with a white handkerchief, and without disturbing the folds in the material, blew his nose and returned the handkerchief to his pocket.

"It's not that bad, Professor Ameen," said his mother. Everyone in Egypt was a Professor, even the local baker and butcher; in King Farouk's time, it had been *Bey* and *Pasha* for Sir and Lord. "It's just a small quarrel between the boys in the neighbourhood," she continued. "One of them was trying to take his revenge on his young friend because he would not stay away from his sister. You know how people are. You must admit that some of the men who helped rescue our church were Muslims, so are the people rebuilding it. There are the good, and the bad, God be praised," she said as she left the room to brew their coffee.

His father had shaken his head. "No. Friend is hostile to friend. You know Professor Gallal, the one you and I used to visit by the railway station? He doesn't come here any more. Neither one of us knew what religious differences were at that time, nor who belonged to which sect. Now, all this hatred is getting out of hand." He lowered his voice. "Your mother likes to put a different slant on things." He nodded his head and bent his shoulders, his back a semi-circle as he slid down the wooden chair he preferred to the sofa.

"Professor Gallal must have his reasons, Father," Monir had answered. "Maybe he's not feeling well. Why not send someone to ask about him? I'll go see him if you wish." His father had shaken his head. *I* know better, and *you* cannot hide the truth from your old father, he seemed to be saying. Monir had continued, "Remember how many times you used to warn us there would be a giant upheaval in our country?" His father's eyes lit up with the memory. He stared at the son he idolized and hoped that the young man's knowledge of history and people would point a way out of his own pessimism.

"Many times! Isn't that so?" Monir asked. "You foretold civil wars between the two religious factions. How many have there been?" he questioned as his father avoided responding. "None! There *will be no civil war*. Our people have avoided violence against each other throughout our history. Of course, this does not stop the few from trying, and failing. Here's your coffee," he handed his father the cup his mother had brought in. Monir turned to his mother. "How are Samia and her husband?" he asked her for she found comfort in talking about her daughter and grandchildren.

Monir had to admit to himself that he had come across a few violent incidents which he felt were significant harbingers of change, and young Coptic men went a step further than their Muslim counterparts. Whereas the Muslims dressed in suits and buttoned-up collars, or in *gallabiahs,* the Copts walked the streets in open shirts to exhibit the mandatory cross hanging on a chain on their bare chests. Confrontation: an I'm-not-going-to-hide-what-I-am thing. You're-not-going-to-scare-me. We were here before you; you know we are the descendants of Pharaohs and you're not going to drive us out of our land. We'll fight you, if need be. We are twenty percent of the population, not the ten percent the government's census claims we are; we'll fight. We'll survive. We've done it before, we'll do it again.

This was the silent Christian message rising in counter-defence against Islamic extremists. Monir had seen his son's friend wearing his cross like a sword, an unnecessary gesture. What chance did he have against ninety percent Muslims? And why was confrontation necessary in the first place? Monir had asked Kareem to stop wearing his cross on the street, for religion was a personal matter, and so far, Kareem had complied. But Monir feared his son's group would sway him into extreme action. Worse, Kareem was bound to be identified with the behaviour of his more aggressive friends. As far as Monir could see, only small pockets of Muslim radicals were forming here and there in sporadic groups. Nothing major or serious. Nothing different from the minor incidents of the past. Would he have the misfortune of seeing more people succumb to fanaticism, an aberration of the human mind? Perhaps. But how misled can a person be to resort to religion as a spur for carrying weapons and destroying others? And how many times would the world have to witness mass-killing in the name of God?

Monir knew the Middle East had very little—other than race and religion—to cement its countries together, but without such bonding they had no chance of withstanding American control of their resources and their lives. The United States wanted power over their oil, so whenever a strong Arab leader emerged, U.S. media portrayed him as a tyrant; then its army attacked his country, or they had him killed at the hands of so-called insurgents. King Faisal of Saudi Arabia, Nasser of Egypt—Monir believed that Nasser was poisoned—Sadat, and the list went on back in history to the Turkish, French and British domination of the area. The official American explanation of the death of these men—in Nasser's case a heart attack, Sadat killed by Islamic extremists, and King Faisal by his American-educated and aberrant nephew—were not true stories. Monir did not think Arabs had a chance at self-determination other than by declaring Islamic *jihad,* and yet were this vision to become real, Copts in Egypt were bound to suffer. Monir hoped that Egyptians, who had withstood violence in the past, would somehow avoid religious upheavals in the future. The next few days within Luxor's ancient marvels, he would escape this tension by taking his groups to the temples and through the market squares that he loved.

He turned on his bed to face the morning light. Since his childhood, his mother had been blessed with an inner peace and a guiding light. Whatever happened, she was steady in her support of her children and husband, and certain that the good sense of Egyptians would prevail. He hoped she would prove to be right.

***

The hotel bar was crammed. Yasser and Selim watched people in the large mirror facing them: it reflected the marble bar-top, crystal chandelier, couples interspersed at tables. Selim said, "The job needs someone who has diplomatic flair."

Yasser slapped the shiny counter-top with his flat palm and set the ice-cubes rattling in the glasses, "I told you I don't want to be involved in politics. I'm a businessman, not a politician." His eyes were fixed on the mirror to where women entered the bar through an open, stained-glass door. One woman's back was bare to the waist. He watched her and sipped his whisky.

Selim said, "Who's talking politics? All I said was, we need people like you who can deal with Egyptians and Americans.

If you don't serve your native country, who will?" He ordered fresh drinks.

Yasser stared at the woman's bare back in the mirror. If he decided to get involved in this arms deal, he had to do so with eyes open. If he were to agree to go into negotiations with the Americans, he had to be sure of the Egyptian viewpoint. The woman smiled at him as she turned on the dance floor, and he smiled back. The prospect of a new business deal with the Americans intrigued him and his own acumen would come into play. Negotiations might involve risk, the risk of angering the Egyptians, the Americans, or both, but if negotiations worked, he would have helped his native country acquire weapons to build strategic power in the Arab world. He had to think this one through.

"If you want to stay with Nadia, you can work in Cairo. You'd be meeting Americans in your office in Liberty Square. It'll be a penthouse, with your own secretary. Air-conditioned." Selim followed Yasser's smile to the woman. His friend attracted even those with partners, but Yasser was lucky the woman's companion had not seen him, or the man would have knocked him down.

Yasser watched the woman's back, straight, slim, curved at the waist. He said, "Give me time to think about it." His eyes in the mirror were puffy and creases between his eyebrows and on his forehead made him look old and tired. He yelled, "I came here for a holiday, for heaven's sake!"

He had no idea why his voice was loud or at whom he was directing his anger. He studied himself in the mirror and realized he was drumming on the marble counter, so he swivelled his bar-stool and announced, "I'm going for a walk."

***

A full moon hung over the upright sculpture like a bulb attached to a dark stand in the desert. From her spot at the foot of the granite column in Al Karnak Temple, Nadia saw the bulb's luminous circle as a halo in the night. Her guide,

Monir, sat beside her on a step at the bottom of a colossal column, his back against the cool stone, his arm on a higher level
at Nadia's back, his legs stretched forward. Facing them, the
strange sculpture was of a headless Pharaoh, his arms crossed
over his chest holding a flail and crook. Another sculpture of
a headless Pharaoh was attached horizontally to the first, the
two Pharaohs' bodies forming the configuration of the cross.
The moon above the sculpture transformed it into a black-
and-white lamp-stand, and behind it, silvery sands stretched
to a midnight sky.

At a slight distance from them, tourists gathered around
the red glow of coal and mingled with local tribesmen in white
garb huddling close to the flames. One of the tribe turned ears
of corn on the grill. The slim man at Nadia's side was silent.
He had told her he was Professor of Archaeology at the
University of Cairo, that he hosted tourists in Upper Egypt
during his mid-term breaks. Instead of taking a part-time job
at another university to supplement his meagre government
salary, he had opted for these trips. "There's a new law that
people cannot hold two government jobs. I can't continue to
teach at the university and be a tourist guide. I'll have to com-
ply with the law, but I'm not sure which job I'd give up! I can
apply to a private tourist company, of course." She asked him
how he found time to keep up with his two roles.

"I take slides on my tours and use them in my teaching,
and sometimes I take students on my trips. Mornings, I teach;
afternoons, I do tourism around Cairo." His low voice swept
away with the breeze. She got up; he followed. Carved lotus
flowers on the top of pillars of the temple formed an overpowering design against the moon's clarity and dwarfed people
into minute particles in the onward flow of civilization. As
they listened to the wind's passage, neither one spoke. Monir's
voice had the quality of wind, distanced, sweeping over time
and space without consciousness of itself. He merged with the
scenery, a passing figure at the foot of lasting stone. Instead of
being overpowered by the monuments, he seemed content to

follow the stream of dwellers whose lives had passed through at the foot of the pharaonic pillars.

He said, "To know what this land means, people need to come to this spot and look up at the sky from between these pillars. How many millions have done this over the years? When they realize how people age and die, but sites last forever in the desert, they know that their individual lives cannot amount to much on their own. Only the work of the group lasts, and the land lives on." He said this to the open darkness.

Nadia recalled how earlier in the afternoon, she and he had gone down some steps outside Al Karnak Temple and crouched underground in the dark tunnels leading to the innermost cove. Centuries ago, ancient oracles had performed their ceremonies there. His flashlight, a dim yellow, had converted the dust and walls into oppressive presences. Crouching low, he and she had taken several minutes to get to the spot where the oracle—often a woman—hid in ancient times. The voice of the oracle would have sounded through the passages to surface at the opening where worshippers stood awaiting answers to their prayers. The place of the oracle was circular, resounding with thousands of years of silence, and its musty enclosure gathered them into its unrelenting solitude.

Nadia and Monir walked up to the tourists and tribesmen, and Monir picked up a corn cob from the grill, cut it in half and offered her a steaming piece. He said, "I've always wanted to live here in Luxor where I was born." He seemed to be part of the earth where he stood. For an instant, she too belonged to this land, in a pre-birth state, where her ancestors surrounded her in the sand. She felt that this is how the group dynamic, the choral sense in Egypt, gained momentum: man and woman—dwarfed by stretching sand and memories of thousands of years—realized that as individuals their lives were inconsequential, but as a group they could leave their mark on time and invoke meaning from stone. Here, you got the sense of being a particle among many in the forward sweep of civilization. Behind them, the columns of the temple loomed large and silent, and beyond these the silvery waters of the Nile River flowed into the Holy Lake. Ancient religious ceremonies were held by priests in processional boats which would have glided on the lake, their voices rising in prayer, keeping rhythm with the oarsmen. Their chants would have mingled with the murmur of whistling sands.

Now the smooth water in the Holy Lake—site of ancient purification—shone with an unrelenting composure.

***

Yasser had told Magda that in Cairo he would be in his office off Medan-El-Tahrir most days of the week, and Magda hoped that even if his wife were staying with him in their apartment off the same Medan, he would come and see her at her place in Douki. Magda glanced across the darkening bedroom in the Luxor Hilton Hotel where Soheir lay on her back in bed, arms stretched out on the mattress. She had fallen asleep hours ago. Magda envied her her deep dreams. Yasser and Selim had decided to cut their trip short and fly back to Cairo. They were leaving Luxor in a couple of days. Perhaps she and Soheir could join them. Did Soheir really have the wild, fearful nightmares she described to Magda? Some people believed their dreams foretold future events, but Magda did not place much value on such superstition, for how can the dead visit the living, when the living were so far apart, boxed into their individual fantasies? She rolled onto her back and settled her head on the pillow. What was it about this man, Yasser, that made her feel so much a part of him? When he was with her, he had the manner of a proprietor who took care of his possessions. Was she one of these? Not possible, for he could not have transported her into such an ocean of wildness if this were his customary behaviour. Never before had she felt so comfortable in the arms of another. Her father believed she had a special place in his life, but how often was he around? All he wanted was an illusion of caring, a proof that he was kinder to her than her mother was. He did not guess that his presence loomed a huge ghost in her life, his muscular arms blocking the day's light. He believed he was his daughter's protector and considered her mother a fallen woman, who had abandoned her child and brought shame on him by running away with a lover. But he had not acknowledged his part in the family break-up, did not suspect he was negligent, nor that he existed in his mind amid incidents in army barracks and violent confrontations in the desert. What occupied him was power. He was consumed by his passion for domination, especially over his daughter, and his declarations of love for her were mere words, not actions.

She recalled the first night she had met Ezzat, when his eyes had analyzed every bone in her body and sent shivers through her skin; his jokes, the harsh wine. Her last night with him was something she could not bear to recall. He drank excessively, even though he belonged to a circle of zealots who believed alcohol was Satan's weapon. On their first night, with the aid of wine, he had seduced her into a tunnel of closeness with him. He had contained her with his eyes and she had felt wanted, because before that, her life had been fragmented and empty. From then on, he had never left her alone. He had shadowed her when she was off work. That was before she knew he was a drunk and before alcohol had unleashed his anger. Sometimes, he was furious with her for being part of an upper middle class; at other times, he attacked her for being the daughter of a General who maintained the status quo of a corrupt government, corrupt because it was not part of what ordinary people, like himself, wanted. Invariably, he was angry, even at the men on the street who watched her walk, angry with her for having attracted their attention. But that night, she had run out on the street screaming when he had picked up a kitchen knife and, circling it above his head, had shouted about a future that would show who the real national was in this country: someone like her who imitated Americans, or someone like him who knew and respected his nation's customs.

She had gone to the police. The following days she had locked out of her mind. The police had ordered him to stay away from her throughout their divorce proceedings, or his job in the army would be in jeopardy. Just the ceremony of Ezzat's drunken eyes spinning with black fire, the frenzied dance when he wrapped his wet lips around her breasts, sucked her nipples, thrust his fingers into her, never glancing at her, just the boobs, the open passageway. She shivered.

And he was sure he was within his rights, was right, and the rest of the world was in darkness.

***

Nadia is sitting up in the dark, crying; she does not want to leave her home. Why has she allowed it to be put up for sale? It has taken them decades to acquire it: wide windows, white walls, and outside it, trees and shrubs. She has allowed it to be sold. A nice couple has bought it. She and Yasser are homeless, wandering through large houses on exclusive streets, searching. None of the mansions are home. She wants the one they have fixed, her quiet sanctum, not an outstanding place, but home. Was her home. She does not want the other houses. She wants their home. But she would never have it. It belongs to the couple who came to see her and Yasser to say how comfortable the house was. Yasser's hand is on her shoulder. "Nadia, you're crying, wake up." His voice is far away.

It has taken them years to put it into shape. That's where their children have grown, each room with a special memory. She enters one huge place after another, the one with the large entrance and living room, high ceilings, crystal chandeliers, upper-storey balcony overlooking the main hall on the first floor. On the second floor, a study. The house has an addition, labs they seem, and above them empty cavities that could have made a studio with a large window. The studio is huge, deserted, full of cobwebs and dust. A forsaken place. Old broken furniture. She doesn't want a home that has belonged to unhappy people; her home has been happy.

She stares into the dark and whispers, "I know I'm dreaming, but I can't get out!" Yasser's palm lies on her stomach. He asks, "What's the matter?" She sobs without making a sound, "We don't have a home, in Canada."

"But of course we do. You're dreaming." He pulls her closer to him. They slip down on the pillow, together. One part of her knows she is dreaming, the other is desolate. She is knocking on doors, crying, because she has agreed to have her home put up for sale. She is entering large houses with wide entrances, huge reception halls, high ceilings, two-storey buildings, dark, unconnected to her life, her children's, Yasser's. Where would she find another home?

She shook herself to get into Yasser's reality, she rocked in his arms, but was half in her recurring dream, half in his world. Their king-size hotel bed hugged their bodies with its fluffy pillows and enveloping mattress. She was glad she had not told him her dream, the dread that filled her. His warmth was unclouded by the shadows haunting her. She did not like the feeling of having left something important behind.

***

Nadia's almond-shaped eyes filled Monir's memory as his footsteps hit the road on the Luxor Cornice overlooking the river. Not a carriage nor a single step other than his own. All he heard was the dry, distanced barking of a dog, crisp songs of crickets rising from the waters flowing in the river running alongside the road. Three in the morning. The streets had discharged their cargoes and opened up their asphalt to his tread. Solitude set his thoughts in order and cleaned the debris of the day's actions. Silence illumined his mind. He had danced with her on the Lotus, run across her at Edfu temple, spent an evening with her at the Karnak. Nadia's eyes—like those of King Akhenaton's mother, queen Tiy, who had a personality to mould granite into art—had a presence that emanated from a hidden source. Both women had almond-shaped eyes, long thin noses, full lips, and hair that bunched out in copious strength. Their eyes held numinous secrets, reflections of inner moments, light of life's energy. No wonder his country-men believed in the resurgence of the spirit; it came to life in a new body with the qualities of the previous human and filled it with zest. Such was this woman's face. It approached him from across the centuries and beckoned him. Her bunched-up hair, thick as a deep forest, accentuated the aura of a spirit that has wandered in from faraway places and was on its way to far-ther skies. What he wanted was to set her essence down on paper. He had to coax the charcoal to deliver the texture of her skin on paper. He wished he were a sculptor, not a mere scrib-bler in charcoal; not a painter in colours, but the real thing, a sculptor in granite. He would have his creation reveal her haunting presence, and it would last, throughout time. Was there a pool of spirits somewhere in the velvet sky, or in the hard road under his feet, in air, somewhere, vying for the bod-ies they would inhabit? Did they hide in swaying palm while they bid for their preferred personalities? Did they choose to be those whom they most resembled in previous lives, or were they mischievous enough to become the opposite of what they had been? Did kings decide to become paupers, and spirits pay heed to gender, or did they jump into bodies of the opposite sex? If his own spirit had a choice, it would get closer to this woman's mind and lie with her in her chamber of silence.

As Monir's eye-lids struggled to remain open, his mind continued to invoke a mythological garden of dreams on his way back to the Luxor Hilton Hotel.

***

Chapter Six

Sea

In the noon sun, Nadia saw the overpowering granite stones of Abu Simbel Temple as a greyish blur behind a gauze screen, yet in her mind's eye was a clear picture of the previous afternoon when Yasser packed his clothes and stepped into the taxi with Selim. Yasser had returned to Cairo, and from there he was going to Damietta on the Mediterranean Sea, where he was to begin his engineering project for the Egyptian government. She was not sure what his job entailed, but it had to do with the sea's encroachment on the land. He would try to stop the waves from taking over the beaches and gardens; but how any man-made structure would harness the fury of the sea, she did not know. He was supposed to have spent two weeks with her in Upper Egypt; he had stayed one.

She sat on a large stone half-way between the escarpment overlooking the Nile on her right and the group of tourists assembled at the feet of Ramses II statues on her left. Throned and seated in a row outside the temple, the colossal granite Pharaohs appeared as though through a long-lens camera; she could not zoom in for a close-up. With their palms on their knees, the statues loomed large and arrogant, the people dwarfed at their feet. The sun was high, but a steady breeze quelled its heat. Nadia strolled towards the edge of the plateau and peered over. The granite rocks below showed no evidence of the original site of the temple which lay covered in water. What a gruelling task it must have been for the workers and archaeologists to have marked and carved into square blocks the statues and temple at the bottom of the hill, raised and transplanted them piece by piece with cranes to the top of the plateau, then re-assembled the structure. The temple behind her seemed intact as though untouched by thousands of years of

ancient sand, but upon closer examination, she detected lines
dissecting the granite where archaeologists had cut the stone.

Yasser had interrupted his holiday with her to start his
work on the Damietta project; he had chosen to enter negotiations with the Americans in Cairo at the same time, but
worse, she had been too resentful of his decision to enjoy their
days together.

A woman distributed wrapped sandwiches to the tourists
sitting at the Pharaohs' feet, and Monir served them lemonade
from bottles dripping cold water from an ice-filled metal
bucket. Nadia returned to the group and sat down on a large
stone at the edge of their gathering, then Monir joined her.
Pressing his back against the stone, he had the satisfied smile
of the proprietor of the site, self-assigned to transcribe its message to those seeking initiation into its mysteries. Pointing
down the escarpment, then up to the temple, he told her, "I've
explained to the tourists how the archaeologists cut and re-
assembled the monument on this plateau. My son, Kareem,
and I were here when the workmen were setting up the temple." She had not associated him with a son, and he, perhaps
guessing her thought, said, "My wife died when our son was
eight. Now Kareem's nineteen."

Young, despite his grey hairs, thin, immersed in his desert
world, untouched by civic anxiety, his books, slides and
archaeological sites were enough for him, yet how could he
live in the middle of sixteen million bodies in Cairo and not
feel dispersed? Perhaps other people's energy formed an insulation against the erratic murmur of his heart. He was telling
her of the difference between Abu Simbel then and now, how
the new building seemed empty of the spirit that had dwelt in
its ancient site. They ate in silence.

The same lady served them Turkish coffee from a thermos
flask. Monir set his cup down, lay full length on the uneven
stone, rested his head on his knapsack, smiled as if he were
lying on silk. He spoke of The Nile Arts Club in Cairo: artists,
writers, musicians, dramatists who celebrated the heritage of

Egypt. His eyes belied his posture, his pupils alive and focused as if he were describing a collection of artifacts he had taken a lifetime to accumulate. "Our club is an oasis in Egypt at a time when political matters are so volatile." Then in an undertone, "Something in our society seems about ready to erupt." He slid down and lay flat on the stone but did not pursue the subject further, his half-closed eyes marbles behind his dark-rimmed glasses. She told him about her paintings of the Delta Barrage, her sense of being an intruder on the peasant woman washing her clothes in the river, her shame for being alien from her people's customs. She would have liked to tell him about running away from the Mansour residence, but his group of tourists were re-entering the temple. He sat up. "Why don't you join our Arts Club?" He scrutinized her for a reaction.

"I'd love to!" she responded on impulse. He did not stand to leave.

She told him about her home at the Delta Barrage, her garden, the jasmine that connected with her roots. "But, since Yasser works in Cairo and I'll be in the city, I may have some time to join you." The hills on the opposite side of the river were far away, yet she yearned to lie on the sand and run her fingers through its warm velvet. "Most of the time," she reflected, "I prefer to work at the Delta Barrage."

"Sometimes our lives infringe upon our work." Monir told her of his fascination with faces on temple walls, of Pharaohs, queens, scribes, the ones who had stories to tell, and as he did so, his eyes outlined her face, almond eyes, aquiline nose, full lips. She was the object of his scrutiny, not the creator of images—as she was used to being—so she shifted her position. He excused himself, got up and entered the temple.

Yasser was in Cairo and she here. He had joined her after almost a year's absence so they could be together, but they were apart. If he were to find a meaningful way to serve his native land, he might achieve inner peace, but would associating with Selim be a way to find peace? Not likely, she thought, but it was Yasser's way. She knew that living without his energy was a solo journey on a road without a tree or a shrub to shelter her from the mid-noon rays. Like the unchecked sun, her solitude was reproaching her.

***

A trip through Luxor at night seemed an inviting alternative to Nadia's thoughts. She would join Monir and friends, plunge into city crowds, smell freshly ground coffee beans, roasting chestnuts, strudel in ovens, see ears of corn on red sparks from coal, buy roasted watermelon seeds, pop them open to savour their salty freshness. She would find a turquoise scarab ring for a charm, see rolls of brocade piled up on shelves in small stores, purchase green silk for an evening dress, then browse through imitation Pharaonic statues.

Monir, Nadia and three American tourists arrived at the centre of town in a horse-drawn carriage: Bob, a big-boned real-estate agent, his wife Rose, a thick gold choker with a rectangular cartouche containing her name inscribed in hieroglyphics, and Peter, a schoolteacher with a thin, myopic face. They chose a café on the pavement on a cobbled street of the village and crowded around a small table with a red-and-white chequered cloth. Heat waves in half-circles of energy and light swirled before Nadia's eyes. Getting used to such movement in warm, narrow places would take time. The road was choked with people. Multi-coloured bulbs on stalls lent their feverish glow to the night. Bob ordered a *narguila* air-pipe for himself and beer for Rose and Peter. Nadia and Monir opted for black tea. When the waiter arrived with the *narguila*, he placed the lit coals on a small tray atop a stand, then Bob drew his first breath of smoke through the air bubbles in the water. Liking his experiment, he passed the pipe on to his wife.

A vendor came to their table to display his jewellery and scarves. The group pushed their drinks aside to study his wares, and Nadia selected a turquoise scarab ring and silk scarf, the greenest, bluest-purple of the lot. The vendor pointed to a store where she could purchase silk. She paid him the amount Monir suggested and stored the ring in her handbag. Hot tea scalded her tongue in burning mouthfuls. From her chair on the pavement, her eyes followed light bulbs zigzagging on doorways of stores and restaurants. People formed a giant, twitching body, its cells vibrating, but she could not forget that Yasser had abandoned her. In agitated voices, people around the table asked Monir about ingredients in dishes on the menu. They had heard warnings about Middle Eastern food, and feared that anything they ate was going to land them flat on their backs in hospital. Monir ordered bottled spring water and recommended broiled foods or fava beans and *falafel*.

Nadia turned her attention to a vendor in a lined grey-and-white *gallabiah*, his face ghost-like, inching in to their table, his arms bobbing up and down with yoyos, plastic monkeys in bright oranges and reds, throwing and retrieving balls. But no one was interested. They were ordering *falafel* and fava beans as the least risky of alternatives. He replaced his toys with a pile of cotton, hand-woven mats for the beach. Rose selected two, and soon she and the vendor were haggling about price, so Monir gave the man a figure he had to accept or leave. The man surrendered his goods, took the notes, gathered the rest of his merchandise, placed it on his back and muttered oaths at Monir for having forced him to give his mats away for free. His back piled with rows of coloured wares, the vendor reached a neighbouring café where he set his load down and worked the yoyos. Rose's face wore the puzzled expression of one who could not understand why anyone would choose an ignoble job, impinge on others' privacy and be so belligerent. By way of explanation, Nadia said, "He probably has six children to feed in a hut on the outskirts of the city."

Sipping his beer while waiting for his wife to return his *narguila* pipe, Bob asked, "But why do they have so many children?"

"Because," Monir answered, "for them children are gifts from God and harbingers of good luck." Bob wrinkled his forehead. His wife surrendered the pipe, then asked whether

Egyptians practised birth control. Monir nodded. "They do, but then we Egyptians are no good at planning our lives," his voice soft, wary, as he sipped his back tea. Rose examined him as she would a frisking fish in a glass bowl. He was sipping a steaming glass of scalding tea, curls of steam winding into his nostrils.

Nadia offered, "Egyptians are intuitive. They live by feelings of the moment."

Rose persisted, "But don't they see the results of this kind of living? People are destroying the land. Isn't the government *educating* them?" Her sleek fingers adjusted the gold *cartouche* on the chain around her neck. Monir nodded. "Yes, it does. Ads about free government birth-control clinics are incessant on radio and TV, but our farmers like to have a lot of children to work the fields."

Nadia thought of Esmat and her children and said, "The problem arises when these children leave the land and move to the cities to work in factories. They abandon the farms and turn the cities into slums because they have little money. But this movement from farms into cities is a universal problem which we are also facing in Canada." A street juggler approached them, his body a hanger for dangling strings with numerous knives, sharp daggers of different sizes and shapes.

"Want me to juggle knives, lie on a sharp dagger? . . ." he spoke hurriedly in Arabic, fearing interruption. Rose gestured him away with the back of her hand. He set his shoulder burden down, took a large kitchen knife from his sack, opened his mouth and slid the razor-sharp blade down his throat. Silent up to now, Peter shouted the juggler away, but the man kept the knife dangling point down straight into his throat. "No, NO," shouted Rose, shaking her head from side to side, her face transfixed with horror at the blade wedged between the gaping lips. The vendor extracted the knife, wiped it on his sleeve, wrapped it in spare cloth, and stored it in his shoulder bag. "Lady, I swallow fire," he grinned, speaking in English. He lit a gas torch and pushed the flames down his throat. The brown enclave of his mouth closed around them. Nadia placed a hand on Rose's arm, and Monir gave the vendor bills and told him to leave. The man kissed the money, stacked it into an inner pocket, picked up his wares and shuffled on. The three tourists' faces reflected the shattered, invisible bubble around them.

Monir broke the silence. "The other day I was talking to my son about the distinguishing characteristics of Egyptians . . ." He examined faces around the table. "Has anyone seen the earliest maps of the world?" he smiled at each in turn. No one had. He continued, "The maps appear as though they were drawn on the surface of a ball." Monir took out a note-pad, sketched a convex drawing of the continents. "The land is seen as from a modern satellite. Anyway, my point is, in ancient times Egypt was represented as the centre of the map, with Thebes, then capital, south of the present Cairo, as the focal point, right here," he drew a star at the centre of the map, "the same Thebes that is immortalized in the works of Homer and other ancient writers."

When no one responded, he continued, "The point is, we Egyptians are at the centre of our world, as was our Suez Canal at one time. Our culture is a link between East and West. We understand the intellectual thrust of the West and feel the mystical pull of the East, and we are able to combine these qualities with a love of life which reflects our Mediterranean heritage. You see, the West appreciates Eastern philosophy, and Eastern people seek Western technology. Today, Japan, China, Pakistan, India are able to equal Western know-how in their individual areas and perhaps surpass it in some—like car-manufacturing computer expertise, hand-labour. East and West are closer to each other than they are to us." Then, in a measured tempo, "I don't think either one understands us." He stumbled into a silence that—instead of healing the wound—had ripped it open.

Rose pushed her chair back and stood up. "Is there a ball-room-party at the hotel tonight?"

Monir signalled the waiter for the bill. "Certainly," he said with a smile. "You go to the carriage-stand down the street, and I'll join you when I've settled accounts."

Bundles in hand, Nadia and Rose trudged between carts on the street and people at the café, the warm comfort of baking strudel greeting them from busy ovens. Shish kebabs on skewers were piled up on tables; in shop windows, wicker baskets of dried figs and dates, candy dolls in rows sat along window sills. Nadia reached the shop with the stacks of silk and darted in. Roll upon roll of bright damask—piled up to the ceiling, spilling over counters—greeted her eyes. A long silk fuchsia dress hung at the back of the store: a simple A-line design, no ornaments. She asked for it, but when she had it in her hand realized she could not try it for the narrow store had no fitting room. She placed it against her body: the size seemed fine. She paid the woman and waited for her to wrap it in flowery black paper, took her parcel and dashed out in pursuit of her group.

She ran into sounds and lights, found Rose and Monir beside a cart with a short metal chimney exuding smoke. Their paper funnels were piled high with hot chestnuts, and Monir handed Nadia the nuts, then went to see the drivers about the carriages. At the buggy-stand, Nadia and Rose climbed up into the back of the carriage while Monir negotiated price with the driver. When the men had taken their seats opposite the women, Monir sat beside the driver, and the horses reared, starting their familiar route to Luxor Hilton Hotel. Monir's back a detached silhouette and the horses' hooves hitting the cobbled road in syncopation transformed Nadia's journey into a hypnotic dance in the darkening street. Wicker baskets of merchandise disappeared; radio songs trailed behind them; men, women and carts dispersed. City noises cushioning Nadia from her relentless thoughts receded, and she re-awakened to the discomfort of Yasser's absence. Their horses swung onto the Cornice. Above the expanse of midnight river, they clumped through silence to the hotel, now bathed in light, looming in silent testimony to the opulence within, in contrast to the mud houses at the outskirts of the wakeful city.

***

A day after Selim and Yasser left Luxor for Cairo, Soheir and Magda followed them. When she arrived in Cairo, Magda—on board the tourist bus en route to the Cairo Museum— relived her moments with Yasser: the bounding gazelle with wavy hair pushed back from his forehead, shoulders open to the wind, body comfortable, herb-scented, his movements lithe, his natural state one of action. She collected tickets from her passengers and conjured up her evening with him on the Lotus, and their other night at the villa in Luxor, neither of which she would forget. A few days ago in Cairo, she had run across Yasser on a packed street off Liberty Square. She could have hugged him right there, but didn't, because the men on the street knew her, and her father owned the Persian carpet store a few feet away from where she and Yasser stood. Yasser was the one lover who had carried her through a forest of wild shrubs and dream animals with his lips on her neck, fingers unlocking springs within her, penis a butterfly fluttering, his closeness a vibrating tremor in her body. Her eyes sank into his as they stood on the street, and he promised to see her in her Douki apartment.

***

Downtown Luxor had refreshed but not calmed Nadia. Back at the hotel, she showered, put on her fuchsia dress and scarab ring, bunched her hair like a sphinx's, wore an emerald velvet head-band, her face pale in contrast to the fuchsia and green, then went down to join the party in the ballroom. The crystal-lit hall was jammed. A small band on the stage played rock on electronic guitars, xylophones and drums. At a table near the dance floor, Monir stood and waved, held a chair out for her. His eyes touched her hair and shoulders transforming her into an artist's model. "You look . . . Pharaonic," he said, " . . . a vibrant sculpture!" She told him that the fuchsia dress was the one she had purchased that morning.

Around the table, men were joking about a belly dancer who was due to start any moment. When the song ended and the dancers left the floor, the belly dancer entered, trailed by a band of musicians playing Arabic tunes, accompanied by the insistent measure of the drummer, his skinny fingers beating rhythm on the funnel-shaped instrument tucked under his left arm. Aware of Monir's scrutiny, Nadia maintained her concentration on the dancer as she wove her way around guests' chairs and at each table bent backward until her head reached her calves. But before an outstretched hand reached her, she straightened her back and moved to the next group. Accompanied by a high drum roll, she circled the floor, went up centre stage and began her performance. Like an electric wave, viewers' anticipation rose and lifted Nadia's spirit.

Monir shifted his attention from Nadia to the dancer whose fingers beat imaginary drums; she clapped and signalled the audience to keep in step with her. Swaying her arms and thighs, she bent backwards until her head reached the floor then slid her back onto the floor until she lay flat, keeping her legs tucked under her buttocks. Her long hair swept in undulations sideways on the shiny parquet, like a slithering, dark snake, one side and then the other, complementing the action of her arms and hips, her well-shaped body bare except for the studded pink gauze sheathing her breasts and pelvis, her thighs apart, her skirt open fan-like on the floor. Pink sequins on her scant triangle glittered. Yells from the crowd spurred her tremulous motions. Monir drummed the table and joined the men in a song. He took off his clouded glasses, wiped them, put them back on. The dancer beckoned men to join her; women remained in their chairs, straight-backed, wide-eyed. Nadia merged with the pulse of the nightclub, clapping rhythm to the music. Flower designs on the dancer's sequined dress shone under coloured spotlights, her hair wove circles in air, her arms bade imaginary lovers to come to her, pelvis conjured up wild dreams of uninhibited men, breasts celebrated waves of desire reaching her. Soon the women were entering her web of dreams.

One by one, the men came up to her and placed their hundred pound bills into her breast-cover. She led them into a dance. Each twirled with her in a circle, returned to his place as another walked into her magic web. Women were mesmerized by their husbands' abandon; men drummed and beckoned the dancer to come to them then lifted her up on their table and sat smiling up at her as she danced, her alabaster legs just above their eyes. When they helped her off the table, they crammed large bills into her scant covers sending the bills spilling onto the floor, then they picked them up and piled them on her abandoned veil at front stage. Lights changed from red and green to blue and yellow illuminating the bare woman: fleshy icon from a world beyond the reach of hands. Then she was gone.

She dissolved in the dark; white light replaced the coloured spotlights. Men and women blinked as they re-entered their world, now denuded of the mirage. A rock band gushed fast-paced metallic sounds to fill the lull left behind by the soft lute and Arabic drums. Faltering couples moved onto the floor, and Monir and Nadia joined them. Emerging from sleep, the couples awakened to an energy that had floated to them from the veins of the belly dancer. Hypnotically, they beat the floor. Nadia reflected Monir's enthusiasm as he twirled her around. She entered his twisting dialogue, then changed partners, and danced solo within a circle of dancers. Above her head, a silver ball cast flashing stars on faces, clothes, ceiling and plunged her into a subterranean swirl where illusion was reality. She moved in and out of people's arms, welcomed Monir's slender hand, floated with him in a dark cave lit by stalactites. The belly dancer had ignited fields of fire that had sprung from her and entered their bodies, and they could not quench their thirst for more. Monir swung Nadia out into the veranda, and the drums they heard were their own heart-beats. He enveloped her in a world of stars; she matched his steps with wild ones of her own.

They descended the cement steps into the garden then stopped and faced each other. She stroked his hair; he tilted her face and kissed her, the way a young man pledges his first love. Night music played, but neither knew where the sounds originated. They swayed to the resonance of drums. When they unwound, he escorted her through the ballroom into the elevator and up to her room. He did not wait for her to unlock her door, but turned and left. As she entered her room, crickets' songs broke in through the open window. She did not want to sleep, but as soon as she was in bed, and before she could form another thought, she did.

***

"Come on Yasser, say you'll go," Magda urged as she rouged her cheeks in her dresser mirror. "You'll like Mariout. Our villa overlooks the desert, and from my bedroom you can see green watermelons under the shrubs."

He lay on his back watching her. She tickled his feet; instead of smiling, he jerked them away. He had no intention of going with her to Mariout. Magda had the habit of including him in her activities as though he were part of her life. He had been with the woman a few times, and she had come to expect him to spend his weekends with her. Apart from her work in the tourist business, they had nothing to talk about. He got up and brushed his hair in the mirror, observed the contents of her room spilling around him. Clothes on the bed, under it, in the corner, on hangers behind the door, an open box of chocolate creams in a dresser drawer by her bedside, lopsided window drapes undone on one side, a couple of flowering plants in the window, their dry leaves showering the sill, the green ones yellowing. Pictures—of water buffalo and peasants tilling the soil—hung from rusty nails on walls, their elaborate gold frames several generations old. Magda had told him this had been her grandmother's furniture: ornate, handcrafted by Egyptian workmen in a manner that defined its age. The disarray was incongruous. Ingredients of life were here, but the disorder turned them into a jungle. Quite opposite of the way Magda dressed, for she designed her face to perfection, her hair glossy, body perfumed, her eyes a sea that drew him in. Her place in Douki had become an easy escape for him at lunch hour. Too easy. In a few minutes, he would be in his office in Liberty Square; yet these surreptitious meetings were taking longer each day, and he had to end them before she became part of his life, and before Nadia returned to Cairo.

"Father never goes to Mariout, I don't know why, at least he hasn't since his mother died four years ago." She watched Yasser fasten his belt and put on his jacket. "I love it there," she continued, "the bedouin bring me dates and *sambousek* filled with Turkish delight. Come on, Yasser, say you'll go: just Thursday and Friday. All you need is to take off early on Thursday!" She spoke with urgency to battle his movements which would take him away from her. She messed his hair, pushed him over the edge of the bed, tumbled over him; he lay on the crumpled bed and he knew he had already spent too much time with her, yet he needed to forget codes and agreements; other men did, without feeling the world crumble. For a few seconds, he relaxed in what he knew would be reason for his inner disquiet.

***

On the upper deck of the *Lotus*, winds flapped the canvas and pushed the boat full-tilt downstream, its hull slicing water as though in a hurry to reach Cairo. Drinks in hand, people wandered around speaking in whispers, stopping to absorb the scenery. Nadia and Monir bent over the rails and watched the river flow. They noted a buffalo circling in the distance. Flat, green terrain ended in a straight line that turned into ochre sand until it reached the blue sky. Soon, city noises would approach. Monir edged closer to Nadia. "This was a special trip," he said, and she nodded.

"If you'd like to see other places in Cairo, let me know." He took his notebook and wrote his telephone number and address and handed her the paper. "This is the number for my studio where I spend my time when I'm not teaching. If you need anything, or if you want to join our Arts Club, phone me, evenings."

On land, rusted machinery lay in piles on sand. Nadia put the paper in her pocket and pointed to the metal. "This looks like an abandoned battlefield!"

He laughed. "It's Russian farm equipment left here since Nasser's time."

"The farmers did not want to use it?"

"They did, but by the time it needed repair, Nasser had asked the Russians to leave Egypt, and since no one knew how to fix the equipment, the farmers abandoned it and went back to their traditional hand labour."

***

Yasser's feet dug deeper into the mud at Damietta, where his job was to save the land from an encroaching sea, but on every visit, he thought the beach had shrunk a little, although he guessed that the erosion could not be happening so fast. Salt-edged wind hit his face, and behind him waters of the Mediterranean broke over the soil. He had to take measurements of the land, come to conclusions about the erosion, but it would have been easier to have had a government engineer with him. He recalled Magda's eyes: was he running away from her? from his life? You should do something useful for the land, he nudged himself into alertness, pay attention to the erosion of the soil, you're here to survey it. But what he felt was the salt on his lips, her tongue searching his. Damn Magda! She invaded him with her constant presence, a signal of division within himself. He had come to fear her power over him. He walked around the field to study the hills. Her soft brown tits, wide shoulders, full hips, earthy reality pushed him into a wild desire to hurt what he found so appealing.

He blocked out the memory of Nadia, her slender body inviting protection; he wanted to hold her and rest there. Why then was he giving in to his base instincts? What if Nadia guessed his betrayal, or someone told her that he had been seen entering Magda's Douki apartment? But none of the hoards of faces in Cairo knew him. Thank God his mother had died a long time ago, a few years after he had married Nadia and moved to Canada. Tall, slim, with rules for everything, his mother would not have understood his actions. But what about his sons? Both men now. He would be brutal with them if they practised his duplicity. Samy would be shocked to discover Magda in his father's life. As for Amir, his worst suspicions of his father would materialize, and he would turn away and never look back, their tenuous connection dissolved forever. Yasser had to straighten out his life and make no more excuses for his repeated deception. He had to pay attention to his work. Soon, he would be meeting the American consultants in Cairo to discuss ways of controlling the sea.

***

Monir and Nadia's last day on deck was warm and bright. Monir asked, "Do you plan to stay in Egypt for good?"

Nadia answered, "I don't know. I'm doing all the things I've wanted to do for years: live in the Delta, visit ancient sites, family, but I feel disoriented. Our sons are in Canada, and we are here."

"But when your sons get here . . ."

"Oh, they're not staying! They're visiting over New Year's."

"And you? Do you want to follow them?"

She shrugged, but when she looked up her eyes were watery. He removed his glasses, wiped them. "I hope I didn't annoy you by asking." He held his glasses against the sun then put them back on. "The other night in the hotel, I overstepped my limits. I was in a strange mood, the music, the place, I didn't mean to intrude. I hope my actions didn't trouble you, and if they did, I'm sorry." He kept his eyes on the fields. She shook her head and mumbled, "Wonderful evening." In her mind, winds of the Mediterranean blew. She was on a beach assailed by gales, overpowered. Her jostled perceptions would find their way to canvas, but how would she withstand the winds of change? Eastward, southward, changing, until she no longer knew her direction.

Monir placed his elbow on the rail behind him as though to pin the moment in place. High buildings approached them on the banks. The overhanging gardens of El Gizereh were just

ahead. Nadia studied his profile: alert young student of the universe discovering constellations and axes of the earth. In his late
thirties, probably early forties, with the figure of a man in his
twenties. Slight body, veined hands, tanned skin in an open
white shirt. He smiled, she turned to face him, took his hand in
her own, traced the skin on its back, the veins, knuckles, then
turning his palm upwards, traced his life signs. They laughed.

"Do I live to be a rich man?"

"Not rich; just vital." He stopped smiling, and studied her
through his glasses.

***

"It isn't like that, Yasser," Magda said. He lay on her bed
in his pyjama trousers, his hair dishevelled on the pillow. She
had come in from the balcony when she heard him shout. She
slid her housecoat off her shoulders to the floor and climbed
into bed. What had she said that had brought this fierce stare
to his eyes?

"I told you, I haven't talked to Ezzat since we were divorced.
He follows me on the street, but I don't look at him. I think he
believes I don't see him, but he's there, and I see him when I'm
alone." She sat by Yasser and leaned her head on his chest. Her
breasts, long and full, lay half-naked in the pink lace nightgown.
He sat up and rested his back on the headboard; she edged in
closer. They stared at each other in the dresser mirror. He said,
"The thing is, you should go to the police and tell them this man
is shadowing you. Get them to take him off the streets."

"But I've told you, he's in the army, and I'm afraid of kicking up a fuss there, just in case my father hears about it.
Anyway, don't worry, Ezzat dares not touch me, he would be
killed. He knows how powerful my father is. The only thing
that matters to me is, my father must never know about him.
Everything else, I can control."

"Don't wait until Ezzat gets drunk and attacks you. You
never know what this bully will do."

"I know, but he's a coward. The police know him, so he

won't dare move. What I should do is change my job, or move to another apartment." She reached out to her dresser drawer, took out the box of chocolates and offered him one. He refused it, so she dug her teeth into it savouring the liqueur with her tongue. Liqueur ran down her lip, and her tongue followed it. She licked her fingers and placed another round chocolate in her mouth. Yasser could not tell if she went through these motions to get his attention, or if she were unaware of the effect she was creating.

"My father bribes me with chocolates. His officers bring them for me when they travel abroad. He thinks he's buying my love!" She shrugged to say, that's *his* business. Then, as though on the same theme, she said, "The thing is, I had a job offered me at IBM, as receptionist. Pays very well, better than what our government doctors are making! But I didn't take it."

"Why? It should be easier than the one you have."

"Not really. I have a cousin who works as computer programmer in an American company. She tells me she starts work at eight in the morning and never finishes before nine in the evening. She gets home about ten o'clock. That's not for me. My tourist job is better; I'd rather have less money and more freedom." She twisted his hair and teased it into spikes, then laughed and turned his face around so he could see it in the mirror. He turned away from the mirror and faced her.

"Does the company pay overtime?"

"No. My cousin gets regular wages. Management thinks twelve hours of work is normal. Sometimes she has to stay longer to finish her work. Besides, my father gives me money. He likes to pretend I belong to him." She raised her arms above her head to examine the soft skin in her armpit, whiter than that of the low-cut nightgown. She stroked her armpit, enjoying its velvety smoothness. "My cousin gets paid six hundred pounds a month, or less than one hundred American dollars." His eyes followed her fingers.

"This money is a pittance, even if employees receive benefits," he told her.

"I know. In America, the poor are better off. But what can we do? I asked my cousin why she does not discuss her salary with her boss. She said, 'He'll tell me, there are many people waiting for your job.' And," Magda continued as she wiped her mouth on the back of her hand, "he's telling her the truth. The reason I got an offer was, they like to have people recommended by their workers. I know English and Italian. I was brought up by Italian nuns!" She laughed then pulled the top of her nightgown down until her full, brown nipples popped out of the pink lace. "And see what happened!" She caressed his armpits and moved her fingers towards his nipple. He kissed her mouth, tasting the chocolate syrup. Magda swallowed the remainder of the chocolate then bent over him and licked his nipple. Her breasts swung across his chest.

She said, "My father wanted the best for me! So he sent me to the nuns. Little does he know!" She sat up, her arms above her head, her nipples alert, their skin a velvety pink-brown. She ran her middle finger in circles around each, teasing them into firmness. Then she pushed her nightgown down, lay back, and her fingers roamed between her thighs. Yasser's hand replaced hers. Words tumbled out of her mouth. "You know the funny thing? My cousin doesn't even have a pension!" She laughed and watched him in the mirror. With one hand she caressed her nipple, with the other she reached for his open fly. She slipped down farther and made funny faces at him. Yasser pushed his trousers down.

But in the back of Magda's mind was the nagging thought that working in an American company would antagonize Ezzat, who told her that those who dealt with Americans in Egypt were traitors and would get their comeuppance. She did not want to trigger his fury. She reached for the cognac bottle and sprinkled drops of the liquid on her breasts. Yasser bent over and lapped them.

***

"Nadia in the jasmine garden." Soraya Erian.
Oil pastels. 1995

"Yasser in the elements." Soraya Erian.
Oil pastels & charcoal. 2004

"Magda at the Nile Hilton." Soraya Erian.
Oil pastels. 1995.

"Monir in Edfu Temple." Soraya Erian.
Oil pastels, acrylics & charcoal. 2005.

Chapter Seven
Chasm

Nadia passed her arms through the sleeves of her black gown and the silk flowed over her head down to her ankles. The large white collar hugging her shoulders was neat, but the complementary flower at her waist drooped, and she had no time to press it. Her heart pounded. The evening promised to be claustrophobic. In the mirror, she looked dressy, with flair. The soirée at the American Embassy was in honour of the Atkinsons, the newly arrived American Ambassador and his wife. Her grandmother's pearl necklace around her neck, her hair gathered at the nape of her neck the way her grand-mother's used to be, Nadia looked elegant, even aristocratic. Yet how much better it would have been to be in her garden at the Barrage, her ankles in mud, Nessim's face impassive as rock, his shoulders hunched in silent reproach of her usurping a man's work in the garden.

Their sons, Amir and Samy, were arriving in Cairo the fol-lowing day, and she would have preferred to stay behind with Esmat to make konafa filled with cream cheese for Samy. Yasser came up behind her to the dresser mirror, and for the third time unravelled and adjusted his tie. This was to be his first meeting with the Atkinsons and McKinnons, and he wanted to create a smooth pathway for negotiations. He was aware that he had left his tension-ridden state in Toronto to come here and rest, yet he welcomed the tightening of his stomach muscles, the tension building up in his body, for he liked being in gear, and disliked uneventful days stretching to infinity. He preferred to be over-wound, life throbbing through his veins, expectancy in his bones.

Nadia's apprehension mounted as she and Yasser climbed the marble steps to the iron-trellis door of the American

Embassy. The building had an aura of calculated opulence: fresh white walls in contrast to the backdrop of grey buildings—trees a bright green, no scarcity of water on *this* compound. The iron-trellis door—immense, out of proportion with gates and garden walls around it—emanated power. These formal evenings were alien to her nature; they set a barrier between her and the people outside the confines of the Embassy, those like Esmat and Nessim who lived close to the soil, those she had come to Egypt to get to know better. It seemed to Nadia that the country was doomed to be the focus of foreign greed and domination, even though the Suez Canal was no longer the main artery of the world joining West to East. The country had been the centre of intrigue through Roman, Greek, British, French, German, Turkish, American, Russian and Israeli invasions, and each nation had driven its stake in the land. Yet the soil and its people managed to steer clear of the colonial grip. Now, faced with American control through technological aid—more insidious than outright colonialism—it was not easy to reject the offering.

Ahead of them were two couples in the receiving line. Two days ago, she and Yasser had had a heated discussion about the help Americans offered the Egyptians in the form of technology to rescue the land from erosion by the Mediterranean Sea. He had argued that the American goal was not wholly altruistic, yet its aim was making Egypt autonomous to prevent it from joining religious fanatical movements in the Mediterranean basin. Nadia was not so sure: no foreign aid came without the clinking of chains.

The Atkinsons were the first couple in the reception line leading into the huge vestibule, the wife in red chiffon, black beads and earrings, husband in black tuxedo, red cummerbund and tie, mirror-reflections of each other, his-her models stepping out of Macy's. Both tall, brown-haired, slim, his upper lip stretched in a smile decked with pearly teeth. Yasser and Nadia introduced themselves, shook hands with the Atkinsons, then Nadia passed her arm through Yasser's, and they proceeded indoors behind a liveried footman who announced their names at the door of a reception hall crammed with visitors. Jazz rippled from the player's fingertips at the piano across the room. His head bent—perhaps to ward off the noise of his admirers clustered around him chatting—he played jazz. High ceiling, bevelled glass windows, nineteenth-century American oil paintings. Yasser escorted Nadia to the piano and introduced her to the McKinnons. The man's layered hair was gelled to stand on end above his forehead but shaved over his ears and the back of his head: probably an ex-Colonel turned Trade Consultant. His wife's green eyes lined with blue mascara, her long nose pointing to thin lips drawn in glossy crimson lipstick that matched her dress, she spoke with clipped precision as though she had designed her lips to stay shimmery in spite of food, beverage or small talk. When she smiled, which was rare, her upper middle teeth gaped in a frank, unabashed separation.

Yasser was telling Nadia, "Our visitors will be staying a few months in Cairo." He turned to the other couple. "And of course, Mr. and Mrs. Abdullah," his Egyptian boss and wife. The Abdullahs extended firm handshakes, the wife smiling through lined, kohl eyes staring out of a face powdered white, her silk dress sequined with grey pearls: a silver fish emerging out of water and slipping back into it. Rotund and balding, his bluish velvety lips the focus of his shiny face, Mr. Abdullah looked as though he had consumed a pheasant with trimmings. Nadia expected him to burp any moment. He had been pictured in *Al Ahram* as Egypt's Minister of Trade.

The McKinnons' open manner suggested an easy liaison for Yasser, and he launched into the must-see sites in Cairo, offered to escort his host and hostess there with his wife Nadia. Judging from his hosts' encouraging smiles he had scored points on appearance and versatility in their language. Nadia felt Yasser's spirit soaring; after all, such parties were *his forte*. People relaxed with him and his mood celebrated their own. As a child in a large family, Yasser had been happiest among his siblings and cousins. When he and Nadia were married, his mother had described to her their family occasions when Yasser, the oldest, had organized his cousins into soccer teams, their laughter echoing back from the beach. At the centre of a group, his true warmth surfaced.

But Nadia was trapped. What was it her mother had said, many years ago, about foreign delegations in Egypt? "They come, use our land and resources then treat us like second-class citizens!" During her first few weeks with Yasser in Egypt, Nadia had not had time to verify her mother's statement, but now in the great hall, her mother's words rang true. Her father had countered her mother's statement by moving his head back and forth, an attendant, ancient spirit rising from the earth. "It doesn't matter what foreigners do when they come here. Our land harbours them; it does not succumb to them. It is they who are overwhelmed by her. They absorb her customs and never want to leave. It's been like this for thousands of years!" For him, his country's soil was unshakeable in its ochre identity, lively in sun, cool and green by the Nile's waters, its sand warm under his back.

Around Nadia and Yasser in the Great Hall, Americans and Egyptians faced each other in stiff formations as if standing on cliffs—divided by a chasm—waving to each other. Beside Nadia, Mrs. McKinnon—using short words and accentuating her *s*'s—was saying, "Cairo *is* lovely, especially at night around Gizereh Island. The Nile *is so* romantic. We've been sailing, and the weather is *so* great. *Isn't* it Cam?"

Cam rose to the call. "Amazing how little one needs to eat in this heat. It's *great* for losing weight!" He laughed and tugged at the Egyptian crocodile belt around a thin waist, patted his non-existent stomach. The Abdullahs, rotund and satisfied, shifted on their feet. Nadia imagined the pan of stuffed vine leaves and pot-roast awaiting them at home. Silence hung like a drugged bat swinging upside-down between them.

Mr. Abdullah offered, "I know you love *za* Nile, so I arranged *zis* Friday party to be at *za* Papyrus Institute in a house-boat near za Meridien Hotel. We will have a few drinks; *Ouzo*! It's great on ice. It makes you see bright stars in *za* sky!" He laughed. "We will have *za* food prepared for us by chefs of *za* Meridien: French dishes, Arabic ones like *kubeeba*, our Egyptian hamburger! And of course, don't forget za belly dancing . . . Last time, you were not able to take papyrus with you." He spoke his *non sequitur* in soft accents of regret, as if weighty political matters hinged on his negligence.

Mrs. McKinnon smiled. "Ah A*kh*med," she sounded a strong guttural in place of the soft *h*, "Thank you *so* much, thi*s is nice* of you. Perhaps we can complete a *s*mall transaction *this* time?" A high trill at the end left a vibrating question in air. Mr. Abdullah bowed, a court Vizier offering his *Amira*, the Princess, his humble service and oath of allegiance.

Yasser described to Mr. McKinnon the renovations under way at the Aswan Dam. He hoped his American colleague would see the similarity between the dam and the upcoming Damietta project. But Mr. McKinnon was half-listening to Mr. Abdullah who was telling Mrs. McKinnon, "We Egyptians take pride in our country and call her *Misr, Om El Donia*, *z*at is: Egypt, Mo*z*er of *za* World. Egypt is our mo*z*er. She has been here since *za* beginning of time." He pronounced the *th* sound as a *z*, unaware of the confusion it created. He smiled again. "Our country is a place where every*z*ing is possible. Here, *all* wishes and dreams come true."

His voice wafted over Nadia and the group and came to rest with meaningful silence on the McKinnons. Eyes shiny wells promising untold fulfillment, full lips pronouncing words as though tasting fresh pheasant, he bowed to Mrs. McKinnon, his bald head gleaming under the crystal chandelier. Alert to his proffered courtesy, Mr. McKinnon responded, "We've worked together in good faith before and have come to realize that our arrangements can be of mutual satisfaction," the straight-backed Colonel, at attention, smiling, awaiting a bugle to summon him to action.

No fresh air. Nadia glanced around the room: all windows were barred and sealed. She was trapped in a bowl of stillness. Surely the place was ventilated, or was the system defective? It couldn't be. In any case, what were they, she and Yasser, doing here, when they were supposed to be enjoying a year of rest? Yasser broke the silence to tell Mr. Atkinson about the Aswan Dam. He described the work he was supervising on the sluices. Renovations, when carried out on time, he said, could save the country immense damage. Nadia and Mrs. McKinnon discussed places they would visit, and Yasser knew he could depend on Nadia for a smooth exchange.

Mr. Abdullah stretched one arm to Mrs. McKinnon and another to Nadia, then with regard to their womanliness, said, "Now, if za ladies would excuse us, we have a few matters to discuss," led them to a sofa, and the men dissolved through a door at the far end of the hall. Air hung heavy in the room. The women sat and smiled.

***

In the small library, the pulled-back red velvet curtains let in a hazy sun onto the mahogany table where the three men sat under the lit crystal chandelier hanging low over their heads. Yasser leaned forward on his arms to listen to Mr. Abdullah and Mr. McKinnon exchange pleasantries about their previous visit. The shiny surface of the mahogany reflected a mirror-image of their faces, and below the crystal chandelier Mr. Abdullah's receding forehead shone like a centrepiece. He placed his hand on Yasser's arm and said, "Mr. Amin is a well-known architect in Canada. He's a native of our country, but he has lived a long time in Norz America. He is a trusted member of our Damietta team. Great experience in Canada. He will be helpful in liaison work wiz your team." He smiled at Yasser who smiled back. Mr. McKinnon nodded, "I'm looking forward to working with you, Mr Amin," then went to the side-board, filled large goblets of port and placed them on coasters before his guests.

Mr. Abdullah gulped the contents of his goblet, took his handkerchief out of his pocket, wiped his mouth and blew his nose with vigour. He said, "We are very grateful for your help wiz za Damietta project. Za diagrams I sent you a few days ago show how za sea has swallowed up za land. We have Egyptian engineers who have followed zis situation. Zey will report to Mr. Amin, who will work wiz you to draw up new plans for za area. I am sure that between our engineers and yours, with Mr. Amin's help, you will find za situation very satisfactory."

Yasser offered, "I had talks with the engineers. I will be going to Damietta to make my own survey. I've visited the area briefly, but this time an engineer from Damietta will be going with me. I know that some data has been prepared, but I want to record my own. As soon as I have done that, I will present my findings to you." Mr. McKinnon topped up the port goblets. "Fine. My wife and I need a couple of weeks to find our way around town." Everyone smiled.

A rush of excitement filled Yasser. This project could yield concrete results for Egypt: he was doing something vital for his native land. Mr. Abdullah scratched his forehead. "Before we go, zere is a matter I need to mention. I'll tell you briefly, zen you and I, Mr. McKinnon, will return to it later." Yasser listened to Mr. Abdullah's reference to some machinery Americans were to provide the Egyptians. Mr. Abdullah did not specify which machines, perhaps some reference to the Damietta project. Yasser did not think it wise to ask questions, so he allowed his mind to roam.

***

"Have you been to the Cairo Museum, Mrs. McKinnon?" Nadia asked.

Mrs. McKinnon smiled. "I've read a lot about it. We were fortunate to see the *Tutt* exhibit when it was on tour in the States." She added an extra t to the name as though she were admonishing a child for misbehaviour. She turned to Mrs. Abdullah. "I'd like to see the small market with the narrow

streets where men hand-craft metal and gold; you know . . .
the old quarter in Cairo?"

Her eyes veiled under thick lashes, Mrs. Abdullah
answered, "Khan-El Khalili." She explained that her husband
had arranged a tour for them of the Bazaar with the best
guides.

Mrs. McKinnon added, "This time, I must remember to
buy a gold bracelet to match the necklace I took last time, the
one engraved with my name? Many people complimented me
on it, and I must complete the set. I forgot to thank *Akh*med
about that." She asked Mrs. Abdullah, "Would you thank
*Akh*med for me?"

"I will pass your message to *El Sayed Abdullah*," Mrs.
Abdullah emphasized her husband's title and surname, for to
her he was Mr. in the traditional Egyptian form of respect.
Her husband in turn called her *El Sayeda Om Khalil,* Lady,
Mother of Khalil, their oldest son, so indicating that his wife
and mother of his children was the revered presence in his
household, the spirit and mover of things.

Mrs. McKinnon continued, "And ask *Akh*med to remember the spring water, because last time . . . " Nadia listened to
the farcical exchange. At least, she had been spared the duty of
ushering the visitors around Cairo, when she would rather be
with her sons. But Mrs. McKinnon turned to her. "Perhaps
you and I can go to the place near the pyramids where the
peasant women make all those hand-woven tapestries."

"You mean El Hourania where the women make their
own dyes from natural plants . . . ?" Mrs. McKinnon nodded,
her eyes focused on a painting on the wall showing white-
washed American suburban homes with expansive verandas,
children in gardens, bright light shining on their golden
heads. A black butler came up to Nadia with a carved
Egyptian silver tray and crystal goblets half-filled with white
wine; another presented cheese and crackers on a more elaborate tray. Alike in appearance, the servers struck Nadia as
identical tin soldiers strutting out of a music box. Mrs.

McKinnon excused herself and joined a group of compatriot ladies by the window in the far corner of the hall. In a few minutes, Mrs. Atkinson returned to invite the two ladies to the adjoining room to watch a movie, a documentary highlighting the architecture and historical monuments in Washington, D.C. When the women returned to the main hall, Mrs. Atkinson discussed the movie with them, hoped they would have the opportunity to visit the capital of the United States of America, then moved on to greet others. Nadia's claustrophobia began to lift when their laughing men emerged from an inner door.

As soon as she and Yasser were in the taxi, they talked about their sons' arrival. He suggested taking Amir and Samy up north to the Damietta branch of the Nile at the Mediterranean Sea, where he was to launch his new project. Nadia added, "We need to visit family afterwards."

"Yes, the boys will want to spend some time with your mother and my brothers," he said.

***

Monir's fingers moved charcoal on paper to capture the aura emanating from Nadia's face, not a photographic resemblance of her, but a representation of the way he felt her to be, illumined from within. Her distinctive, almond shaped eyes, more slanted at the edges than was customary in Egyptian faces, clear space between her eyebrows, gave her an open look. Her hair, copious waves surrounding her face. No makeup. What an expanse of restful silence, hardly the face he saw among women in Cairo who—even when veiled—wore heavy eye make-up, like prototypes in ancient Egyptian reliefs but lacking their subtlety. Nadia's face—like an untouched canvas—summoned him to create on canvas what was in her mind. Her eyes spoke of vast terrains of solitude where the wary foot stepped lightly on earth, a kindred presence in Egypt, not an alien one as she believed herself to be. He set his charcoal down. He had to go slow: the woman was married, and he had his own ideas about how one should treat another man's wife. He had to block his heart's excitement from carrying him away, as it had in the ballroom at Luxor. Yet, she had reciprocated, touched his hair, kissed his lips. But that was his fault; *he* should have observed his limits. Did she like him, or was she responding to the evening's call? For some reason, he could not imagine her doing this with other men. He shaded in her hair. In any case, what business had he to dream on like this? She had rejoined her husband in Cairo and would not cross his path again.

Nonetheless, on paper her eyes had to shine. He steadied his hand to keep the tip of his pencil clear of the white gleam in the centre as he filled in the dark pupils around it.

***

The early morning sounds of Cairo held an immediacy for Nadia. Her sons had arrived the previous night, and when Samy had teased his brother to divulge his personal news, Amir had announced he and Laura were getting married. A new light filtered into Nadia's life and filled it with hope. As she punched dough in the kitchen, she heard Samy call his brother to the balcony. She rolled balls of the soft dough between her palms then patted them flat, her fingers moving in circular motion to create the best loaves she could make. She remembered how in Toronto, she had made ginger-bread men for her young sons, and they had drawn their initials on the dough. On their last visit to Egypt, they had been in their teens, now they were men. A symphony of vehicle horns came in through the open balcony: Cairo at dawn, awakening giant stirring her limbs, her murmurs turning into grating lurches. An orchestra of human noises: cars, bicycles, carts, metro horns, the sounds alive with energy for she was sharing them with her sons. Her earth, the soil of Egypt, was theirs as well. She sipped her tea and was comforted by the aroma of baking bread, a wholesome constant in a world of moving trucks and exhaust fumes. Baking early in the morning redeemed her day

and camouflaged the city's tired air with the smell of freshly
rising dough, harbinger of family reunions around her table.
She could not imagine how sixteen million people survived in
Cairo. A couple of million poured into the metropolis in the
morning for work and left at night, or on Thursday evenings,
to return to their nearby villages and towns. The only thing
that could compare with this congestion in Toronto was the
Chinese quarter at the corner of Dundas and Spadina streets:
crammed with people, shops, carts, open cartons spilling
oranges on pavements, people eating, their shops overflowing
with colourful artifacts to entice Sunday's pedestrians to buy
their tea-cups, soup bowls and paper lamps. She loved their
hot egg rolls and wonton soup.

Amir and Samy were laughing on the balcony. The next
two weeks would be a time of peace: Nadia's family re-united,
her body whole, her heart and mind at rest. Samy entered the
kitchen, Amir close behind, and Samy pointed to the balcony.
"You won't believe what's walking down there, Mother, sheep
are going through Liberty Square! The herds-woman was trying to keep them away from the buses and headed them down
the narrow street to Douki."

Her sons sat across from each other at the kitchen table.
She checked her bread in the oven. "I find it reassuring," she
said, "that animals are still around. If *they* can exist in this congestion, so can we!" Her sons smiled. "Bread will be ready in
a few minutes. Call your father, Samy." She wiped the flour off
the table as Amir set the cups and plates.

By seven, the four were in the car heading north out of
Cairo. The air smelled fresh on the outskirts of the city and
became fresher as they moved farther out. It had the quality
Nadia remembered as a child, of dew rising from the sleepy
earth, a new creation stirring, an airy freshness, the early sun
warming moisture on petals and releasing their perfume.
Flowers exuded a lush scent, grass and leaves lent a freshness to
the air that she and other natives of the land believed came
from the sediment of the Nile. The silt had a fecund quality its

people celebrated through the years, rich earth moving through waters, thickening and enriching it with its dark, secret recipe. How much of this fertility had remained in the soil after the Aswan Dam, she wondered. In the front seat, Yasser's excited voice told Samy about the new project at Damietta and Samy's voice, in full volume, responded. These two expressed their affection by challenging each other. Amir turned to Nadia. "The farther we go from Cairo, the more incredible the land becomes. The green here is vivid, even though it's not as deep and as thick as in Canada." She nodded and watched the land from the window on his side: no brown soot from cars, small white houses with flat roofs dotting sides of the road, the occasional palm branch waving in the breeze. This was her earth, the native land she remembered. She explained to Amir, "The peasants make their homes from Nile sediment baked dry in the sun, and they claim it is the best insulator against heat and cold." She laughed and told him how, as a child, she had rolled down the hills at Ras-El Bar, had loved the feel of the warm earth, how she did not mind her mother chiding her when she returned home covered with sand and pieces of palm leaves. Soil had been her cradle, her rocking chair, the grandmother's lap she had never known.

"And *your* news?" she asked.

Amir smiled. "After our wedding, Laura and I plan to travel. Perhaps we'll come here later for a couple of weeks to take a good look around."

"It would be wonderful to show Laura the ancient sites in Upper Egypt," she affirmed.

Around them the land lay in a carpet of green, a jubilation that mirrored Nadia's heart. Her three men were here, her oldest son engaged to be married. Her earth was whole. Was it not the same earth that had endured through Pharaonic, Biblical and Islamic times, and had not its agricultural methods survived since the original systems depicted on temple walls? The sun warmed her shoulders, nurtured plants, reminded her of generations coming and going, the land remaining a jubilee of green outside the cities. And in the middle of the fields were the bent backs, brown hands working the soil as they appeared on Pharaonic temple mosaics. She wanted to see her grandchildren lie in the brown earth. She told Amir she could see his son's naked body lying on a carpet of ochre sand. He laughed and said, "I'd like to see *my daughter* in a thick woolly coat kicking around in a mound of snow!" She laughed.

Yasser was saying to Samy, "The Americans have promised us help. I'm certain we'll find a solution." Samy told his father about his correspondence with the researchers at the University of Western Ontario. "I want to work on the artificial human heart. Perhaps they will invite me to join their team. I can do their programming on the computer. That's my dream anyhow." Like trains on parallel tracks, father and son rushed to see who reached the station first.

Fields widened as the city receded; ahead, the world was green. Nadia was used to travelling south by the main artery of the Nile where fields were a thin strip of green and the sand dominant. But as they travelled north, plantations hid the sand. Villages dotted the Nile border. Women washed their clothes in the river and men travelled on foot or rode donkeys. Low mud houses lay scattered outside the towns, modest high-rise loomed at the centre. The hardened, muddy road was fringed with open-armed acacias, drooping willows, water buffalo on the banks of the river. There were brown hands turning the soil. Nadia told Amir, "The strongest trait of the people here is their tactile bond with the land."

Yasser announced, "We're almost at El Mansoura! It's a beautiful sea-side town. As a child your mother used to come here to visit her maternal grandparents."

"I'd like Amir and Samy to see my grandparents' home on the Cornice," Nadia exclaimed on impulse, not knowing if the house was still there.

"Just for a few minutes, then. I have to be at Damietta before nightfall," Yasser answered her.

They stopped at a restaurant on the Cornice, and ordered *fetir*. The thin strudel dough arrived puffing hot, filled with cream and honey. Their sons had to wrap their handkerchiefs—the only item they had adopted from their father's background—around their steaming tea glasses to drink. Yasser felt his sons' presence protect him from guilt and cushion him against his attachment to Magda, the woman he feared because of the division she caused within him. When his sons leave Egypt, he would straighten up his life. Now he would not see her, and she would understand he was busy with his sons. Later on, he would explain his situation to her and end his obsession. He could no longer carry on with an affair he had no reason to begin in the first place; besides, it was time for him to come to terms with what was driving him in this feverish way to seek involvement with a woman much younger than himself. He could not harbour Magda's anguish and deal with his own, and he was finding it difficult to face his sons. He drove past Nadia's grandparents' home on the Cornice before she recognized it, and he had to drive back. The villa's walls were battered and discoloured, its outside layer of lime chipped, revealing broken stone beneath. They could not see trees in the garden. The balcony was at the back of the house, but they did not want to walk around it in the bramble to check it out, and she could not tell if the hand-carved iron rails of the balcony were still there. Despite the aging condition of the villa, Nadia saw a stately mansion of some ancient prince whose followers had neglected. But she could not associate this place with memories of her grandparents, and felt pity as though a part of her had been destroyed when she was not looking. Her sons observed the debris. How could they imagine the harmony that had existed in this garden and shone in her grandparents' marble halls?

Yasser relaxed. Now that he had made his initial decision to break with Magda, he felt lighter. Nadia was sensing his malaise; his sons were too. The previous night in bed he had been so dissociated from her, or from himself, that when she had wrapped her arms around him, he had shifted away. He could not remember his having to turn away from Nadia before. She was the connection that made sense to him. He would resolve his dilemma and be worthy of Samy's trust. He drove on to Damietta. As they approached the sea, the air became cooler, the humidity and salty smell more pronounced. They called at the home of the engineer, picked him up, and drove for a kilometre towards the sea. The engineer—a short thin man with eyebrows that met in the middle—leaned forward in his seat and gave Yasser directions. "We can turn to the right here, the exact spot where the sea poses the greatest danger." His voice was apologetic, as though he were responsible for the disruptive swell of the sea.

Before Nadia understood what he meant, she saw a wide area of flat land unfolding and stretching until it disappeared into the sea. Agitated waves foamed over the land. Yasser jerked the car to a stop. Nadia did not want to step down. Around her, the soil glistened with water, its green a soggy olive, the smell of sea water high, but higher was the odour of rotting fish. When the men got out of the car, their feet sank ankle-deep in mud. She followed and her feet dug down in wet soil. They ploughed closer to the waves. High foam dashed onto the land as the frothing madness unleashed its fury. Gaping, dead fish lay petrified as waves attacked the swaying green. Winds moaned. The salt spray was a surrealistic nightmare, and the chilly wind penetrated their skin. Nadia wanted to draw her sons to her to protect them from the sight, but they were in front of her, nearer the thrashing water. Winds broke against her uncovered neck; she pulled her collar up, buttoned her jacket and reached the men, head bent against the sea's salt spray, eyes shut. She was sinking in this brine madness. This *was* her land.

***

Magda took the large circles of paper-thin strudel from the bedouin, placed them in a white cotton towel inside the refrigerator, came back to the door of her villa, took the plastic container of goat cheese and thanked the man. The bedouin grinned. He handed her a jar of fresh honeycombs as a gift. She called him *Amou Nakhla*—Uncle Palm—because he was tall, thin, brown, his thick sun-burnt hair riotous over his head; he treated her as he would his own child. He laughed at his nickname. He was older now, with grey sideburns, but she remembered him when he came to their villa in Mariout and her grandmother was alive, ten years ago. Then he wore bright head coverings, white top and jumper-like pants. Now, he wore dark trousers and a striped shirt. His wife did not come with him. She tended their sheep and stayed close to their shack. They had several boys, but Magda did not know where they were, perhaps tending sheep near their hut. She knew *Amou Nakhla* would be around her villa in Mariout whenever she needed him, and that he was more aware of her existence than her own father was. What would she do if she were to look out this window and see the sand, the palms, goats scattered and nonchalant around the walls of her villa, yet know her *Amou* was not there? She was secure when he was, for around here, an unwritten code dictated that when a bedouin was responsible for a villa, it would be out of bounds to local men and looters. The bedouin had clout; intruders and thieves knew they could not trespass on a bedouin's domain. She was safe from the people who knew she was here alone, without a man in the house to guard her.

She closed the door, switched the radio on and stretched out on the sofa. Yasser would be here in two days. He had promised. She was supposed to get the place ready for him, but *Amou Nakhla* had done that. He was happy with the money she gave him. Now he owned a radio and a car. But she did not give him that kind of money, so where did he get the extra thousands his car must have cost? Hopefully, not by selling drugs. She got up and poured herself some whisky, a habit she had nurtured in the evenings. This is what her nightmarish marriage to Ezzat had taught her.

She settled in the dusty cushions and stared at her grand-mother's portrait hanging on the wall in the middle of the room. Yasser would be here before she realized. Would he stay for more than two days? She had not asked him about his wife because he would not like it. She hoped the days she and Yasser spent together would lead to more days, even though he had been irritable the last few times he had visited. Perhaps he worried about his wife finding out, but here they were safe from intrusion. Magda unbuttoned her house dress, allowed the wind to brush her nude body. She touched her nipples. Salty wind from the sea, a lively feel of satin on her skin. Wind, extra fresh, and balmy.

She recalled the time she was with her paternal uncle on the bench at the highest point of the roller coaster. She was ten then, her uncle sixteen. They were suspended for an instant with the Mediterranean Sea lying at their feet. On the tip of the roller coaster, they came crashing down to the dark sea below them. A few miles away from her villa, the Alexandria fair was their hideaway. He did not tell his older brother, her father, that this was where he and Magda went in the evenings, for her father would have prevented them from going. Her uncle had been fun; he had allowed her to ignore her father's rules. "He's as ancient as these hills," he would mumble at the cottage, pointing to the surrounding hills of sand and would nudge her as a fellow conspirator. He was twenty years younger than her father and had disobeyed him with the impunity of a teenage son. Magda and her uncle were truants, and the fair on the Cornice in Alexandria at Sidi Gaber Station overlooking the sea was their favourite spot, for her father would not be there, by mistake or with visitors, because he considered the fair a den of vice, and gambling booths—where you shot your ten *piastre* piece to come to rest on top of an object in the stall—a fraud because the tops were slanted. Her father considered gambling booths and alcohol evil activities inciting people to do worse evil. Yet she and her uncle had played games at the stalls. They had driven electric cars, and her uncle had manoeuvred them to crash into others. The impact would rattle their bones, yet they loved the fear at the moment of collision. But it was the instant at the top of the roller coaster, suspended in the dark sky—before their hearts sank in terror at the incline—that she loved most, when her body tensed before she shivered down the descent screaming, her eyes glued to the sea across the road. It appeared to her then, that the coaster would keep hurtling down until it plunged into the sea.

When her uncle died of cancer at thirty-eight, she realized that he had drunk and smoked himself into oblivion. But she knew him as the young man who had dared his brother and taught her to salvage moments of danger and delight that were taboo in her restrictive world.

***

Standing before the roaring waves at Damietta, the engineer pointed his chapped finger-nails to a pole bending into the sea. "That pole over there," he shouted to Yasser and Samy above the roar of the waves, "this is where the street used to be. Beyond it was the beach. Now, it's water."

Yasser shouted back, "How much does the sea gain on the land in one year?"

The man shrugged to say, "Who knows?" Then, "About one metre, I would say. There's no keeping it back. It's swallowing the land."

"What started this?" Samy's voice fought against the wailing sea.

The man yelled back, "The Nile sediment, it doesn't pour down the river as it used to. When the Aswan Dam was built, the sediment was checked back at Lake Nasser."

Samy said, "But how does this affect the sea?"

The man positioned his back against the wind, planted his feet in the mud, and with his hands enacted the movement of sea on land. One palm pushed back the fingers of the other: "When the sediment of the Nile poured into the sea, it pushed the sea water back from the beaches. The sediment nourished plants and fish; it protected them from being pushed out to shore. Since the fresh Nile water is heavier, it formed a barrier between sea-waves and the shore. Now, the sea has no natural barrier to separate it from the beach." He coughed hard as though to clear an obstruction in his throat. "See those fallen trees over there?" Trees sprawled on hills of mud, their roots protruding in air. "Destroyed by salt water." He grimaced with shame as though he was responsible for the disaster. As the engineer's voice battled the sound of waves, Yasser remembered he had promised to see Magda at her villa in Mariout, but he had agreed to that before he knew his sons were arriving. Would she understand he was not going to show because of his sons? Perhaps he could go tell her he was leaving her, was cancelling the liaison between them: ferocious sea lions hacking away at each other's hearts.

Foam filled Nadia's sight. She was not prepared for the sea's rage. Her sons had stumbled unprepared into this devastation. Amir's arms were wrapped around his body, his head bent against the wind. This *had been* her land; the earth she wanted her sons to know lay under the sea. Her body trembled as waves rolled over the shrubs. She felt like a gored plantation. The roar of water was an endless threat. She turned her back to it. Her men sank ankle-deep in salt disintegration. She worked her way back to the car. She had given birth, promised life, but instead had delivered death. Amir touched her shoulder and took her by the arm. Behind them, Yasser's voice bellowed to the engineer, and Samy's questioning voice rose higher. Amir held the back car door open for Nadia; he tightened the car windows shut. He had never seen his mother's back so bent.

"Do you want some tea?" He poured the steaming liquid from the thermos into the plastic cup and handed it to her. She bent her face as he wrapped her shawl around her shoulders. She pulled it over her ears to shut out the noise. Rotting fish. Not the fish, she thought, the last free life on earth. Fish stranded in mud were the most sordid devastation. Her heart lay exposed on the ground alongside the fish. Amir supported the cup in her hands: "Take a sip, Mother." She sipped and glanced at her shoes oozing mud on the carpet. Doors of the car opened; a louder roar of waves engulfed her. Men climbed in. A car door slammed shut. The roar receded. The men talked about rocks, cement, heightened earth, mobilizing labour, as though these words would intervene between a gaping land and the devouring sea. She could not make sense of their sounds. Amir's hand lay on her arm. The way back was dark; it was long.

Yasser asked if she wanted to rest at a hotel. She said she wanted to go home to the Delta Barrage. She was shivering and could hear the salt waves long after Damietta; she heard them all the way home. They gnashed the earth; the fury of that sound. When would the noise end? How much of the soil would it swallow? She sank into her raped body, her eyes crying. She had come to the sea full of joy and was leaving it blinded by despair. Samy glanced back at his mother; Amir gazed ahead as he told her about his work, his dreams to be a paediatrician. He realized she did not hear him but knew he was there.

*** *** ***

Soft wind blew in through the open shutters at Mariout. The villa was dark, but at the top of the open window the sky was a melon red. Sunset. Magda stretched her body on the sofa under the window, her nightgown open, cool air brushing her skin. She liked to be in Mariout because it had the freshness of the Mediterranean Sea but the dryness of the desert. The sea was a kilometre away. The huge salt lake outside Mariout cooled the area even as the hot dry sun on her skin filled her with desire. Her body was striped white under her bikini straps and the rest was a mahogany brown. She would take Yasser out on the sand dunes into the small nook and they would lie together, naked on a cotton carpet. Sun would shine on their skin. Their bodies would rise to the heat, her arms would reach out for him and she would watch desire deepen in his eyes. He would touch her, roll with her in the alcove, enter her in the setting sun, bury her in the warmth of earth after sunset.

Her skin would feel the cool air, her naked limbs would be protected by the dry earth, his hair like waves would be combed with sand, his eyes covered with the shiny particles, so he would frown the way he did when she made him do things he did not like. But this was when she wanted him most, and this was how they would start all over, their feet in sand, their lips struggling free of the grains, but neither would care, for here in the heat they would merge skin to skin and he, tall and comfortable, would hold her to drown her sorrows. He would be here, to run his hands over her, inside her, make her forget, just his fingers teasing, over and again, outside and inside, his scent fresh herbs from the desert, his mouth the juice of purple grapes, his strength a surge inside her, holding her to a bargain they had not spelled out but had exchanged in silence, over and over, in the silence of the night, over and again.

***

The family arrived at the Delta Barrage at midnight.

Nadia is searching for her home, the one she wants but cannot find. It is wedged between rocky hills close to the pyramids. The sand is a reddish brown, the colour of blood, her sleepy brain tells her. The front of the house is of glass. How can a house in the desert be made of glass? This frightens her because anyone passing by can see through it. A stone would shatter its windows. Pine furniture, white kitchen, Jacuzzi-bathroom with skylights and plants. It's like a home built in Canada and transported here, spacious, white, serene like the desert, between reddish-brown rocks in a cul-de-sac. Rocks protect it from blowing sands; glass allows sun in. A sunny-spot of peace.

Until she allows it to be sold.

It's that dream again. Nadia sat up in the dark. I'm dreaming the dream, she thought. Why had she allowed her sun-home to be sold? Had she not learned from her previous selling of her home in Canada? Why did she not want to stay in it? This was the dream. She had to get hold of herself. She opened the window, breathed cold air, climbed back into bed and slept holding Yasser's warm back close to her.

Walls of her grandparents' home in El Mansoura are falling, crumbling. Men are using bulldozers. Sea is devouring the street, pouring into the garden, rolling over it. Waves are rushing in. She is standing on one side of the building watching waves attack the stone. She is not perturbed, just watching the fury. Waves are human furies, fighting.

She is in a noisy home giving birth to a premature infant: very small, almost fish-like, mouth soft and pouting. Girl? Boy? Relatives are around. She does not want a child again. Yet she does. She wants to know whether it is a boy or girl, but it is too small to hold. She is falling asleep, she is waking up. She remembers she has a baby somewhere: has anyone remembered to feed it? Where is it? Too small to be seen in the crumpled bed-linen. She searches between the folds of the sheets, horrified. Has she not remembered to feed the little pouting mouth like an open snail? Have they forgotten to tend the infant? Where is she? Then she sees this small creature the size of a pebble. It is her infant. Thank God. She does not know how to pick it up with her fingers to place it on the palm of her hand. She shakes it to find out if it is alive. It is a girl! Hair flows around her tiny visage, she has to be fed. The tiny infant is opening her eyes. Thank God, she's not dead. She suckles her infant, but her nipple cannot squeeze into the mouth, yet milk trickles in through the lips, and the infant grows. Its eyes open, cheeks become smooth, but the body is still so small as to be invisible. If she nurtures her infant, she would grow. She feeds and feeds. After a time, the infant grows and becomes a real child. What a pleasure to nurse a child again; now, she would concentrate on the feeding and not allow anyone to disrupt her, for if she forgets to feed the baby, she would die.

But she does, she forgets. Someone has thrown a pillow over the face; the unnatural mouth is open, and the baby dies.

Screaming, she runs toward the small infant who is a gaping fish.

"Come on, wake up. Look at the sun on the balcony. I'll get you a glass of tea." *Yasser's voice is a blur.*

She sat up, her teeth rattling, her forehead burning, her thoughts far away. Yasser handed her a cup, but she could not hold it. "Your face is flushed, I'll call a doctor."

Amir put wet compresses on her forehead. A defenceless barge on the sea, voices pushing her, eyes of creatures watching, fish with gaping mouths gasping, moving. She was not sure her eyes were open.

"Stop!" she yelled, "Stop! Don't let them move, or I'll jump out."

"Steady, Mother," rolled over her from Amir.

"Make them stop!" she cried.

***

Chapter Eight
Vortex

"Say something, Mother!" Samy urged. Nadia sat with her feet stretched on the sofa, a bowl of green beans on her lap, head bent, fingers moving fast preparing green beans for Esmat. Her sharp-paced actions reflected her troubled mind. Sitting on his wicker chair at the other end of the narrow balcony, Samy contemplated his mother, his arm flung on the rail behind him, an English-language *Al Ahram Weekly* untouched on his lap. Nadia avoided his eyes. Unable to explain why she had been shaken by the sea's attack on the Damietta shoreline, she bent her head over her work. She knew her son was on an opposite shore viewing a mother he could not understand, but she was not sure what she could tell him: that she was the soil and when it was gored her world was eroded; that she wanted him and his brother to see the Egypt of her youth, the one she knew existed or should exist, but is no longer there? That she had a sense of rootlessness, of foreboding about approaching disaster? Her fingers moved slicing beans.

"You've been quiet since Damietta," her son probed.

"I feel badly for keeping you and Amir here at the Delta Barrage when you have little time to spend in Egypt," she answered with face averted.

"Mom, you know we came here to see you and Father. Anyway, Amir and I have decided we're coming back to Egypt to take another look around. I enjoy the noise in Cairo, the vendors, the smell of food on the streets, the baking bread in the ovens, the chaos, even the dirt shows it's a place being lived in!" He laughed. She smiled. Her son reminded her of her paternal grandfather who enjoyed the sensual moment; he had had sixteen children, and she hoped Samy would have several. His enthusiasm was genuine, but she knew he was embellishing

Cairo to cheer her up. The sounds and smells he experienced were real, but he had said nothing about hovels on streets and mud-alleys. Perhaps he had not had a chance to see the city's slums.

"Besides, I love the women here," he teased, knowing how to garner her attention. Nadia was aware that Samy took Yasser for a model and could, perhaps, find happiness with an Egyptian girl, but Amir and Laura loved Toronto, and she hoped her sons would not be separated by miles of ocean.

"You find Egyptian women attractive, but can you *live* with one?"

"When I'm here, I *think* I can. Who knows?"

"I can see you with five pairs of dark eyes jumping around you."

"You wish!" he said, his voice high at the prospect. "It's a dream, Mother. Can you imagine Egypt, or the world for that matter, supporting half-a-dozen kids in one family?"

***

Nadia's sons left the Delta Barrage with Yasser to visit Cairo's sites, but her cold had settled on her chest and prevented her from joining them. Esmat was baking *baklava* and *konafa* desserts to serve the men upon their return. Nadia pushed her bedroom shutters open and the early sun poured in. Moderate heat, a golden, bright sky. Jasmine branches and leaves obstructed her view out of the window; they needed trimming. She wanted to be outdoors, her feet bare in soil, her shoulders basking in sun. She picked up her garden scissors and stepped out onto the hardened garden path. Fewer chickens pecked at her feet, which made her suspect that Nessim had helped himself to a few in her absence. Her feet sank into the earth and silence filled her. The soil was cool, the sun on her hair and shoulders warm, comforting. In between clipping her scissors, she listened to the pecking chickens. Her last two weeks in the Delta Barrage had been busy baking bread at dawn, stuffing vine leaves, watching Nessim barbequue chicken on the grill of his make-shift wood barbeque. Amir, Samy and Yasser had helped Nessim in the garden, and Esmat had corralled them after meals to help her clear and stack dishes.

Jasmine branches spread out beside their bedroom window and surrounded it, pushing leaves up to the nurturing sun: only three weeks remained before April's budding. Nessim was near her before she sensed he had come in through the iron gate. His head bobbed up and down like a giraffe in slow saunter as he intoned something, perhaps the *sourahs*, merging his feet with the soil, his body so thin that not a wisp of air breathed as he reached her. She smiled to him, but he shook his head in disapproval. Someone who did not know Nessim would think him sullen with thin face, sunken cheeks, piercing bullet eyes; but Nadia knew his look of shame reserved for a woman who ventured into man's territory and made him feel inadequate. "Nessim, I like to work with my hands, you know *that!*" She cajoled.

He maintained his silence, picked the dry branches with eyes averted, adamant that *this* was man's work. His wife obeyed him and stayed indoors, did not venture out to the market alone, and his fifteen-year old son ran errands for his mother and four sisters, the younger son only eight, soon to be looking after the women as well. Nadia's fingers lingered over the jasmine. She climbed up the garden steps onto the balcony fence to trim the top of the climber and to design each part to be head upright in sun, then she stepped down and contemplated her work. Nessim's spade lay against the stone wall, so she picked it up and dug around the plant to make sure the plot was aired. Tiptoeing around him, she replaced the spade, turned the corner of the house, picked up the hose and switched on the water. She sprinkled the jasmine branches, beads of water sparkling on green leaves, but all the while, Nessim muttered under his breath as he collected larger branches and spaded around trees, turning the soil as Nadia would rice in a pan. To mask his disapproval, his eyes stayed glued to his work, because in his Upper

Egyptian rural background, watching a lady at work was a
brazen intrusion on her privacy. Sculpted in sharp angles, his
impassive face topped a scrawny neck, his stealthy posture sug-
gesting he was listening to sounds of leaves in the desert or
seeking shelter from the sun in his mind. Even so, Nadia liked
working by his side, for he and his folk were the essence of the
land they loved and nurtured, the country whose rituals they
had preserved throughout the ages.

Noon rays burned her head. She set her clipper down: her
hands scraped, her toes mud-soaked, her face dusty, but she
was at peace. The aroma of baked dough hailed her as she
cleaned her feet and stepped into the hall. Esmat came out of
the kitchen tossing a steaming loaf from one hand to the other
to disperse its heat. "Here you are, Madam Nadia," she
declared. "I kneaded the dough to make you this loaf for
lunch." She placed the bread on a towel on the table and folded
it, then brought other loaves from the kitchen and spread them
on another towel. "I baked a lot while the oven was hot." Nadia
knew that Esmat offered her employer food when she herself
wanted to eat, but custom dictated that Esmat not taste the
bread until the mistress of the house had had her share. Nadia
recognized this ritual decorum, so she took Esmat's invitation
to eat seriously, washed her hands and face, sat at the table, cut
the loaf into a small and large half, offered Esmat the bigger
piece. Sighing as though reluctant to start, or relieved that time
for food had arrived, Esmat pulled out Yasser's armchair and
squeezed her body into it, tore into the warm pita bread and
set to work on the chunk of cheese—soaked in virgin olive oil
and hot red pepper—balanced the suspended pyramid and
folded it into her mouth. Bread she had a lot of at home, for
she baked it, but cheese—this double-cream luxury—she did
not, so she ate it with abandon. The women dipped their pita
in the same plate, and more than any other, this sharing broke
through the social barrier between them.

***

A few days later, Nadia's sons and Yasser returned to the Delta. Intrigued by his escapades in the city, Samy told his mother, "In one of the tight alleys in Khan-El-Khalili, there was this strange man following us. Dark features, long beard. When we went into a shop to buy a shoulder bag, I pointed him out to the store owner, who warned us the man might be a pick-pocket. Later, someone cried, 'Thief, thief!' and people started running down the alley. They caught a man with a bunch of stolen gold necklaces, knocked him down and kicked him. It's weird! If this man intended to steal from us, why did he follow us so openly?"

"Maybe he was dodging you because he knew you were foreigners carrying American dollars! Stealing American money is justifiable in his mind," Nadia answered.

"I don't know. I'm not even sure he was the one they caught! It's all so bizarre!"

Amir and Samy stayed for a day at the Delta, then left for Canada, but promised to be back in Egypt within the year. The place Nadia had created for her family became vacant when Yasser left for Cairo to team up with American engineers and builders for the Damietta project; he was determined to find a solution for the sea's erosion of the land. Now Nadia's space waited to be filled with the stored energy in her mind. In the first few days, she cleaned her home as she would sculpt a forest into liveable shape—a prelude to entering her imaginative world. The place had to have a certain arrangement, aroma of flowers, feeling of expectancy, before she could appropriate its rooms and balcony as working studios. She gave herself a few days to exit the home of her family and to re-enter a space where she could construct an existence to protect her from life's noise and intrusion, her readiness an incantation to gods and goddesses of the unconscious. Esmat knew her mistress's ritual and did not enter her room but waited for Nadia to emerge before setting food on the table.

As she washed windows, Nadia hoped that Yasser would achieve satisfaction from harnessing the sea's force against the

land at Damietta. She arranged furniture and cupboards and
Esmat scrubbed and waxed hardwood floors. Cleaning went
fast. They made jams. Nadia wrote her mother to thank her
for her sons' visit to her, and her mother wrote back that the
young men had loved being in Heliopolis at the edge of the
desert. All was as it should be in Nadia's world. Yet within the
cycles of her concentrated energy a nexus of dread grew.
Imminent danger followed her. She set up her easel in the bedroom balcony and painted in oils. What came out on canvas
were gaping fish, purple waves sweeping over them. A violet
sunset lit the surging foam and brown fish lay shrivelled on
slippery, mildewed rocks. As her brush swept over the canvas,
she realized she had stored, not resolved, her shock at
Damietta. At night, she dreamed of the sea-shore.

*The fish are dead, yet moving, they are trying to get back to
water, but can't. They are stifling under weed and rock in full glare
of the sun. Their skulls with mouths atrophied in open mask-like
fixtures litter the earth. In the company of a strange hunchback,
Yasser is in a stony area, hauling out a fishing-net: brown, coarse
threads knotted brutishly in his hands. Their fingers, weather-
beaten and bleeding, pull at the rope. Winds are attacking their
bodies; they are swaying, falling on rock, bleeding, hauling. They
have a big fish in the net and they are pulling it in to shore. They
are panting and pulling, but the net is drawing them out to sea.*

Nadia awoke, her forehead damp, her cheeks wet. Turning
on the light, she poured linseed oil in her small jar and
resumed her painting on the balcony until a faint light
appeared in the sky and the first rooster broke the sound of
stillness. A huge weariness filled her, so she climbed back into
bed and slept. But the dense smog of her anguish thickened.
The more she tended her home and garden, the more she
needed to paint. Esmat came and went, happy to have light
work, enjoying her own freshly cooked meals, indulging in
hearty portions as a child would enjoy a long-awaited slice of
chocolate birthday cake. At noon, she slept in the garden on a
wooden bench under the sycamore tree, but her nap delayed

Nessim's work, for he would not pass by the sleeping Esmat, her bosom high at her neck-opening, her stomach well-rounded, her thighs half-hanging off the bench, inciting a ready hand to adjust her spilling flesh. As she lay asleep, she pulled her feet up on the bench, and her long underpants in flowery cotton and black lace trimming around her ankles embarrassed him. Once Nadia glimpsed Nessim in the corner of the garden taking pot-shot glances at the sleeping queen of flesh, but he would have left Nadia's service had he realized she had seen him. His Upper Egyptian pride would not have accepted the notion of his own surreptitious pleasure. In the afternoon, as he finished his spading and weeding, Esmat fed the chickens and swept the garden.

Away from her husband and children, Esmat was happy. Neither of the women had said it, but they had declared a truce about their families: husbands, children, parents, they had left them behind in the city. Here at the Delta Barrage, silence was a space they shared together. Esmat's somnolence and quiet surrender to day and night helped Nadia remain in limbo, suspended between green shoots in her garden and a storehouse of memories. In the afternoon, the two women sat on the balcony sipping strong tea with fresh mint leaves plucked from the garden patch. They watched the chickens flutter under the guava tree.

The telephone rang. Nadia jumped up and ran into the house.

"Nadia? This is Selim," his hurried urgency was a warning signal.

Expecting some twisted story, Nadia asked, "What's happened? Where is Yasser?"

"Yes, well, it's . . . Yasser. You've heard?"

"Heard? Heard what?"

"He's been hurt."

"He slipped off the rocks at Damietta?" she enquired, recalling her dream of Yasser standing on rock, pulling a fishnet drawing him into the sea.

"He's had an accident . . . "

"An accident? Where?"

"In Cairo. He's in Kasr-El-Einy Hospital. He fell on the pavement . . . broke his arm."

Nothing could be more unlike Yasser for whom movement was a natural state. She told Selim this. How had it happened? But before he could answer her, or she could ask him further questions, Selim had said goodbye and ended the call. Fish gasping on shore, Yasser pulling coarse nets in her dream, everything was with her now. She had been apprehensive about something, and it had revealed itself. Yasser was hurt, and in her mind it was connected with Selim. She had to see Yasser, so she hurried back to the balcony and asked Esmat to pack a few clothes for them. Nessim was cleaning his tools in the shed; she told him to get a taxi. She rushed back into the house, washed and dressed. She would be in control of her panic if she knew what had happened. Her mind raced into a jumble of unanswered questions. She did not know where she could reach Selim. She did not know his last name, and hundreds of Selims would be in the telephone book, since Arabic listing was by first name.

In a navy sequined *gallabiah* and black veil, Esmat awaited Nadia with their packed bags at the front entrance. The two women climbed into the taxi; Nessim handled their bags and waved them goodbye, his hand raised in salute until the taxi disappeared from sight.

The way to Cairo was a pounding in Nadia's heart. Visible from afar, a dark cloud over the city, a huge bat, its wings lowered over the buildings. On the city's streets, exhaust fumes filled the air with their tired gasoline smell, but Nadia's wandering mind was yearning for glittery snow, its white fluff silvery in the street lights. She wished she were back home in Canada, where brisk winds refreshed and cleansed her soul, not here startled by jammed cars, exhaust fumes and thoughts of Yasser. Carrying copies of the morning edition jammed under their arms, newspaper boys jumped between cars and,

in lilting cadences, cried the name of the paper, *"Al Ahram, A-
a-h-raam."* Nadia rolled down her window and a boy shoved
an issue through the open glass. She pushed the money back
at him, and he snatched it and ducked between the rushing
cars. She rolled the window up again. Tucked between longer
articles on the bottom of the front page was the title, "Attack
on Foreign Delegation in Cairo." On page four, she saw
Yasser's picture with those of the three Americans.

Esmat cried, "What's Mr. Yasser's picture doing there! Tell
me, what happened?"

Nadia's voice said, "He's been shot,"and inside her someone cried, "Oh my God, my God." Cars, newspaper boys,
Esmat's questions, honking horns, but the loudest irritation
was the pounding of her heart. The car moved in spurts.
Traffic was transfixed. Dusk. Tears coursed down Esmat's
cheeks as she took Nadia's hand between her own and recited
souras from the Holy *Koran*. Nadia stared out the window. The
two women sat pinned against the seat of the taxi. The car
stopped. People came to the door. Policemen. One of them
shoved his face near the open window and shouted, "Move on,
move on, no parking here."

Nadia found her voice. "My husband is in the hospital.
He's dying. I must see him." The policeman motioned the
driver on. "Move, go on, no one is allowed to stop here."
Behind them the horns of cars were loud and insistent, and
policemen peered into their windows.

"Isn't this Kasr-El-Einy Hospital? My husband, I mean
Professor Yasser Amin, is in there. I have some identification
. . ." She fumbled in her purse for her passport.

"No one is allowed here. Move ." The driver pressed the
horn and the crowd separated in front of the taxi. He asked,
"Where to, *ya Hagga?*" Nadia gave him the address of their
apartment in Liberty Square that Yasser had rented for them
on his return to Cairo. Yellow street lights glimmered through
the window. She dreaded the thought of Yasser bleeding on a
hospital bed and dying, all alone. They had not yet bought

their cemetery plot in Canada. If something were to happen to him, what would she do? The thought was enormous. Her mind raced back to the snowy night when she and Yasser had gone out in the ravine at the back of their Toronto home and tobogganed down the hill to the stream. Above their heads, branches of old oak were twisted in ghost-like shapes, a few stars sparkling in the dark sky and peeping through the leaves. Across the ravine and through the dense forest, Christmas lights beckoned from neighbours' homes. The car stopped. Esmat paid the driver, helped Nadia out of the taxi and took the luggage up the stairs, mumbling souras and stopping to blow her nose with venom.

On the sofa in their apartment, Nadia re-read the paper and remained seated for hours. When she had showered and dressed, she went into the kitchen and ate of the cheese and bread that Esmat had prepared. As she cleared the dishes and Esmat sipped her Turkish coffee, Nadia remembered Monir's offer to call him if she needed anything. She dialled his studio number.

He answered. "I've been trying to get you," he said, "I read about Yasser in the paper."

She said, "They won't let me see him." He asked for the name of the hospital, then, "I'll go there. I have friends who are in the police force. I'll call you when I have some news." The receiver clicked.

Nadia's mother called. "Thank God you're in Cairo. I don't understand what happened to Yasser, but Sherif, your cousin in the army, is going to you to see what he can do."

When Sherif arrived, he said he could not do much, since the matter was in the hands of the local police. He had to wait until Yasser had been turned in to army personnel, before he could take any action. The telephone rang. Monir had obtained permission through one of his police friends to visit the hospital. Could she meet him at the Kasr-El-Einy Hospital? Sherif offered to go with her.

Monir met them at the front door of the hospital. He said a few words to the policeman, then they walked in through a corridor and up a flight of stairs. Monir had Yasser's room number on the second floor. They passed through a maze of corridors, then reached the room and entered it. An old man lay on the bed. Monir asked the nurse in the corridor about Yasser. She confirmed he had been in this room but was taken to another hospital in the morning. The head nurse on the floor confirmed the story. Events spilled over them in electronic waves manipulated by an unseen programmer. Was Nadia the subject of a hoax? Who had found her life so important as to play this twisted game? They rushed back down to the Director's room and Monir entered. Yasser had been moved to an army hospital, but the Director did not know which one. Bullets had been extracted from the patient's arms and shoulders, but he had no further details. The nightmarish search had turned Nadia's dreams into omens of disaster. The three descended the stairs to the front door of the hospital. The policemen at the entrance did not glance in their direction. They must have moved Yasser out one door of the hospital as she, Sherif and Monir had entered the building through the other. But why? And where to? Sherif left them to go seek an army contact.

No vacant taxis. Nadia and Monir got into a taxi with other passengers and returned to Nadia's apartment, made tea at the kitchen table. Esmat, huffy about the strange man who had accompanied Madam Nadia into the apartment in the absence of her cousin, went to fetch the evening paper, and Nadia and Monir turned television news on but found no reference to the incident. Nadia re-read the article in the morning edition of *Al Ahram*. Three Americans and Yasser were getting out of an Embassy car in Ramses Square near the railway terminal when two men fired at them and disappeared into the crowds. By the time the police arrived, the aggressors were gone. The first American out of the car was pronounced dead on the spot; the other three men were taken to Kasr-El-Einy Hospital. Nadia found no mention of Yasser's condition nor that of the other wounded men. Bizarre, for if an attacker appeared on a street in Egypt, he would be overpowered in seconds by the men surrounding him; there was no shortage of people clogging the pavements. People took pride in rounding up culprits on the spot. With so many pedestrians, it would have been impossible for anyone to flee the scene, unless the crowd had allowed him to; he would have had to shove his way through the gathering crowds, so why had the bystanders permitted the attacker or attackers to escape? Were the Americans in the car members of the Damietta team? Did people stand there while the aggressors disappeared because the victims were Americans? What was she to tell her sons?

She turned to Monir. "I don't even know if Yasser is alive!"

"Let's find out from the Canadian Embassy," Monir suggested. "Are you Canadian citizens?"

"Yes."

Her head kept saying, "I have to tell our sons, but what? They have barely returned to Canada, so they cannot come back now." She would have to wait until she had found out Yasser's location and condition. Hopefully, Canadian news media would not carry the item before she had informed her sons. "If you want to go to the Canadian Embassy, I'll go with you," Monir offered.

"What about your work?"

"I'll arrange with my colleague to take my place. I'm free most afternoons, anyway." Then he left.

The doorbell rang. A big veiled woman whom Nadia had seen on the landing of her apartment offered her a basket of food. "Good evening, *ya Hagga*, I'm Rana, from next door. I've brought you some supper." She turned to go, but Nadia asked her in, placed the basket on the round table and unpacked it. Rana said, "I read about your husband in the paper." She folded her arms on her stomach. "Have something to eat while it's hot." Nadia knew the food was an offering of comfort, so she brought in dishes and cutlery and served it.

Rana continued, "People are saying the gunmen are fanatics from an underground organization called *Al Wihda*. They call themselves 'the union,' because they are part of a militant organization. Allah save us from their violent ways." She arranged her white veil around her face and placed the rest of it over her left shoulder. Then she took her plate and ate a spoonful. Nadia swallowed a few spoons of hot rice. Rana resumed, "I saw your husband with you a few times on the landing. My husband and I would like to help you. He's an army officer and has connections. Please come and have coffee with me when you can." She ate only a little of the food she had brought, since she had enough of it at home and had the time to prepare meals at her leisure.

Esmat burst in through the kitchen door and into the living room waving an evening newspaper above her head. "They've caught one of the attackers!" she cried. "The news is all over the cafés. The police caught him as he was stepping into an aeroplane to go to some foreign country. It's in the paper!" She handed *Al Ahram* to Nadia and placed her pudgy hands on her high-backed chair to listen. Nadia read two paragraphs confirming Rana's words. The men were members of *Al Wihda* group and one of the attackers had been rounded up for questioning. Two wounded Americans were flown home after their treatment at Kasr-El-Einy Hospital. No mention of Yasser.

The women moved to the balcony and looked out at the Nile. Darkly flowing, its waters mirrored swaying lights from the street bulbs; a symphony of horns, sirens, radios and voices swelled, lulling their minds into a hazy somnolence.

***

Magda knocked on the door of her father's house. Anger stifled her. She had forgotten her key to her father's house and had to wait for the servant to open the opaque glass door. Her father had to help her find Yasser; she would have to face him with the truth about her affair. She contemplated the silent door. Now that she did not live here, the building looked dark and abandoned. The door remained closed, the vestibule unlit. The servant was old, but Magda had no time to waste, so she kept her hand on the bell.

While on a trip to Luxor, she had seen the article on Yasser and his picture in *Al Ahram*. Over and over in her mind, she kept saying, "Just when I've found you, Yasser, you're gone. When I think I have you, you go and get shot. I knew we had little time together, but not so short a time. They shot you, and I don't know what those bastards have done to you." The servant turned on the light in the vestibule and opened the door. Magda pushed past him and burst into her father's sitting room.

***

Nadia awoke at dawn. At eight-thirty she called the American Embassy. The secretary's voice whimpered in nasal tunes, "I'm sorry Mrs. Amin, Mr. and Mrs. Atkinson are in New York. They will be away for a few weeks. Can I help you?"

"I'd like to make an appointment with Mr. McKinnon. It's urgent."

"Mr. and Mrs. McKinnon are also out of town. I will let them know you called. What's your number please?" An hour later, Nadia and Monir were in the Canadian Embassy talking to Mr. John Spencer, Attaché for Canadian nationals in Cairo. Nadia pleaded with him, "I don't know where Yasser is. I just want to know if he is alive. He's a Canadian citizen. The Egyptian government might tell us where he is." She told Spencer all she knew about the incident. He knit his brows and passed his fingers through his glossy brown hair then, placing his forefinger upon his lower lip, tapped it and said. "I knew about the incident but did not know that Mr. Amin was one of our nationals until early this morning. I thought he was an Egyptian."

"We've been in Canada for twenty-three years and have been Canadian citizens for twenty. I have to find out if Yasser's alive." Her tired voice dissolved into the powder blue walls; everything in the room remained in suspended motion.

Adorned with a brass pen-holder and a marble paper weight, Spencer's desk shone like an armour, establishing a shield between him and his visitor. No books, papers, open drawers, or untidy magazines hinted that anything moved in this room; even the flowers on the side table in the corner were of blue and white wood.

Spencer summoned his secretary by intercom and requested all available information on Mr. Yasser Amin. He swivelled his leather chair in Nadia's direction, opened his side desk-drawer, picked up a gold Mont Blanc pen, turned it from top to lower end, tapped it on his desk to punctuate his words with rhythm. "In the meantime, Mrs. A*h*min," he pronounced her name with a sigh, as though he were ending a prayer, "be assured we will leave no stone unturned to ensure your husband's safety." Spencer had no clue what to tell the woman. He had been in touch with Mr. Abdullah, but was unable to extract any information from him. Egyptians' sense of time lagged far behind his own and their rules of protocol changed with the direction of the wind. He had nothing to tell Mrs. A*h*min, so all he could do was waffle until he had had a chance to talk to Egyptian officials and obtain some information from them. Now, he would pacify. The secretary called back with, "No information to date".

In her mind's eye, Nadia saw Yasser squashed under rocks. The monotonous rhythm of Spencer's pen on the desk was the swish of brine over rocks where Yasser's body lay buffeted by waves. Yet, all this official could do was keep vigil over his own time-clock. Spencer set his gold pen down, placed his palms on the polished desk, pulled his torso up by his elbows, stood up, rocked back and forth on his heels, his grey suit and upper body mirrored in the shiny desk. He walked over to Nadia and Monir, buttoned his jacket, patted his lapel into place with the air of one whose business was to make sure things lay in their proper places, then escorted them to the secretary outside his office. Nadia did not know whether Spencer was going to speak to Egyptian government personnel, to army officials, or if he would demand to know Yasser's whereabouts. He had promised nothing, and Nadia did not ask. This was her first encounter with the man, and she would have to save her questions for her second meeting. Besides, something inside her warned not to expect much. The way Spencer rocked on his heels, buttoned his double-breasted jacket suggested that the status quo was good enough for him. Standing midway between his office and the hall, he offered her his hand then disappeared abruptly into his room. The brass handle of his door turned and a lock slid into place.

The secretary offered them coffee, they declined, so she ushered them to the front entrance of the Embassy. Monir and Nadia faced the harsh sunlight. A crowded bus pulled up at the station, and they wedged their limbs between the stacked bodies. The distance to Monir's studio downtown was a few minutes, but as the bus beeped its way through the noise of cars and people it seemed like hours. When they got there, they elbowed their way through congested bodies on the pavement. Crowds barred their view of the street. A seller of carob juice rattled his brass castanets to announce his presence on the pavement, but other pedestrians pushed Nadia and Monir, and they bumped into the seller. Dark juice sloshed inside his circular glass container, and white foam rose to its surface. They stopped and bought drinks from him. Nadia raised the glass to her lips and wondered if it was good practice to drink from a container she did not know was washed, or if the man had prepared the carob juice, and if so, where. Yet she allowed herself to seek comfort from the pungent froth she had dreamed about on hot July days in Canada. When she saw the man's nails and the way he wiped the container's edge with a soiled cloth, she could not finish her drink, and she handed him the half-finished glass, a gesture the seller did not relish.

As they walked away, she wondered when she was going to have concrete details about Yasser. They reached a narrow doorway of an old building, its paint and limestone worn off, revealing half-broken bricks underneath. The building stayed together by an invisible force, for the cement that had held it together had crumbled away leaving gnarled holes gaping like fresh wounds in a body in a battle zone. Monir ushered her up a dim stairway to the third floor. The way was filled with the smell of dust and chicken feathers. Someone must have delivered live chickens in the building this morning. Perhaps the porter responsible for cleaning was an old man who could not climb more than one of the ten flights. On the third landing, Monir unlocked a door and reached in for the light.

Nadia was in a room crowded with a sofa, chairs, paintings, books, plants and a television set. Monir threw the shutters open and sunlight poured in. Colours greeted her: green, orange, purple, white, from furniture upholstery, paintings and plants. In haphazard combinations, items were bright against the ochre walls and well-worn maroon carpet. He turned off the electric light and opened the balcony door; sunlight flooded in accompanied by street noise. She lowered her body onto the sofa as Monir put on an old record of a song she had heard and loved as a young child: Abd El Wahab's classical "Al Karnak." Its flute and drums piped through her body, conjuring up childhood memories when a radio was first installed in their home, and more recently the high stone pillars of the temple in moonlight, the eerie stillness of the Sacred Lake. Monir brought her hot tea and set it on the small table in front of her, then he settled into a chair beside her. He asked if she would like to see his drawings, and when she nodded handed her a black book.

She leafed through its pages. Sculpted faces surfaced, halfway between the stylized features on carved reliefs of temples and the faces on streets. Eyes commanded the drawings and spurted the central energy of the pieces. But instead of the torsos being two-dimensional as in temple reliefs, they had depth, inviting the viewer to sink into the body through the gateway of the pupils. Creased foreheads and grooves below the eyes reflected sadness. A twist of the head, curvature or an angle of the neck expressed character. Hair design spelled status, or jewellery did. Every portrait had detail and skin texture. Faces spoke through half-open mouths, their smiles clashing with the sadness in their eyes. They belonged to a family with the sensitive features of a religious people who harboured secret sorrow. Plaintive music wound through her consciousness. Abd-El-Wahab's voice contained thousands of years of sadness, which sprang from an ancient soil that had borne much and survived. She was not aware her cheeks were wet. Her sorrow had merged with those of the singer. She stared at the haunted faces in the drawings. She was a wood plank drifting down-stream and did not know whether her sorrow was for Yasser, the land, her two sons, or herself as she faced the world without a husband. Everyone was homeless, disinherited, thrown out of the traditional ways where the body was comfortable in familiar terrain. Waves, open mouths of fish, uprooted trees, and Yasser somewhere, a pawn in a land whose rules had changed. They should have stayed in Toronto where they understood life's events, and where they would have been near their sons. A hand lay on her arm. She heard the noise from the street and realized she was in a small room, Monir in a chair by her side turning over the pages of a magazine. He smiled. A glass of cold tea stood in front of her on the table. She got up, went to the telephone, and said, "I have to make a call. I need to speak to someone who can tell me where Yasser is." Selim was not the person she could trust, but she believed he knew of Yasser's whereabouts. At least he would be able to tell her about the incident. She dialled a number she had found in a small telephone notebook in their Cairo apartment. He answered.

"Selim, this is Nadia. I want to know what happened to Yasser. Where is he?"

He said, "Why don't we meet at Le Meridien Hotel on the Nile?"

"But why can't you tell me now?"

"Look, I don't know much about Yasser. I will make a few phone calls and meet you."

"In an hour?" She put the receiver down. "He doesn't want to tell me, but I think he knows."

"None of us likes to discuss such matters on the phone," Monir offered. She studied his face; after a moment's silence she muttered, "I can't remember when I was moved as I was by the people in your drawings. They are strong, sad, as if each one has an irrepressible tale to tell. They are as immovable as stone. Their faces remind me of a dream I've been having for years. I don't understand why this dream has been bothering me. I don't even remember when it started. It's our home, but I'm not sure if it is in Canada or in Egypt, because every time I dream it, it's in a different place. At first it was in Canada, now it's in the desert by the pyramids, or in Mansoura or in Alexandria with the sea-waves flooding it. At any rate, I dream that I have allowed our home to be put up for sale, as though I'm the one who has permitted it to be bought from me. Perhaps this is what bothers me, that I stand by and let it be sold. If this is a reflection of my life, then am I a bystander watching others determine my fate? But this is impossible. I'm an artist, I report on what I see, I'm not a passive observer. My home is dear to me, and when it is sold, I'm desperate. I feel I'm without a place to put my head, that I'm doomed to wander like a refugee, no clothes, no people, just the search, the weariness, this terrible yearning for its walls to wrap themselves around me, to protect my family from wind, sun, waves, sand . . ."

She was in a dark tunnel and his eyes were focused on her. His hand lay on her arm, so she covered it with her own.

***

Chapter Nine
Scarab

The wide expanse of the Nile River meandered around the terrace of Le Meridien Hotel where Nadia—at one of the few occupied tables—searched Selim's face for clues to his evasive words. At three in the afternoon—when people were working in private company offices or having siestas – the terrace was abandoned. Selim reclined on his straw chair, hands on his knees, face fixed in a grin more suitable for a horse-dealer showing off his prize steed than for a man comforting his missing friend's wife. So far, he had divulged nothing that she did not know. She glanced on her right where the river flowed silvery in the afternoon sun, and on her left at the hotel's open wings hugging the water flowing below its walls, but for her, the terrace and air were fraught with tension, and the water's babble an intrusive warning.

Selim bent his head, with grey hairs standing on end and pushed sideways by the wind, skewed his neck at a stiff angle, patted his stray hairs down over his bald spot. He circled the beer glass with his fingers, crossed his left leg over his right knee, held himself straight to check his words, his actions stiff, almost rehearsed. Like steam erupting from a pressure cooker, Nadia's anger surged and she struggled to curb it, took small sips of foam off her Turkish coffee, set her demi-tasse down and said, "All right, I realize you can say nothing on the phone because you fear it is being bugged. But why should it be? We are not involved in politics, are you? Where *is* Yasser? He was shot two days ago, and I still don't know where he is. *Is* he alive? Was *he* involved in politics?"

"Of course he's alive! And no, as far as I know, he has nothing to do with politics. I realize how difficult it is for you to wait for his news, but what can *I* do? I only know what's in the papers." She didn't believe him. He slurped his beer, pressed his back against the cushions, tapped his fingers like a faucet dripping on the table. In the deserted terrace, his words slid over the ceramic floor and floated out onto the water. He stroked his balding forehead and, holding his hairs down against the wind, looked around for the waiter.

"If Yasser's alive, where is he then? Why all this secrecy?"

"The secrecy is *routine!*" he stressed in a hushed voice. "Anything to do with foreigners getting shot—and remember one American was killed and two injured—means army intervention until things are settled." He looked triumphant as though to say, "There you go, it's simple!" He snapped his fingers, got the waiter's attention and signalled for more beer.

"What exactly was Yasser doing at Damietta? Was he involved in some deal? Who were the Americans with him in the car?" Rage choked Nadia at the sight of Selim's smirk, as though to say, "If your husband has not told you, how can *I*?"

She bent across the table and focused on his shifting eyes. Yasser had kept his actions secret from her, worse, she had accepted his silence when she should have probed him to know more. Her anger turned inward, for she had been too busy resenting her solitude to talk to Yasser, and now she had to be careful to check her rage before it blocked her from taking meaningful action.

"All I know is, they were specialists called in to raise the land against the rising sea at Damietta. *I* never met them," Selim told her. A slim possibility existed that the man was telling her the truth, but why were his shifty eyes checking the veranda and avoiding hers?

"How about Mr. Abdullah, *he* would know." Her stomach churned with coffee and hatred. What a toad! The waiter brought another bottle of beer. Selim lifted his hand high to coax the froth to build up until it spilled over the table-cloth. He slurped the foam, slipped his tongue over his lips and allowed a muffled burp to escape. "When I talked to Mr. Abdullah, he assured me Yasser was safe. They have to remove bullets from his arms and shoulders, and his wounds are superficial." But, Nadia thought, the bullets had been extracted at Kasr-El-Einy Hospital!

Selim continued, "Yasser's fine. Now he is in a military hospital where he is getting good care, but Mr. Abdullah did not say which one. I don't know if Yasser was the target of this attack or if he happened to be in the car with the Americans, most probably the latter." In his mind, Selim thanked his stars he had not been with Yasser the day of negotiations; good thing he had trusted his own common sense and spent his time with Soheir. His gut feeling had been to avoid the meeting just in case something went wrong: instinct and good common sense. Bless Soheir, for whenever he was with her, she brought him good luck.

Nadia pushed her demi-tasse away. "I want an appointment with Mr. Abdullah," she demanded.

"I'm not sure it's a good idea, just in case." Selim rubbed his fingers on his forehead as though solving a complex mathematical problem.

"Just in case *what*?" she snapped, her palm hitting the table.

In hushed tones, "Take it easy! These cut-throats who shot Yasser may have friends, and they may hurt you." He bent across the table and placed his hand on her arm to warn or to steady her. She withdrew it.

"Do you think such a threat will stop me?" She set her back against the chair cushion to preserve the distance between them.

"Everything is fine." He inspected the terrace. "If some of these thugs know you, this would be dangerous for you and for Yasser." Another transparent ploy. "Look, don't threaten me," she said. "I'm asking for Mr. Abdullah's address and telephone number," she told him in a hushed voice. She passed him a paper and pen and he scribbled, spelling letters and numbers as though trying to recall them. He handed her the paper. "Now," he said beaming, "why not have a beer and relax?" He signalled the waiter, then watched as she placed his note in her purse.

"No thanks." She pushed her chair back and stood up. He added, "Just as a brother, I have to tell you this is not a woman's field. You have to be careful. In a few days, everything will be clear. Remember, you'll see Yasser soon!" he called out at her retreating back. This is all he could do, tell her to wait and be careful; after all, he had given her Mr. Abdullah's address and telephone number and taken the risk that this might spoil things between him and a boss who insisted on secrecy. But she did not appreciate his efforts. Like Yasser, Nadia did not realize how things had changed in Egypt since they had left two decades ago.

Fearing the violence within her, Nadia rushed out of the veranda to the street. If she had a sharp pocket knife, or a nail file, she would have dug it into Selim's stomach. The thought horrified her and, as if pursued by a pack of wild animals, she ran into the traffic, signalled a taxi, and went straight to Mr. Abdullah's office in the building of External Affairs in El Gizereh. The streets on the island were wide, lined on both sides with acacia trees. How ironic, she thought, that the most beautiful part of Cairo housed foreign delegations, government buildings and was the home of political intrigue. She pushed the trellised, iron gate open and hoped Mr. Abdullah would be in. A soldier checked her identification. Indoors, the receptionist at an untidy desk outside his office asked if she could be of help.

"If you please, *ya hagga*, I want to see Mr. Abdullah."

The woman studied her itinerary. "I'm sorry, *madam*, you need an appointment."

"It's very urgent," Nadia explained. She recognized the emphasis on *madam* as a way of identifying her as one of *them*, not one of us. "Mr. Abdullah's very busy."

From within the contours of her white veil, the woman's made-up eyes glared. Two large golden hoops swung from her ears, and her brilliant red dress with puffed sleeves formed a startling contrast to the white veil embroidered with lace flowers and covering her hair. Thin black eyebrows arching high hugged her eyes in a naked, sexy look; her crimson nails clashed with the red dress, her numerous tinkling bracelets complemented her wide earrings, her clothes clung to her body to emphasize the slim waist and round bosom: a playful cat, irritable, about to spring into action, fleshy puzzle within the circumspect white veil. Crimson bride-to-be.

"I'll wait here until he's available," Nadia announced and sat down in the chair facing the woman's desk. If Mr. Abdullah were in, Nadia decided, she was not going to move before she had met him. Watching the secretary, Nadia sat upright in her chair, hands folded on her lap. The woman pressed a buzzer at the side of her desk. A man hurried in and asked Nadia to leave. She announced she would tell the news media how the Department of External Affairs was treating an expatriate. The secretary got up and, strutting on her high heels—in a click-clack and a wiggle of thighs—left the hall in unmasked disgust. Another man, accompanied by the one who had stood earlier beside Nadia, appeared from an inner corridor and left the building. The secretary returned and, without looking at Nadia, resumed her work. Her left hand swung the gold hoop in her ear back and forth, and her right played with the computer keys.

Some time later, Mr. Abdullah emerged into the reception hall, his face breaking into a smile at seeing Nadia. Pointing to his office door, he said, "*Ahlan wa sahlan.* Welcome! Come in, come in, Madam Amin. *Zey* didn't tell me it was *you* waiting here." Brown leather furniture crowded his room, and gilt frames—of glossy photos of the Nile at the heart of Cairo—hung on the wall behind him. He offered her a chair and assured her that Yasser was recuperating well in hospital. She wanted to know which one, and he answered, as though it were common knowledge, "But of course in Helwan!" He advised her to wait until her husband got well and returned home. But she wanted to see Yasser right away. He informed her that he would let her know of the appropriate time she could visit him.

"When would that be? I need to know he's all right."

"Certainly, certainly. But if you'll excuse me, Madam Nadia, I have a *very important* appointment." He hurried her out of his office, his unsmiling face peering out from between the closing door and wall. Rather than comfort her, he had triggered her fears. Why was Yasser at the military hospital in Helwan, and what had he done that required such secrecy? When she arrived at the apartment, Nadia found an angry Esmat at the door: a woman, she admonished Nadia, should not go to a government office alone; Madam should have taken Mr. Sherif with her. Knowing Esmat's belief that the codes of propriety in her village had to apply to Cairo as well, Nadia patted her shoulder, then withdrew to her bedroom to recall the day's events.

She could not see Monir before evening, so she waited. He called her at eight and offered to come and accompany her to his place. She said she would rather walk. When she arrived at his studio, he asked if she would like tea. No, she had come to talk. What did she know about the *Al Wihda* group? He shook his head. "Not much. They're extremists who want Egypt for Egyptians. They don't like Americans, and they make their point by attacking them." His eyes were those in the portraits he drew, full of age-old sadness.

"But why would they shoot Yasser, who looks typically Egyptian?"

"I am not sure. They may have thought him a traitor because he worked with Americans." She noted the lines on his forehead and the speed with which his fingers moved to arrange the counter top. Monir was unsettled by the news. He went up to the window, glanced down the street and mused, "Most of our women are veiled. Religious extremists want it this way, a return to fundamental Islam, with its traditional clothes and way of life." He smiled as he came into the room and sat down beside her, a quizzical look in his eyes as he asked her, "Why need we think of such matters?"

Nadia pressed on. "Yasser was a member of the rescue-the-Damietta project . He had dreams of stopping the waves from encroaching on the land." Tears clouded her eyes.

Monir placed his hand on her shoulder. "Extremists are a small faction in Egypt. Most of us do not believe in an insular homeland." He picked up her hands and passed his fingers over them. "These violent people are not going to succeed!" When she did not respond, "Do you want me to swear to this?" They laughed.

She shot back, "They attacked Yasser! And now I don't even know if he's alive!"

He nodded. "Our history is full of such fanatics. They rise and they fall. But no major change takes place in our country as a result of their violence," he said, skirting the issue of her husband's situation. He picked up two decks of cards from a bookshelf, shuffled them, came back to the sofa, placed the cards on the small table in front of them and began to build a card-house. The foundation stayed in place on the rough wood surface. Afraid to disturb the configuration with his breath, he spoke softly, "Most of us are just busy living." His subdued voice was of a spiritual leader delivering a sermon half to himself. "We have to work hard to keep our plants growing or the sand will cover our fields, and the sun will scorch them. We have no energy . . . " The card he was placing in the third row fell and the whole structure collapsed. They laughed at the timing. She helped him reassemble the deck.

"I was going to say, we have no energy for political hysteria. But never mind that now!" He laughed, his eyes dark pools, his fingers hovering over the first row of the card-house.

"You know we Egyptians are pacifists," he continued. "Even at the height of Nasser's power—when he saw himself as a Pan-Arab leader—the Yemeni episode didn't last long. Incidents of violence are short spurts in our self-contained history. I'm not sure why we are pacifists. Sometimes I think it's because our history is one of colonial take-overs and we are fed up with turbulence, or we have been conditioned into pacifism by the colonialists and by our own leaders who share the power with them. Now, it seems, all we need is to live. Perhaps we're just lazy and want to lie back in the sun!" He chuckled; she laughed.

They were silent as he set up the fourth row of cards. He placed the last one on the pyramid, then looked at the house, took her finger and pushed it over, toppling the rows. They laughed and sat back against the cushions. Nadia accepted Monir's words for their intent to calm her. She rested her head on his shoulder. "I hope you're right." His shoulder blade was thin and bony under her cheek.

What Monir did not say was, he could not see how his country could exist without uniting with other Arab nations, for how else would they survive in the face of Western design on the region's oil? If they failed to be one force, there would be more than one Palestine, but he worried that religious fanaticism, now on the rise, was a heavy price to pay for unity. He pushed the thought from his mind. Nadia was here and his moments few. He touched her hand, realizing this was the only spell of peace she had known in days.

He thought aloud. "Look at the '56 Triple Alliance attack on Egypt. After the Americans, French and British had done their job on our country, Nasser emerged as political victor. Today, the Suez Canal is ours. You see, somehow, we manage to survive! We don't have to win military battles; our victory is the survival of our identity."

She said, "I worry that hunger and homelessness will drive people to join militant extremists in other Arab countries. A while ago, Yasser and I passed by the Cairo Cemetery at the heart of old city, and we saw people living in what they call the City of the Dead, pigeons flying among the plants on the roofs of the mausoleums! These destitute people might be driven to violence, then Egypt will erupt into a seething pot of fury." What Yasser felt when he was gunned down, she did not want to dwell on; she had to find him.

Monir turned to her. "But our people don't *feel* these tombs are places of death; they believe them to be houses of ancient spirits." He got up, rummaged in one of the drawers in an old buffet and returned with a photograph. "Here, see this man? Professor Ismail!" A broad face, eyes spurting energy, thick eyebrows meeting in the middle, lips open, visage stark and pronounced: "Ismail! What a bundle of contradictions! He's married but goes around seducing women—some of whom are married—is a remarkable engineer yet very superstitious, religious yet drinks whisky wherever he finds it!"

He showed her other photographs of Cairo, and her eyes came to rest on the large burial site. The place had deteriorated since she had last seen it. People's washing hung on lines between crumbling walls of the shrines. No longer did the poor crawl into the tombs and hide their tell-tale signs of life, Monir explained, they usurped the place openly and the government was powerless to do anything about it; and because it could not provide them with shelter, the government has introduced electricity inside and outside the tombs. Nadia thought the small bulbs in the night photos ghoulish.

Monir continued, "Ismail told me a strange story. He swore it happened to him on the road outside the tombs. His car was out of order, sputtering, jumping and stopping. Then, just parallel to the tombs, it moved easily *up* the hill. As it passed by the cemetery, it floated along as though propelled by spirits. Then when he had passed the tombs, his car slowed down and stopped, and he could not get it to move. He thinks this miracle is due to the spirits of the dead who roam the area and are the energy that propels his car up the incline. If he made up this story, it is not important because he believes it. The point is, people here do not *mind* living in the houses of the dead, it's better than sleeping on the streets or in the garbage dump site on the outskirts of the city, where Mother Teresa does her work. They sense benign spirits roaming around them here and they take shelter in the stone mausoleums. Of course, the rest of us realize that these shrines cannot be an excuse for indifference about these people's poverty, for they should be set up in government housing, like the ones which exist on the way to the pyramids in Giza. But there are never enough units, and people have learned to cope with life in their own way."

"I burden you with my fears," she said, realizing the effort he made to pacify her.

He did not answer; his silence an acceptance of her problems and worries. He got up, took a lemonade bottle from an old Westinghouse fridge, sat down and poured the fizzy drink into her glass. He said, "You know how ancient Egyptians venerated the beetle because in dry spells it rolled over in the sediment of the Nile and survived to the next season? Well, I think we Egyptians are really scarabs." He laughed. "My colleagues make fun of me when I say this, and some are disgusted because they take my words literally. But the fact is, no matter how improbable the conditions for survival, we manage to duck under the mess and re-emerge." He laughed again. "No wonder most of our craftsmen reproduce the scarab as a good-will charm and make ornaments of turquoise, the colour of the Nile!"

He spoke with elation as though this exchange with Nadia was an oasis in the desert of his mind. Expressed aloud, his thoughts were the spring from which he drank and quenched others' thirst.

"Tomorrow, all being well, I'll go with you to find news of Yasser. But the day after tomorrow, I am busy with the Art Festival at the Exhibition Grounds in El Gizereh." He went to his desk, picked up a poster in Arabic and handed it to her. "Our club is having a group show. Its theme is 'Artists' Views of Eternity.' If you wish, you can enter your work." Nadia studied the page. "We'll see what tomorrow brings," she said.

He gave her the key to his studio so she could deliver her paintings.

***

Yasser's mind whirled in confusion: shots, murderers, Americans wounded, killed. Why was he in this hospital? How was *he* guilty? He wanted to see Nadia, but he also needed to keep her separate from this sordid affair. And who was going to help him get out? He had sent messages via Selim to his brothers and cousins in Ismailia, and they had come to this building a number of times, but were not admitted. This fellow Ahmed, with his drooping moustache and greasy hair—the only human popping in and out of his cell—had told him that his relatives had to have the proper connections and papers signed by some army authority.

Yasser's head and arm hurt. The room smelled foul; it was narrow. Where was Selim? Had he put Yasser into this predicament then withdrawn from the scene? But what would Selim gain from such treachery?

***

Early next day, Nadia took her paintings to Monir's studio. One painting was of the Nile pouring its waters into the sea, its rich brown-turquoise contrasting with the light aqua of the salt water; another portrayed the River Nile at sunset; a third, the Nile at sunrise. She expressed the spirit of place in white light over the river in the paintings she had done at the Delta Barrage, before her life had become surreal. The following day, Monir would take her paintings to the exhibition.

When she returned to the apartment, she found her breakfast ready on the kitchen table. She ate fava beans with Esmat, and they cut the whole-wheat pita bread in bite-size pieces to dip into the fava bean plate. They did not speak; just the motion of their hands falling to the plate and rising to their mouths was a shared moment. Starting her day in quiet partnership with Esmat strengthened Nadia's hold on reality, kept her in touch with the solid stream of life that marched on, no matter what the events of the day. Esmat's big body and fleshy movements were a reminder to Nadia of the way the woman and her folk survived in resourceful ways, her size a bulwark against catastrophe, or so Nadia sensed as she dipped her bread into the fava beans topped with tomatoes, cumin and olive oil. Her six o'clock walk to Monir's studio had ener- gized her. At this time, Cairo was beautiful, when street sweepers were out, there were only a few pedestrians, and cars sirens were subdued.

Shortly after breakfast, Mr. Abdullah called to say Nadia would be able to see Yasser in the afternoon at the Helwan Military Hospital. She would need to have an army man with her and identification papers; her Egyptian passport would help. Nadia's heart raced, but she pushed away any glimmer of hope in case something fell through. She called Sherif, but he was out on duty. She knocked on her neighbour's door. Rana opened it. Nadia could not wait for the customary salutations to be over before she asked if Mr. Soliman could accompany her on a trip to Helwan Hospital.

"Of course, Madam Nadia, Mr. Soliman would be glad to go with you. Please come in."

Nadia thanked Rana and declined the invitation, for she had preparations to make before she travelled. Would Mr. Soliman please knock on her apartment door when he was ready? When he arrived an hour later, Rana was with him car- rying a straw basket of food which she handed to Nadia. "This way, you do not have to make a long lunch stop." Rana blessed Nadia and withdrew into her apartment.

Mr. Soliman said, "I made a few calls to reserve a jeep, and by the time we get down the stairs it will be at the door." He started ahead of her, and Esmat stepped between them, bal- ancing the basket of food on her veiled head with one hand, and with the other carrying her own parcel of home-baked biscuits and *ghoraiba*, shortbread that Mr. Yasser loved. In a few minutes, the jeep pulled up at the door of the apartment building.

The road to Helwan ran alongside a narrow stretch of Nile. The farther they drove from the city, the quieter the way became, between interspersed willows and acacias that drooped in air. Nadia dared not hope. At her side in the back seat, Esmat held her hand, while Mr. Soliman commandeered the vehicle from his perch beside the driver. Before Helwan, they stopped for lunch and Esmat served the sandwiches but declined to eat, Nadia suspected, because she did not think it her place to be forward with a man of Mr. Soliman's station. But when the two had finished their lunch, Esmat offered the driver his share of food, then took the basket, climbed into the back seat of the car and munched on the rest of the sandwiches as she looked out of the window. She reminded Nadia of a bird hatching her eggs, somnolently, as though the world were contained in and close to her body. Esmat cuddled her sandwich, her look serene, her actions surreptitious, mouth savouring each morsel. She did not appear to be chewing, for her cheeks were relaxed and she sucked on her food, a soft peace filling her as the flavours slid down her throat. She was still eating when they reached the outskirts of Helwan.

At the army hospital, they stopped at the gate. Mr. Soliman showed his card and exchanged a few words with the guard, who checked Nadia's identification, but Esmat had no papers. The guard would not allow Esmat in, so they left her at the gate talking to the young man in dulcet tones, her body rocking, her hips vibrating, her face aglow with a soft smile. Nadia and Mr. Soliman drove into the yard, filled with palms and acacias. Inside the sparsely furnished officers' room on the first floor, the men and Mr. Soliman exchanged a few words. Nadia understood that Yasser was in this wing of the hospital, maximum security for people involved in incidents which threatened the country. Mr. Soliman stayed behind with the officers.

Nadia and her escort took an elevator up many storeys, then passed through several half-lit corridors smelling of latrines. They stopped at a dark metal door at the end of the corridor. The guard knocked vigorously, then took out a bunch of heavy keys and jingled them, selected one, and put it in the keyhole, then turned it. The few seconds before the door opened were eternity. Finally, through the slice of space between the metal door and wall, Nadia saw a bandaged Yasser lying on a narrow bed in the middle of a small cell, the right side of his face, left shoulder and arm bandaged with soiled gauze. She hurried to him and surrounded his head with her arms, pressed his face to her body, rocked him. "What are you staring at you lout?" Yasser flung at the guard, who scowled and retreated, banging the heavy door behind him, then clinking his keys loudly as he re-locked the door.

"Yasser!" She sat down on the edge of his bed, touched his shoulder, kissed him on the left cheek and brushed his lips. Afraid to jar his solitude, she hovered close to him in silence. His watery eyes examined her as they would a stranger. "You're finally here," his voice said. She moved farther away to give him space. His eyes puffy, one side of his head unruly with greying hair, the other side bandaged, and in her mind, "My God, what have they done to you?" Aloud, "It seems ages since we've been together!"

She had heard of people greying suddenly, but she had not expected it of Yasser. His eyes looked through her. What had they done to him? She did not ask; enough for now that he was alive, the getting well would follow, and later she would know. She stroked his left arm. He did not ask her about their sons and she did not volunteer information. She held his hand. Sensing her unasked questions, he said, "They are not ill-treating me. But it stinks in here. The food is foul."

A loud female voice filled their space as it bounced in with the sound of jingling keys. The voice declared, "Yasser, here is some orange juice I asked Mahmoud to get you!" and the woman with the long black hair, whom they had met on the *Lotus*, entered, one hand outstretched carrying a glass of juice, the other carrying her black purse. In black slacks and red top, she wore long gold and black earrings swaying within the folds of her silky hair, which fringed her forehead and emphasized her dark eyes. Her lips, a golden crimson outlined with a deeper pencil, were held together in simulation of a rosebud.

The woman stopped at the door and scanned Nadia, then she nodded to her and went up to Yasser. Bending over the bed, she placed the straw in his mouth as though she had done this often, her eyes holding Nadia's across the bed. The women examined each other. In the green pupils was a silent message for Nadia, a stare emerging from a world she was not party to and to which she knew she was not welcome. Nadia encountered the shadow in her own mind; she reclaimed the glass from the woman, who surrendered it then sauntered out of the door as though *she* had no wish to be there. Yasser pushed the straw away. "You know Magda: she's Selim's friend and has high connections in the army. She has tourist business in Helwan and dropped in for a visit." His hand wove circles in air, but his eyes juggled focus and settled on the dark blotches in the yellowing wall. As he adjusted himself on the bed, he grimaced with pain, but Nadia did not offer him help. One thing was necessary for him, that he take control of his situation.

"We met her with Selim and the other lady on the *Lotus*," she offered his apology for him and felt diminished. Then, "I'm here now!" She thought, why do I adjust his mask for him? No wonder he's interested in that animated female. Beside her, I am a snail retreating from shame and pain. However, I'm holding his hand and he's *alive*, so what more do I want?

In a voice harsh with resentment, or with pain, he said, "It was bad: one moment I was getting out of the car, the next I was slumped in the back seat, bullets in my body. No one has told me what happened. I haven't seen anyone. What's the official line in the papers?"

She told him the little she knew, but her mind skipped back to the green eyes examining her across the bed.

"Which one of the Americans was killed?" he asked her.

"I don't know, the newspapers didn't say," she answered.

"How did *you* get here? Through Selim? I asked him to let you know."

Not wishing to burden him with Selim's errant behaviour, she nodded. "How long will they keep you? I want to take you home." The moment she uttered the words, she started trembling and her anxiety bounded ahead in leaps.

"Perhaps in two weeks," he answered, his forehead lined with thought.

"Two weeks! You can do better at home." Two weeks with that woman by his side?

As from a sense of duty, he said, "I suppose it's the best way. I don't want to burden you."

"You're not burdening me! How do *you* feel?"

"I'm okay, except that I don't know how much use I'll get out of my left arm. But I suppose I'm lucky to be alive." Then, "How are the boys?"

"I'm calling them tonight. Now that I've seen you, I have news to give them." She held his fingers.

"I tried to get in touch with you, but you know these army hospitals, they don't treat you like a human. All this security and red tape!" He passed his fingers over his head as though warding off a blow.

Nadia thought, how come they let *her* see you? And aloud, "Don't worry, I'm here now; I'm going to stay with you," she said.

"No, no. I don't want you out of your home. This whole mess will take time. Where would you stay in Helwan? I'd feel much better if you returned home."

Home? Home where? Helwan? Cairo? The Delta Barrage? Heliopolis? Toronto? How could she be at home when she was so alone and dispersed?

Esmat's voice burst into the room with the orderly close on her heels. "Mr. Yasser, Mr. Yasser!" and before she reached his bed, she motioned the orderly away. She kissed Yasser's hand and flicked tears from her eye-lids. Then she searched her breast-pocket for a handkerchief. Blowing her nose, she returned it to its place, placed her goods beside Yasser, unwrapped the package with a fierce jab at the string.

"I baked you some *ghoraiba!*" Esmat tore at the paper wrap, opened the box and offered him shortbread with peach jam filling. He refused it. She put it back in the box, extracted her handkerchief and wiped her eyes. Yasser held his hand out to her, and she covered his fingers with both hands.

She turned to Nadia and whispered, "That young man over there gave me a hard time. He went through the whole parcel and messed up the sugar on the *kahk*. He didn't want me to come in. But I found a way, and he caved in." She winked and pointed to her ear to indicate he was within earshot.

Mr. Soliman entered the room and looked askance at Esmat. "It's time to go, Madam Nadia," he spoke with authority, not unkindly, but as a man used to giving orders.

Yasser said, "It's best you go home. I'd feel better knowing you are safe."

Nadia stood up and looked at Mr. Soliman, then at Yasser. They avoided her eyes.

"Fine," she said, "but I'll be back."

***

The moment she set foot in her apartment, Nadia knew she had been foolish to leave Helwan. The green eyes across Yasser's bed taunted her. She was being displaced by a woman who had surfaced from the shadow in her mind, who appeared to own the hospital, and Yasser. The woman's voice had an assured ring, her gestures arrogant. So how high were her connections in the army, and how far was she entrenched in Yasser's world? Nadia recalled the stained walls in Yasser's cell, the single bed with the protruding wires, the discarded yellow plastic tray with uneaten fava beans, the cockroach in the corner, the dirty toilet and washstand. She recalled the corroded urine stench, decades old as though it was caked into walls and floors, details she had registered before, but had not absorbed till now. She telephoned Amir, then Samy in Toronto and told them their father had been hurt and was in hospital. She could not give them details on the phone, but eventually she would. Their sons wanted to return to Egypt, but she convinced them it was difficult to travel to Helwan, and encouraged them to wait until their father had been released from hospital. Amir asked why Yasser was at Helwan and she told him Cairo hospitals were overcrowded, but when she put down the receiver, she was overwhelmed by the weight of her lies.

Soon Mr. Spencer called to tell her she could go visit her husband. He had been trying to reach her for days. She thanked him, said she had been to see Yasser, and promised to stay in touch. Her trip to Helwan had filled her with dread. She was separated from Yasser and feared this was his doing rather than the army's. He had decided to block her out of this part of his life. She wanted to be with him, but instead, she had accepted the conditions he and Mr. Soliman had imposed upon her. Although she had no place to stay near the hospital in Helwan, she wanted to be in the city to deliver Yasser to his sons.

***

Nadia dressed and went to the Exhibition Grounds in El Gizereh to see Monir's art show. Late afternoon, and the sun shone red between the acacia trees. At the crowded entrance music blared through the iron gates. Inside it, people were packed skin to skin and she merged into the crowd yearning to lose herself in their intensity. Vendors of peanuts and water-melon seeds called out their wares from carts with small metal chimneys exuding smoke. She wound her way through moving bodies until she reached the Painting Exhibit Hall, bought her ticket and pushed in with the crowd. Shouting voices met her, shuffling feet, excitement, as though people were entering a place where an ancient king was to be enthroned. Inside the building, they gathered in groups around exhibits. She could not see her direction and had to wedge in at each corner to peak at the exhibit.

Paintings depicted various leaders, religious or political figures portrayed in the middle of crowds. Many works were of people, few of scenery. Some paintings portrayed the rise of nationalism, with soldiers in battle, farmers in fields, people in green spaces near the Nile's banks. Faces of men and women shone with private dreams, and light shone on trees and flowers. Colour united the paintings: vibrant greens, ochres, reds, violets and browns, while the turquoise of the river expressed an energetic life-urge. The olive green of the fields in one painting unleashed the strident orange of a girl's dress and her lustrous black hair. Nadia found the stall where Monir's paintings and hers hung. Her oil painting with the onrush of the Nile waters into the Mediterranean Sea had been sold. She noted that people here bought art the way they shopped for personal clothing or food: if they liked it, they bought it, even if they had to use the last piastre of their month's earnings. They did not question if the work was well-considered in the art world, or if it was a good investment; they did not care to save for a rainy day. The energy she received from their purchases gave her incentive to buy two paintings, one of an oval-faced woman standing in front of a wall, bearing the replica of the woman's eyes engraved in the stone behind her: Monir's work. The other, by another artist, portraying young men in bright orange, green and black standing beside a shelf of male and female candy dolls in shiny clothes. For Nadia, these works reflected the two sides of the national psyche. The eyes in Monir's work were the gateway to the soul, and people in the other painting were the communal sense expressed in the life-style of those who shared their waking moments in close proximity and survived to celebrate Ramadan and other feasts with vigour.

Her excitement soared as the man wrapped the works in newspaper and placed them in a plastic bag, then she hugged her finds and went outdoors, careful to avoid a stray limb hitting her parcel. The sinking sun—a red melon—hung behind the trees; large light bulbs on poles illumined the dusk sky;

balloons in children's hands and banners on top of buildings flapped in the breeze. People blocked the narrow pathways. She recalled Yasser's distant eyes, the way he stared at his cell wall. Torn between wanting to be with him and resentment for his having placed her at arm's length, she pushed her way between the moving bodies. Years ago, she and Yasser had attended the July Festival des Arts in Quebec City, and had stayed in the Old Quarter in a small room with a large bed, and small washroom shared with occupants on the basement floor. From their bed, they had watched pedestrians' legs and feet shuffle by. At night, they opened their window and listened to the French phrases and the laughter. They had walked arm in arm to concerts, watched clowns in side alleys, talked to artists exhibiting their wares in the narrow streets, contemplated works displayed on the ground and covered with plastic. Later, they had sat on a raincoat under one umbrella to listen to rock music in the park until they were drenched: only eight years ago.

She headed off with her parcels towards the central square of Exhibition Grounds, winding between bodies. The sky darkened. She reached a circular area surrounded by tables in rows outside café windows, but all the chairs were taken. Hungry, she watched the *shawerma* meat swivel on a pole over coals and realized she had had nothing to eat since breakfast. People pushed her towards the *shawerma* stand. She wanted a slice of the barbequed lamb in a pocket sandwich but needed to set down her parcels. A hand touched her arm and Monir pulled her towards a crowded table, their encounter natural, as though their lives moved in concentric circles into each other's. He took her parcels into the café to keep them in an inner room with the proprietor, a friend of his, and came back with a stool he set down beside her, sat and bent his head close to hers: "Now, let's celebrate."

Scattered stars dotted the velvet sky, and light bulbs on trees reciprocated with colour. Yasser had abandoned her for the feline green eyes across his bed. A vendor close to Nadia sold balloons to children who popped them and did not know whether to laugh or cry. People engaged in the serious business of eating. Monir bought them two *shawermas* and tea. They shared the pickles. At the centre of the square, a band of four played Arabic music on an electric xylophone and Egyptian guitar, the *ouod*. Children ran up to the musicians and danced around them, but their parents captured them and set them on their chairs. People in the square became a giant body, belly-dancing to the beating drums. Some of those in *gallabiahs* remained at their tables and watched, the women drumming on the tables, the children swaying their feet under chairs. Tucked between Monir and a woman, Nadia was comforted by the warmth and laughter cushioning her against pitfalls in her mind. His shoulder touched hers, but he did not interrupt her thoughts with words. Suddenly the crowd was on its feet cheering its favourite singer who had appeared on the small platform in the square. Clapping reached its highest when he picked up the microphone and began a slow song. Spectators joined in the chorus and beat the tune on the tables. Every lyric comes to life with its chorus, Nadia thought as she joined in. The singer spoke of a young lover who searched for his mistress with hair flowing like the sea, but the soothsayer, who had read the lover's destiny in his coffee dregs, warned him that his mistress was unreachable, for she had no name and no fixed address and wove her way in sky and wind to appear in people's dreams. The audience clapped and asked for more. He sang into the dark hours of night, and when the first light of dawn revealed the sky, he was reluctant to leave the stage. People came and went, but they did not stop clapping or whistling. Time ceased. The sky turned a light pink, signalling five in the morning. Monir bought Nadia several cups of steaming tea from the ushers. Her hair dripped with dew, so he spread his coat over their heads. The singer's voice cracked as he finished his final stanza, but the flowers continued to shower his feet and urge him on. His clothes clung to his skin, his hair fell onto his forehead, yet his audience would not let

him go. The crowd knew that this frail man's life hung in tenuous balance and his next trip abroad to his doctor could be
his last. He was a scarecrow on a long drooping stick. He
shared the audience's awareness and repeated his last stanza as
they urged him on with their clapping. Afraid to let him go,
they held on to him as though the force of their energy would
keep him alive. He gave them his best, his apparent wish to
expire on the stage at dawn. Then he stopped. The crowd
moved onto the stage, lifted him above their heads, carried
him towards the parking lot.

Nadia and Monir retrieved their parcels from the room in
the café and followed the crowd, moving with them as one
body behind the uplifted singer. Then they turned in the
opposite direction from the crowd onto the Cornice, where
they bent over the rails to contemplate the river, two storeys
below them. They waited until the pedestrians had dispersed,
the horizon became a clear blue and the rose tint of sky in the
east turned a pronounced red. They shared a passenger taxi
with others. At her apartment building, Nadia paid her fare,
pressed Monir's hand, got out and he continued home in the
taxi.

As she climbed the stairs with her parcels, Nadia braced
herself for Esmat's questions, but when she pushed the apartment door open, she found Esmat asleep on her pull-out sofa
in the glassed-in balcony, so Nadia tiptoed into her room and
set her parcels down against the dresser. As she towel-dried her
body, put on her nightgown, lowered herself between the
sheets, her last thoughts were of Yasser sitting hunched in bed,
waiting, waiting . . .

***

Chapter Ten
Rock

"What do you *mean* you don't know where he is?" Nadia asked Sherif at the door of her apartment at eight o'clock in the morning. Sherif came in, settled into an armchair, focused his eyes on the open balcony door and tapped his fingers on the mahogany arm rest.

"What do you mean, you don't know where he is? Yasser is at the Helwan Hospital, I saw him there." Her voice was shrill, even to her ears.

Sherif's shamed expression confirmed he·had made no mistake. He coughed to clear his throat, his trademark way of distancing himself from bad news. "No, he isn't," he continued, "Yasser is no longer at the Helwan Military Hospital. That's what I'm trying to tell you."

"Where is he then?"

"I don't know. They've moved him again."

Nadia bent her head and waited. Sherif continued, "The army people want him in custody until they've completed their investigation."

"Investigation? What's he supposed to have done? Is there something you're hiding from me?"

"No. I, too, am surprised. Some army people think there are reasons for the attack on Yasser: he may have given away secrets to the Americans, or he may have engaged in double-dealing of some kind. They want him in custody until after they have tried the attacker and weighed the evidence against him."

"Yasser give information? What information? When? He's just arrived in Egypt!"

Sherif nodded. "That's why we need a lawyer," he said and bent his torso forward, placed his elbows on his knees, knot-

ting his fingers together, "one who knows international law
and can connect with army personnel. I'll find him." He stood
up, adjusted his army jacket over a distended stomach. "In the
meantime you go to the Canadian Embassy and find out the
story from them. He is one of their nationals! *They* can ask the
army for information." He headed for the door.

Like other army officials, he was tall, rotund, aware of the
image he was projecting, strutting with legs slightly apart, his
stomach making way for him, full of the knowledge of power
in his bones. Nadia's world closed in upon her. She had to get
to Yasser before things deteriorated further. She dialled
Monir's studio, then his home, but got no answer. By eleven
o'clock, she was in the Canadian Embassy talking to John
Spencer. His lips compressed as though he had just heard
unpleasant news, Spencer got up from his leather armchair
behind his mahogany desk and extended his hand to her. "I
called you, Mrs. Ahmen, but you were not in. Please," he
motioned towards a chair facing his desk, and continued,
"About your husband's latest situation, a surprising turn of
events and quite confusing, one might add." He frowned, his
eyes squeezed into green marbles. "Mr. Abdullah says the man
who did the shooting says he has proof that Mr. Ahmen had
secret meetings with American personnel, which, the man
claims, involved the exchange of arms reportedly not in working condition, and therefore posing great danger to Egyptian
soldiers. That's a pretty serious charge. I suppose Government
officials want time to examine the evidence." As though back
from a marathon race, he panted, straightened his back, rested
his elbows on the arms of his chair, interlocked his fingers,
rotated his thumbs and, in a deeper voice, explained that taking circumstances and conditions of this country into
consideration, Yasser's detention could be seen to be in his
favour, at least right now, since he was safe from further
attempts on his life until, of course, he had been cleared of
charges.

"Who's the man who did the shooting?" Nadia asked.

"Brother of an Egyptian soldier who was killed at Helwan
. . ."

"Killed?"

"It seems the soldier died while unloading ammunition
from a truck. In any case, the man who shot Yasser is the dead
man's brother." He cleared his throat and kept his thumbs
rotating in precise motion.

"So the attacker was avenging his brother's death?" She
asked, not knowing what this had to do with Yasser.

"We're not quite sure the motive was revenge. Perhaps, as
I understand from the Egyptian newspapers, the attacker
belonged to *Al Wihda* group, a right wing organization
opposed to the presence of foreigners in this country. This is
also what I understood from today's briefing with key people
in the Egyptian government. Some right wing faction, not significant in numbers or power, I am told, is claiming
responsibility. But rest assured, we have the situation fully
under control. We're exerting pressure in the right places."

The large print of Lawren Harris's mountain-landscape
behind him—expansive sweep of navy blue lake, solid white
peaks, crystal air—was the antipode to his stuffy office with
iron bars at the closed glass windows. Spencer emphasized that
he could do nothing that Egyptian officials—or worse, the
Americans—might misconstrue as interference or obstruction
of the due process of law. "We must not only abide by the justice system of this country, but we must also be seen to abide
by it," his teeth broke into a smile as if he had coined the trite
phrase. She picked up her purse from the floor. "But, before
you go, Mrs. A*h*men, if you know of any way we can help you,
please let us know." He stood up, folded his arms over his
chest to protect himself from further forays into the subject.
She heard herself say, "I'm going to need financial help. I have
to have a lawyer."

"We'll see to it that you get suitable aid," he answered. She
wondered if he meant he would pay the necessary expenses,
but knew enough not to push him. "Thank you, thank you

very much, Mr. Spencer." She shook his hand, and on her way out the door glanced at the Harris snow-peaks, wished she were on a Canadian snow field with white fluff hanging from tree branches, icicles shining from window frames of her home, ice crackling under her feet, wind smarting her cheeks. But she was out on the street in Cairo, in front of the Canadian Embassy, hot sun raiding her head, heavy air around her, with no idea of Yasser's whereabouts. She took a taxi to Mr. Abdullah's office. He was not there, so she booked an appointment to see him in two days. She taxied to Monir's studio and let herself in with his key, threw open the shutters, took a long breath of Cairo's exhausted air, then exhaled it as if she were letting her burden down. Her life was a surrealistic nightmare from which she could not awaken. Where in this maze would she find Yasser, and if she did, how would they continue on their way through these knotted entanglements? She made Turkish coffee and carried it to Monir's desk, where she found a graphite pencil and loose white paper. Her pencil moved over the page sprouting ears of corn, swaying and reaching up towards the sky, the cobs dwarfed by high shoots, strangled by weeds, struggling to move above the forest undergrowth to assert their freedom. She put in darker lines at the lower levels and lighter shades on top where the leaves were exposed to light. When she lifted her head it was dusk. She turned on the light and called Esmat.

"Madam Nadia, don't forget tomorrow is Afaf's *katb-el-ketab*," Esmat's oldest daughter, Afaf, was to be betrothed to her first cousin. Esmat explained their vows would be tied, but the bride and groom would not live together until months after the wedding celebration. "I will be leaving your place, Madam, in a few minutes to help my children with preparations." Nadia brewed another *demi-tasse* of Turkish coffee and brought it to the sofa, just as Monir's voice came in through the studio door. "I saw the open balcony shutters and knew you were in," he said joyously, but when he saw her face, he asked, "What's the matter?"

"They're holding Yasser under arrest on a new charge of collaborating with Americans against Egyptians," she told him in a nonchalant voice, as though events in her life were not happening to her. She brought him a cup from the kitchen and poured him coffee. He sipped its rich froth and set it down. In a monotone voice she recited the day's events, but in her mind she was asking: what has Yasser done, and if he has, how could he? Has he betrayed his native land? Not the Yasser she knew. "Are you all right?" Monir asked without looking up.

"I'm okay, I guess, but I feel as though I've fallen a long way and continue to fall . . ."

He turned to her. She continued, "I'm going to call Magda: *she* may know where he is."

"Who?"

"Some woman we met on the *Lotus*. She has *high connections in the army*," mimicking Yasser's voice, "and special designs on Yasser." Monir thought through the unanswered questions in his mind.

"I'm looking for a lawyer," she continued.

After a few moments he suggested, "I may have one. He has his law papers from Egypt but he has also studied in Switzerland and in France. He knows about the problems of expatriates. If you want, I'll ask him."

"Yes, please." Then she asked, "And you? How are things with you?"

"Fine, just puzzled by the recent turn of events."

Setting her anxiety aside, she asked, "Your son, how is he?"

"He's going for Computer Engineering," he shrugged and laughed. "He thinks I work hard and get little pay. He wants to earn a lot of money." He went to his desk where a bunch of her drawings lay in disarray, so he picked one up, then another, and studied them. "These cobs are stifled," he announced, leafing through the sketches.

"They are?"

"They are strangled, yet there's hope: they're reaching for the sun." He smiled. She had not had time to study her drawings. He took his desk-chair over to her, "How about your sons? Do they know about their father?"

She bent her head. "No. They know he's hurt, but I didn't tell them the rest. When I find out where he is, I will tell them." Through the balcony door, the sky stretched in a smooth darkness, no stars visible because of the glaring street lights. She went out on the balcony, contemplated the jostling crowds, then called through the door, "I'm hungry; do you have cucumbers or cheese and bread? Tomatoes?"

"No, but there's a small café on the street that has great *foul medames* and *falafel.*"

Their fingers entwined, they walked one behind the other through the crowds. Lights from stores and lamps shone on the packed bodies of shoppers. Shop windows—displaying gaudy shoes with silver and gold buckles—lined both sides of the street. Nadia knew that Egyptian women had an obsession with shoes and spent large amounts on eccentric designs and high heels. Many of their shoes—imported from Italy and Spain—sold for high prices. Femininity was spelled out in shoe design, in silver or gold buckles, in high steel heels. She would understand their fascination with steel heels if pavements were not riddled with potholes, broken stones and sellers with carts of hot peanuts on street corners. Vendors exhibited their illegal wares: leather belts, combs, mirrors, *loofas*, shoe strings, necklaces, assortments of threads, thimbles, needles scattered on straw mats on the pavements outside posh stores, and watched for police cars. Sellers called out to Nadia, "Necklaces, rings, leather soft as butter, *ya gameel*," in sing-song tunes ending with, "you beautiful"; children stopped to stare at the toy trucks in small boxes on carpets before their parents hauled them away. Cars honked in steady procession; sounds of engines, horns and voices rising above the din bombarded Nadia's ears. They reached a door leading into a narrow room with wood chairs and tables, where through the vine trellis a navy sky harboured a few stars. They sat at a small table in the middle of the narrow café.

On their way back to the studio, they held hands. In Monir's apartment, Nadia remembered that Esmat was spending the night with her children, so she stretched on the sofa and closed her eyes. Monir turned on the television, sat on an armchair by her side and fidgeted with a pack of cards. When the news ended, he switched off the machine, stretched beside her, his back to the vacant screen, his head and arm higher than her head and shoulders. She snuggled closer to him and he gathered her to his chest bending his head on her cheek. His body trembled. She touched his eye-lids: he was her twin whom she had discovered after decades of travelling, her half who had been severed—she could not remember when—from their symbiosis. Now re-united, she wanted to surround his thin body with hers, to lie with him in a large bed under silken sheets, wind blowing over them from the open balcony. But such a thought was too close, as though her longing ravished the silence that united them in an intuitive perception of each other, for she was within his soul and he within hers.

Monir's heart lay by his side. His was an ancient body whose spirit had travelled into a *shawabti* vessel that adorned Pharaohs' tombs to lodge travelling spirits after death. He had died and was now in another life. His heart lay in Nadia's body and he had to reclaim it to become whole, but he knew that if he did, he would lose her. Night held a promise it could not deliver, an unsettling bitter sweetness. This promise was all he knew, and holding to it his only hope. He yearned to share her breathing, she, the spirit of his dream, the only one he had. When their limbs felt cramped, they shifted, broke apart, and he slipped back into his abyss. Later, he accompanied her to her apartment.

Back in his studio, he saw her drawings scattered across his desk and collected them.

***

The next day, Nadia called Selim for Magda's telephone number, but he did not have it and told her Magda was out of town. A day later, Magda called Nadia to meet her at Groppi, the *patisserie* near Soliman Pasha Street. They arrived at the crowded delicatessen almost at the same time and wedged their way to a table by a window beyond which pedestrians' bodies blocked their view of the street. Nadia ordered their coffee.

Her face vibrant with tension, Magda explained in staccato phrases that she had returned to Cairo sooner than she had planned and that Selim had told her about Nadia's request. Dressed in purple, green beads outshining her pupils, crimson lips trembling as she spoke, dark shadows emphasizing her eyes, she said, "I know the building where they keep him. I have friends who will let us through. We'll go see him." She spoke in rapid syllables as though the two were co-conspirators in a dark plot. Nadia had not remembered the woman to be so thin, wan, or excitable; was she imagining this to ease her own torment, or was Yasser in deeper trouble than she thought? But she had to forget Magda's liaison with Yasser and concentrate on what lay ahead. "Thank you," she said.

But where was Yasser and how far away? Afraid to hope, she avoided questions. Magda told her, "Buy a black veil. My contact says no one there should know who we are. Perhaps we will be mistaken for cleaning women!" Was she implying that soldiers at the building knew Magda as Yasser's woman? In any case, why was she helping Nadia?

"Tomorrow night, about eight; we should be there by nine. I'll make arrangements." Magda spoke with a vitality that set her at the centre of action and in command. Nadia held her eyes down to veil her hostility and to bide her time. She would make a pact with Esmat's clandestine spirits if they would return Yasser to his sons. She paid the waiter and— mute in her willingness to accept things until her husband came home—she nodded her acquiescence to Magda, but her nod was temporary, for Yasser was hers and she would reclaim him.

***

Exhausted and in no mood for celebration, Nadia dressed to go to Esmat's daughter's *katb-el-ketab*. She remembered her own father's words when a relative died before a wedding in the family. "When it's a choice between a funeral and a wedding, choose the wedding. There's always time to mourn." Since then, Nadia had recalled his words, but even though her mind ruled that going to this celebration was necessary, her feelings were rebelling. She wished she had someone to accompany her. She had to go to Old Shoubra at dusk and find her way through the narrow alleys. Sherif was busy. To be seen at a wedding with someone other than her cousin—at a time when her husband was away from home—would have been scandalous in Esmat's circle or any other. Nadia took out the dress she had bought for the party, a shiny midnight blue with more sequins than she was accustomed to wearing. Weddings among Esmat's people had to be celebrated with glitter; a simple dress would be perceived as an insult to the bride and an underestimation of the solemnity of the occasion. She wrapped herself in a shawl and went out to the street and took a taxi. The small houses on the dusty street were unnumbered. She leaned over to the driver, "It's supposed to be number eight, but I don't see any numbers. There's a wedding there." The car swung to a halt at the corner of a tight path with shoddy buildings. She paid him and stepped out into the middle of the bodies spilling out of a narrow alley. Loudspeakers blared a wedding song, and women's ululations rang out as guests poured from the dusty, dark alley, between three-level apartment buildings that keeled towards each other. Floodlights focused on the middle of the throng where Nadia glimpsed the top of the bride's white veil. Dust rose whenever Nadia moved her feet and pebbles littered the way. A whitish film surrounded them. She recalled how Esmat had said that she, her daughters, her stepson and people in the neighbourhood had taken days to clean the alley from garbage, rocks, abandoned utensils and cans, and they had swept and watered the street.

Men in dark trousers and white shirts surrounded Nadia. As they awaited the bride's procession to come out of the lit alley, they followed Nadia's movements with cats' eyes. She was not sure she was in the right place; she knew no one and they observed her with watchful, dark irises, but a loud voice rose from the moving body of people and Esmat emerged out of the dust and went straight for Nadia. In shiny green *gallabiah*, sequined red flowers on her breasts, Esmat elbowed her way through the crowd, her head wrapped in a black embroidered kerchief, her neck adorned with the only piece of gold she possessed, a chain with her name inscribed in Arabic, gift from her stepson. She hugged Nadia and glanced over her shoulder at the crowd as though to say, "See who comes to attend *my* daughter's wedding? My friends are from high places. Do any of you know such people?"

She took her time to kiss Nadia on both cheeks, then eyeing the crowd to make sure people were paying attention, she held Nadia's waist and propelled her along. They were surrounded by bodies, long perfumed clothes, waist-length hair shining with cream, cemented curls augmented with jewellery, ears with dangling gold flowers, arms lined with traditional gold bracelets, fingers of each hand decorated with several large rings. Nadia knew gold was women's insurance against poverty, but she had forgotten how the ones with no steady income and no reliable husband would invest what they had in gold and wear it for safe keeping, as though carrying their bank accounts along with them. The men stood at the opening of the alley, their thin backs thrust against the broken limestone buildings. No fresh air in the place as dust rose in a cloud above the jammed bodies. Esmat led Nadia into the centre where under a floodlight the bride stood awaiting her mother's arrival with the honoured guest. Esmat swept her daughter's friends aside and planted Nadia on the left of the bride, who reached out for Nadia's hand. Now the ritual would continue.

People dangling from narrow balconies popped their heads down and called the bride by name. "Afaf, *alf mabrouk ya* Afaf! Many best wishes of the day, Afaf, may you find joy and happiness in your husband's arms!" Their ululations overpowered the tinselly music, and the combined volume pressured Nadia's eardrums; loudspeakers bellowed tunes mixed with electronic hisses above her head. The procession came to a halt in the middle of the airless alley so the photographer could take pictures. He photographed Nadia at least as many times as the bride. On Nadia's left, Rasha—the rescued sister, dark haired instead of peroxide blonde—wore a brilliant blue polyester dress, faux satin glitz gathered at the waist and falling to the ground. She smiled at the guests to imply, my turn is next.

The groom, Afaf's first cousin, was very much in love. He had courted Afaf for seven years during which she had spurned him, because she had assumed she would be marrying the young doctor for whom she worked as receptionist, and with whom she was having a touchy-feely flirtation. She gave the groom a disdainful smirk so everyone would know she was marrying him to please her mother. In fact, she had accepted him after she had discovered that her young doctor friend wanted to bed not wed her, when he appeared in the clinic with his betrothed, a fair girl with highlighted, kinky hair. Her fair-skinned bridegroom was well-built, immaculately dressed in black suit and tie. Nadia knew that his clothes were rented from the best shop in their neighbourhood. In their circle, this man was a god of immeasurable beauty, and he owned a mechanic's shop.

Afaf, taller and heavier than her fiancé, was dark with a cluster of kinky curls decorating her forehead, face sprinkled with sparkles, eye-lids, forehead and cheekbones. The bride's clothes—rented from the same shop as the bridegroom's—

were circumspect with long sleeves and skirt, the veil hanging to the dusty ground in waves of sequined gauze, glittery earrings touching her shoulders and swinging with each movement of her torso, her mouth crimson, the sequin-studded gown fitting her body like a glove, emphasizing her swollen, melon breasts. On this night, she would put aside her virginal shyness—everyone, especially the bridegroom, assumed she was a virgin—and exhibit her charm to people who had congregated there to witness it. Her groom was proud of the rented jewellery he had provided, for he never stinted any expense to make her happy. Her single gold wedding band was hers to keep. Meanwhile, the bridegroom's green eyes mesmerized the girls, who appeared to lust after him in their sleep. He was immaculate in his borrowed black and white tuxedo, except for the yellow smudge of nicotine on the fingers of his right hand, and the ochre teeth exposed in a hapless smile.

Their backs squashed against the walls of the old apartment building, trumpeter, drummer, musicians stood ready to strike the first note of the wedding march, yet the march did not ensue. Instead, the crowd separated—where they found the space to move Nadia did not know—and facing the bride they formed a semi-circle into which arrived, after much shoving and pushing, a young flute player, not more than eight years old, and with him two male dancers. As soon as the boy struck his first note, the two men started *rakset-el-tahteeb*, sticks held above their heads as they circled each other, lifting their legs in complementary motions so when one raised a right leg, the other his left, forming a unit with four limbs moving in harmony. Everyone clapped in rhythm. A variety of dancers and singers hired by the bridegroom followed. Guests pushed closer into the alley to watch the magician draw birds out of the bride's veil.

Then it was time for the much-anticipated bride's dance. Throwing her timidity to the wind, she gyrated her well-formed hips, swayed her breasts, hung her head low before male watchers, stayed away from her bridegroom, who smiled and waited; he waited during the rest of the dance. What he would do later was not clear to Nadia. He might wait and smile as he had done for seven years, or he might pounce on his bride that night and demand immediate acquiescence to the rights assured him by the law of his country. There was the slim possibility his bride's disdain was a seductive come-on sign, or a public statement about virginal innocence. She completed her dance and returned to her spot beside Nadia. By this time, small stones had dug their way into Nadia's soles, and she realized the celebration would take place here, as she stood with her hand captive in the sweating grasp of the panting bride. Packed among others in the perspiring crowd, Nadia's body grew sticky with the heat as loudspeakers continued to pour their jubilation over her head.

When it was Esmat's turn to dance, all present clapped and shouted her name. Eager to command centre stage, she moved in, eyes half shut, arms and hips swaying to a hidden music. Her stepson, a few years younger than herself, stepped up to her as she tossed her accustomed control aside, shimmying her breasts and hefty midriff, and exuding a simmering hunger. Her hips and breasts jiggled. The stepson moved to and around her, every sinew in his body swaying to hers. The alley gyrated with their energy, people clapped and drums punctuated their steps. Men drank Esmat's voluminous charm and suppressed sensuality. Her partner—tall, well-built—followed her hawk-like, and in drunken abandon called forth innate energies dormant in her all the years she had been married to his old man, now too sick to attend his daughter's wedding. At last, Esmat was rid of the old man's bad breath. The liquor she and her stepson had gulped down before the ceremony was a matter of strict secrecy. Other people smelled of alcohol, but as far as those dangling from the balconies were concerned, no bottles were in sight. Everyone knew that indulging in alcohol was sacrilegious. When her daughters had reached marriage age, Esmat had curtailed the clandestine operations she had enjoyed when they were young. Now, locked in her stepson's arms, she gyrated with uncontrolled sensuality. They lusted after a triumphal dance that would outdo the best and youngest in the crowd. This was legal and permissible, for to enact a dance with flourish for the bride was right and respectful, since it would help launch the young couple into a life of copious fertility, as should be the case among people of moral rectitude. Deafening applause and whistles followed the spectacle.

Now the procession was to begin. The over-heated bodies pushed forward and like steam from a pressure cooker surged from the lit alley into the dark, towards the new couple's apartment where more celebrations awaited.

On her way home in the taxi, Nadia thought the bride would return to her mother's place until the groom had saved enough money to take her to his new abode. A year later, on their formal wedding night, the groom and his bride would enter the plush bridal chamber and change into their shiny night clothes, prepared for them by their families and exhibited for visitors on their hot-pink satin bedcover with silk embroidery. The bride's gear would be the most minimal and the most suggestive. Her husband was entitled to this abandon and to the most serious seduction from her, in contrast to the circumspect behaviour expected of her in public. Under their pillows would be special herbs tied in a kerchief by the area's female wizard to ensure fertility of the man and fecundity of the woman. Only then would the bridegroom have the right to shed his vestments and—with the alacrity of the famished—consummate his wedding rites.

Afterwards, people waiting outside the marital chamber would be assured by the re-emerging, re-clothed, blushing bride, that all things had come to fruition. A celebration with ululations would ensue, the bridegroom's father being the most pompous and the most relieved. His son was a man, and people were witness to that. The group had been blessed with the fertility of the young, but the guests would have to wait months for the birth of the new child. On that day, all being well, principal family members would congregate outside the same room while the midwife set about her business.

From then on, each ritual day in the new couple's life would be cause for jubilation to both families.

***

The following night, dressed in dark *gallabiahs* and black veils Nadia and Magda set off in a taxi to Helwan. Magda's crimson lipstick and wild rouge glowed from within the folds of her dark satin hair. Nadia noted the woman's stark look, similar to those portrayed by Egyptian artists, like hibiscus flowers bursting with colour from green shoots. She was so much *there*, that the eye had to register and celebrate her. But now was hardly the time to dwell on that. In the dark, they arrived at a large fortress within high stone walls. Inside the compound dense acacia trees choked the building, the first time Nadia had seen trees blocking out the world.

An orderly awaited them at the door. The place was packed with soldiers. They passed more soldiers outside a room filled with officers seated on wooden chairs drinking Coca-Cola, and sipping Turkish coffee from small gold-rimmed cups, indicating the rank of officers who wielded power and made decisions after the briefest recourse to a higher official. Magda spoke with the heaviest, moustached man in charge, and he sent a thin young orderly with them to the elevator. As in ancient Egyptian reliefs, the size of people reflected their status. The women and the soldier walked through a well-guarded dark corridor, past locked doors until they reached the one at the corner. The orderly pounded on the door then opened it with a key from a chain around his waist.

Except for the sling on his right arm, Yasser's bandages were off, and he was sitting on the edge of a narrow bed, staring at the opening door. A large scar slashed the right side of his forehead. When Nadia came closer, she saw the wounds on his left arm fresh with red stitches. His eyes followed hers. His room was empty except for a brownish, smelly latrine and a dark wash-stand in the corner. When she was near him, she realized his face was fixed in panic, his eyes moved as though expecting an onslaught from a combined enemy. Within one dark veil was Nadia's face and within the other, Magda's. Yasser felt defenceless before this firing squad; his breathing accelerated. Nadia's heart was seized with pain. She took him in her arms, ran her fingers over his spine and along each rib. The bright red scar across his forehead had changed the effect of his features, from serious to stern, even old. But the greatest change was his hair, grey on sideburns and temple. On her previous visit she had noticed the grey, but now it seemed abundant, adding pallor to his haggard face. She had believed that like his father, Yasser would retain his black hair into his sixties, and he could have, she thought, had he not fallen into this trap. The grey had picked up readily. She had been cheated of this part of his life, which had happened without her, or in some strange way without her consent. He had struck out into unknown territory and situated himself far away within this tangled jungle. She sat by his bed and asked how officials were treating him. Magda stood at the barred window looking out at the dark sky, undecipherable as coal.

Nadia touched Yasser's hair and whispered, "Tell me how they treat you. Are you all right?"

"They don't ill-treat me, but I've been shut in too long." Her fingers stroked his hair, her heart pounded as she listened to him. She offered him the packages Esmat sent him, but he set them down on the stained table by his bed.

"We'll have two lawyers handle your case," she whispered to him, "one through Sherif, the other through a friend of mine. Whenever I get in touch with you I'll call them 'your cousins.' The Canadian Embassy is exerting pressure; the Egyptian Government is going to have to release you."

"I've done nothing wrong."

Magda came over. "Anything you want, you let us know through Ahmed." Smiling, she nodded in the direction of the young orderly who slouched against the door, his vacant stare focused on the barred window. "We'll send you what we want through him, and he will deliver your letters to us." *Us,* Nadia pondered. What cheek.

Yasser studied the dark man in uniform, tall with wavy hair and lean face; jealousy jabbed at Yasser. What was this insolent soldier doing with Magda? Rage overpowered his other pain. Magda took Ahmed by the arm and stood by the door.

Like a fish in a glass bowl, Nadia had no place to hide from the woman's eyes. She bent and kissed Yasser's hair, brushed his scar with her lips and whispered, "I'm not telling our sons anything, until you are well. We'll send you baked goods." She smiled. Feeling the woman's eyes on her back Nadia said, "Eat well and stay healthy." She hugged Yasser but knew he had not heard her. He nodded and kept his eyes down. He did not know what he was accepting: to stay healthy, everything, anything, just to be alone. He did not like the triple scrutiny from the women and the sullen man. He mumbled, "This small window brings in fresh air," then sank into irrelevance.

Nadia squeezed his hand. "Send me messages. Don't be silent, Yasser, please." Then she got up and walked out without looking back, a habit which she had had since her youth. She believed that if she did not look back, her chances of seeing this person soon would be higher. Magda and the orderly closed the door behind them. They talked as they followed Nadia along the corridor. When the three reached the entrance of the building, Magda sent Nadia ahead to the car and went into the officer's room.

In the moving car, the women sat side by side. They did not talk. The dark veil hid Nadia in her corner of invisibility. She thought, the wife does not exist. She had allowed the fleshy woman at her side to displace her. And after Yasser had

gained his freedom, what then? Would Nadia sink into irrelevance, step aside so the shadow who had emerged into light
would become the reality, while she receded into the shadow's
place? She would not allow this to happen. She was going to
accept her hooded position until Yasser was released, then she
would reclaim him. He and she shared twenty-five years of
marriage and two sons. This woman could not step in unless
Nadia let her.

Magda said with assurance, "They're not going to ill-treat
him. I have this on highest authority. They're trying to make
sure he's clean."

Nadia acquiesced to the dark shadows around and within
her. All she wanted was to see the light of day and know that
Yasser was re-united with his sons.

***

Yasser folded his arms and faced the barred window.
Night. Far below him was asphalt he could not see, and all
around him heavy acacia trees. In the dark, he could not see
those either, but he could hear their leaves rustling. Beyond
the trees was a high wall; this and the acacias he saw well in
daylight. Night was quiet. The nervous man on the other side
of the wall of his room did not make a sound. Within Yasser's
body, silence. A vacuum had replaced the commotion. The
women's presence had been sudden, the two together. He had
not imagined Nadia and Magda as a team; he must be in
greater danger than he suspected. Recent events had left him
numb. He could not cope with the forces that had taken over
his life. Nadia's oval face was strained, shadows underlined her
eyes, a dark veil covered her hair. No familiar landmark in his
world. How did Nadia team up with Magda? Had Selim
betrayed his trust? Yasser did not have need for anything:
food, rest, feelings, all were useless. Outside his room was a
vacuum. Far away, Amir and Samy, though extensions of himself, were incongruous shadows. Nothing made sense in this
world. Which world? He was far removed from humanity.

And where did he think he was going when he was gunned down? Running to what? He turned on the light, walked to the window, examined his face in the dark glass: scarred, middle-aged skin, lined forehead, tired eyes, greying hair. They belonged to the person in the glass. He was at a distance from that man as he was from the darkness out there, and from the black-veiled women. He recalled his anguish when he discovered Nadia's face under the veil and his maddening jealousy of Ahmed's slim figure and glossy hair. These people were silhouettes in a play that drove him to despair. He could not find meaning in the charade. He was on an island, far from shore, and they were moving figures playing a mime he could not understand. Had he loved these women who collaborated in their silences as though they saw him beaten by eagle's wings? When had he belonged to anyone? What use were his sons to him when they were ten thousand miles away? And if they were here, what good would they be?

He turned out the light, opened the glass window and looked through the bars. Cool air defined the contours of his face. He yearned for clear snow on open fields, endless vista of white receding from white until it became the pale blue sky. He threw himself on the narrow, wired mattress, careful not to touch the crumbling wall, no bed headboard to protect him from the cockroaches that ran up and down the wall at night. Sometimes, one flew down on his uncovered face. He placed a handkerchief over his features when he lay in the dark. Mattress wires stuck into his back; the pillow was an odd, smelly assortment of cotton balls bunching under his head. A brown stain on the wall beside the door took on the characteristics of warped men: old, wrinkled eye-lids, a beard, a man's head twisted on a scrawny neck. Shapes appeared in the ancient paint like an army of dispossessed souls emerging from the ochre-brown dirt.

Replays of recent incidents spilled out of his mind, heavy waves battling for dominance on shore. He had kept his thoughts empty of images so he could see his way. Now, he was in this bizarre room waiting, for what? Gun-shots, like children's toys, rang through his head. He was stunned, then he awoke to street noise and pain, intolerable pain on his right side. He could consider himself lucky to have been spared serious injury, even though the scar on his face made him look like a warped warrior. His left arm was useless, it might still contain shrapnel, or the shoulder and elbow might. The replay had begun a week ago and had not stopped despite his efforts to block it. He heard parts of his conversations with Bob and Tom—he dare not think which of his American colleagues had died. He recalled discussions about arranging an arms deal with Americans. He was the one who had let Selim and Mr. Abdullah convince him the transaction was a simple undertaking. Despite his own misgivings, he had gone along with the negotiations. Had Selim set him up? What did he, Yasser, think he was doing anyway, and what was he going to achieve for Egypt that other men had not achieved? But he had to stop his head from thinking, for the recall was tumbling out in fast succession, and he could not stop it. "We'll need teams of American technologists to teach Egyptians how to use the equipment." Was it Bob, or Tom?

"Raise the level of the land, use rocks, stones," Ali, the Egyptian engineer, said, mouth open to the wind, teeth blackened by chain smoking.

"You cannot launch missiles from this terrain and direct them at another country in the Middle East," Yasser had said, on whose authority? Of course they could, the Americans had replied, if they built suitable camouflage to hide the machinery. But what right had Americans to dictate to Egyptians how to use their soil? And did they believe they could use one Arab country with impunity against another? Were the arms imperfect? How could *he* have known? But why had he become involved in negotiations for arms he knew nothing about?

Conversations in the American Embassy, in Egyptian offices, handshakes, his gullibility made him sick. Marble halls, slides of weapons, anti-aircraft missiles on desert land—

flat like a table, so difficult to protect the soldier or the tank—
all the hardware for which he had been used as a middle-man
between the two countries, air-control toys now revolving in a
merry-go-round with planes for horses, automatic cannons for
arm rotators turning the wheel fast, faster, until it shred into
explosion. Off go the bullets, and the pain surfaces. He had
allowed himself to be used. Did Selim know the hazards of the
job and not warned him? Would Selim come here after that
one time with Yasser's brothers? What use was his own family
without contacts in higher places? With the kind of minds his
relatives had, they would think him a traitor for making deals
with Americans.

Acacia leaves outside his window rustled and reminded
him of the outdoors he could not reach. He pressed his head
with his right hand and placed his face between the mildewed
pillow and his hand. When he was a child his maternal grandmother had told him that headaches were helped if he pressed
his forehead between his two palms. His mind had been quiet
for a few days. Now it took over, absorbing energy from his
limbs and using it to ignite shooting-off points in his brain.
Like a revving engine, his brain had picked up speed and distanced him from familiar scenes in his life. He was an alien in
an underworld teeming with figures beside which everything
paled. He could see through a long-distance lens, darkly.
Objects at the other end were jumbled merry-go-rounds,
guns, toys, jeering faces of Egyptians, soldiers guarding his
cell, officers summoning him to justice. But he could not
plead innocence for lack of caution, forgive his own insuffer-
able arrogance for believing he knew his machines or his
stupidity at collaborating with Americans where the man on
the street was hostile to them. What he saw with his outward
eye was dwarfed by the glare of the deserted star he had landed
on, a hard white rock. He could have been deceived by
Egyptians, or by Americans, or both. Even now, he did not
believe that the quality of arms was up to him to ascertain.
Egyptian specialists should have checked the delivery when

the soldiers unloaded the ammunition and weapons. If blame were to be placed on his shoulders for imperfection in the transaction, then he was being used as a scapegoat. Even the Canadian Embassy staff had disappeared. He had received a message from one of them, a Mr. Spencer, who was looking into his case and would soon have something to tell him, but nothing had happened.

Yasser spent days trying to block out his vibrating head. He avoided involvement with others in the yard. He was in a bubble of horror which no recognizable outer incidents interrupted. They might find him guilty and shoot him. He might be imprisoned in another cell for a long time, or left to rot in a dungeon. His family would not have the energy to set him free from this torture. His nightmare would be endless. He had to control these images; he had to stay calm. He could have asked for a recorder and musical tapes from the orderly with the wavy hair, Magda's man, who had insinuated that Yasser could have them for a price, but he had no need to listen. No music could block out his inner monologue. As minutes passed, for he did not count days, he became fascinated with the images in his head. They became the new adventure. He had not opened the parcels Nadia had sent him; food was sawdust. He didn't need it since his meagre exercise was confined to a daily walk in the yard under soldiers' vigilant eyes. Exercise was useless, aimless motion was not for him, neither did he believe in the efficacy of the sun, Egypt's sun, that scorching ray glorified in ancient myth. He could not understand modern sun-worshippers lying on sand, their bodies open to the rays. No goals, just lying there. Something anti-life in it, for life is meaningful motion. He had enough fresh air and light from his barred window, and at night he had the brisk cold air; this was all he needed. He slipped into sleep.

He was allowed meals with three men who were in temporary detainment. They ate in a small, bare room on the same floor and they used their fingers and bread instead of utensils. He did not enjoy the sight of other men's greasy fingers, nor their open, chewing mouths. When they talked, he followed the action in his mind. Sometimes the replay was of the shooting, or of the days before. He heard his sons' voices. Amir, "But I need to take this year off, Father. I don't want to wait for another two years." Yasser never quite understood this son of his. Samy, "You're not listening, Father, the guy was not interested in new ideas. All he wanted was to get me to follow his command." Samy seeking control, but not ready to deliver a complete project. And Nadia, "Don't be silent Yasser, please . . ." as though they had not been silent for, who knows, how many years?

He let the sounds take over. Into a fathomless corridor—soundproof, no other noises checking inner ones—in damp, rough terrain. He liked the challenge of new and difficult situations that taxed his energy, but he was not equipped to deal with this uncontrolled switching of gears. Why was he re-living meaningless events, and how low had he fallen to have nothing better to do than sit here re-dreaming his life? What was the point of feeling close to his sons when they did not know where he was? And if he were to be released, and Samy would see his scars and grey hair, would he say, "Let's go to the Sheraton Hotel and have a couple of beers and look around," with the half-wink in his eye, as though to say, his father was too old but he would take him along anyway? Now Samy's light-hearted gibes would come too close to Yasser's truth.

Keys sounded and his door swung open. The orderly threw a package on his bed then went out, slamming the door shut and locking it. Yasser ignored the package; it would contain more food from the women. But when he opened it before his cell-light was switched off at night, there was a letter in Nadia's handwriting folded and tucked under the food. He pressed the letter with his right hand over the bandages on his left forearm, then he ripped it open and was surprised to see his fingers shake.

"Dearest Yasser,

"It's hard to write across this empty space. I wish I had stayed in Helwan where we could have seen each other. I see your face and recall your expression.

"Sherif and I have met your cousins. They want to see you . . ."

His eyes relaxed; he could not keep them open. The light in his cell went out. Must be ten. He did not want to sleep with the letter in his hand, so he slipped it under his head and the mattress. Musty mildew nagged him somewhere in the distance. He fell asleep.

He did not know that several times in the night he cried out to ward off his assailants and other intruders.

***

Chapter Eleven
Camel

Light shone through the bars of the small window above Yasser's bed, sending their lined shadows across the yellow wall facing him. Nadia's letter waited to be read. He propped himself on his elbow, dug the letter out from under the mattress, re-read the first two paragraphs then sat up to read the rest. Her handwriting was not clear: the previous night he thought he was falling asleep, but now he realized he needed reading glasses. He pressed his eye-lids together to focus the words.

"Your cousins want to see you. As soon as your wounds heal and by the time you are ready for physiotherapy, you will be back home. Amir and Samy know; I told them that you had an accident, were hurt and are in hospital. Samy said he's coming in a week's time; Amir will make arrangements with his professors.

"Do you exercise? Eat well? I miss you. Write me. Ask Ahmed for pen and paper.

"So far, you and I, Yasser, have rushed to fulfill our obligations and postponed living as if we had all the time in the world to be together. Always later, never now. But now is the only time we have. In Toronto, I remember I waited for you to come to me, thinking you needed your freedom, and I did not want to invade your privacy and make you feel chained to me and the boys. I was anxious for your love, so I held back believing that the moments you gave me freely were better than the hours you offered me from a sense of duty. I would have undone our vows if you would have come to me with the eagerness of our first years.

"When our sons were growing up, our life was not our own: you were immersed in your work, and I was listening to a voice cautioning me against playing dice with our sons'

Canadian identity, so I spent time adapting to our new way of
life. Perhaps this is when our paths separated, perhaps this is
how I fell short of my love for you. I did not express my feelings because, as you know, my upbringing did not prepare me
for such openness. This must be where I failed you. Some day
you will answer my questions, and so bare your longings,
something you do not like doing. One thing I know: we will
be re-united. When our sons arrive, we will celebrate your
release.

"And then we can go on the trip to the source of the Nile
that we've dreamed about, and retrace the river from its first
trickle at Lake Victoria down to where it pours into the
Mediterranean Sea. We would take Nubians with us and we
would dress in their long white robes to protect ourselves from
the sun. Let's go and see the Cataracts, Lake Nasser, the
Temple of Philae, which we haven't seen in its new site on top
of the hill. Remember our first visit to Philae? The Temple was
in the valley inundated with water to within a few feet from
its ceiling. Remember how dark it was when we entered it by
canoe and bent our heads to pass under its archway?
Remember our siestas in the Old Cataract Hotel at Aswan in
hot weather, tucked between silky cotton sheets, the breeze
caressing us, how we made love as though the sun, the river,
the breeze were there for *us*. You took me for walks on the
Cornice to see the boulders on the river's bank which dropped
down sheer into the water. Exhausted from the heat, we
returned to our room for more love-making. I can still feel the
sun provoking our skin like sultry mangoes in full season. We
had champagne, papayas, pineapples, cherries, strawberries, a
feast of fruit. Yes, it sounds as though I'm dreaming, but it was
so, wasn't it, and it will be again.

"And we went out in the scorching sun to walk around El
Begum Aghaghan Mausoleum! Above us the rocks formed
mountains, and far below us the river was so wide, between us
and our hotel on the other bank. On the lower plateau of the
mountain, the white-domed home of Aghaghan's domestics,

its arabesque design sheltered by a few palms. I remember how
the men in feluccas looked like miniature oarsmen, the sunset
a brilliant crimson, and we shielded our eyes as we stood over
the granite escarpment. These days are dear to me, Yasser. You
are my first love; together we sailed to the old Nile meter,
where we anchored our felucca at the foot of the high granite
boulder, which ancients used to gauge the height of the Nile
flood, and we saw how far the water level had been lowered by
the Aswan Dam. You remember how our oarsman—like a
Nile beetle—climbed the rock in bare feet, and pointed to a
higher water mark and said, 'For thousands of years the Nile
has flowed at this level. This mark here,' he said, 'is an ancient
reminder of the story of the Nile,' and all the while we were
worrying about his fingers slipping off the rock and we'd lose
him in the water! When he climbed down into our boat and
resumed his rowing, he told us about the checked-back river
gathering into Lake Nasser, flooding people's homes in Nubia.
We heard him but did not listen to him, for we were holding
hands and sensing the warmth enveloping us. Then he started
his Upper Egyptian chant, to a rhythmic beat with his rowing:
'Oh land of my fathers, thousands of years old, oh river,
energy-giver, source of my children's lives.' His words were
fantasy to our ears, and little seemed important other than the
man's hypnotic voice, the turquoise water, the ochre sands, the
sun on our skin, the love we made in the afternoons, in the
mornings, no routine to mar our days. All of this plays in my
mind like a recent film-strip. I remember how this trip drew
us close, the river hugged us, and we were contented to lie
there rocking between light and dark. I know this is not a
dream, it *was* so: it *is* our reality and it will always be part of
us. But we need to renew it.

"And that one time in the boat with other travellers, I
shall never forget, when the old woman sitting across from us
said, 'Your young man loves you; he never lifts his eyes off you!
You're so lucky to be so in love!' And I, embarrassed, thinking
she was old and had forgotten, assumed that everyone in the

world had what we shared. All I can do now is hold on to these
memories and realize that no matter what comes between us,
no one can take your place. When you come back home, we
will plan this trip. What do you think? We can start from
Uganda and Lake Victoria and spend a month going down the
river to the Mediterranean. I would love to wash your scars in
the river, at its source, where the water is diamond-clear.
Crazy? Maybe, but it would be fun.

"Write to me, Yasser. I can't live with your silence. We
need to share who we have become. As the years pass, we
change, and we learn to be what we are not. Yet, as I go
through my days, and no matter who I meet, for me you are
my love, warm, yearning to fill earth with the abundance of
your energy. No number of years or scars can change you, no
amount of solitude can destroy your faith to move boulders
and raise monuments. I know that when this is over, we will
see it as a time that drew us close. We will have lived it, and
our sons will have seen that even if we have not done it in the
best of ways, yet we have experienced it together. This *is* a long
letter, but I needed to talk to you. Write to me, Yasser."

He was watching a film he had seen before, its incidents
blurry. Had he been that young man in this love-letter? Such
energy, such life? Had they shared so much? Or had he engaged
in a make-believe routine, gone through a series of masques in
the mirror, without making choices, just going through the rituals? Had he arranged his life in technicolour to portray what
he wanted to believe? Had he given Nadia what she appears to
have received? Did he *know* his wife? He pushed the letter
under the mattress; it betrayed his emptiness. He got up,
washed, dressed, analyzed the face in the glass at the barred
window: drooping eyes, grey hair, lifeless skin and across his
face the shadow of bars separating him from the outside world.
And *this* sex-hungry husband was Magda's lover? Strange how
his sexual appetite had petered out, for Magda now seemed like
a cloying hyacinth, bees buzzing around her, her perfume
musky, her presence unnerving. He resented the young soldier's

glossy hair, but that was another matter, the man's thick hair was a mirror of youth, of which he, Yasser, had little. Magda he disliked. The way she rolled her hips suggested she had probably slept with half the soldiers in the Egyptian army. His days of hunger were over: for a woman's body, for food, sun, fresh air, he did not need any. He stared at the man in the glass. A good thing his father had died, for how would the old man have handled his oldest son—and head of the family—incarcerated in an army detention centre? His father had been an *Omda*, a chieftain or mayor, in his home town and everyone in the extended family heeded his words. He chastised men and women wrong-doers and they acknowledged his right to enforce rules on their children. None of them dared face him when he was angry; all were struck dumb in his presence. How would *he* have faced Yasser's failure? Better dead, than alive to see his son in this shape. As a young man, his father had consumed alcohol, been with women, made a lot of money, engaged in surreptitious trade with the British to keep his people fed with hard-earned navy supplies, yet he had not collaborated with the colonialists. He had risked many dangers, beaten up a few men, young and old, when they became friendly with the British. In his middle-age, he had given up alcohol, remained with one wife, assumed moral leadership of his town, was acknowledged law-maker because of his hardiness, his ability to keep his community alive and united. Even the colonialists recognized him as leader and dared not touch him. But that was then.

"The man had muscle," his youngest uncle had said to the teen-aged Yasser, "he knew what he was doing. Didn't fear a thing. By Allah, *he* was feared! Obeyed to the death. Especially when the British were in control." With a knowing smile, his uncle had intimated that his father was a bit of a rogue, and that this was the reason for his success, but he, the uncle, was a gentleman and, if not a leader, at least *nice*. These insinuations had not amounted to much for the young Yasser who knew his father's mettle. And now he—this man's oldest son—had gotten himself into a jail-hospital. Where along the line had he missed his footing? And yet, he had inherited his father's genes, his fierce desire to live life to its dregs, his assumption of power, his love of alcohol, the old man's roguishness—that's why he resented his father's claim to piety in his later years.

The cell door swung open and a hand shoved Yasser's breakfast tray, sending it rolling to the corner of the room. The door banged shut. Yasser picked it up: turquoise tray, fried eggs, pita bread. The orange plate was a dirty plastic, the bread a muddy bran, its bottom layer caked with a rough-textured substance. Probably some sand in it too. He munched a piece of the crust with a mouthful of eggs and the food crunched under his teeth. He stopped eating and put the tray back in its place on the right side of the door where the orderly would slide his arm in and pick up the tray without stepping into the room.

At exercise time in the yard, Yasser shuffled his feet on the gravel and avoided everyone. He paced by the wall of the building and counted seconds, concocted an imaginary game of backgammon and played one side against the other. In the afternoon, two lawyers, the cousins in Nadia's letter, arrived. Middle-aged, dark grey trousers, white shirts, one overweight, the other thin and balding. Yasser had expected them to be young and energetic; he was sick of middle-aged men, their flaccid bodies, their rancid dreams. The thin, bald one took notes. When the fat one spoke, the bald one finished the sentence, his fingers scratching words on paper. Yasser dismissed them from his thoughts. They asked him questions, inquisitors expecting dark revelations, but the person they interrogated, this middle-aged, greying—already grey—man was tired of their faces and those of humanity. They promised him freedom; he did not believe a word they said. Anyway, he was too tired to care. All was sawdust.

None of Yasser's brothers or cousins had his father's guts. Otherwise, contacts or no, they would have been here a long time ago, and they would have stood up in his defence, created a row, muscled him out or bribed their way through. Instead, they came, visited and left, mumbling something about going to the *Mogamaa,* Cairo's Central City Hall, to get something done. You'd have to be an illiterate moron not to know that nothing ever happened there, in the *Mogamaa.* Even *he* knew that. Yasser shuddered to think how his father would have shaken earth to get him out of this stinking hole; but better his father was dead than alive.

The heavy-set man—stomach hanging over legs set wide apart to accommodate the dangling flesh—said, "Level with us, Mr. Amin: what exactly *were* your agreements with the Americans?" then mopped his forehead with a large, white handkerchief striped with navy blue.

"Especially the ones who were shot," continued the bald, thin one, his eyes a network of red veins behind thick glasses. When Yasser said nothing, the thin man complained, "You're not co-operating with us, Mr. Amin," then removed his glasses and rubbed his eyes with vigour.

"I am, I am," Yasser answered. "What *is* it you want of me? I just carried out what Mr. Abdullah told me to do. I did my job. I was liaison man. Go ask him."

The one with the bulging stomach said with the patient voice of a parent humouring a five-year old, "We have, we have. Mr. Abdullah said he asked you to import construction equipment, not *weapons.*"

"Mr. Abdullah did not authorize you to buy *weapons,*" reiterated the thin one. "Do you have papers, memos, letters to prove that?"

"No."

"*No letters* to tell you your line of duty?" the fat one asked in despair, rummaged his pocket and came up with a couple of candies he unwrapped and dispatched into his mouth, his jaw moving in stabbing jerks. He offered a candy to Yasser, but when he refused it, the man unwrapped it and stuffed it along with the others into his mouth.

"None," repeated Yasser raising his voice. "You know how work is done here: everything by word of mouth, *you* know that." The lawyers stared at each other, past patience.

Peering through thick glasses, the red-eyed one spoke. "How would you describe the deal then, Mr. Amin, the one between the Americans and yourself . . . I mean, between the Americans and the Egyptians?"

"How do *I* know?" roared Yasser. "Go ask my boss."

After a moment's silence, he continued in a tired voice, "Americans were to supply aircraft bombers, the Egyptians to allow them to use an air-base in Sinai. But Mr. Abdullah was to negotiate these details. I created working lines between the parties."

The big man scratched his hair then rested his arms on his stomach. With benign smile, he nodded to Yasser to encourage him to keep on speaking, but Yasser had nothing more to say, so the man explained in a soft voice that he had been abroad, to Switzerland, Austria, knew how difficult it was to return to one's homeland. The bald man took notes, even during silences. Their questions poured out: witnesses? Selim's address? enemies?

Events were jumbled in Yasser's mind. Had he told Selim about the details of the arms shipment, or had Selim given him directives from Mr. Abdullah? He was not sure at this point whether he, Yasser, had gone ahead and made the agreements, or the Egyptians had worked out the agreements with the Americans. Probably the latter. What did he have in common with either party? Like a dithering fool he had allowed himself to be wedged between these two aliens.

The fat man reminded Yasser to tell the truth, and if what he was saying was the truth, then he had a good chance of being released, for the lawyer had won a number of suits for other expatriates who, like Yasser, had been caught between the laws of more than one country. If, for example, Mr. Amin had read the papers perhaps two years ago or so . . . Yasser found it impossible to concentrate on the man's words. These lawyers did not have sufficient clout to sway the courts. A military court? Which of these two rogues was strong enough to face a military that shielded Mr. Abdullah and found Yasser an easy scapegoat to save face with the extremists who shot him?

***

Standing in the noon heat before the Sakkara Pyramid, Monir noted its crumbling stone, its granite scattered over the sand, its ascending steps, the first in the world to rise in decreasing width to reach the gods, the likeness of this structure imitated in pyramids of South America. The steps narrowed into an apex symbolic of people's desire to reach divine power above, they did not know where, just up there towards the infinite, thought Monir, although, more likely, the infinite was down here, within them. Monir feared that Yasser would be freed, but he checked his impulse and remembered he could not build his happiness at the expense of another's. He left the tourists resting in the shade of the pyramid and wandered off into the sand: a hot desert ochre stretched to the horizon as did his loneliness, and the sun's heat. His roots went deep into this soil, but he needed to merge them with another's, with the woman who had lived more than two decades in Canada married to someone else. He must be mad, but he felt that Nadia and he were meant to be together. Even with his wife, Samia, he had not had this connection. They had had a reasonably happy life, but Samia knew little of the world he lived in. When he had started out with her, all he had was his job as professor, and they had struggled on a limited salary. Eventually he had discovered art, and this had led him to make visits to archaeological sites. He needed to know the reliefs first-hand, to be near old stone walls and colossal statues, to immerse himself in the haunting faces of ancients, vibrant on the walls of tombs. Samia only knew the walls of her home. Nadia was another matter: she had her world structured and whole, and all he had to do was walk by her side, his reality clear to her. When they shared

each other's worlds, it seemed to him they had met without
boundaries, had kept on walking to meet on the same stretch
of land. How many times in his life would he have the chance
to feel like this? In the years since Samia's death, he had not
realized the extent of his alienation from others. He had been
busy caring for his son, but now that Kareem had gone on to
continue his studies and to travel abroad, Monir came face to
face with the stretch of sand that unfolded relentlessly in front
of him. Nadia had been the catalyst. Her body beside his
awoke feelings he had not shared for years, for with other
women his sexual forays had left him empty. And now that his
mind was close to another's, these rolling hills seemed to hold
promise. He noticed details: the camels, granite statues in the
distance, dark olive shrubs interspersed on yellow, reliefs on
walls in tombs touched with light, but his feelings did not stop
here, for her body was near his. To pass his fingers over her
face instead of just exorcising it on paper as he did almost
every night would realize his images in the flesh. Dare he go
further and initiate physical intimacy between them, so he
could achieve wholeness?

He watched camels stand at attention, listening to an
inaudible sound sweeping over the desert. What engaged their
minds as they sauntered in the heat, unattached, no shelter in
sight? When they found a small oasis, they ate heartily and
travelled for days storing their nourishment in their stomachs.
They survived without moisture for a long time, longer than
any living creature he knew. What endurance, what majesty,
patience, but more, what acceptance of life exposed to
extremes, truly the epitome of survival in his country, where
people lived for life, endured for endurance, welcomed the
moment for its riches without paying attention to the discom-
forts they faced, just happy to sense the sun on their backs and
to watch the sky until it glowed turquoise above their heads,
or until it dwindled into a satin-cool shade.

He would have liked to be a monk. A monastic life for a
few months would enable him to follow the day's rhythm

from sunrise to sunset and would do him good. But he could not see himself giving up his archaeology and his son, Kareem, even for a day. Yet, the idea was intriguing.

His eyes hurt from the noon rays. Recently, he had begun to feel the sun too bright on desert sand.

***

Since she sent him her letter, Nadia had not heard from Yasser. She was uneasy about his silence, needed to shock him out of his remorse, to hold him to her, for in his absence her life was bare. Yasser, she talked to him in her waking moments, how long do I search for you? Do I only encounter you for brief moments, as when I meet a face approaching me on a bridge in a fog at dawn, a face covered with dew which I touch and taste, but by then it will have disappeared, because it will have gone past me as I stand in the middle of nowhere, uncertain whether to keep on walking or to turn back and follow it? Can we meet, hold hands, agree to travel in one direction? But she must not ask these questions. She must concentrate on what she had to do and to re-double her efforts to get him out of there. Who was in confinement, she or Yasser? Why did *she* feel confined when he was away? She rested her arms on the kitchen table. She had to exert pressure through the Canadian Embassy, but how could she, all alone, achieve this? Where would she get the money for the lawyers? Was Spencer serious about footing the bill until she repaid him? So far, she had not seen any money from him. She might have to find a job to make up for the loan.

Esmat breathed audibly as she entered the kitchen door; her steps pounded the tiled floor as though each movement were her last. Nadia wondered how the woman could climb four storeys carrying groceries *and* hauling her body up. In her own building, Esmat climbed eight storeys. Now she entered the apartment, heaved her bags onto the kitchen table, placed her fleshy hand on Nadia's arm, and in a subdued voice said, "I'm going to get her to unwind her charms," as her body thumped into a chair and her hips hung outside its confines.

"Who?"

"That wicked woman who came here to pick you up the first day you went to see Mr. Yasser. I *know* it's her doing. She worked an evil charm on him." Esmat wiped perspiration off her forehead. Concerned about Esmat's threats, Nadia watched her wind her kerchief around her head, then move to the stove to brew Turkish coffee. The energizing coffee—mixed with fresh nutmeg that Esmat had pounded the day before—poured into the cup with its rich foam. Sitting across from Nadia, she began, "Ahmed, the orderly, you know the young upstart who thinks he owns the president's palace, the man we saw the other day when we went to visit Mr. Yasser, I met him in the market today. He knows that woman and says Magda is a follower of the Evil One. She gets men in her power, but when she cannot have one, she destroys him. You may think his story strange, but these dark acts exist, Madam Nadia." She sipped her coffee, then pressed her aching forehead with a hand on either side of her head. Nadia frowned at her housekeeper's words.

Esmat got up, placed her hands under her *gallabiah* at her back, reached for her bra's hooks and released her breasts, then juggled them inside her clothes until they settled on her stomach. When she went to the market, she liked her breasts high, so her admirers could get a full display of her riches. Comfortable, she sat down again, and resumed, "You don't know these evil doers, may Allah, the Beneficent, protect you and yours from such types!" She sipped foam off her coffee and rocked in her chair, muttering prayers to protect the family from envious eyes. "I'm going to undo her evil charm, trust me," she said, her eyes containing ocean secrets.

Nadia patted her arm, but Esmat would not be pacified. She shook her head and announced, "I have one of the woman's blouses. Don't ask me how I got it. I have friends. I took it to the soothsayer, the one who helped me find my daughter, Rasha." She glanced at Nadia's face to see how the story was working. Nadia bent her head. To try to get Esmat off this track

was like trying to dislodge an old steam engine from its well-beaten path, yet Nadia felt compelled to react, so she said, "We don't want to get involved in these shady deals, Esmat."
It was Esmat's turn to patronize Nadia. "The soothsayer can do these things. Just leave it to me. People like you need to be protected from evil. The soothsayer will make a doll in Magda's likeness out of the blouse I gave her. She will sing chants and rituals over the doll, then she will do the rest of the ceremony before me and my friends. We have to get together to witness the casting out of the spell. Tonight, we go to her place in Old Shoubra, and we will chant the destruction of the evil snare that Magda has set up for Mr. Yasser. You wait and see, right always wins. As sure as Allah is the One and Only, this jinx will be overpowered and destroyed."

***

Magda's brief weekend with Yasser at her villa in Mariout had not worked out the way she had planned. They had not tasted the dough and honey, he had not wanted fresh cream from the village. Instead, they had made sandwiches and gone fishing, the very first time in her life she had been in a boat. That's what Yasser wanted to do. They had gone to Alexandria and rented an old boat, its sails tattered, but the oarsmen moved it smoothly through the waters of the round harbour. And when they had passed through the small opening in the stone circle and gone out to sea, they had met a fierce wind and the boat had risen sharply at the prow, then dipped to one side and drenched them with waves, threatening to overpower the boat. The oarsmen shrugged and laughed, and Yasser had not wanted them to turn back. He had sat there for hours struggling to keep his line straight in the water and talked to the old man at the helm. She did not like being soaked in fishy water, yet she had said nothing. This is how she wanted to remember him, as he was one week before he was shot. She did not know who had done this to him, but perhaps her father would find out. At least Yasser was alive.

During their weekend, Yasser had not wanted any of the food she had prepared for him. They had not walked out on the hot sand, nor drunk the red wine with the leg of lamb she had prepared. He had preferred salad, but she had had him to herself that night. She had held him after he had gone to sleep, heard him breathe, her head on his chest, her legs entwined around his. The window had brought in a musty freshness. Her hand had rested on his arm and her eyes had remained open to avoid the pain in her stomach and to ward off the frightening whisper of her heart. Now all she had was pain. As soon as she left Mariout this time, she had to go see a doctor. Her father, after much shouting and frowning, had promised to help get Yasser out of confinement, but would the man deliver, or would his jealousy—she had not told him Yasser was married—tie his hands and make him fail her one more time?

Here at Mariout, everything was still. This is where she felt at peace, lying on the sofa, her grandmother's portrait hanging on the wall above her, the round face looking down with calm expression, as though the old woman did not mind hanging there to smile down at her granddaughter. Her greying hair wavy and short—for she did not wear a veil as most women her age did—her ankle-length flowery summer dress with the long sleeves and intricately fashioned gold earrings with a diamond at the centre. Who had taken these earrings? Her father had never mentioned them to her. Had he given them to one of his lady-friends? Magda would soon have to go to Cairo to follow up on her plans for freeing Yasser.

***

Esmat closed her eyes and rocked her torso. She started chanting. "Don't take part in these dark acts, Esmat," Nadia cautioned. To distance herself from Esmat's murmurs, Nadia did what she saw many women in her native land do after they drink their coffee: she turned her cup over on its saucer and left it for a few minutes until the dregs dripped down the sides and formed an intricate lacy design on the porcelain. Then she turned it up to interpret the open face of her destiny. She had seen her mother and grandmother spend evenings of mirth deciphering events depicted in the brown designs inside their coffee cups. They only half-believed their own interpretations, but they proceeded with caution, just in case what they deciphered was real. Now Nadia hoped this method would deliver her from her abyss.

"Madam Nadia," Esmat persisted, "if one is silent about evil, one encourages it to take possession of one's loved ones. Knowing what I know, I will fight back to reclaim Mr. Yasser for you and his boys."

Esmat became more agitated as Nadia rolled her cup sideways to make sure the dregs covered its inner surface. "We must fight evil with evil. The sooner we unlock Satan's grip, the better for Mr. Yasser. That woman wants him there, broken, so she can have him. Leave it to me, I'll make sure she does not keep him." Somewhere in the back of her mind, Nadia knew action was the answer, but evil charms? Did one have to assert one's hostility, act out vengeful schemes to push back the sinister schemes of another? Esmat closed her eyes either from frustration or with determination.

Nadia studied the designs in her cup. A dragon, forest, man on a horse. Yasser. The dragon, his love for Magda. A woman cheats another of the love of her husband. Yet, she, Nadia, had no right to judge Yasser, for her own attachment to Monir was questionable, at best. Yet, she and Monir had not made love; they had been restrained. She had told Yasser the truth, although, perhaps not the whole truth. She was sure Yasser had cheated on her; she had reason to seek companionship, especially because he had kept her out of his present predicament. She could not mention Monir to Yasser while he was under such duress. With time, this period might draw them together, or separate them, and she did not know which would prevail. But none of this mattered; she wanted Yasser safe. In the coffee dregs: a snake, entwined around a tree, a valley, mountains. Her mother would say after valleys, there would be mountains and joy. Around the rim of the cup, the clear part was an expanse of sky: perhaps, a place of hope. That night, Esmat stayed out till dawn.

Alone in her apartment, Nadia listened to the silence pushing her inward. None of her plans for helping Yasser had materialized. She had listened to Esmat's superstitious voodoo, but this had nothing to do with freeing Yasser. She had not heard anything positive from Canadian or Egyptian sources. She and Yasser had come to Egypt seeking renewal of their marriage and re-discovery of their roots; they had hoped that by returning to their native soil they would somehow recover their identities. They had come here to re-emerge with people and events, and perhaps, when the time came, they would retire here. Most of all, they wanted to live in the sun, revisit ancient monuments, drink the water of the river, bathe in the waves of the Mediterranean. For the Arabic saying goes, "He who drinks of the water of the Nile will always return," and the words had lingered with her and with Yasser—or was it only with her? In any case, their hopes had seemed to work.

Now, Mr. Abdullah's statement, "Misr Om El Donia, Egypt, Mother of *za* World" rang spitefully in Nadia's ears. How would her native land be a mother fulfilling her daughter's wishes, when Nadia and Yasser were in such a predicament? Was Egypt good for those who had persisted and lived on her soil, and bad to others who were born on her soil but had opted to live elsewhere? Perhaps she had betrayed her native country by leaving it, and in so doing had forfeited its protection. She and Yasser were hanging in mid-skies over oceans, under clouds, blown by alien winds from one continent to another, no land claiming them as her own. No one cried for Yasser. Their sons had not yet discerned the truth about their father, and when they did, they might reject association with this land and be alienated from parents who had come to it seeking re-initiation. Canadian Embassy people would not be willing to risk their smooth relations with the

Egyptians to take a firm stand on Yasser's situation. Mr. Abdullah—the Minister of Trade who had hired Yasser—would not go out of his way to vindicate him. He and others would be afraid to do that in case they angered the fanatics who had attacked Yasser. After all, even in Mr. Abdullah's mind, Yasser was the one who had given up his native soil. He had lived in Canada for decades and made money, dealt with Americans. No reason to mourn *him*.

She did not know where she and Yasser would locate their niche, and she hoped they would not be homeless forever. They needed to be together in their own corner. Most of all, she did not want the same fate to dog their sons' and grandsons' footsteps.

***

Chapter Twelve

Lamb

After a restless night dreaming of a barefoot Yasser racing on burning sand with rabid dogs chasing him, Nadia got out of bed, dressed and knocked on Rana's door to ask if there were fresh disasters her neighbour might have heard through her husband's grapevine. When Rana ushered her into their living room, Nadia had little time to voice her questions and waited for her neighbour to rush into the kitchen to squeeze the mandatory fresh orange juice. Nadia could not get to the reason for her visit on the doorstep, an indiscretion considered the height of indecorum. She looked around her at the living room: beige damask upholstery, red velvet curtains, mother of pearl plates on walls, rubber plants in the corner.

When Rana returned to the living room, Nadia waited until they had sipped their orange juice before she asked about Yasser. Rana had heard that a high-ranking officer had hinted to her husband that Yasser's release was imminent; police had found no proof of his dealing with Americans without the approval of Egyptian officials. Rana had also heard that Sherif had made successful contacts with top rank officials in the army, but that since neither rumour was certain, she had to wait until they were before she divulged news to Nadia. "Our hearts are with Professor Yasser. Allah never forgets the blameless, Allah, the One and Only." Rana cleared the juice glasses, and they watched television. But Yasser's scarred face stared out of the screen, and somewhere in the background was the smelly latrine, dark and cracked in the corner of his cell, cockroaches running up and down the wall at night. Nadia had to get him out of there before Amir and Samy arrived, before his confinement played havoc with his mind; yet all she could do was wait.

In the next few days while roaming the streets in dense crowds, Nadia kept seeing his eyes staring at her from windows of moving cars, peeping out of shady corners of streets. She glimpsed his greying head, his back in a dark suit bent over coffee inside the open doorway of a dim café. Eager to steady her rambling mind with the invigorating images of Ramadan, she peered through shop windows, but often stared at her own eyes. She knew that government officials would not take action on Yasser's case because people were fasting the holy month of Ramadan, an undeclared holiday from pressure. Their fast lasted from dawn till sunset, not a drop to drink nor a morsel of bread, no cigarettes, no coffee. Some did not brush their teeth until sundown. Their energy was sapped. Meanwhile, their supervisors looked the other way, and no one did any work unless he was employed by a foreign company, and even then, employers exercised forbearance when workers interrupted their work to pray, a practice Nadia respected, since remembering their faith five times a day was an exercise of the will and heart. In the meantime, nothing happened in government bureaus.

On a few occasions on the street, she sensed someone's footsteps behind her, but whenever she turned around, she saw no one. Her nerves were jumpy, but once she was sure she had glimpsed a bearded man in a *gallabiah* glaring at her from a café, and questions flooded her: did he know her? Was he one of the attackers' supporters? Did he realize she was Yasser's wife? Worse, was she imagining all this? Another time, a uniformed man hanging from an army jeep, shouted at her: "Cover your hair, woman! Aren't you ashamed of walking on the street without a veil?" followed by a chorus of curses from his comrades. These belligerent types expressed chauvinism, not piety. But Yasser's bandaged body on the narrow bed was painful reminder of the danger of trespassing on others' beliefs. From then on, she wore dark long sleeves and ankle-length skirts on the street, covered her hair with a scarf. Esmat was exuberant about this change in Nadia's appearance and prophesied that only good would emerge from her mistress's pious behaviour. As days went by, Nadia adapted to her veneer and felt exposed when she walked on the street with one inch of her arms or legs showing: how quickly one adapted to convention and how little it meant! But the advantage of the attire was envelopment against the harsh rays of the sun and the dust that flooded the air whenever the cars' tires screeched on the edge of the road or blew up accumulated garbage. No street washers could cope with the sand that poured into the city from the outskirts of the surrounding desert, although shop owners daily splashed their part of the street with pails of water they had used for washing the pavement. With time, she came to understand how women behind black veils with small slits for eyes would be seeing the world from within their shroud of safety, yet they were a small number, who had arrived with their men from Arab sheikdoms.

Ramadan fare filled shops with dark dates, sugary sweet, pistachios, figs, *konafa*, dried apricots, but Nadia's mind was on Yasser's pending court appearance. She had not heard a word from his family in Ismailia. On stalls, inside and outside shops, were walnuts, fresh oranges, bananas, Ramadan sugar dolls, yet her eyes were trapped by the freshly slaughtered lambs, hanging in tight butcher shops, spilling their blood on sawdust to prevent it from spreading. Had Yasser been with her, he would have been offended by the carcasses hanging from huge iron stakes dripping pools of blood on the sawdust. Meanwhile, festive lights adorned the doorways of shops, loudspeakers announced the *muazzin*'s evening call to prayer summoning the faithful to end their fast. But in her mind was the bleating of lambs who awaited their turn in courtyards, or were confined in stalls of slaughter houses, their sounds high-pitched, their wail insistent. At night, they cried. Someone had told her that animals knew when their time had come.

She hailed a taxi and went to the Canadian Embassy, up two fights of stairs to a secretary who announced her through the intercom. Mr. Spencer met her with a broad smile at the door of his office. He looked askance at her attire, but courteously held out a chair for her then took his own, knotted his hands on his shiny desk and offered her his pearly white smile. She dared not ask him questions. He volunteered that the two lawyers she had hired were doing remarkable work, and he was optimistic that it would be a matter of a few weeks before Yasser's release. Mr. Spencer would pay the lawyers until she was in a position to return the loan, but she needed to be patient while awaiting results. She had not expected news during Ramadan and wondered whether Spencer was preparing her for a long wait, or if he had heard specific information, but she knew that questions from her might trigger ambiguous responses. So she hung on to hope. At least he had promised to pay the lawyers. She shook his hand, mumbled a silent prayer as she slipped out of his office onto the Cornice. A few metres down the bank, the river flowed. She ran down its grassy incline to the splashing rhythm, soft and subdued, a symphony of tears. In ancient times, before the building of major dams, waters of the river rose in May and June inundating the surrounding land with its rich silt. After the construction of the Aswan High Dam, everything was harnessed into unnatural routines, and instead of rising and falling in thanksgiving and ritual baptism of the earth, the river lay low all year. Today, no celebration, just the sluggish flow in a uniform tempo. All year, the river lay dormant. How perverse, how far removed from its natural state.

Mumbling prayers for Yasser, she recalled Edfu Temple where she had experienced a sense of ancient presences. She sat down on the grass, removed her shoes and dug her feet in the wet soil, then washed them in the cool river. Her tension seeped out into the water. Wiggling her toes, she drew images in the water. The anxiety that frustrated her and created visions of disaster was filtering out through the tips of her toes into the soothing flow. No threat existed that baptism could not cure. Her tense spine relaxed and her body gained comfort from its interplay with the river. The youthful days she had spent with Yasser surfaced: at the pyramids, on the escarpment overlooking the city at night, the small stars, cool evening air, lights in the distance, miniature diamonds in a sea of black except for the twinkling lights of the far away city. Huddled together in a tent, they peered through the open flap at the wavering silhouettes on silvery sand, the sphinx, pyramids, immanent presences on the star-lit sand. No nearby sign of civilization then, no high-rise, restaurants, food shops, trinket shops which were now travesties of this ancient land. She remembered being in the tent with Yasser at the foot of Cheops pyramid, lying side by side, not touching, enjoying their closeness, cool wind brushing their skin. The tent-cloth phosphorescent in the dark, whispering silences ministering to them in the wind swishing over sand. Then, your eyes, Yasser, asking me, your arms holding me, your heart pounding like a trapped bird yearning for larger space, perhaps you have an extra strong heartbeat, or I am attuned to the listening. We were lovers then. Now at my feet, street lights are dancing in the river, they remind me of our felucca at old Semiramis, nothing in sight but wavering lights from other feluccas. It was quiet then. Just the flip of oars, glimmer of lights dipping and rising at the prow of boats, tall, dark silhouettes of oars-men standing, their chants inaudible tunes. Now hooting sirens, voices, people turning and staring at me as I bathe my feet in the river.

If prayer worked, her silent words would usher in hope. Whether she was calling upon Jewish prophets, Christian messengers, Islamic deity, there was no difference, they were and are essences inhabiting this land. They had sprung in the same area of the world and had come to rest in it. Her father, like others of his generation, had received instruction at the feet of a Sheik, learned his fluent Arabic by reciting *sourahs*. Once, he had said, "Read the Koran, Nadia, its classical Arabic will teach you to sing!" She had read it years ago in Toronto, evenings, while she waited for Yasser to come home. What poetry flowed through its lines, what wonderful insights into the region and its people. Yet a few militants had interpreted its scriptures to condone violence, paradox being the essence of religious patriarchies.

Daily, her father had listened to the Sheik render the Koran on the radio. At best, his friends had thought him eccentric, but at worst they feared he was a traitor to the Copts, yet they kept their suspicions muffled in deference to his social status. He had been at peace with other holy books, like the Bhagavad Gita. Standing on his head for meditation had been his practice throughout his life, and she had seen him practise Yoga on his bed days before he died. He knew that ancient spiritual presences co-existed in Egypt: in the Coptic Church, the Islamic Mosque, the Jewish Temple, ancestral holy places sharing the ancient background of Pharaonic belief in an afterlife.

Akhenaton's ancient granite statue sprang to Nadia's mind. Seated—not on one of those huge golden chairs that Tutankhamun was noted for but—on a backless stool, his unadorned right hand carrying a *crook*, his flabby breasts on his midriff, his stomach dangling over a short, tight tunic: the first person to declare one deity in the universe. He believed the Sun-god Aten was supreme, not the many gods Pharaohs before him worshipped. The high priests had denounced him as heretic. Monir had said to her at Al Karnak: "In ancient Egypt and in India, as in a number of other countries, there were many gods, one for each aspect of life. Today, these aspects are sacred but they are combined in One Person. People overburden God with personas created in their own likenesses."

She got up, climbed the grassy slope and crossed Medan El Tahrir to get to her apartment. People, cars, houses meshed into a loud din. Wearily, she climbed the stairs, reached her apartment, entered and found Esmat in the sitting room awaiting her with the latest news. For once Esmat forgot to chide Nadia for going out alone at night. Nadia flung herself into an armchair.

As though afraid to be overheard by lurking spirits, Esmat drew her chair close to Nadia's. "Remember what I told you about this woman, Magda? I and my friends went to the soothsayer's house last night." Her story promised to be a long one, so Nadia got up and stretched out on the sofa. Esmat pulled her chair close, held Nadia's foot in her hand, massaged it with extra rich skin cream from a jar she kept under the sofa, and in hushed tones said: she and her women friends were known in Old Shoubra—a quarter of Cairo where narrow alleys harbour energies and superstitions from long ago—as psychics with connections to the spiritual world. Old midwives, they had delivered babies in their youth and were training younger women to do the job, so they, the psychics, could communicate with unseen powers. They knew how to combat evil and protect themselves against harm. They had taken the art of magic from their mothers and grandmothers. In the narrow alleys of Shoubra, this power was known to preside in special families. Esmat had gone to Hagga Aisha, the best psychic in their quarter. She and her friends had huddled together in the Hagga's apartment and prayed over the Magda doll. The soothsayer mumbled evocations as she pierced the doll with pins, then the Hagga shrieked, rolling her head from side to side as the Evil One entered the doll's jabbed blouse.

"But I swear to you, Madam, and the other women swear it too, the sound she made was not human. The shriek was unearthly, like the siren of an ambulance carrying a dead body, or a chicken whose throat is being sliced with a blunt knife."

Minutes had passed, then Esmat and her friends recognized a dark presence—big as a cloud—hover over the doll, which trembled as darkness took her over. A shriek rent the air. The doll tossed and bounced across the room metres from where, cross-legged, they sat huddled together holding hands and chanting to ward off the Evil One. The doll shivered, swayed, shuddered as the Evil One entered her, and she pounded her head on the floor until her clothes were in shreds. Then she lay still.

"I swear, Madam Nadia, everything happened like that, for nothing is impossible for Allah, the Mighty One." Relieved that the doll had stopped moving, Esmat and her friends chanted their evening prayers while rocking, holding vigil until the first rooster crowed at dawn, then they slept, knowing their loved ones had been saved from dominance by the Dark One. Having finished her story, Esmat went to bed, satisfied that the day's actions had been fruitful; but Nadia was worried about the violence in Esmat's story and her association of dark forces in people with the light of faith. How the disenfranchised, as well as some of those who were not, used their faith to justify magic acts, evil spells, wandering ghosts and harm they wrought on their fellow humans, mystified her, but it was not a strange phenomenon for her when she considered the number of wars waged in the name of God all over the devastated world. She went out on the balcony and sat contemplating the horizon until her eye-lids drooped.

***

Selim had brought Yasser a new suit, shirt and tie for the court hearing, the second time the man had shown his face. Yasser had accepted the clothes, since his other option for his court appearance was to wear the khaki one-piece jumper which he wore in his cell, and which he hated because when he sat on the toilet it lay on the dirty floor. Even the washing accorded it by the prison wardens did not change its offensive smell. He had learned to hang it up before he sat down. Now he had new clothes. The ones he had been wearing at the time of the incident—with the bullet holes and the blood—had been thrown out at Kasr-El-Einy Hospital. Selim had hinted to him that the purchaser of the new outfit was someone else. Who but Magda? Yasser tidied his hair with the brush Magda had bought him. A court hearing in Ramadan, a new twist of justice lay in wait for him. The jurors would hear him while people were fasting, so they could sentence him in secrecy when no one was looking. But this had not been what Magda had said: her father was the intermediary in the case. She had assured Yasser that everything was going to be dealt with, in time, but in whose time?

***

First thing in the morning, Nadia put on her walking shoes, cotton shirt and skirt and set off on a pilgrimage to the ancient quarter of the city. Passing narrow and muddy century-old streets fringed with sporadic mud houses, she reached the Hanging Church in Old Cairo. Carts piled high with watermelons and oranges dotted the side-road, the turbaned vendors' faces—enveloped by stark white head-wraps—were burnt umber in the sun. The church stood on top of a first century Roman fortress. The same spiritual force that had worked for her ancestors, and for those before them, formed a lasting power to which she would add her voice. The door of the church stood open: she climbed the refurbished stone stairs into its dark interior. Under reconstruction, the ancient ceiling was supported by wood scaffolds. She forgot the workmen and their tools and wandered around to the icons inscribed on walls. Twelve marble pillars, elaborate and hand-carved, six lined on each side of the aisle, led up to the holy of holies. Moslem craftsmen were carving meticulous renovations in wood. The new doors were a mixture of Coptic domes and Islamic designs. Nadia felt ancient faces rise from the pillars and cast their protective presences around her. Light came from a bunch of candles lit by visiting worshippers, who stopped at a life-sized icon of Madonna and Child to pray and to ask for special blessings. There, Nadia lit her candle but her lips did not move; only her thoughts registered her prayers. Having circled the interior, she glided out of the dark into the flooding sun. In the front vestibule, a few feet away from her, the floor was ripped open and a wood fence protected her from falling into the gaping hole. At first, the lower level seemed pitch black, but seconds later she discerned in the deep cavity an ancient Roman amphitheatre, housing pillars surrounded by thick stone walls. She stared into the half-concealed underground; millions of spirits had inhabited this space, and their silences enveloped and soothed her. Yasser, release Yasser, her heart spelled out.

Outside the church, a small path led around the stone building to a narrow alley lined with boutiques, stocked with hand-woven carpets, pottery and brass goods. A sudden bend in the alley revealed an ancient building, the Ben Ezra Synagogue. She climbed its well-preserved steps and entered a small hall, at the entrance of which stood an old custodian. He guided her through the place, its bare walls a yellowing cream, the altar decorated with gold designs. The north side was elevated by a couple of steps from the rest of the hall. The place seemed abandoned: no chairs nor benches for the invisible congregation, but the man was proud of the walls that his community and his family had re-painted and of the re-built mahogany door. He boasted that this synagogue was maintained by Jews who lived in the area and who had not left Egypt, even when in 1948 many others had joined the exodus to the newly established Israel. Designs on walls and pillars were similar to, though not as ornate as, the Coptic ones in the neighbouring church. A large stone altar stood in the centre of the hall, where he rested his hand and told Nadia the story of the shrine which, he was proud to say, had remained intact throughout numerous political changes. "All my family lives here. In fact, this area is the home of my people since hundreds of years ago. My nephew will take over my duties when I'm gone."

Nadia slipped a few pounds in the box by the side of the altar. Through the court and out into the light. She walked back to the church and circled its stone walls. The sun beat down. April. Yasser had been confined for eight weeks.

***

Dressed in officer's clothes, wig and glasses, Magda pushed past soldiers at the door and sat in the third row of the small courtroom. Her father had not arrived, but he had assured her he would be there. Yasser stood inside the box, his hands hanging over the top of the rail separating him from the rest of the courtroom. On one side, ten army jurors sat on a platform facing him and on the other the presiding judge sat on a chair elevated on a higher platform facing Yasser. Magda did not care that her father had admonished her against attending. She had borrowed officer's clothes, brown wig, tan suit, dark glasses and she carried a forged passport. One of the men at the door had let her in: knew who she was, thought she might consider him a likely paramour. *That* was *his* business.

The familiar pain in her stomach reminded her she had to take her pill, so she swallowed it without water. At least the doctor had given her temporary relief so she could attend the trial and find out what was to happen to the only human who mattered.

***

Nadia trudged through a muddy street by the Hanging Church to a group of sellers to ask for a telephone. They directed her to one at a fruit shack. She called Monir and told him she needed to go to Mohammed Ibn Qalawan Mosque. He was scheduled to meet a group of tourists there at four and said he would wait for her. When they arrived, she was waiting for them on the wide steps of the mosque. They removed their shoes, and she re-arranged her scarf to cover her hair. Inside the expansive dome, hand-painted baroque designs greeted them; Persian carpets covered the floor. Small groups of men, their heads bowed to their knees, their hands on the floor, recited their prayers. High walls under the main dome were a sky-blue covered with pastel arabesques. Light from windows in the high dome filled the interior, illumining bursts of green, blue and yellow. She lingered on the women's side of the hall, beseeching mercy for Yasser. This was his religious home, and she prayed on his behalf.

Later, the terrace was bathed in a white light, and the expansive veranda opened wide over the ancient city. Five in the afternoon, blue sky and rocky ochre hills rolled to the horizon. Monir joined her to point out the stone walls of the Citadel surrounding the ancient fortress. If the fortress fell into the hands of attacking enemies, the whole city would fall with it. Nadia derived solace from the old stone and avoided words. Down the granite stairs to the streets of Old Cairo. The sun hid behind yellow buildings as the group wound through the narrow alleys. Monir put his arm around Nadia's shoulders and drew her close. They walked through alleys packed with boutiques, gold and precious stones locked behind glass.

One of their group wanted to buy a gold bracelet for his wife. They entered a small store where three men sat behind glass counters. On the walls of the shop were large mirrors displaying the tourists to themselves and to the vendors. Lights from elaborate, antique crystal chandeliers bounced off mirrors in a rose-pink, maroon and cream-white sheen. Monir explained that the chandeliers with their amber rose tint and sparkling gold had hung in one of King Farouk's palaces. The store was barely wide enough for the group of five to stand side by side in the surreal glow of a world under glass, where what counted was beyond reach.

A German man, the size of three, was in the store when they arrived. In front of him on the glass counter lay heavy gold bracelets and necklaces displayed on black suede. His gaze did not waver from the gold exhibit. He punctuated his heavy breathing with slow words in German, and the vendor answered him in his language. The Greek tourist in Nadia's group asked a vendor to take out a group of necklaces from under the glass. Nadia watched as the salesman in the corner, probably the owner, studied each tourist in the multiple mirrors to determine the price he would quote each of them. As soon as someone showed interest in a piece of jewellery, he exchanged glances in the mirror with the two other vendors. One spoke in Greek to a tourist and quoted him the price of four hundred pounds. When the Greek decided he would take the bracelet, the vendor in the corner snapped in English,

"Seven hundred pounds." Confused, the man turned to Monir who intervened, but the one in the corner said in Arabic, "It's eight hundred, but we are giving him a special price." Nothing Monir said mattered.

Instead of leaving the necklace and walking out, as a local person would do, the purchaser counted out his seven hundred pounds. The owner of the store lost interest in the Greek man and turned to study the German who, still examining the heavy gold pieces with attention to craftsmanship, had so far shown no preference. The owner, staring at no one in particular, maintained his fixed expression of unmitigated boredom. As the group was ready to leave, two American women with white legs flashing in mini shorts entered the store and asked for the price of some bracelets. The vendor in the middle of the store gave them a price, and without hesitating the women handed him their dollars, took their gold and left, as the men's eyes ogled their backs and naked legs. Meanwhile, the vendor in the corner turned his nonchalant gaze to the German, the prize catch of the day, then swivelled towards the window to watch the tight alleys and the tourists who would push open the swinging glass door to his well-crafted shop.

Outside, the alleys were packed. Monir led the group to a small sidewalk café, wood chairs and tables, where the tourists ordered *fetir*: a light strudel filled with nuts and covered with icing sugar.

***

Yasser's lawyers flanked him in the courtroom, took their time repeating their meaningless jargon. Selim was nowhere; there was no familiar face. Two women officers in the crowd. Yasser did not know they allowed women high positions in the army. Few civilian clothes. Words, loud remarks, everything was meaningless. A huge man stepped into the room from a side-door and slipped into a chair in the front row facing Yasser. Steel magnets, his eyes dominated the room and he fixed his stare on Yasser. Eyebrows heavy, nose long, five stars on his chest, perhaps one of the upper echelons of the army. Yasser turned his gaze to the judge, round face, double chin, bald head, kinky hair around the ears. The jurors in army uniforms, his own lawyers in funereal dark-blue suits, beads of sweat rolling down the fat one's forehead, no candy bulging from his cheeks, the thin man's watery eyes laced with blood-red veins.

Faces crowded Yasser and jammed his brains; bodies suffocated him. He was doomed. All this was a deadly charade.

***

Selim escaped to Alexandria alone but found no rest. On the Cornice, the rocking waves fomented his surging fears. He had not brought Soheir with him because she had to work. He had taken a few days off, but no one in the office would miss him during the month of Ramadan. He had a small room in San Stefano Hotel on the long stretch of Cornice between Stanley Bay and Gleem, the nicest and quietest part of the seaside road. He needed a few days of peace, but rest he could not find because he was worried about Yasser's fate. Selim had managed to stay away from the scene of negotiations, but he could not avoid the aftermath of Yasser's incident. He had been in to see Mr. Abdullah, but his boss had been cagey, his face had that swollen look as though he were hiding something. He had intimated that since Yasser was unwell, they should consider replacing him before his sentencing.

Selim's job was arid; he could not face up to the possibility of Yasser's conviction. Curse the day he had convinced his friend to take the job, but he was fasting Ramadan, so he had no business to swear. He did not eat a morsel of bread nor wet his lips until *El Esha* when the *muazzin* chanted prayers, but he stole cigarettes when he was alone, as he was doing now on the Cornice so, in fact, his fast was a lie. He did not drink, so his lips were parched, even cracked from smoking. His nerves were on edge and there was no sleep to be had. Even so, he should not be swearing. Perhaps what was happening to him was punishment for the mistakes he had made in his life. Nothing was for free. He had wanted Yasser to be in Cairo but had not wished him to get into trouble, not that kind of trouble. Selim would not be able to resume his normal life if Yasser were . . . But he should not entertain such morbid thoughts. He had to relax, for Yasser could get people to work for him. Magda was running around to get her father to take action. Selim had known her for years, but she would not raise a finger to help him should *he* be in any kind of mess, and he had known her ever since he had known Soheir, about eight years. This is how he had learned to be cautious, for no one would help him if *he* were to fall into disfavour.

***

The group at Khan-El-Khalili asked Monir if it was proper to place their orders before the crowds had ended their fasting. Monir answered that foreigners were exempt from social codes. But when the *muazzin's* voice sailed out of the microphones with the chant that released the fasting congregations from their abstinence, his voice jolted the tourists and awakened their guilt for ordering food a few minutes before the sanctioned time. Monir contemplated the faces around the table. They were jarred by the impact of the lilting voice that rose and fell in the alley. He imagined that the sung prayer itself, without the high volume, would sound strange to their ears. They had set their drinks down on the table as though they were poachers caught in well-watched territory. Naturally, for they came from countries where prayer was private, but here prayer was communal. Allah was manifest in the solidarity of His worshippers. No wonder Westerners, accustomed to solitude, were baffled by the prayer carpets spread on the ground, men bending on their knees to pray, heads down, shoulder-to-shoulder, their chants rising in the dusty air; then silence. Suddenly, all hands jumped to life across the tables.

Nadia was contemplating an inner field of ice shining silver in the noon sun. She and Yasser were sitting in a small wood hut, their nylon lines disappearing in a hole at their feet. They were ice-fishing on the frozen waters of Lake Simcoe. Even when sitting close to Yasser with many layers of wool clothes and parkas, her teeth were chattering. He was teasing her about her red nose, his parka open, his head uncovered. The line tugged at their hands, but they pulled out an empty hook and had to replace the bait. A thermos with hot tea was their solace, but even that got cold. Yasser did not catch many fish, but this did not matter. They did not go out on a frozen lake in the middle of winter to catch fish; they went for solitude and scenery. Out of the chink of window in their hut, her eyes roamed the snow-bound lake. She was resting her eyes on its pure white, earth as it was meant to be. Unrelenting brisk air came in through the opening door, but she awoke to the tight, noisy alley in Khan-El-Khalili at dusk, voices shouting everywhere. Around her, between ancient, dark walls, were the tinkling of plates and utensils, shouts to waiters, aroma of lamb on charcoal, the stir of people drinking, downing glasses of apricot juice, their spoons plunging into mounds of rice and chopped lamb. Laughter.

At her table, strudel and Turkish coffee, powdered sugar from fluffy dough settled everywhere on the chequered cloth. They ate. Microphones blared voices singing new songs of Ramadan. Cats wailed in alleys and waited in stealth under tables. Life flaunted its sounds, people chewed their meat with gusto, tourists watched the scene with quiet resolve; they were determined to understand.

A rising cacophony of sounds, purring cats feasting on pieces of lamb they snatched from surreptitious hands under tables, utensils on plates, singers, music, voices shouting orders for more food, and Nadia, sinking in the tidal wave, surrendering to those who were thankful to be breathing and dreaming.

***

Chapter Thirteen

Carnation

Nadia's trying to go home. She's shouting, shouting louder, her words echoing in a dream telling him, "Come on let's go or we'll be late! La . at . e . . Let's go o . o . . !" Her voice is reverberating from bare walls, bouncing back and re-echoing. "O . . o . . o h."

Where are they, in an apartment? They are getting dressed, rushing to go home. Would they get there? Is she in that dream again? She wants to find her home, the one she has allowed to be sold, the one with the white-washed walls, large windows and forest trees.

"Hurry up!" she shouts.

They are there. Which home is it? She has no time to ask before they are rushed in through the front door by the real estate agent. Here is the garden she loves in the street she has left behind. They walk into the vestibule: it's not the house, it's another, a small one they had rented a long time ago, the one with the rock garden and the willow tree. But the willow is not there, a maple is. The house is changed. A circular staircase replaces the straight one. The new stairway is not gumwood, it is white wrought-iron. She hates white wrought-iron. This is not the house they had rented. Its bay windows in the living and dining rooms are painted brown instead of white.

"They've changed it!" she's shouting up the staircase to her companion. Her voice drowns her ears. Who are they, these people who have changed their home? Does he hear her? He does not notice the changes, nor does he seem to mind. He looks around the second floor, comes down the stairs to the first and joins her. Smiling, her companion approves walls, rooms. They have agreed to take it. She awakens. She is between the house in her dream and the bed where she lies.

In this dream, they were able to return to their home, the one they owned and wanted, only to find themselves in the one they had rented. The rented house had also been good for them, but *it* too had changed. With its iron stairs, metal kitchen cupboards, painted gumwood doors, it was new and cold. No longer the soft glow of gumwood she had spent hours polishing, the solid oak cabinets where her children had sat at her feet, pulled out pots and pans from lower drawers and banged them into a terrific din. Even Yasser in her dream was an unidentified "he," although she sensed that "he" was her husband, though her mind had not spelled that out. She knew he was walking upstairs or downstairs, where she was not, and coming to conclusions about the house, making his decision without consulting her, without being aware of her bewilderment at the transformation of their previous home. This "he" was out of touch with her.

Nadia got out of bed. Her dream had taken a new and disquieting turn. The new home in her dream was a cold house; its special features had been camouflaged, and no one had given these trespassers permission to smudge its identity, but then, *she* may have. While *she* was wavering between personas, the house was defaced into something less than itself. Her home was a reflection of her uncertain identity, imperfectly rubbed out on a messy blackboard. She had been weak; she did not know whether her home was in Canada or in Egypt, with her sons and husband, or without them, where she would find it, and on which side of the globe.

The telephone bell was a short, urgent ring. Long distance. She rushed and picked up the receiver. On the other end, "Mother?" Amir's voice. "We'll be in Cairo in four days. How are you?"

Hanging between two worlds, she thought out loud, "Fine. How's Samy?"

"He *and* Laura are coming with me. We'll be there soon. How's father?"

"Laura's coming?" Her heart fell. "Great!" she hurried on, "Your father's well. Recuperating. Except, he thinks he should stay in hospital until he's recovered. Doesn't want to burden me." Soon they would be here and have to face their father's situation. What Laura would make of this mess remained to be seen. Nadia wished Amir a safe trip and put down the receiver. Then she panicked. She and Esmat had so much to do to get the apartment ready for the boys and Laura. Esmat rallied; Madam Nadia was not to worry, Esmat would do the cleaning, then they would do the baking together. Rolling her sleeves up above her dimpled elbows, she took her pail from the kitchen cupboard, placed it in the sink, filled it with warm water and grunted as she lifted it over the edge, heaved and carried it into the living room. She scoured the tiles with brush and soap, poured water from her pail onto the floor, took a burlap cloth and, between great huffs of breath, swung it over the tiles. She washed the cloth, twisted the water out over the pail and repeated her motions. The floor had to shine for the young visitors. Between heavy breaths, she kept her commentary going. "I told you, huh ... something good will come out of the casting out of the Evil One. And I was right ..." Folding her *gallabiah*, she tucked it between the layered flesh of her legs and it stayed tucked as she bent down to the floor, her rounded backside like a buffalo's. "Only two weeks since I went to the *Hagga*, and now your boys are coming ... uh ... May Allah bring them home safely ... uh ... Wait and see what happens to this witch, Magda!" She bent down to mop the water from the floor and her breasts overflowed the sturdy black brassiere, and rose towards her chin under her *gallabiah*. Her face reddened and beads of perspiration dripped onto the floor. Her dress got stuck at her back between her thighs, and as she swung her arm sideways to wipe under a chair, she lost her balance and fell, pulling the pail down with her, sending dirty water splashing over her bare legs and bunched-up *gallabiah*. She hauled herself up, reached her handkerchief from her bra, wiped her face and blew her nose. She replaced the kerchief into her bosom, re-tucked her wet clothes between her legs, and started drying the floor. Nadia moved chairs out of her way then returned them to their places. She knew that by the end of the day, Esmat would disappear into the bathroom, scrub herself under the hot shower, wash her clothes and emerge shiny, made up, and perfumed, but there would not be a drop of hot water left in the gas heater. So Nadia pre-empted her and entered the bathroom to shower.

The following day, Esmat punctuated her whirlwind actions with prophecies and loud singing. The woman doubled her energy, scrubbed balcony floors, shouted hilarious *salaams* to passers-by on the street, entered the rooms, changed bed-sheets, washed and put them out to dry on lines on the roof of their apartment building. She brought in her favourite electrician to fix the hot water heater in the bathroom, which he did on his first attempt, a feat only she could achieve, since workmen had to be called in several times to repair the same gadget, and each time they would find something else wrong with it, their way of breaking even with soaring inflation and the devalued pound. Only Esmat's work was perfected on the first visit.

She sat in a lotus position on the tiled floor of the bathroom, rocking, regaling the electrician with love-lyrics by the popular, now deceased singer Mohammed Abd-El-Wahab. Her *mezzo soparano* began with, "Stop kissing me in my eyes, for such kisses perplex me," her eyes and silver-black lids hinting at years of yearning, intimating she was amenable to kissing, if only from a distance. Her breasts heaved and her humming whispered secret longings. The electrician's tall, muscular body.lay back full length on the floor, his eyes glued to her, his arms stretched above his head to work on the water pipes tucked between the bathtub and the corner of the wall, his natural endowments bulging like a tempting feast in full view of Esmat's hungry gaze. His wife and four children were his security in a one-room flat, but Esmat was pleasure. In Ramadan, though, this kind of joy was illicit for a fasting man, an edict that gave him a bitter-sweet taste of guilt, rendering

Esmat's actions all the more desirable. His nerves sank into her husky voice, his eyes glued onto her heaving breasts, his forbidden pleasures a savoury richness. Nadia was talking to her mother on the telephone. "When the boys arrive, we'll come and see you," she promised. Something had to give. Nadia shouted out, "Esmat, we need a party!"

***

The two women bustled around making their preparations. People came to visit: Rana, Mr. Soliman, Sherif, Nadia's cousins. She had not heard from Yasser's family, but she knew, via Esmat and her grape-vine, Ahmed, that two men, brothers or cousins of Yasser, had gone to visit him, had been refused admission and were hoping to get in to see him. Nadia suspected they avoided her because they blamed her for not dissuading her husband from working with foreigners. Her relatives brought her Coptic icons; friends took Yasser's clothes to the Sheik to bless them; neighbours presented her with dried figs and dates of Ramadan; they gifted her coloured sugar dolls as harbingers of good will. Perhaps Yasser would be freed during the month of Ramadan, they declared, when the government releases some of its political prisoners. Other neighbours brought her baked goods for her arriving sons and bride-to-be, surrounded her with the enthusiasm widespread in the most joyous month of the year. Yet in spite of these preparations, Nadia sank deeper into anxiety dreams.

She is in a cottage in Canada. She does not recognize the area, a combination of Sauble Beach and a windy, treed sweep of sand. She wanders alone, comes upon a cottage on a stretch of land nearest the lake, or is it the sea? The Mediterranean Sea? No. Why does she think of this sea when she is looking at a cottage in Canada? A local person takes her to see a front-row cottage which she likes and she convinces Yasser to buy it. They do. It is a divine spot, but when she goes back to see it, she cannot find it. Then she sees this place for rent, a dump with small rooms occupied by vagrants. She has no recourse but to take one of the rooms. Where is Yasser? She discovers the room is uninhabitable, too close to the vagrants who come and go with strange companions, the space small, dirty floors infested with insects and cockroaches. She wants to get away. She does. She cannot remember when she wakes up.

She is in Garden City at the Kasr-El-Einy bridge in Cairo, near exotic houses of foreign delegations, immaculate gardens lush by comparison with those of local people. She chooses a lovely villa, a cross between a residence and a cottage-cum-greenhouse, on a long stretch of front-row property overlooking the Nile. The roomy house sits flat on the ground and its plants are everywhere. Pots of snapdragon, pansies, and daisies bloom in sun, ceramic pots of hibiscus and tropical plants—heavy with oil—decorate the floors and window sills. A haven. One day she returns from work and cannot find her home. It has moved, or it has been moved. Where to? Who has taken the liberty of taking her home without consulting her? Someone informs her she still has possession of the house, but it is now on another site. Who took it, she asks, which site? But he does not know. Some people came here and moved it, he says. In the meantime, in place of her home there is a wide medan *or a circle in the middle of many streets like a host of rivers pouring into a central lake. And what makes her loss so agonizing is, instead of her home with the plants and flowers, there are asphalt streets and cars and millions of vehicles like ants swallowing up the* medan. *It is no longer a sanctuary but a hive of activity, cars criss-crossing each other as they do at grand junctions of highways in Canada. Streets are not set above each other as in overpasses but pour into a central vortex. She runs away from the place and goes in search of Yasser. "Yasser! Where are you . . . o . . . . o !"*

***

Nadia called Monir and told him about the expected arrival of her sons and Laura; he informed her that two of her paintings had been sold at the exhibition, and reminded her to pick up the third and her money. She promised she would the following evening. She called Selim to inform Magda that

Amir and Samy would like to see their father. The following day Magda called and asked Nadia to meet her in a small café near Medan-El-Tahrir, close to the main shopping area, downtown Cairo. When Nadia arrived, she sat near the door at a window table. Ten minutes later, flushed and hurried, Magda burst into the café, pulled her chair out in jerky movements and sat down. Nadia sensed a new disaster lurking in Magda's worried face. Outside, the wind was high, the air dusty, the day foreboding. Nadia watched the congested crowd on the street, waited for Magda to catch her breath and break the silence. When Magda did, she placed her trembling hand on Nadia's arm, her fingers thin, the red nail-polish garish against her pale skin. In disjointed syllables, Magda told Nadia, "I have a surprise for you."

Nadia retorted, "I'm afraid of surprises. Another one would kill me," suspecting a new and felonious blow, just when her sons were arriving.

"Don't worry, it's *good* news!" Magda placed her trembling fingers on Nadia's arm. "Imagine: Yasser is free!" Tears surfaced in the woman's eyes. Nadia's spurt of energy doubled her heartbeats, flooding her mind with images of a bandaged Yasser lost on the crowded streets of Cairo. "The two lawyers you hired presented a good case, and we were able to arrange for a hearing before a private court in these last two weeks, even though it is the month of Ramadan." Magda did not specify the "we," and Nadia did not want to know. "The army ruled he had no illegal connections with the Americans," Magda continued with a smile. She dipped her hand into her crocodile-skin purse, took out a kerchief and mopped her forehead.

"The two lawyers that *I* hired?" Nadia asked.

"Yes. And Yasser had high backing in the army as well."

"Who? Mr. Abdullah?"

"No! Some people we know, from the army."

That "we" again! "When is Yasser coming home?"

"In a few days . . . two, three at the most." Magda selected a cigarette from her gold case, with trembling, manicured nails and lit it with her gold lighter. So the woman had attended the trial and Nadia, Yasser's wife, had not. Even Mr. Spencer had not been in touch with her.

"How is Yasser coming home? Who's bringing him?"

"The army."

"Are you sure he will be freed?"

Magda nodded her head several times to emphasize there was no doubt in her mind. She looked over her shoulder to check the window as though she were expecting someone to show, glanced at her watch and puffed the smoke in circles. As tears escaped from her eyes, Nadia placed her hand on Magda's arm. "Thank you. Thank you very much. You have given me wonderful news." Then, "Would you like coffee?" Magda nodded.

Would Yasser be released, or was this another hoax, Nadia wondered. Yet Magda had never given her false hope. The waiter came to their table, and Nadia ordered two cups of Turkish coffee, no sugar. The women were silent until the coffee *demi-tasses* arrived and the waiter set them down with the mandatory glasses of iced water. Magda's fingers fidgeted with her hair strands at the nape of her neck and in an inaudible voice stated, "He's a wonderful man," as though congratulating herself, or Nadia, for some attribute she did not recognize in her husband. In a louder voice, "I thought I should tell you I'm moving out . . . out of town." Her cup clattered into the saucer.

For how long, two weeks, three months, forever, Nadia wondered. Would Yasser never see Magda again? Was the woman serious and if so, what had motivated her selfless act? Lines under Magda's eyes suggested she was serious, her powder caked with perspiration. Nadia respected her will to action, but how important was she in Yasser's life, and who was her highly placed helper?

Nadia said, "If there's anything I can do for *you*, I'd want to know . . . " The woman shook her head. They sipped their coffee. The woman's pallor suggested exhaustion, or worse.

What kind of life had she had, and why was she willing to move away and surrender Yasser? When they had finished their coffee, Magda fumbled with her cigarette case and started to say something, then changed her mind. She smiled; Nadia smiled back. Magda crushed her cigarette into the ashtray, opened her handbag, took a red comb and matching brush, fluffed her hair and renewed her lipstick, actions few women did in public. She set her image in order with scrupulous attention to detail, as though her expected rendezvous was important, and what people thought of her was not her problem. She smiled again and Nadia nodded in acknowledgement. They watched the crowds out of the window until the waiter came and Nadia tipped him, then Magda left the restaurant and Nadia followed the woman's back as it receded on the pavement. Soon, the emerald green dress was swallowed by the crowd.

Nadia hoped this would be the last time Magda would cross their lives, but she did not know whether the woman had made such a promise. Like a well-rooted mint, Magda could take hold and re-surface in their lives. Yet, as the green dress vanished, Nadia felt a chunk of her life was passing away. She had not thanked the woman nor taken proper leave of her; she recalled her own unanswered questions. Which day would Yasser be released? What time? What had he done? What happened at his trial? Would there be a penalty attached to his freedom? He was *her* husband and *she* did not know. She leaped out of the restaurant in pursuit of Magda. But the green dress reached the curb and disappeared into a taxi that merged with the procession of cars. Disquietude settled in on Nadia. She wondered if Selim had the information she needed. She caught the bus home.

As she entered her apartment, the telephone rang. Mr. Spencer wanted to inform her that his negotiations with the Egyptian Government had been fruitful. Yasser would be returning home in a few days, but he did not know which one. Then Mr. McKinnon called: did she know that the American

Embassy had been able to extract Yasser from his difficulties? An hour later, Mr. Abdullah called to congratulate her on her husband's pending freedom and to emphasize he had gone to army and police officials and delivered Yasser from a very unfortunate misunderstanding. He was happy to tell her that Yasser would be arriving home the day after tomorrow. By this time, Nadia knew that each official would claim credit for Yasser's release, and she would receive no insights into the events leading up to his freedom. *Would* he be released? She did not know what had happened behind the scenes, if there had been a formal hearing, how the charges against him had been resolved before the army high court hearing which was scheduled for the week before the feast of Ramadan; and, perhaps, she would never know. Did Yasser know? Why was Magda at the centre of the action? She wondered what the newspapers would say, after the fact, whether *Al Ahram* would acknowledge Yasser's release, say he was incarcerated as a political prisoner, or define his time in hospital as a period of recuperation.

Nadia wanted Yasser home. She would prepare for his arrival without fanfare until he was safe in their apartment. When her mother and Sherif called, she told them she wanted to keep things quiet until after Yasser's arrival. When Esmat heard the news, she flopped down on the kitchen mat and wept. She held out her hands, palms facing the ceiling in supplication to heaven and said, "*Ashkorak, ya Rub, Allah* be praised, God Almighty is merciful!" She wiped her eyes and nose with her handkerchief and rocked, prayed and mumbled words about the soothsayer. Then she pressed her head between her palms, closed her eyes, and recited her *sourahs*.

Nadia called Monir. "I need to see you."

"I heard the news," he affirmed. "My friend in the police force told me about your husband's release." His voice reached her from a distance. She told him she would be at his studio that evening to pick up her money and unsold painting.

***

At night, after her life's commotion had subsided, a nagging silence oppressed Nadia. Esmat was spending the evening with her children. Filled with a strange sense of foreboding, Nadia got dressed and went to Monir's studio. He stood at the door, his eyes avoiding hers. She knew she had no right to be there, yet she needed to be near him. She walked to the sofa and sat down, stretched her legs on the cushions and lay down. He turned the radio on to a local station and withdrew behind his desk, his pencil scratching paper. A flute moaned on the radio.

"Is your son coming home? It is the end of the university year," she began.

Monir maintained his concentration on the drawing for a while, then he put his pencil down. "No. He isn't. He wants to travel and do some free-lance reporting. He wants to go to Lebanon, with all its upheaval! Perhaps this is its attraction." He studied his palm as though examining his life signs.

She surrendered to the silence, got up, picked up *Al Ahram* and leafed through it without deciphering the words. She murmured, "I feel there is something coming towards me, as though the sky would open and deliver much that is unwelcome. I don't know why. Yasser is coming home the day after tomorrow; Samy, Amir and his fiancée, Laura, are arriving the day after. What more do I want?" A wave of excitement rolled over, drowning her; she had to go away, avoid everyone. She was saying, "Maybe I should take Yasser and our sons to the Delta Barrage to avoid the mess here." He nodded, his eyes down.

"But I will miss you," and before she had said the words, she was crying. She had crashed the silence between them, ripped the translucent veil that shielded them from each other. He bent his head over his work. His voice came out of limbo. "Trying to be what others expect us to be is difficult." He was in a space she dare not touch. He continued in a subdued voice, "When I was a teen, about sixteen or so, my friends spent afternoons walking on the Cornice in Alexandria. You know how the rails overlook the sea high above the beach, so you can perch on them and watch the girls on the sand below, then you can turn around and whistle to those passing by you on the pavement."

He sketched for a while then said, "We—my friends and I—used to sit on the rails with our backs to the sea. We watched the girls go by on the pavement. They brought their friends and paraded in sexy clothes for our benefit, or perhaps for their own. Of course, this was before women wore *gallabiahs* and veils. We sat on the rails, and as wind hit our backs we whistled to them and told loud sexy jokes to get the girls' attention; when we failed to get it, we made disparaging remarks about them: how ugly this one was, how fat the other, and this rankled them, so they answered back, and we provoked a conversation. A great pastime for young men who were not permitted to talk to girls. My friends loved it."

He looked up. They smiled. "But," he said, "I was frustrated. These encounters were meaningless, and I began to avoid my friends. I was uncomfortable because at that age, I did not like what we were doing but believed I had no alternative." He pushed the sketch away from him and examined its lines. He resumed drawing. "I had one good friend. He was shy, not loud and brash like the others. Sometimes we went with fishermen in their sailing boats outside the harbour into the open sea. Although we knew nothing about fishing, we wanted to handle the ropes and clean the fish. The fishermen gave us a few of their catch, and with the money we got from selling the fish, we bought second-hand books that vendors sold on straw mats on the Cornice. We spent afternoons reading Naguib Mahfouz and Tewfick El Hakim, and the torrid sections in the works of Ihsan Abdel Khodous. After three years of closeness with this friend, I turned my back on him, because others made fun of us, and I started to fear I was gay, since we were close, and I did not like the preoccupations of my companions. Years later, after I had met my wife, and when we had had our son, I realized why these diversions had not appealed to me. I discovered art and *it* was world enough for me. Even now, there are days when I prefer to be in my studio than with others, for the world of art and exhibitions can stand between me and my work. Yet, it's a lonely life." He concentrated on his sketch. Now he had spoken, she felt less desolate. "So when a person fills my life with her presence, I'm grateful for the hours and minutes she spends with me."

She responded, "And *she* stepped into your world and found it hers, discovered in you a long lost brother and lover." Fearing she had said too much, she stopped but was compelled to continue, "When I'm here, I'm at rest. My life is coherent. I do not hear the noise on the street, nor notice the flurry in my life. You have a torch and the corners of my life are illumined!" He came over and sat beside her, his knee brushing her leg. He bent his head over his hands. She continued, "But this closeness between us is unreal." He looked at her and she added, "Yasser and my sons are flesh and blood. They are my reality. They prove I'm here on this earth, in this body, part of our moving species. You know what I mean when you talk about your son, or mention your wife." He nodded. "With Yasser, my reality comes alive for he is the father of my children. We struggled together, and I find I can put my art aside to look after him, although, now that he is broken and distant, I don't know . . ." She was rushing downstream. "When I'm here, I look around your studio and wonder if I've abandoned my life and camouflaged it with an acquired one. Right now, I feel that art is real, that the life I made for myself—my husband and children—is a smokescreen to hide reality. Are we, artists, staying on solid ground so we do not get too close to the centre—as did Icarus, or Jackson Pollock, Van Gogh—and like them burn at the edge of fire?"

A vortex pulled her inwards. She struggled to untangle meaning. "I ask, am I an escapist running away from my destiny and from the razor edge of my isolation, or is my life with my husband and sons real? I don't know any more." Images accelerated in her mind; pictures she had stored spilled out. Moving closer, he touched her hair and passed his fingers over her face, outlining her mouth, picking up her hands in his, bending his face over them as if trying to find the origin of life in the lines of her skin. "For me you are both. You're my reality, and you're the woman in my life." After reflection he said, "But I must let you go." His touch steadied her, but his words sent a shiver through her. She mumbled, "Both of us have to let go," and removed her hand from his grasp. But then her fingers moved towards his face, removed his glasses and he winced, as though someone had taken away his shield. He brought his head closer to hers. Now he could not study her face, he would feel it. Their foreheads met. His hair lay on hers, their hands rested together, their faces close, their shoulders getting closer. The half of her that had been missing was merging with her. Their lips touched, their hands sought each other's backs, their bodies met. They swayed, picked up a rhythm complementing their lips and hands. They held on as though afraid to let go, then they peeled off each other's clothes; face to face they were unaware of the narrow sofa, she in a flow that commanded her body, sinking her into the river, lulled by the rushing currents, he embracing her into his world, taking her into himself, her hair, cheeks, eyes, shoulders, navel, back, knees, toes, pacifying her in a limbo where he and she existed for each other and felt the wholeness of their being. Their union was to last and be contained forever. Her breasts, her hair, he took into himself, until she became his, then he entered her, holding and seeking the woman he wanted. Neither felt the cold tiles on the floor where they had slipped off the sofa. They were safe and at a distance from tangible objects. Sounds from the open balcony door did not reach them. She floated with his love. She was chaff on the river moving towards the ocean, rushing, resting, at home, knowing that in this action lay her peace and quiet. She did not want to get to the ocean, because in getting there she would have to return. So she flowed, touching every muscle in his body, feeling his ribs press her abdomen, her legs locked around his, her toes pushing against his holding her up to him. His soft hair fell on her forehead. Their interlocking transported her to a place, somehow familiar, also unknown, because never before had she felt so much herself. They held each other and did not move for fear of disrupting their configuration. Cold air brushed her skin; she lay on the carpet, his body over hers, his face on her neck, his eyes closed; she did not awaken him.

When she opened her eyes again, she was covered with bed-sheets and Monir was at his desk. She got up, wrapped the bed-sheets around her, tiptoed to the bathroom. She had no business being there. On her way back into his room, she stood by his chair, but he did not look up and continued drawing. Her leave-taking would be smooth, as though this were one day of many they would spend together, so she picked up her handbag and turned to leave. His scattered things in the room sheltered her, his paintings, drawings, sofa, radio, plants, books, cushions, the half-faded maroon carpet, wicker newspaper holder, were all here, and *she* had to go. She walked back to his chair, pressed her palm on his shoulder, fluttered her fingers over his hair, brushed her lips over its strands, turned and went out of the door. He continued drawing.

***

Nadia woke up at daybreak and blocked the previous night from her mind as she baked bread with Esmat. At eight, she went down to see a florist. A big man in a tan *gallabiah* greeted her at the door of his tiny shop and showed her variations of gladiolus, snapdragon, roses in large pots on the floor. Wild flowers and green shoots lay on wet moss at the back of the store. No refrigerator, nor air-conditioning, some flowers wilting in the heat. She asked if she could choose a dozen roses, and he nodded, but by the time she had picked three he had completed the bunch with others that were open or drooping.

"*Someone* has to take the open ones," he grumbled, not by way of apology, but assertively as if she had plundered his shop. What indeed would the man do if everyone chose the fresh flowers and left the not-so-fresh ones to die? The same thing happened when she asked for red and white carnations. Yet the man relented a little and let her choose the jasmine to show her he bore her no ill will, and he added half fresh leafy stalks and decorated those with baby's breath, then offered to wrap the whole with a large red ribbon. She declined the ribbon. He asked, "Where do you come from, Lady, from America?"

"From Cairo," she said with a smile. "I was born here; I grew up here."

"No Madam, you're not from this street. You arrived a few months ago. I know all the people who live in our quarter."

"I've lived here the first part of my life. Now, I come from Canada," she admitted, nonplussed. The man nodded with satisfaction.

"I hope you hear good news about your husband, *Kul sana wa enty tayiba*, many happy returns of the season," he said as he wrapped her flowers in cellophane paper instead of the usual newspaper. He knew her, so how many others on the street did? Men sitting on chairs on pavements at cafés had watched when she walked by. This would explain why she had this uncanny feeling that someone was following her. Perhaps they had known her all along. She might look different from local women, or Esmat might have blurted out the story to a local admirer. The florist knew she was not from Cairo even though her features and skin-tone were typically Egyptian. She did not know if she was safe or if these people were hostile towards her. The man appeared sincere in his good wishes. She took her flowers, paid and tipped him, left the store, and hurried past the cafés to her apartment building.

On her way home, she dared not look at the seller of carob juice ringing his bells with his big round glass container strapped to his shoulders, its white foam topping the burgundy drink; she did not pay attention to the sugarcane juice seller who carried his ware in the same manner, neither did she stop to buy her watermelon seeds from the small shop—a one-person Canadian telephone-booth size—for all she wanted was to get off the street. Back in her apartment, she arranged the carnations in earthenware pots on side tables in the hall and balcony. She blocked out her memory of Monir sitting at his desk; she had betrayed Yasser on the eve of his return, but she knew she would not return to Monir's studio. Selecting a flowering jasmine, she placed it in a small vase on Yasser's night table. She showered, brushed her hair, swept it to one side, attached a jasmine to her left shoulder, put the remaining jasmines in a ceramic vase on the dresser. The flowers were to remind her of her nights with Yasser at their Delta home, but all they did was spell out her duplicity. From the kitchen, Esmat's baked lamb and potatoes filled the apartment with its homemade aroma, Yasser's favourite meal. Nadia waited on the balcony, her eyes registering a blueness.

Towards mid-afternoon, an army jeep screeched to a halt at the door of her apartment building and before it stopped, soldiers jumped out and hollered at each other in raspy sentences. Neighbours bent over their balcony rails to check the action; children gathered around the jeep. Finally, Yasser's head appeared out of the door of the vehicle as he stepped down to the street in a brown suit, no bandages.

"Esmat!" Nadia yelled through the open balcony door, "*He's here!*"

Esmat's ululations pierced the air as she burst into the balcony rolling her tongue and producing a shrill sound that travelled down to the people on the street. The uniformed men looked up, smiled, jumped back into the jeep, roared away in their vehicle sending the wheels spiralling dust into the air.

The two women rushed down the stairs and met Yasser at the door of the building. Nadia opened her arms and drew her husband in; Esmat wiped her eyes on the corner of her shawl and sobbed. She bent and kissed Yasser's right hand, then held his arm and helped him up the three flights of stairs. As they

reached their floor, neighbours' ululations poured out of the
open doors, heads bobbed over the rails. Yasser nodded and
waved to no one in particular, then entered the apartment.
Nadia stayed behind to thank the neighbours for their baskets
of dried fruits and home-baked goods left at their apartment
door. Once the three of them and the baskets were inside the
apartment, she drew the door shut. Yasser was safe on the sofa,
his hair almost white. Placing the gift baskets on the table, she
sat by his side, her body trembling. Her inner spring of energy
alerted her she had much to do. She hugged him, placing her
hand on his ailing arm and asking, "Do you want something
to eat? Esmat has lamb and potatoes in the oven."

He shook his head. "They gave me a big breakfast of eggs
and coffee in the officer's room before they packed me off!" he
said, his lips parting in a stiff smile. She pressed his arm. He
bent his head forward but did not touch her, his face thin, his
hair uneven at the nape of his neck.

"Nobody's going to come here until you've rested!" she comforted him. He nodded. "Besides, we need to give you a hair-cut
and face-lift!" Nadia continued with a half laugh. He shook his
head as though to say, you have no idea. Esmat brought a large
plastic bowl of warm water, a bar of soap, a jar of moisturizer, a
towel, and set them at Yasser's feet. She untied his shoes, took off
his socks, set his feet into the bowl and massaged his toes in the
soapy warmth. Then rinsing them with fresh water from a jug,
she dried, turning them over as though they were short bread,
she spread cream on his skin, put his socks back on, set his feet
into his slippers. She heaved a sigh and pushed the bowl under
the sofa where she sat at his feet. Nadia served iced mango *sharbat* reserved for feasts. The three drank.

***

Monir stood on the balcony of his studio looking down at
the crowds below him in the street. He would lose her forever,
that he knew. He would never return from work to his studio
and smell her coffee brewing.

***

Magda watched her father as she told him of her illness. Like shooting bullets, his eyes pierced hers and held them. He was angry with her, for being *sick*? Or was he mad at the powers that plagued her with cancer in her thirties? "Which doctor did you go to? Why did you not tell me?"

"Doctor Aziz," she answered, ignoring his second question. He glared at her. "*When* did you go? Why did the man not call me? I saw him ten days ago at the grocer's!" He pounded the table and a blue vein stood out on his temple. Dr. Aziz was not crazy to tell *him* the news, thought Magda.

"I went to him last week," she lied. Her father must hold her responsible for contracting cancer, as he believed, from her lovers, or he could be frightened at the possibility of getting the illness himself from some creepy reptile that would slide off her over to him, the way he had behaved when his brother was sick. People tended to believe that cancer was infectious so they do not hold themselves responsible for a life-style that might have helped trigger the dormant illness. They avoided thinking of their genetic weaknesses because they reminded them they too were at risk. She must have drunk and smoked herself into this abyss. She remembered her favourite uncle who had died of cancer, but she had not heeded the warning of his life. Her father stomped across the room but did not utter a word, just like him to fail her when she needed him. He did not touch her, not that she would have wanted him to. He stood by the window of his living room with his back to her. He might get into another fit as he stared at his face in the glass, or he might ignore her. She was in a jungle surrounded by wild, poisonous shrubs, her body in pain, her father a fierce animal king who ruled by sheer power, carried a grudge for no reason; she would lie and die without his turning around and seeing her.

***

Nadia and Yasser entered their bedroom. The jasmine triggered in him a faint memory of a forgotten past. She knew he was too tired to shower, so she damp-clothed his face and hands, helped him into his pyjamas, held the bed-sheets up as he slid in, covered him, drew the balcony and window shutters together, kissed him.

"We have so much to talk about. When you've had a good sleep we will. Happy homecoming!" She placed her hand on his arm. He held his other arm up to her until his fingers reached her head, brought her face down, placed a kiss on her cheek and let go. She tiptoed out the room and telephoned people to let them know that Yasser had arrived. To relatives and friends, she said she would be having a celebration as soon as he had recuperated. Magda was not in when Nadia called to thank her.

Down the street Nadia went from shop to shop to pick up her groceries, filling her arms with mangoes, cucumbers, lettuce, apricots, everything that had the flavour of the Nile. She bought steaming Arabic loaves puffed up with heat and ran back home, careless of honking cars, unmindful of onrushing buses, not worrying about a strawberry falling from her nylon mesh bag, not even fearing the stray dogs, nor men's suspicious eyes, just focusing on the road ahead, her urgent need to get the food to her apartment for her husband and sons.

***

Chapter Fourteen

Gladiolus

Nadia threw open the shutters of her bedroom window and a burst of sunshine lit her bedroom, but a thin veil of dust covered the scenery. Even here at the Delta Barrage, in the fourth week of March, the *Khamseen* winds were tangible with desert sand. The family had decided to leave Cairo and return to the Delta Barrage to avoid the hot winds that had swept the city and filled their rooms and balconies with sand. A beige film had settled on floors, furniture and window sills; even though Nadia and Esmat had swept daily the sand piled up on the balconies and blew in through the wood shutters into the apartment. They decided to move to the Delta, but Esmat remained in Old Shoubra, in Cairo, for a couple of weeks with her children.

Nadia waltzed about their Delta home dotting it with pots of jasmine, re-arranging furniture, dusting shutters, cleaning floors, her hands revolving around the rooms as on a potter's wheel, her fingers creating harmony of furniture, garden and food. The jasmine she arranged with care, even though it reminded her of her vulnerability. She began early in the morning so Amir, Samy and Yasser could have a quiet time together in the afternoon. Laura—shy, soft-spoken, tall, with hazel eyes, light brown hair, bangs over her forehead, soft sandals which she had purchased from Khan-El-Khalili Bazaar—moved around the kitchen preparing vegetable and fruit salads, and Nadia allowed her the space to get used to her new environment. A biologist, Laura conducted experiments in Canada to create ozone-friendly products for the garden; her cotton dress sprinkled with forget-me-nots, her bronze hair in shiny strands rivalling the polished copper of carved plant-holders, her brown sandals displaying clean-cut toe-nails, no polish.

At their Delta home, the Khamseen winds were subdued; numerous acacia trees surrounded their walls protecting
them from dust. Amir helped Laura prepare salads and wash
dishes, the type of house-work his father was under no compulsion to share. During meals Amir studied his father, and
after, kept his distance from him by reading a medical book
under the trees. He did not think it right that his father had
kept his business connections secret from him, from his
brother and their mother, had not shared his thoughts with
them, nor taken time to explain his situation. When Amir and
his brother were young, he remembered his father as aloof, lost
in his world of work, even though he sometimes found time
to accompany Samy to his soccer games. A gulf of silence had
grown between Amir and his father ever since he could
remember, but Samy's sense of humour had broken through
their father's smoke-screen even if for a few moments. Yasser
preferred the way Samy cajoled and needled him, but Amir
refused to coddle or humour, since he deserved to be taken
seriously, and his father had had no time for that. His mother
had listened, but his father followed what went on in his own
mind.

Recently, when Samy talked to their father, he too
received short answers as Yasser murmured under his breath
and deflected his questions. Once, as Samy and his father sat
on the wood bench under the acacia, he raised his voice at
their father, but Yasser had bent his head and said nothing.
Most of the time, he preferred to be alone on the balcony. On
the rare afternoon, he went down to the garden to help
Nessim water climbers and trees, to feed the chickens, but
these activities were a recent phenomenon he had acquired to
camouflage his preoccupations from his family.

Nadia did not know what Yasser had told their sons about
his detention, but she had explained to them that after the
shooting, army personnel had questioned Yasser in hospital
about his role in the Egyptian-American negotiations and had
found him innocent. Amir's face had distanced itself in

despair; Samy's hurt expression revealed he was in a sea deeper than he had contemplated. Nadia examined the cultural gulf that separated Yasser's predicament from his sons' sympathy and realized that her attempts at bridging the gap between them were futile. Their sons demanded to know the compelling reasons that had driven their father to involve himself in a scene so alien, and to what purpose? Was he planning to single-handedly change the customs of thousands of years of history, or the way seventy million people lived? For them, Egypt was an experience, not a soil harbouring generations of family roots and decades of nostalgic memories, and this gulf was bound to remain part of their family dynamic.

Most days, Nadia began painting at six in the morning in the bedroom balcony. When she placed her brush on canvas, Yasser's face emerged with a scar on the left of his forehead, grey hair on temples, caged look in his eyes, shoulders bent as though he had been on a year-long safari in the desert, unwashed, un-cared for. The background in the paintings—a desert, a cave, the turquoise-brown Nile—contrasted with Yasser's aura, his grey hair emphasized the shadows under his startled eyes. The orange-red of the flowering poinsettias, the deep olive of palms, the crimson dates, aqua sea, opaque brown-turquoise of the Nile River rose from the canvas like songs of praise. She filled her painting with yellow flowers, lilacs, blues, snapdragons dancing Chagall-like in a midnight blue horizon. Land, sea, sky hugged his pale face with their startling hues, anointed him with energy, re-created new life in his wary eyes. Painting is magic, Nadia thought, and a shaman uses it to heal a person's body and mind, her own and another's. She was casting a spell on Yasser, to lift him from his dejection, to merge him with the land of the living, make him re-enter his family circle with peace. One painting she lingered over was of his face emerging from the Nile, water drops splashing his smooth, brown skin, wrinkles washed away. Moved by energetic winds from the river, crimson hibiscus shot out of the water and danced around him. When would his suffering end? She recalled an afternoon a few days ago at the Delta Barrage, when she had taken Yasser to the river, washed his face, hands and feet with water from a bucket Samy had lifted from the Nile—Nadia's ritual act of cleansing Yasser's suffering. Amir and Laura stood apart, unsure of the ritual, until Samy pushed his brother into the water and Amir retaliated, then both carried Laura in. Their splashing had rid them of the heat, left them sticky, so they had fought for the shower upon their return home.

Afternoons, when the sun shone between acacia leaves, Yasser sat on the garden bench, surrendering to the warm rays. His skin changed from pale to tan. Nadia brewed mint tea, sat by him and reminisced about times when Samy—joined on occasion by Amir—had played soccer, and Nadia and Yasser had driven to parks to watch them play. These had been their least self-conscious days.

Nadia awaited the jasmine buds to release their fragrance, even though their aroma filled her with an uneasy peace. Yasser had yet to share with her the events of his shooting and incarceration. She painted faces of men and women, eyes sinking inwards, working out insoluble puzzles. Yasser's movements had slowed down, his head hung low as though contemplating great theories of the universe; he was quiet during meals. When she looked up from her canvas or pulled bread out of the oven, she surprised a look in his eyes as though remembering something, but he interrupted his thoughts to give her a fleeting smile. Other times he winced as from physical pain. Was his arm bothering him? Were his memories? She wished he would join her on the trip to the source of the Nile. Whenever Monir's image broke into her world, she set it aside, like packaging jewels in a safe, or placing them under a loose tile in the basement. He was the river that had mirrored her reality, but perhaps its crystalline clarity was a narcissistic mirage.

Yasser had reading glasses made and in the afternoons perused the paper or played backgammon with his sons. He challenged Laura to a game of cards, and she offered him tea with biscuits. They drank and ate together, the game a bond of peace between them. She helped him in the garden. When she and Amir went out, Samy played chess with his father. Esmat arrived and filled the house with the aroma of her daily-baked bread and cakes. Laura picked up Esmat's recipes, and Nadia became used to Laura's presence in the kitchen.

When Amir and Laura's wedding announcement came it turned the house into a whirlwind. They would be married in Egypt in ten days, then upon their return to Canada they would hold a reception for her family. The household rang with joy. In ten days! Little time left for invitations and preparations. The Khamseen winds had died down and the family returned to Cairo where Nadia's world opened up. She would prepare the finest wedding for her first born. Esmat broke out into ululations; Yasser discussed arrangements for the wedding with Laura and Amir; Samy regaled them with his corny jokes. Looking at his brother then at Laura, he said, "Just before we came to Egypt, I was in a restaurant and a man and a woman were eating fruit. The man attacked his apple as if he could not wait to get to its core, while his wife peeled her banana and ate it in lingering bites, as if she did not want it to end!" He paused and stared at them, "It occurred to me that when people eat fruit, the man opts for an apple, the woman for a banana. Why?" Laura and Amir laughed. Mimicking his brother's baritone, Amir answered, "Because a circle and a rod fit well together!" Samy laughed the loudest.

Amir and Laura ran out to visit Nadia's mother and Yasser's brothers; they toured Cairo Museum. Yasser had not seen his brothers and cousins since their visit in hospital, so he called his family in Ismailia and invited them to the wedding. He called Nadia's mother, her cousin Sherif and other relatives to apologize that, due to the slow pace of the mail, they had had no time to send out proper invitations. By accepting this hurried wedding, he was conceding many of his expectations for his son, but its taking place in Egypt had made up for the concessions. Between phone calls to relatives and friends, he moved around the apartment, head bent, legs stiff, bandaged left arm painful, propelling himself to action, his energy and will too weak for life. But something beckoned him on: for Amir's sake, for Samy's sake. Through hazy days, gun-shots burst into his consciousness; images of a pale Magda followed him, her footsteps tracking his path as in fog, sounding in the crunch of gravel under his feet.

Nadia invited those who had supported her in Yasser's absence: Rana, Mr. Soliman, even Mr. Spencer and the Abdullahs, although she suspected the last two would not show. Her good-will gesture was her way of thanking the people in power. She wrote Monir a hasty note about the wedding celebration, suspecting he too would not attend. With help from Esmat, Rana volunteered to make flower arrangements for the bride and bridesmaids; Nadia's mother offered them her home for the reception; Sherif arranged for taxis and limousine; Yasser reserved a date for the ceremony at the Mena House Hotel at the Pyramids; the reception at Nadia's mother's place in Heliopolis would be on the opposite end of the huge metropolis. Esmat began a marathon baking session creating a six-tier wedding cake with white icing, sugar dolls and copious flowers. Nadia made arrangements with a Heliopolis caterer for dinner to be served under a large canvas tent in her mother's garden. Sherif set up the canvas, a hand-painted stitched cotton, with multi-coloured arabesque designs for wedding celebrations. For two days, Esmat and Nadia prepared *kahk* using a *manaash*—a decorative tweezer—to pinch the dough into grooves which they would fill with icing sugar. As their hands patted and pinched the designs, Esmat wiped the flour off the table, filled her mouth with roasted almonds, crunched them with zest, bent over to Nadia and whispered, "May Allah be praised. The day of the wedding will be the first day of the feast of Ramadan. We think things just happen, but Allah has reasons. Blessed be the One and Only." Esmat had ended her fast and eaten her copious meal an hour earlier, but she continued snacking on the almonds, an expensive luxury. "You know that wicked woman, you know what I hear? She's very ill. May Allah protect us, but she's in hospital with that vicious illness. May Allah never have reason to visit us with such misery! She has a bad growth, and they cannot do anything, because it has spread all over. Allah, the Gracious One, has punished her for her sins!" Nadia's stomach twisted into knots at the thought of Magda's illness; but Esmat, with the air of one secure in her faith, smacked the dough into an oval shape on her hand, picked up the *manaash*, pinched the dough into a floral design, placed it with loving care on the greased baker's sheet which she would bake in the local oven. Order was restored to her world, she would pursue her life with confidence in the key role she played in the universe. Nadia thought, so this is why Magda had lost so much weight: she was dying of cancer. Guilt swept over her, as though she had wished this illness upon her rival.

When she climbed into bed that night, she gathered Yasser to her with renewed awareness of his pain, even as she felt a lingering hatred and jealousy of Magda. But the woman was dying; she would slip out of their lives as she had come in, without announcement or reason. Nadia pushed the thought of Monir away: that chapter was closed. At the time she had been under duress. She lay her body over Yasser's, supported herself on her elbows to avoid pressing his arm and shoulder. She caressed his scar, kissed his lips. He responded. She changed places with him, her fingers fluttered over his shoulder and back. He gave and received with an intensity she had not felt since his return from hospital. She was closer to him, he to her. Yasser accepted Nadia's love as his mind wandered to Amir's wedding, a landmark in their lives. He drifted into sleep.

Magda is standing on the deck of a drenched boat, in a dark see-through Pharaonic tunic with a burning diamond tiara in her black hair, her body lithe and warm, her eyes other-worldly. She approaches him, bends close, her hair falling over his fore-

head, gives him a crunchy kiss, her teeth spilling out of her gaping mouth. She presses his back against the rails and sea foam splashes up into the boat and drenches his back and feet. His head is thrown back so his neck almost snaps, but his body surges back to life. He snatches his arm away from her, then feels pain running through his muscles. She opens her mouth and reveals her crumbling teeth. She is a panther, a jumping hyena wanting to lie with him, she would throw him into the waves. He shouts, "No, no!" and stretches his arm to avert her animal spring.

He awoke and sat up in the dark. Nadia touched his arm. "Are you okay? Do you want some tea?"

"No, I'm fine," he answered, his limbs trembling. He shook his head to wake up, then said, "I'm the one who used her." He had spoken aloud. Nadia withdrew her hand from his arm. "I convinced myself she was an easy woman, but she was unwell, and she may have known this all along. I hated her!" Words tumbled out, "Her father is the high-ranking General in the army who helped me get my freedom. He's the one who arranged for the hearing." Yasser had not referred to the woman by name. So Magda's father was the army man behind the scenes making arrangements with the army, and Yasser's freedom was *her* wish.

"She's dying," he said. Nadia lay back. "I've messed things up!" he concluded.

Guilt stifled Nadia. She had not told him about Monir and would not tell him now, yet he had to know. She had made a terrible mistake sending Monir that note with her mother's address and an invitation to the reception. A stupid act; an impulse.

"So have I," she answered him. "I'm not faultless. When people have been married for as long as we, temptation is bound to pop up." He did not respond, perhaps he had not heard her. She pressed on, "We'll talk about things as soon as Amir's wedding is over. Do you realize it's the day after tomorrow?"

***

At the foot of the Giza plateau, the old mansion of the Mena House Hotel sparkled with white bulbs hanging over its front door, and sprinkled through the branches of its acacia trees. The *mashrabiah* designs of the windows grounded the building into its Islamic history, so you could almost envisage a veiled woman standing behind the elaborate wood design, peeping out on the world from a small opening in the wood, her face and body barred from the eyes of watchful men on the street. Around the tables near the swimming pool, guests glimpsed the three pyramids across the road on the hill in the distance, the three dark triangles towering over the surrounding low land, and between the pyramids and the hotel palm trees fringed the view down to the foot of the hill. The wedding party gathered around the gilt bridal thrones to congratulate Laura and Amir. Inflated with pride, and aware of her stately dignity, Esmat wedged her body between the tables, held her breasts out, conscious of her new wedding dress and her regal appeal, flaunted the gold necklace and earrings which the family had given her. She saw herself as proprietress of the evening and conducted herself in like manner. Re-arranging Laura's satin dress and gauze veil, she stood by her side as though she were the mother of the copper-headed bride.

Wearing a white carnation, Samy, as best man, ushered the visitors to their tables. Although he did not know many of them, he greeted each person with the same cheerful *"Ahlan wa sahlan"*—the few words he had mastered in Arabic—with the gallantry of an honoured lord. He led them to their tables, recognized some of the members of his father's family, for he had seen his two uncles in Egypt several years ago when he was a teenager. He recalled the dark eyes, thick eyebrows, tall bodies that had grown up in the salty air of the Mediterranean Sea. Unlike Amir, he could not speak Arabic but he understood it; his father's relatives did not know many words in English, so he communicated with them through gestures and a sprinkling of words from the two languages. He waved to the seated guests as he passed by.

Esmat was satisfied with her choice of bridal chairs—imitations of Tutankhamun's ancient gold throne—behind which she and her girls, Roda and Rasha, had placed arrangements of giant gladiolas and jasmine fanning out like peacocks' feathers. They had arranged the green leaves in the shape of an extended feather fan, then decorated them with the flowers.

Samy chatted in English with the guests around Laura and Amir. He seated people in groups around the pool to drink orange *sharbat,* a special drink for festivities, and to eat the *kahk* Esmat and Nadia had prepared. Esmat spread out the tulle of Laura's veil in a circle, patted it into position, arranged the bride's curls at the nape of her neck, tucked in her headdress of baby's breath at her forehead and to one side of her face. Laura's blue eyes and pale pink make-up contrasted with the dense pearl designs of her dress and veil which Esmat had helped her choose. The bride was decked out like a Ramadan sugar doll, frills and pearly twists included, the way Esmat envisioned her, except that the bride's copper hair was a unique feature. Amir, handsome and slim in his dark suit, translated the guests' remarks to his bride. Surprised by Laura and Amir's decision to hold their wedding in Cairo, Samy concluded that his brother concealed a grudging respect for the city, or he may have made this decision to cheer up their father. Samy seated his father at the head of a long table with his brothers and relatives on each side of him in clan-like manner. He was proud of his father's status as oldest member of his family. Glowing in her lilac outfit, his mother sat at his father's immediate left, and Samy's chair was farther down the table to his right.

Signalling the end of the formal part of their wedding, Amir and Laura moved to one side of the garden to the small table where they signed their documents. Guests gathered around the entrance of the hotel garden to fill the waiting cars and to form a procession from Giza to Heliopolis on the south-eastern edge of the city. As Esmat's ululations sliced the cool night air, Samy, with help from the bridesmaids, ushered the couple into their carnation-decked limousine. Behind them, visitors' vehicles formed a long line, their honking horns filling the air with their dissonant jubilation. Samy climbed into his parents' car and headed the procession out behind the limo.

***

In her father's house, Magda tore her letters, pictures, old clothes into shreds and threw them into the kitchen garbage can, where she was sure her father would not see them. She did not want him to get into her cupboard later. Her father's handling of her things would be a travesty of a life she had lived alone, away from his ominous shadow. She packed her nightgown, toothpaste and brush, make-up, and a Chanel Eau-De-Toilette bottle that Yasser had given her in Mariout. She placed a few personal needs in a small air-flight bag to take to the Italian hospital. As her fingers moved to destroy what she owned, her mind lingered on Mariout. She meandered through the dream she had shared with Yasser in her hide-away, the place she liked even though she had spent lonely summers there as a child. It was where she had invited Yasser to stay with her for four days, while her father was on army duty in Sinai. That was one week to the day before Yasser was shot. In the small, one-floor villa, they had been close.

The ochre walls of the villa were smudged from unrelenting neglect and the furniture dusty, even though the bedouin porter had cleaned it. The place was her paternal grandmother's, a woman Magda had loved as a child. Her grandmother's huge photograph hung in the main hall: a small woman, her clothes flowing to the floor, her home full of comfortable, flowery sofas and chairs. Even then, dust had curled under her furniture and in the corners of rooms, cobwebs had hung from ceilings. In her grandmother's time, the villa was far from immaculate, but their days together were peaceful. They had sat on the veranda or walked in the sand dunes behind the villa, and Magda had sat on the floor as her grandmother knelt on her prayer carpet five times a day. Her grandmother had not been one to worry about material details, but she cared about essentials: prayer, food, solitude. She had not pushed Magda, as though she believed her own prayers were strong enough for the two. The place harboured her grandmother's peaceful presence. Magda and Yasser had sat on the balcony, looked out on the palms and cacti that spotted the sand. Yasser had not talked much, but late at night, they had made love on the couch in the veranda, lain side by side in the huge bed, and she had had that strange feeling that they would always be together, asking for everything in love, needing little else.

***

Nadia sat close to Yasser in the limo. Inside the carnation-decked car ahead, she could see the bridal veil and Amir's dark hair. The two cars remained close to battle downtown traffic, a bridal procession being one of few rituals for which Egyptian drivers conceded the right of way. Women rolled down their windows and shouted good-wishes to the newlyweds then rendered their shrill ululations of joy; a girl popped her head out of the window of her car, held her hands up to the sky, and shouted, "Allah grant it be *my* turn next!" then broke into a string of ululations, rolling her tongue and holding one hand to the side of her mouth to direct her hopeful wish to heaven. When she gyrated her belly at the window, an older woman pulled her down by the sleeve. A young man, his torso out the back window of a car, clapped and led a song in honour of the groom. Other passengers sang the chorus and clapped. Passers-by crossed the street in the middle of the procession, jumped on the front and back fenders of cars, and clapped. Vendors in food shops interrupted their chores to step out onto the pavement and watch the bride go by, their arms akimbo, towels over their shoulders, smiling, clapping in crackling bursts.

Behind Yasser and Nadia's car, Esmat was in the back seat of the taxi which Selim's brother drove, her two unmarried daughters, Rasha and Roda, beside her, one in red the other in blue satin, their black hair stiffened straight as cardboard by the hairdresser, their faces aglow with make-up. Decked in an emerald satin, Esmat sported a black sequined kerchief on her frizzy hair, her dark eyes double-lined with *kohl*, her gold necklace and earrings glittering, the latter—a gift from Amir and Samy—hanging long and entwined in thin lines to her shoulders. She was proud of her jewellery and had made sure her female neighbours—spying on her from behind their drawn shutters—had had ample time to see her walk the alley swaying her hips, her shiny daughters flanking her sides.

Nadia's joy would have been complete had her mother been there, but her frail parent was at home awaiting the arrival of her guests. Her mother had spent days with her maid cleaning her villa, supervising the men whom Sherif had brought in to set up the canvas tent in the garden. Her anticipation of the bride and groom's entrance into her home would be high, for Amir was her first grandson to get married.

Yasser wished that Samy too would find his mate. Nadia looked well in her lilac dress, her figure trim, her white gauze hat decked with spring flowers. Amir's contentment was vital to her well-being and her radiance reflected it. For him, people's jubilation alongside the wedding procession was unreal, reminding him that this was the first day of the *Eid* of *Ramadan*. He pressed Nadia's hand; his own still hurt, but that did not matter. The other pain mattered, because he could not dismiss it. Magda's wan face travelled alongside him; he had used her for no good reason. She might have been unfaithful to him, but he could not tell for sure. She was not like Nadia, independent, able to survive in her mind as well as in the world; Magda needed to be with another, even though she existed in a self-absorbed space of physical needs; she realized reality through her flesh, especially her sense of touch. The way she ate on the balcony in that smelly house in Luxor was the way she enjoyed his body: through taste, how things touched her skin, her tongue, the here and now was the woman's strength. But she was also being destroyed by the flesh. Ravaged, consumed. She had kept her illness hidden from him until he had begun to suspect something was wrong, and she had told him on his last day at hospital. Now, she was dying, and he had to visit her. To thank her, or to assuage his guilt. Better than nothing. He feared that at any moment his mind would erupt into a string of actions he had or had not done. He would need some peace of mind to sort things out. A few months ago, before that terrible day, he had thought he was in control of his life; now, he knew he was rudderless.

The wedding procession slowed down. Cars jammed the road. Behind them the car with Esmat and her daughters bumped into theirs, but Esmat continued her singing and clapping. Ahead, a red light announced a busy railway crossing, and the cars came to a standstill. Two men jumped out in front of the bridal car and began a traditional *tahteeb* dance using their sticks above their heads and performing a duo-dance. As long as the wait for the passage of the train lasted the men continued their ritual, but as the freight pulled away, the dancers jumped aside and the cars surged forward like a dam flooding the ground. Soon after the crossing, the clogged traffic reached Roxy Square, where the bridal car headed off towards the photographer's, and the rest carried on to Nadia's mother's place in Heliopolis.

On Tarik El Sarayat, the banyan trees lined both sides of the road, and a strip of garden ran through its centre; traffic eased as a cool breeze came in through the windows. Dusk.

***

Selim examined his skin in the mirror, bluish, rough, haggard. Although Yasser's looks had changed after his ordeal, his was still dynamic. It might be the cool weather in Canada or the absence of sun, but Selim acknowledged to himself that Yasser had this handsome ruggedness since their days at university. Alone at his shaving mirror in his apartment in Cairo, Selim talked to an imaginary Yasser; the man was so much on his mind. Selim had to block him out as he had banished memories of his own awkward twenties with his short body, kinky hair thinning on his forehead—although kinky hair was not supposed to fall out. Yasser's unspoken suspicions about him rankled. You did not know, Yasser, Selim addressed his friend in his mind, that I am blameless, and how can you, since you think me a negligible acquaintance, something like a cross-breed donkey with bull's horns. I did not know they would use you, but you, my friend, blame me. That time on the phone, days after I had slaved to earn your release through Mr. Abdullah, you blamed me for what happened. There's a lot you do not know. For example, do you know that Ezzat, the mad man who fired the bullets, had been Magda's lover? Did you know he had a fight with her days before he shot you, that he had threatened to kill you before he would dream of seeing her with a man who had deserted his country to become an accomplice to the Americans? She did not tell you, but she told me. You see, I get women's confidence, even of those who love you yet are afraid to tell you. Does this mean I am less, or more human than you? Women are a mystery to me, so I don't pretend to know, but would you have listened to Magda had she told you the man, Ezzat, had meant every word he had said? You did not know that Ezzat tried to kill himself in prison, but the clothes-line he used was flimsy and broke. A macabre joke, isn't it?

In a way that I can never be, you are self-sufficient, unaware of people, perhaps because you do not need their friendship. You are the hero of your own story. You do not have to stagger through life idolizing others, being second to those whom nature has favoured with dashing looks. You think yourself better than me and you may be right, but I wish you would not show it so much. Tell the truth, Yasser, you believe yourself superior, but just because you live in another country does not mean you're better than I, who have stayed in this country and served it since my birth. Your wife blames me, but I can't fault her, for she knows little of your activities.

Which brings me to my point: you did not invite me to your son's wedding. Never mind, I would not have gone; I don't go where I'm not welcome. I have my pride. I found out through Magda, who got it from Ahmed, who got it from your house-keeper. Roundabout way for a friend to know about your son's wedding, don't you think?

I've been eager to please you, and you accepted my friend-ship, but you do not tolerate me, and *I* went along with that. Some day we may talk about this; perhaps you will have learned something about your compatriots, the ones who have lived here and been faithful to their native land and to their childhood friends. I'm afraid to tell you about that animal, Ezzat: he's a drunk and he's dangerous. If he's released a year or two from now—for who cares about the lives of a couple of Americans who did not have the right to be here in the first place—I hope you will have returned to Canada. When this furious beast is released no one knows what he will do. Magda has not told you about him. Perhaps *she* will be spared the sight of Ezzat's ugly face, for no one knows how long *she* will live.

***

Nadia put the last touches to the centre-pieces on the din-ner tables. A densely designed tent material covered her mother's back garden, the top of the young mango trees touching the ceiling, their green fruits of guava and orange promising a rich harvest, their buds delivering garden-fresh-ness to the air. In April, nature is full of promises. From the top of the two-storey building, the canvas angled down to where it was held up on the last pole in the back garden. Sherif had arranged the tables and chairs around the trees. On a plat-form near the house, he had placed the two bridal thrones where guests, seated below and around it, could have a good view of the bride and groom. The buffet ran alongside the canvas walls. If Monir had received her note, Nadia hoped he would not show. She welcomed and seated the guests at their designated tables. Yasser supervised the caterers and serviced the drinks. The street in front of her mother's villa was packed with cars, and late guests had to park on faraway streets.

Nadia's mother—in pale pink, her silvery hair trim, a white boutonniere attached to her dress—re-arranged the flower bouquets behind the thrones, then moved to the bevelled-glass front door to await the bride and groom. Neighbouring villas glowed with coloured lights on the front porches and balconies in celebration of the *Eid* of *Ramadan*. On the street children in festive clothes of traditional satin and taffeta with flowers in their hair gathered by the front door of the villa to snatch a look at the bride. Inside the tent, as soon as the band members had set up their instruments near the bridal thrones, their leader announced the songs the choral entertainers would perform. Yasser offered mango *sharbat* to Nadia's mother. They clicked glasses and she kissed him. They drank. When Amir and Laura arrived, Esmat serenaded them with her ululations, and Samy and Yasser ushered them to their thrones. A belly dancer signalled the start of activities by shimmying in front of the young couple, causing Laura to blush when the dancer paid her homage by bending from her waist back and jiggling her hips with enthusiasm. Nadia's mother explained the bride's ritual dance to Laura who smiled her embarrassment away. Amir joked with Laura, but she held his grandmother's hand for reassurance that what was going on was an acceptable part of the ritual. His bride's confusion alerted Amir to the attention the performer was about to focus on him; when she came close and began shimmying he was embarrassed by her insistence that he belly-dance with her, but at his grandmother's bidding he stumbled into a jittering exercise with the dancer, holding his arms above his head and imitating her moves. Samy clapped his appreciation of his brother's self-conscious efforts and the audience followed suit. Amir entered the spirit of the dance knowing that if he performed well, this would be a compliment to his bride. Forming a circle around him, couples joined in, and he moved to claim Laura for their first dance. He imagined her daughter, small and naked on her breast.

Yasser had not figured out Selim's role in the arms charade, and this uncertainty plagued him. Whenever he and Selim had exchanged words in the past, it had seemed that the man held something back. He, Yasser, had to come to terms with Selim's actions, but right now, he had to block him out of his mind.

Face impassive as granite, Nessim stood at the open flap of the tent looking out at the desert at the back. He did not care for the fanfare going on behind him, for he preferred the somnolence of desert places and regarded noise as alien to the land; and when the dancer started shimmying, he knew the show had gone too far. The woman's gyrations were aggressive and lewd, not in agreement with the teachings of Islam, for women had to be covered in the presence of strangers. They had to be modest, self-respecting. Their bodies were private, holy places ready for their husband's call, not flaunted naked before men's eyes. Woman was man's niche; she had to be modest and hidden from the glances around her. Only loose women flaunted their flesh like this in public. A man's body was different, for he could have three or four women if he was able to treat them fairly. That was the way of Islam. A woman had to be subdued and faithful, but this sinful pot of flesh flaunted her body before young men and girls. He left the tent in disgust, sat outside under a mango tree in the afternoon light, his stern face focused on the desert.

Esmat's daughters, Rasha and Roda, twin handmaids of the bride and groom, sat on the platform nearest the couple. They could not participate in the action, but their bodies vibrated with the tension of the *tabla* beat. They managed to stifle their urges but allowed their feet under their long *gallabiahs* to tap along with the music. Their mother had forbidden them to talk to men, and they knew enough not to eat until the guests had finished their supper, certainly not to participate in belly-dancing. This wedding was not for one of their own. Esmat went to Nadia's mother and whispered in her ear, then the old lady went up to Laura and Amir and proceeded with them to the buffet. When the couple had carried their plates back to their table, bridesmaids and best men followed, then visitors converged on the dinner table from all sides. Hands shot out and piled the plates high with a mixture of delicacies.

The choral group's music was soft, then it rose to the feverish pitch of electronic instruments. Esmat hugged the bride, planting a wet kiss on her cheek, causing Laura to blush and bend her head. At the forefront of the platform, Esmat blessed the young couple and rendered her ear-piercing ululations which other women picked up and made the tent resound with joy. Wedging her body between tables, Esmat served wine, delivered second helpings, her bulging thighs jiggling up and down, hitting the green silk as she went up the steps to the kitchen balancing a pile of plates on her arms. There she gulped mouthfuls of the half whisky bottle Samy had given her to dispose of as she wished. He knew she would not admit to alcohol indiscretion, so he gave her a gift she could not refuse. Between kitchen and tent, she shuffled back and forth, pointing her fingers to her two girls to direct them to carry plates and serve non-alcoholic beverages, disappeared at intervals to swig a mouthful below the kitchen counter. As she passed the front door, she saw a man's shadow behind the opaque bevelled glass. She had not heard the bell ring. When she opened the door, she discovered Monir on the doorstep. Esmat frowned. She did not want to remember the sad days when Madam Nadia had consorted with this man for help. She wanted those days forgotten, so Monir had to go, but he was popping his head in through the hallway door. He had no business to be there. Monir changed his weight from one foot to the other. "I just want to deliver this parcel to Madam Nadia. Can I see her for a moment?" Esmat showed no sign of inviting him in but took the parcel, nodded, mumbled something about everyone being busy, and closed the door.

Monir tapped on the glass. She peered through the half-open window. "There's something I would like to explain to Madam Nadia, and I'd like to wish her happiness for her son." This last admonition he knew Esmat could not ignore for she would perceive a refusal to deliver it as bad omen. In a huff, she asked Monir to wait, left the door half-closed and disappeared.

Nadia was talking to Laura when Esmat signalled her to follow to the front door. When Nadia saw Monir, she had to push Esmat out of the way to invite him into the kitchen. At the kitchen door, Esmat glimpsed Yasser approaching with an empty glass, so she went to him, placed one hand on his arm and took his glass, "I'll serve the father of the bridegroom today!" she said happily, "You go and sit down, Mr. Yasser, and I will bring you a glass of iced water."

"It's all right, Esmat, you have enough to do!" Yasser took his glass from her hand, entered the kitchen and saw them standing together, her back to him, the man facing his way, smooth hair touching Nadia's hat, dark eyes blazing through the spectacles with an intensity Yasser recognized. This man was in love with his wife. When had *that* happened? Yasser moved up to them and Nadia held her arm out to draw him in, "Yasser, you remember Monir? He's the archaeologist who showed us around the temples at Luxor," then realized Yasser had not been with them.

Monir nodded to Yasser; Yasser stared back. Monir turned to Nadia. "Now that I've delivered your unsold painting from the exhibition, I must go. Don't forget your envelope inside the parcel with the money from the sold paintings. Congratulations on your son's wedding," he said to the air in Yasser's direction.

Nadia asked, "Won't you like to come and meet the bride and groom?"

"I have to rush. I'm on my way to catch the train to Luxor to see my parents. Then I will be going to Lebanon."

Monir shook hands with Nadia, nodded to Yasser, then turned to leave. Esmat stationed herself behind Monir and

Nadia followed. Yasser remained in the kitchen. Nadia pushed Esmat aside and ushered Monir down the stairs of the villa to the crowded street and disappeared with him behind the parked cars. Esmat swung on her heels mumbling to herself as she returned to the kitchen. She saw Yasser fill his glass with cold water. "Here, Mr. Yasser, have some *sharbat*." He shook his head.

"Madam Nadia's mother asked me to tell you to go into the tent and say a few words for the bride. You need to speak in Madam Laura's language."

Yasser returned to his place in the tent and set his glass down. He needed to go home. He had not seen Nadia's face, but her hat had touched that man's hair, and she had gone out with him on her son's wedding night. Yasser's brother, Ali, clicked glasses with him and asked when he was going to give a speech. Yasser stepped up on the platform, raised his glass and toasted the bride and groom in English and in Arabic, then he praised the bride in English. Samy stood by his side. "Where's Mother?"

"She's around," he told his son. Then he passed his arm through Samy's, and they went to the buffet to slice and serve cake.

***

When she returned to her place beside Yasser, Nadia kept her eyes down. She had travelled to a deserted country and come back in a daze. Yasser served her cake, and as he set the plate down, his eyes met hers: there he saw a wilderness without flowers, not even a wild shrub. What was this man to her? The words she had said a couple of days ago rushed back to him. "I'm not faultless," she had said, "When people have been married for as long as we, temptation is bound to pop up!" He had been blinded by his misery and not picked up the signs. She must be leaving him. He did not hear Esmat's ear-piercing ululations, he saw the man's head close to Nadia's. Nadia with another man, after all these years, but she was not like that; perhaps because of his own guilt he suspected something that was not there. The threat of losing her invoked his pain. Shots went through his body, toy guns and bullets tore through his shoulder and arm. That young man was self-contained, did not seem much older than thirty. Dark hair, slim body, intense eyes. That look: the man shared a part of Nadia that Yasser did not know. That conspiring glance. A sexual link would be understandable, the man young and she alone. But Nadia's body close to that man's suggested she knew him; they shared a secret. The man had mentioned an unsold painting from an exhibition, this was how Yasser would lose her. Nadia would plunge into the art scene, become one of those artists living God knows how, visiting alleys, leading bohemian lives, and thinking they had a hand in righting the ills of the world, by putting paint on canvas, by writing words in magazines people did not read. Her hat had almost touched that man's hair. Their bodies were aligned as though separated by force. It was more than a sexual bond. Yasser had not seen her so poised, alert, and ready to jump into life, like a bird about to fly, but duplicity was not one of her traits, not the wife he knew. Her actions had not suggested she was going to leave him, yet she may have learned to be deceptive. Perhaps he was going to lose her anyway. As if in captivity, she was ready to escape to her new world. She may have come to Egypt for a change, to get out of a rut, but now she sat quietly as if she lay at the bottom of a river. He ate cake. His wife lived in a country he had not visited. He sat, a middle-aged, grey-haired man, his body and mind riddled with pain, his life ended, his ally leaving him, she at his side eating white cake decorated with white carnations.

Samy was talking to him. Yasser nodded, went over to Laura, took her hand and led her in a dance. Amir danced with Nadia. A toy soldier, Yasser felt, as he turned to the beat of drums.

Nadia regained her glow as she danced with Amir, her head high, her pride in her son evident. Now he, Yasser, an outsider, contemplated the actions of his family, not knowing what to expect.

***

Nadia went to the back of the empty tent, looked out through the open fold at the dark desert, listened to the sand whistling its own solitude. Monir had come to say goodbye, but she hated goodbyes. Structures, beginnings, endings were not for her; they were obstructions like the Aswan Dam holding back the Nile's flow. The last time she had been with Monir, she had left his studio without a word. Goodbyes were final, and yet she felt there would be other moments. She did not like locking doors behind her. Monir's arrival at the wedding party had disclosed their attachment to Yasser. He had guessed. She had not counted on that. Perhaps it was just as well, since they had to talk about Monir anyway, yet she had not wanted Yasser to find out this way, not during Amir's wedding. She had made the mistake of sending Monir that note; then she had felt she wanted to share her joy with her friends. Esmat suspected the worst, for the woman remained aloof and avoided Nadia's eyes. Neither Esmat nor Yasser would understand or forgive, and perhaps they shouldn't, because what she and Monir had enjoyed was not right. Yet Yasser and Esmat presumed that a woman's guilt was worse than a man's, and this Nadia could not understand.

The bride and groom had headed to Heliopolis Sheraton Hotel. They were going to Sharm-El-Sheik on the Red Sea for two weeks, then they would be returning home to Canada. Samy would be staying for five days then leaving. Behind her, Yasser was clearing the tent with Samy, and Esmat was packaging food and left-over cake, keeping her back turned towards Nadia.

Nadia went upstairs with her mother, helped her to bed, turned off the lights, secured the doors of the villa. In the next few days, they would return her mother's home to its proper shape.

***

Chapter Fifteen
River

Yasser sat on the edge of their king-sized bed as Nadia came and went between cupboard and suitcase packing her clothes. He stared into the cupboard mirror: his tan camouflaged the scar on his forehead, his hair had turned grey yet it looked reasonably well against his dark skin. He looked better than he felt. At the Delta Barrage his strength was coming back, and the minutes that had been racing in his head were moving at a slower pace. Nadia was getting ready to go on the trip down the Nile which she had mentioned to him in the letter he had received in prison; she had discussed the trip with him after their sons' return to Canada, and now, she was packing her things to go. He felt no need for change; besides he had to go to Cairo to tie up some loose threads. He reminded her, "Remember your thermos and walking shoes."

"And my hat and sun-glasses," she muttered. She piled her clothes in the suitcase and placed her sketch-pad and water-colours in her handbag. She had decided against oils because they were impractical for a sailing trip. Her actions appeared to him to rise from an unknown source of solitude, and she showed no hesitation about going away without him, a new stance. She had gathered moral strength, whereas he seemed to have lost it. He asked her, "You are sure you do not want Esmat to go with you to carry your equipment and keep you company? You know how she feels about you setting off alone."

Nadia shook her head. "I won't be alone, Yasser. I'll be with archaeologists from Canada, Sudan and Ethiopia, a regular United Nations trip!" she laughed. Just like him, she thought, putting words into Esmat's mouth instead of claiming them as his own. He frowned. Was that man going with her? She came to the bed, sat by his side and surrounded his shoulder with her arm. Her eyes held his in the mirror. "And you? What are *your* plans?"

His gaze steady, he said, "My brothers and cousins are coming to visit me. I don't feel up to the trip now, and I want to be in Cairo. I have a number of things to do."

She swung her legs onto their bed and he turned to face her. "There's the Damietta project," he said, "I don't want to give *that* up. It's important, although I'll do it differently, that is, if they'll let me carry on with the project." He chuckled, then scowled.

"Are you sure it's safe to go back *there*?" Damietta was a fearful word for Nadia, but she should have guessed he was not going to give up on that project.

"It's what I *want* to do. I'll be working with Egyptians. I need to finish what I started."

"I hope you don't do any work unless you have a written directive," she cautioned then thought, how silly, things don't work like this here.

"There's something else I have to do," he continued. She knew what that was: they had not mentioned her since the night he had had his nightmare. "I want to visit Magda," the first time he had used the woman's name! "She's in a private hospital downtown Cairo. I haven't seen her." Now they were talking about her it was easier, yet Magda's name intensified Nadia's guilt, for here was a woman, young and attractive dying of cancer, and Nadia had not guessed Magda's illness nor cared to ask when the woman appeared haggard and suffering from pain at the café. Yasser had not talked about her in the three months since Amir's wedding. Once, Nadia had tried to tell him about Monir, but he seemed distracted, or perhaps he had not wanted to listen. He *knew*. As if by acknowledging his wife's lover, he would have made real what he was reluctant to accept. Nadia had let time pass. She had not unwrapped the gift Monir had placed within the parcel containing her unsold painting which he had delivered on Amir's wedding night.

"Do you understand why I'm taking this trip?" She placed her palm on Yasser's scarred arm. The darkened stiches clashed with his tan and seemed like a macabre joke that someone had played on him. He shrugged. She continued, "My original feeling was to go with you on our second honeymoon!" She did not say that her second instinct was to set out on the river alone, to retrace her life-stream, to come to terms with her own future. "I realize you cannot go," she continued, "but this trip is important to me. If I go to the source of the Nile, I'll be discovering the nucleus of my energy. Ever since I was a child, I've wanted to take this trip." She had not understood her need until now. "I heard this group of archaeologists was going, so I joined them."

"This man," he probed, "this archaeologist, what is he to you?"

"Which man, you mean the tourist guide in Luxor? He's the one who helped me when you were in hospital." In the mirror, her hair was in disarray, so she pinned it up. "He took me to embassies, and made useful contacts for me at Kasr-El-Einy Hospital." She placed her legs in lotus position, her arms on her knees and waited. Yasser set his back against the head-board and stretched his legs. "What else is he to you?"

Did he want the truth? "You know we entered our work at El Gizereh Exhibition together." She played for time, raised her knees, placed her arms on them, rested her head on her arms. She knew what was coming. He raised his eyebrows as if to say, that's it?

"We were intimate . . . once." It was out, the reality he could not accept: she was his, but had allowed another to know her. Why was it so difficult for him to accept what he himself had done? She continued, "I was afraid," part of the truth; but he might not realize, if she told him, what it was for her to lose him in a sea of bodies, in millions of lives in Cairo, to have no clue where he was, whether she would see him again, nor what she would say to their sons.

Yasser saw the man's eyes embrace his wife's, his hair touch her hat, her back poised for flight. Now that he, Yasser, was regaining his strength, she wanted to go away with this young artist. Yasser acknowledged to himself he had not reached this part of his wife, neither had he understand her love of art, which he saw as something ephemeral. Then again, perhaps her art was the reason for her strength. Where he failed to be excited about anything, she was passionate about something and that helped remove her from mundane humanity to a self-contained place of peace. He had no clue what this passion meant, except that she was happy to be on her own. If that man was going with her, this might be the reason why she did not want Esmat to go.

"That night sprang out of despair," she consoled him, but she could see him standing on the brink of a mountain gazing down an abyss, and she could not touch him. She had slept with Monir *once*, but surely Yasser could understood that the years they had been together were more important. "All this is behind us," she told him, "Monir is to me what Magda is to you. Perhaps we had to live this part of our lives to be able to carry on. Did we have to come to Egypt to discover this?"

***

The boat was to start from Lake Victoria. The passengers were assembled at Owen Falls in Uganda. On the plane there, Nadia studied the map to re-discover the Nile's smaller tributaries pouring into Uganda, Ethiopia and Sudan before it reached Egypt. She knew the Nile was Egypt's life-line; now she realized it was the source of life for a number of countries south of Egypt. Where the cataracts blocked the river, the archaeologists planned to board planes. Nadia did not expect such a small boat to await them at Owen Falls, smaller than the ones she had taken at Cairo, but here the river was narrow. Most of those who crowded into the two-level boat came from Canada, France, Italy and Ethiopia.

In early September, the heat was unbearable, even when she wet her hair and covered it with a straw hat to keep the moisture in. She wore a loose, white cotton *gallabiah,* no underwear, so the streams of perspiration ran down her back. Many years back, before they had had their sons, she was in a hot sauna with Yasser, their first in Canada, on a friend's farm, in December, with a group of ten or twelve others all huddled in a hut, wood logs crackling, heat so high that streaks of sweat poured down their bodies. Nothing matched the wood sauna for its immediate impact and texture; the electric one in their home in Toronto never did the same job. Whenever their bodies reached an unbearable temperature, she and Yasser would run out of the hut with their bathing suits steaming in the cold air, trip over mounds of snow to a crack in the pond and jump into a hole of darkness. For a few seconds, they felt nothing, then the slow consciousness of ice made them shiver. When they had made it back to the hut, their wet bodies sighed in the high heat, although at first they could not register it. On these trips to the pond and back, they lost track of time, and when they got dressed, they walked back to the farm house, their bodies zinging with released energy, the night air new on their skin. Snow glowed and guided them to safety on top of the dark escarpment, where an open space ran across the fields up to the farm, the moon's rays streaking the snow with silver. Behind them, couples coming out of the sauna climbed up the dirt road to the top of the escarpment, yodelling and laughing, their echoes bouncing down the valley through the leaves and rebounding.

Now on board the boat in the middle of the crowd, Nadia listened to the traveller's voices rise as the prow of the boat dipped into the water. Dark-skinned people in white flowing clothes stood on shore waving to departing passengers, most of whom were hanging over the rails on deck, in khaki shorts and white shirts, when they would have been better off to shield their skin with the locals' long, white garments. Women mingled with their colleagues taking photos and moving from one side of the deck to the other. At night, everyone crowded around the small bar on the lower deck.

The following morning, Nadia sat on a bench on the upper deck. Her handbag in the cabin contained the parcel Monir had given her. It would be his goodbye message, not a letter perhaps, but something in the shape of a book. She had found this parcel inside the wrapping of her unsold painting with the paper money she had earned from the sale of her two paintings. The parcel was a gift from Monir; she would find time on this trip to unwrap it. In front of her, shrubs, struggling green branches twisted with time, acacia trees, water buffaloes drinking near the bank, the river narrow and silent. She bent over the rails to contemplate the sliding water—its colour muted and shiny—and followed the ripples as if she were searching for hidden reasons for the Nile's existence, but she had to remind herself she was not in search of anything. She was at the source of the river, its lapping water punctuating her heart and she was fifteen again, unrelated, alive, neither wife, mother, daughter, nor lover.

Monir had told her about the trip and she was relieved he had decided not to come. Instead, he had gone to the Red Sea. After Amir's wedding, she had not seen him, but he had helped her book her ticket by telephone. She had not wanted to think she would never hear his voice again, and when she did, it seemed an echo of a distant past: still the incestuous guilt, the brother she had discovered, the one she enjoyed touching, but she was not going back to that. She had wandered into this place of longing, as into kindred soil, where she could touch her imaginative world and share it with him, but now that she could live her art and divulge its secrets on canvas, she had no need of engagement with another. They were too close. She had made love to a part of herself. He *was* herself, in hiding. But when her creative self became real, she had no need of acknowledgement; she would live her life by the strength of her vision, the sound of her internal sea. Distant rumblings of the Mediterranean Sea rolling over the land of

Damietta were far away, she had no need to rescue that shore, but if Yasser wanted to, that was his choice. Anyway, the encroachment of sea on land was part of the apocalyptic cycle of the world and the question was, can fresh life spring from this destruction? It was her role as artist to discover new seeds in the devastated soil. Yasser was the man whose energy had sustained her in the years of nurturing their sons. Their shared life was one. He was battling to reclaim his dream for Damietta, and she her creative life, his search parallel to hers—antipodes of the same world—and between them the universe hung in a balance.

Yasser, she told him in her heart, you are my limbs plunging in soil, you are the blood coursing through my veins. I honour your resolve to return to Damietta; you need time to deal with your anguish, and I need time to deal with mine. I'd like to believe you did not love her, although she is love-worthy, but I know you did, or perhaps you needed her kind of love. Did she help set up the Damietta project so you would be near her? Yet, you have always gained energy from movement and new projects, and you would not have surrendered to lethargy. No. What you did is yours to claim; you would have gone to Damietta of your own accord, as you are doing now, because you have to, because you want to be moving at the vortex of energy.

***

Yasser took the chickens by their wings and put them back into their coop. Time to retire. Late dusk. The sky promised rain. He watered and trimmed Nadia's jasmine. He was tired. After his visit two days ago to the Italian Hospital in Cairo, he had returned to the Delta Barrage, his energy seeping out of his body, yet he was glad to be at their home to pull the pieces of his life together. His mind carried the imprint of Magda's sunken cheeks like a flagstaff on the prow of a doomed ship: death's grimace, no hint of blush or life in the skin, the final confrontation. He had not seen his own father on his death bed; his mother had died two years after he had left Egypt, and his brothers had not told him until after her funeral. In Canada, he had shunned open caskets, not that there were many occasions to see them, just an elderly man, father of his friend, and an old lady who had babysat his boys. The second had been painful. He was careful to avoid the masked faces even though Nadia insisted that they attend these ceremonies. His office had been a sanctum in which he could avoid such duties; he had not gone to the morbid events and could not understand how Nadia endured them, but then, she knew, long before he did, that rituals were etched mirrors revealing our fate.

***

Even on the river the air was still, and Nadia had heard that the next day would be hotter. Dense stars shone in the sky. Mornings, she basked in the heat, as though by getting into it she was jumping into the eye of the sun. The Nile has such a perfect journey, she thought, it starts at the equator at the centre of heat and meanders down mountains and hills to flat land to pour its waters beyond the Egyptian valley into the warm sea. Close by, the Nile's junction with the Mediterranean, the Suez Canal—an artery of movement—allows ships to pass from one side of the globe to another. She had been there too. The river throbbed near the nucleus of existence as it did at the centre of her own consciousness, and in spite of the political upheavals along its borders, it would persist. Nadia was at its source, the source of her forebears' lives, of her own life, of her near and ancient past, and this river would flow through Egypt's parched land to nourish and to provide. It would withstand inroads of salt waves, it would always be, regardless of the drastic changes that have rocked the social fabric of the country.

Nadia realized she had not had her search dream for weeks, perhaps months, she could not remember the last time she had had her homeless nightmare. The dream had vanished as enigmatically as it had begun. At some point, days or weeks after Amir's wedding, she had become aware that home was where she was: you carried your shack along with you, the way bedouins did, the way the Inuit in Canada had done for generations, and you re-created it wherever you went. Structures were expendable, not inner space. The second was not part of buildings nor of earth, not part of houses, nor people, only a part of you. Perhaps what had bothered her in the past was she did not fit in anywhere. How many times had she made friends, nourished, loved, sensed a special place she could call her own within the vast land of Canada, only to realize that this space was not hers, that it had been granted her for a while, or she was renting it for a price. She had belonged to buildings, structures, groups, social configurations until the day her friends dispersed and her world crashed, then the void was filled with another friendship, group or identity surrogate. So continued her sense of oncoming doom, as though no matter how long the friendship, there would be a time it would end, for at the core of everyone was a central dungeon of difference: of colour, shape, mouth, nose, hair texture, anything that can destroy the tenuous connection between one person and another. This had disturbed her. Now she knew that these differences were inevitable and what was important, they did not matter. They were landmarks of reality, like hurricanes, floods and snow storms, they would occur when least expected, but they did not matter. For somewhere from within her she had abstracted the truth that other people's perception of her was not her concern, and ideas others espoused would not explain away the forces of life. Theories were sterile mindwaves that people jammed into their consciousness so they could forget they were alive and that some day, they too would die. Ideas fizzled out before biology did, for biology was, is, and inevitably will cease to be, but it would re-create itself. So what was important was art, consciousness, nearness to the soil, life itself. On this boat, she felt peace, time, the river, earth, all in an infinite continuum, and she a coincidental sojourner. While I'm alive, she thought, I'd like to hold the world by its umbilical cord. Where oceans splash, where river's undercurrents swirl down mountain tops, I'll be there. In snow avalanches, I'll hide. In spring, I'll surface.

***

"Nadia I'm losing you," Monir thought as he watched the waves roll over the sand at the Red Sea. "I've lost you. Forever. I cannot reach you. How do I live?"

***

Yasser wondered whether Magda had told him, "You're the one I love," or he had thought it upon his return home. Had her parched lips, death's grimace, uttered these words, travesties of his dream? Eight months ago, his heart would have flown at these words, but now, through the powder-white lips, letters formed on the contorted mockery of human flesh. He had recoiled from contact with the meaning cracking open on her broken lips, had resisted touching the hand that opened up asking for hope as it lay on the green hospital sheets. But at least he had gone to see her. What a self-centred fool he was, thinking he could evade death's clutch. So this is how he would flirt with the dreaded image. In his own way, he had tried to comfort her but was not sure she had understood his garbled sounds. Words are a noise meaning nothing, and he had never cared to muster them. Too late for him to say what he could have said months ago and meant it, when saying it would have touched her. He had run away from the important moment to reap its fruits after they had shrivelled. Would he chase phantom dreams forever, until his dreams became phantom skulls? In his Cairo apartment, cars and humans hummed below his window, and he yearned for the smooth vista of Lake Muskoka. He wished he were on a craggy rock looking out over still water, in bare feet on a dock or in a canoe sliding along the lake in lapping movements, he and the boat synchronizing their rhythm in the stillness. Hours of quiet fishing, the occasional tug of a fish, cut off from humanity, breathing his own solitude.

Here on his bed, what visited him one more time were those eyes—her father's as he discovered later—in the courtroom, hating, accusing him. The man, dark-haired, well-built, nose commanding his face, eyes dark wells, going through the motions of defending his daughter's lover. But Yasser was not worth defending. His ignorance of protocol aside, he, Yasser, had gone ahead and made transactions with the Americans to import weapons into Egypt, thinking he was making outstanding deals for his native land. But he had been drunk with power, so he was culpable, not with malice afore-planned, but with pride, a self-centred love that had filled him, made him incapable of distinguishing smart deals from risky ones, unquenchable lust from genuine caring, love of his sons from real understanding. He was the skeleton. The empty husk.

***

Late afternoon. Nadia had hoped to catch a glimpse of a crocodile, the sacred spirit of the river at the time of Pharaohs, but on the opposite bank, a man squatted, then waded at the shallow edge of Lake Kioga. She could have obtained earphones and tapes for a running commentary on the sites, but she wanted to register the view with her heart. On the bench by her side, a short man with a heavy belly, bald head, kind face, sipped beer as he watched water slide under the hull of the boat. "It's peaceful here," he said. "Imagine what it was like at the dawn of civilization!" His words wavered over the surface of water. He mopped his perspiration, then took another sip from his bottle. She smiled at the thought of untouched earth: "It reminds me of a trip I took with my school many years ago. We were on a boat at Luxor. I don't know if the water was clean, or if this was part of my childhood crystal vision of the world; but it was perfect, no snakes squirming around, so to speak."

He smiled and nodded. "Tomorrow, we'll be going on a trip at Wadelai. It's going to be hotter. Let's drink all we can to store for tomorrow's sun," he chuckled, clicked his bottle against her soda glass and drank.

At night, Nadia looked out of the window of her cabin and felt at peace with the universe. Damietta, with the sea gaining on the land, was far away; Yasser's turmoil remote; Monir, a delicate mirage on desert sand. Somewhere she had sons, but right now they were beloved silhouettes seen through long-distance lens. Water lapped the boat and shone in the silvery darkness. The bit of sky she could see through her cabin window was studded with stars. She had started at the source of the Nile and was sailing along the edge of desert terrain, until the river fell into the arms of the Mediterranean. These waters had been the same for thousands of years, and their undulations flowed through her blood stream.

***

Magda stared at the red alarm clock that ticked, ticked, each click thunder in her ears. Morphine was water in her veins, the pain constant. A reminder, always a reminder, constant; always in her mind, days that do not end, and no one caring to stop them. Not Yasser, not her father, not even the doctors whom she implored to give her larger drug doses. Everyone left her to shrivel. Her father had been in, but she had avoided his eyes. She hated him. Yet he had helped, a lot, by setting Yasser free. Sheer force of power. Wanted to prove he could do anything. Still anxious to show he was masterful. His big frame, decisive eyes: he wanted something of her. What? To live her life for her? He was healthy, unbreakable. Wasn't that enough? A few days ago she had glimpsed fear in his eyes, but she knew he was sturdy, and his vigour shamed her. She had seen his rejection, reproaching her for dying, she thought. They would never have a truce when all would be done between them. She wished she could see her mother, and she had asked him for her photograph, but her father had not brought it in. When Magda was eight her father had told her that her mother had died, but her great-aunt had said her mother had run away with a naval officer, and her father wanted Magda to consider her dead.

Yasser had been here. Through her pain, she knew he was. He had changed: tight-lipped, stern, even haggard. She dared not glance in the mirror to see what made him look so grim. She had to work on that young doctor, perhaps a hefty needle is all she needed, just a needle, he would not begrudge her that. All these years, the men she had known. Was cancer infectious? Perhaps she was being punished for her love-life, so unacceptable to Allah. Almighty was punishing her for what she had done, but what exactly, hunger for love? Since her childhood, she had been left with one servant after another, their lewd jokes, waiting for her father to come home, but he had been away on army duty, or with some woman. Pain. Always pain. His behaviour was no different from hers, perhaps worse than what she had heard her mother had done, run away with a man who loved her, even if he were years younger. Magda had found Yasser and felt cradled in his arms knowing he would not hurt her. He hadn't, but he had gone and got himself trampled on, caught in a web he could not understand. And Ezzat taking shots at Yasser, wanting to kill him. Perhaps Ezzat had been set up by a higher authority who wanted Yasser implicated in the arms deal. She knew there had been no defective weapons; perhaps Ezzat and his brother had manufactured the incident to carry out their revenge on Yasser, as Ezzat had threatened.

Pain, always pain, even before cancer, pain. She wanted to see Yasser, to remember him on the villa balcony in Luxor, before she had discovered that what throbbed in her abdomen was a serpent eating her guts. The gnawing, the enduring loneliness of it, never relieved except when she had met the man she loved, and he was married. The one she wanted, but then, as though he were too good for her, Allah had struck her down. Now, when Yasser came to visit, he sat on the chair near the window, not by her bed as he used to, and his fingers did not touch her nor caress her hair. He smiled as through glass and his eyes reflected pain at seeing her. His look was hard even though his mouth stretched into a smile. He did not know how strange he looked with his face twisted into a smile. She wished he would just be himself.

People thought her infectious, as if by touching her fingers they would contract the disease. Had she taken the disease from someone else? Yasser come and see me.

***

Nadia woke up with the knowledge she had to open Monir's parcel. Through her window, the sun's orb was a faint pink. Dawn. She showered, dressed, went out on the deck to see the early rays brighten the sky. The day would be hot. A thin film of dew covered the bench, but soon it would dissipate. She walked around the boat. Breakfast would be served in half an hour. She had a few minutes to open the parcel. She returned to her room, took it out of her handbag and opened it.

Soft, flexible paper with lilac flowers on a black background wrapped the small, black leather book. She turned its cover open and saw Monir's handwriting, "For Nadia: drawings of happy times." No signature. Each off-white page was filled with graphite intensity. Miniature faces, carved reliefs of scenery, men, women, guava fruit, mango, palm, acacia, faces filled with detail of vein and skin carved in granite. Light shone from an unseen source, eyes projected character, and ethereal energy sprang from them as from clear water. He had given her his drawings, illumined, bright, not the sad faces that had drawn her tears, but pieces of wonderment, as if he had dived into a stream and brought out pearls of ancient origin. This could be the book he was working on the last time she was in his studio: he had been preparing it for the day she would leave. She wandered through its pages, but if she stayed too long, she would be blinded by its clarity. She did not know he could draw such uplifting subjects, dazzling in their certitude. She re-wrapped the parcel and returned it to her handbag. She would study it later. Enough now that it was hers.

Enough too that she could create her own world. This limbo was hers, her identity fluid. She was anything she wanted to be, not threatened by solitude, her silence nourished and sustained by her energy. She was no longer desperate for companionship to shore up against loneliness. Consciousness was sufficient. She recalled her father's words the year before he died, "Those who want to return to a special place do not wish to return to a space that is no longer there, but to a previous self they cannot relive. They come face to face with their present selves."

She was looking ahead for a reunion with Yasser, not with the fear of rejection, but with the joy of expectation, her way intact, her cherished moments bouncing with excitement springing from the earth.

***

Monir piled his books on the floor of his studio, then carried them to the shelves and arranged them in colour schemes. He needed energizing forms around him, each book part of the mosaic of the harmony he was creating. He would go through his objects, re-arrange them, make room for large papers he had set up for the series of water-colours he was doing: Nadia in fluidity, each work portraying her in motion, soaking in water, no harsh lines, no specific shapes in the background, Nadia as he remembered her, on their first evening on the *Lotus*, in the Al Karnak temple, inside Abu Simbel, in dance at Luxor Hilton, on the boat's deck, on streets of Cairo, in the narrow alleys of Khan-El-Khalili, here in his studio. Each painting dripped with water beads, merging facial expression with the feel of her face, pinks dissolving into purples, greens, his silhouette near hers, the two flowing into each other, no lines between them, fluidity in colour and raindrops. He was containing the woman who had lifted him from his grey monologue to float him into a turquoise dialogue of long ago, when they were young, energetic, rushing through time, touching in a space where he harboured visions, the spirit he had known since he was young, his other self that had appeared as an apparition and set him free to dream in the world of hard objects and lonely corners.

***

Alone in his Cairo apartment, Yasser talked aloud to himself as had become his habit since he had begun visiting the dying Magda at hospital, "Hold on Yasser, you've almost made it, stand firm until the old hyena carries his prey away. You've been to see death's mask three times, on each round its grimace whiter, but you're getting wiser, holding her hand, not showing your fear of the creature gaining power over her. It will not be long now. Guilt. Do something you may be proud of, move, practise for a manly life, so you can face Samy and Amir."

But, he thought, this terror of Madga dying strikes waves within me. I'm being carried away with her on a stretcher into nowhere. Nadia faces the metal bed much better than I do. This silence is strange after the noise that had been raging in my head. Perhaps staying here and visiting Magda will serve some purpose. One repays one love with the strength one gleans from another. I take from Nadia and give to Magda, who takes from her father and gives to me, and her father takes from his women to give to her. One hardly returns power to the person to whom one owes it. The world is a merry-go-round where energy received from the rider behind is passed on to the one ahead, a race where one takes the torch from one hand and passes it on to another. Nadia, I owe you so much, I hope some day you will know.

***

Magda's room in her father's home was empty. Her father pulled out each drawer of her dresser, threw some of them on the floor, snatched open the door to her cupboard: where had his daughter put her things? Neither servant nor porter knew. Neither one of the men to whom he had entrusted his only child knew when she had come in, nor where she had placed her things. What were these stooges doing eating at his expense and taking wages? They pretended they knew nothing, even as his daughter's life was ebbing. Now he would have nothing of hers to keep. She had come into his house, taken her things and left. She did not want him in hospital, he who had taken care of her after that woman, her mother, had brought shame upon his head. If he had known where and how to reach that woman and her lover, he would have destroyed them. Some said they had left Cairo and gone to a remote village near Tanta. But where? Perhaps he could hire a detective. But not now.

His daughter, Magda, was dying. Dying. He could not believe that she, the only person he loved, was dying. He had done what she wanted, freed her lover, even when he was convinced that this fellow, Yasser, was guilty along with the Americans. Now, the man was free, and his daughter dying. Magda's father folded his arms on the desk, placed his head down on them and wept.

***

The boat was approaching Adelaide. People sipped their cold drinks and gathered their parcels for descent. They were going to see the buffalo herds graze. Nadia picked up her handbag, balanced her feet on the wooden steps, jumped onto the sand where a few yards away, jeeps and guides awaited. She climbed into a jeep with three men. The cars moved in a convoy. The air was misty from early morning dew, and noon would be hot. With the slight breeze, the sun broke in waves on the travellers. She wet her hair with water from the thermos, tied a kerchief around her head, adjusted her hat as perspiration streamed down her body. Out of the warm limbo within her, she yearned for the green stretches in Algonquin Park, the open roads she and Yasser travelled in Canada. But she was in a car moving along the bank of the Nile, its water narrow so she could see men on donkeys on the opposite side.

She could have swum across. In a few minutes, they saw the first water buffalo coming out of the bush. Cars reduced their speed and crawled forward alongside the rim of the bank. No one spoke. Some of the buffalo emerged from behind the acacias then stopped at a distance. Cars halted. After several minutes, two water buffaloes started their slow progress towards the river. The first buffalo reached the bank and waded in, went down with a splash, blowing bubbles to the surface as she sank. Then the other. Having determined it was safe to go on, the buffaloes did not look back. They swam, raised their heads and snorted, moved in slow motion, ducked into the water, blew out fountains of sparkling water.

Nadia stepped out of the jeep onto the ground and went towards the swimming buffaloes. She watched from afar. A couple of tourists went closer to the animals to take photographs. The alarmed buffaloes waded away to the opposite bank to get out. Nadia moved from the group alongside the river, her back to the animals.

***

"Madam Nadia, Madam Nadia," Esmat's voice spiralled through palm branches at the Delta Barrage, "come home, what are you doing out there on the river? Come home and reclaim Mr. Yasser. That evil woman has died. Allah be merciful to us all! Come home. Come and see your jasmine tree, the flowers are big and beautiful. Mr. Yasser has been taking care of it as though it were a newborn baby. What are you doing out there on the river?"

***

Monir recalled Nadia's worries about the poor in Egypt turning violent; her point was valid. He would represent his countrymen the way he feared they might become, and he would dedicate his paintings to her. Grapple with the here and now, trap the day's reality. Stop thinking of the past. Create your art in honour of the woman who pulled you into consciousness. After the water-colours, I will do a series of oil paintings of men and women caught in waves of fundamentalism, my people, pushed into an abyss of misguided religious fervour. Perhaps I can paint their figures in strong browns, violets, blues, greens, in yellows to show their struggle against poverty, their need to survive. I can place them in the City of the Dead, or in small alleys around Khan-El-Khalili, children running barefoot, trusting their elders whose anxieties are mirrored in their banners of religious activism. I'll show my people's strength, how they enjoy the moment, I'll draw on their common sense and their love of laughter.

I'll switch to oils, create these works in bright tones, depict the strength of faces around me on the streets, all those who possess me by day, and visit me by night, their energy whispering in the darkness.

***

Sun shone into Nadia's eyes. Short shrubs scratched her feet. In the distance, the silvery olive of the water reflected light. On the opposite bank, a man squatted observing the herd then bent and washed his hands and face in the river. He shouted to the guide of the group across from him on the other bank, the crouching figure brown against the glare of light. Then he stood up and walked away. Nadia remembered Yasser, arms and legs in the river at the Delta Barrage. You could not live on this land and not believe in the river's power.

Yasser, I'm close to you. I take trips away from you, but I turn corners and find you. "Yasser," she called, her voice carrying across the water. Open light. Exhilaration of sound. She was shouting into the eye of the sun. Her voice travelled the intervening kilometres. "Yasser . . ." she shouted, unmindful of those around her.

Each part of her life was listening to the other; sea waves were flowing each to each, bouncing off an ocean, echoing in a central valley from a distant hill, crossing, rising, falling, listening, hearing the other in counterpoint. She was the river pouring into the sea, she the valley, receiving, attentive to time and consciousness.

***

The day is new, Yasser thought, dig the land here at Damietta. Have the men dig deeper and keep on digging. I need to do something tangible before Nadia gets here. Magda is dying, or dead. The last time I saw her, she was a shadow, blue skin under her eyes, gazing at someone, not me, at a shadow on the wall. I must save this land. Nadia will be here soon.

***

Yasser, I'm coming! We'll be lovers. I'll surround you. We will rent our Delta Barrage home not sell it, in case we want to return.

***

I haven't told you about our grandchild, Nadia. You're going to be a grandmother! Laura phoned me at the Delta Barrage to tell us she was expecting our first grandchild.

I told her, "Call him Noor!" She laughed and I continued, "What name better than 'Light'!"

She answered, "Maybe his second name will be Noor. But what if his sister gets here first?" I said, "Call her Manar, for 'Lighthouse'!"

Time to return, Nadia. Time to go home.

***

We'll fly together Yasser, wait for me.

***

Night. Waters glistened. Stars shone. The source of the river fed its tributaries as they raced to meet the sea.

THE END

Glossary

Chapter One

p. 1. *Jasmine*: white aromatic flower threaded into necklaces and sold as a traditional gift of love on the *Cornice* in Alexandria.

p. 1. *Alexandria*: city founded by Alexander the Great on the Mediterranean Sea, north west of Cairo.

—— *Ras El Bar*: seaside resort on the Mediterranean Sea, north west of Cairo.

p. 2. *Delta Barrage*: situated at the conflux of the two arms of the Nile—the Rosetta and the Damietta branches—a relatively small dam, one of the original controls of the annual Nile flood, before the construction of the High Aswan Dam.

—— *Luxor*: situated in Upper Egypt, the original capital of ancient Egypt after Memphis. It is the site of the famous Valleys of Kings and Queens where numerous royal tombs are dug in the side of granite mountains. Homer called it "Hundred gated Thebes".

p. 3. *Gallabiah*, a traditional long garb, often in white Egyptian cotton, worn by men to protect them from the sun's rays. Women wear black *gallabiahs* as a form of modesty.

—— *Cactus pear*. Fruit with rough green skin, white sweet flesh and large brown, smooth seeds.

p. 4. *Serwal*: male farmer's garb, a shorter form of *gallabiah* in Egyptian cotton, worn over long full pants. Sometimes includes a vest.

p. 6. *Cornice*: long shoreline road in Alexandria overlooking the Mediterranean Sea running across the entire breadth of the city.

p. 8. *Metro Cinema*: located in the center of downtown Alexandria—originally showed Metro Goldwyn Mayer films—was a meeting place for lovers. Plush, red interior, air-conditioning.

—— *El Mansoura:* city north of Cairo.

p. 10. *Gamal Abdel Nasser,* President of Egypt, had the High Aswan Dam built according to Russian architectural designs.

p. 13. *Khan-El-Khalili:* a bazaar in the ancient core of Cairo, renowned for its narrow cobbled streets, historic buildings, buzzing market of gold, silver and copper smiths, hand created jewelry and household items. A center for gold and silver jewelry, copper ware, materials, spices, towels, leather goods.

p. 15. *Sham El Nessim:* a traditional feast of spring and fertility of the soil following Easter, held in gardens and parks, and celebrated with *pita bread,* onions and *feseekh,* fish covered in the warm sand for a month then cleaned and preserved in olive oil.

—— *Mariout:* a town in the desert near a shallow salt lake south west of Alexandria

p. 16. *El Khanatir:* a large park near Cairo where people picnic on Sham El Nessim.

p. 18. *Ismailia:* sea-side resort on the Red Sea.

Chapter Two

p. 24. *Alf hamdoulla alla el salama:* a thousand welcomes and a safe arrival.

p. 29. *Nile Hilton:* a hotel, several storeys high, overlooking the River Nile at Kasr-El-Einy Bridge.

p. 32. *1967 war:* the year Israel gained control of Sinai and kept it until the Egypt-Israel Peace Accord of 1973.

p. 35. *Abu Simbel:* the site of two temples, the Great Temple of Ramses II and the Temple of Nefertari, his wife, raised with the help of international aid to the top of the plateau, to save them from the flooding waters of the River Nile after the construction of the High Dam at Aswan.

p. 37. *Abd El Halim Hafez:* popular Egyptian singer who died in his forties.

p. 41. *Cairo University,* in Giza: the most renowned university in Egypt and in the Arab Middle East.

Chapter Three

p. 46. *Fedan*: the Egyptian parallel of an acre, but smaller in size.

p. 59. *Cheops*: Pharaoh buried in the great pyramid of Giza.

p. 61 *Mastaba*: taken from the Egyptian word meaning an elongated bench, refers to a rectangular shaped rock tomb and granite coffin which housed the Pharaoh's body.

Chapter Four

p. 65. *The Lotus*: white and blue lily regarded as sacred in Ancient Egypt.

p. 72. *Douki*: old quarter in Cairo with narrow streets and keeling buildings housing numerous occupants in tight apartments.

p. 73. *Sakhia*: since ancient times, a method of irrigation in which a buffalo turns a water wheel with spokes which carry pails that raise water from the Nile and pour it into man-made canals.

p. 79. *Ouzo*: aniseed-flavoured alcoholic drink.

——— *Ramses II*: Pharaoh known as Ramses The Great. Reigned from c. 1292-1295 BC. Built vast monuments and statues including the rock temples at Abu Simbel, remarkable for their size and numbers.

——— *Amun*: chief god of the Thebans, (in ancient Luxor), from the beginning of the Middle Kingdom, and dominant divinity of the New Kingdom. He was a hidden god associated with the wind.

——— *Al Karnak Temple*: the great temple of Amun-Ra, which includes the famous Hypostyle hall of immense granite columns built by Ramses II.

Chapter Five

p. 87. *Edfu Temple*: built by Ptolemies around 300 BC, it remains one of the best preserved temples near Luxor.

p. 88. *Hathor*: female goddess bearing cow's horns, known as goddess of love and fertility. When Queen Hatchepsut's mother was expecting her daughter, she was led into the birthing chamber by animal headed gods, and her wet nurse was cow-headed Hathor.

—— *Nut*: sky goddess associated with the soul.

—— *Isis*: creator god Atum fashioned the gods from his spittle or semen. One pair of these was Isis and Osisris, sister-brother, wife and husband. Osiris, god of resurrection, was murdered by his evil brother Seth, and his limbs were strewn all over the land, but Isis managed to conceive a son by him posthumously. Their son Horus, associated with Re, is god of the sun. Isis travelled far and wide to collect Osiris's scattered limbs and assembled them together. Osiris became associated with fertility, resurrection and rebirth.

p. 96. *Valley of Kings*: situated on an island west of the Nile River at Luxor, this valley houses many tombs of Pharaohs including the treasure trove of King Tutankhamun.

—— *Kebab halla*: beef stew.

Chapter Six

p. 109. *Damietta*: the eastern tributary of the Nile pours into the Mediterranean Sea at the city of Dumyat.

p. 112. *Narguila*: water pipe from which the smoker inhales smoke after it passes through water and emerges relatively clean of burnt tobacco residue.

p. 117. *Cairo Museum*: near *Medan El Mahata*, or the Central Train Station. It houses most of the ancient Egyptian artifacts.

—— *Liberty Square*: a large square close to the Kasr-El-Einy Bridge and down town Cairo.

p. 121. *Sambousek*: a soft dough filled with dates made in the shape of a crescent.

—— *Turkish delight*: a sweet made of a chewy, jelly roll, filled with nuts, covered with icing sugar and cut into slices or squares.

Chapter Seven

p. 129. *Konafa*: a dessert made of shredded dough, filled with nuts and dipped in a lemon and sugar syrup.

p. 131. *Al Ahram*: national daily newspaper in Egypt.

p. 135. *Tutt*: reference to King Tutankhamun's international travelling exhibition which raised money for a new museum to be built in Cairo to house numerous new artefacts waiting to be housed.

p. 136. *El Hourania*: a quarter in Giza close to the Great Pyramids where the Wissa Wassef family factory is located. It employs illiterate bedouin and peasant women who create world-renowned tapestries which they weave on a loom without master-designs. These tapestries are bought for thousands of dollars and hang in the Louvre, in London, and elsewhere in Europe. The women receive no instruction, and they create their designs freehand as they weave. The colours for dyeing cotton and wool threads they extract from plants.

p. 142. *Fetir*: filo dough filled with feta cheese or minced meat.

p. 145. *Sidi Gaber Station*: central train station in Alexandria.

———— *Piastre*: one hundredth of an Egyptian pound comparable to the Canadian cent but one-fifth its value.

Chapter Eight

p. 154. *Baklava*: filo dough filled with a nut mixture and dipped in a sugar and lemon syrup.

p. 161. *Ya hagga*: translated literally, "Oh blessed woman who has taken the sacred pilgrimage to Mecca."

p. 170. *Abd-El-Wahab*: popular Egyptian singer and composer who dominated Egyptian music for at least four decades in the twentieth century.

Chapter Nine

p. 180. *City of The Dead*: huge historic Islamic cemetery situated near Gabal El Mokatam in the centre of Cairo contains numerous above-ground buildings serving as family tombs. Today, this cemetery shelters the homeless. Having tried and failed at evicting the squatters, the government has introduced electricity and water to the site.

p. 189. *Kahk*: a dessert for festive occasions like a soft short-bread filled with nuts or Turkish Delights, pinched into festive designs and covered with icing sugar.

p. 192. *Shawerma*: lamb barbequed on a spit, thinly sliced and piled into pita bread with *humus*.

Chapter Ten

p. 200. *Foul medames*: fava beans with olive oil, lemon and cumin.

—— *Loofa*: a natural plant used as a body scrubber.

p. 201. *Shawabti*: small vessels buried with Pharaohs to receive their souls after they sojourn in the underworld.

p. 202. *Groppi*: dessert restaurant in the center of downtown Cairo.

p. 203. *Old Shoubra*: an old quarter in Cairo, with narrow streets and old, dark buildings.

p. 206. *Rakset el tahteeb*: folk dance enacted by men holding sticks and synchronizing their movements to dance as one entity.

Chapter Eleven

p. 220. *Aswan*: city south of Luxor on the River Nile. Aswan is one of the most popular winter resorts in Egypt, known for its beautiful scenery, mild weather, dry heat, daily sun, rolling rocky mountains and sandy hills. Situated at the widest point in the Nile River, it is the ideal site for the High Dam.

p. 221. *Old Nile meter*: marked on high granite rocks at Aswan. This was the old Nile meter used to gauge the elevation of the river during its annual flooding season.

p. 227. *The Sakkara pyramid*: a step pyramid of King Zoser, 2816 B.C., the most ancient stone building in the world.

Chapter Twelve

p. 239. *Muazzin*: the chanter of *surahs*, or sayings, from the Holy Koran.

p. 241. *Semiramis*: a large, expensive hotel on the bank of the River Nile at Kasr-El-Einy Bridge in Cairo.

p. 242. *Bhagavad Gita*: an Indian poem composed between the second century B.C. and the second century A.D. in the form of a dialogue, stressing the importance of doing one's duty and of having faith in God.

—— *Copts*: Christians of Egypt estimated by the government to be around 10% of the population, and by the Copts to be 15%-20%.

—— *Akhenaton*: King Akhenaton of the Middle Kingdom masterminded a religious revolution establishing Aten sun disk as the only god of Egypt, thereby instigating a backlash from the High Priests who labelled him an atheist.

—— *Crook*: a hooked staff of Pharaoh which was a symbol of kingship.

—— *Medan El Tahrir*: a major square at the heart of Cairo near the Nile at Kasr-El-Einy Bridge. Translated literally, it means Freedom Square.

p. 247. *Mohammed Ibn Qalawan*: mosque at the Citadel in Old Cairo, built in 1335 by Salah El Din for the protection of the capital of Egypt from incursion by the enemy.

p. 250. *San Stefano Hotel* and casino: situated on the Cornice facing the Mediterranean Sea—between Stanley Bay and Gleem beaches in Alexandria—was considered an elite haunt for famous visitors.

—— *El Esha*: Muslim call to prayers, chanted by the *Muazzin* in a mosque at sundown, and announced through loudspeakers all over the streets in the community.

Chapter 13
p. 258. *Garden City*: a green area at the heart of Cairo known for its large, old trees and beautiful parks.

—— *Medan*: square.

p. 264. *Naguib Mahfouz*: Egyptian novelist who won the Nobel Prize for Literature in 1982 for his depiction of core Egyptian culture of the less affluent areas of Cairo, as well as the daily lives of people who enjoyed manifold vices and clandestine affairs. He aroused hostility from fundamental and conservative citizens of his country.

—— *Tewfik El Hakim*: Egyptian dramatist and essayist famous in the fifties and sixties for depicting daily Egyptian lives and customs.

—— *Ihsan Abdel Khodus*: an Egyptian writer whose novels—published in serial installments during the sixties and seventies in *Al Ahram*, the Egyptian national newspaper—were well known for what were then considered to be passages of torrid sexual descriptions, a relatively new phenomenon in the newspapers of the day. Avidly followed by the sex-denied young people of the time.

Chapter Fourteen

p. 273. *Khamseen winds*: warm March desert winds, carrying volumes of sand, and ushering in a short spring season.

p. 281. *Mashrabiah*: historic Islamic intricate designs of wood doors, sequestered balconies and windows in arabesque designs, including window screens behind which veiled women hid and watched the street below unobserved by passers-by.

p. 286. *Roxy*: square at the centre of the original Heliopolis, before this suburb of Cairo sprawled out into subsidiary urban developments reaching far into the desert up to the Cairo Airport.

—— *Tarik El Sarayat*: a road, which translated literally, means Road of the Palaces. A long, beautiful street in Heliopolis flanked by upscale villas, divided by a wide boulevard of grass with two rows of banyan trees and evenly spaced stone benches.

p. 289. *Eid* of *Ramadan*: a three-day Muslim feast celebrating the end of fasting during the Holy Month of Ramadan, during which Muslims abstain from food, drink, cigarettes and sex from dawn to sunset.

—— *Sharbat*: a traditional drink for feasts and weddings, made of concentrated fruit juice and sugar, then served diluted with iced water.

p. 295. *Sharm El Sheik*: a sea-side resort on the Red Sea, known for its beautiful coral reefs and exotic fish, great sandy beaches, popular among tourists from Italy, Germany, France and other European countries.

***

Acknowledgements

My late publisher, Professor David Knight of Victoria College, University of Toronto, urged me to write fiction. I had been creating and publishing poetry, the occasional short story, and drawings and paintings. David's enthusiasm for writing and all things imaginative inspired those who knew him, and for me, fiction became an engaging journey into subterranean caves of discovery. My belated gratitude to David, and a hearty thanks to my fellow Toronto writers who read my manuscript at its inception and offered me insightful comments: Susan Aihoshi, Frank Beltrano, Fredric C. Ford, Gordon Brown, Diana Armstrong, David Blostein of University of Toronto, and David and M.L. Knight. My special thanks to the late Glenn Clever and to Frank Tierney of Borealis Press for their unwavering support of my work. To Janet Shorten my sincere thanks for her invaluable editorial comments, and to George Bayne, designer of the book cover, for his insightful response to the author's intent.

Canada inspired me with the core theme for *The Jasmine Garden* and Egypt with the vibrant locale: two landscapes entwined in my mind and heart, enriching me with their melodic counterpoint. I am privileged to have grown up in the venerable land of Egypt, with its distinctive ancient culture, its contrasting landscape of desert, green fields, the grand Nile River, the Suez Canal, Sinai, the Red Sea, the turquoise waters of the Mediteranean Sea. I am grateful to have had the opportunity to choose peaceful Canada for my home. Here I met my husband, Mohammed, had our daughter Madiha and our son Hisham, pursued my teaching career, engaged in my twin passions—writing and painting—and enjoyed the exuberant company of my grandchildren.

To the Canada Council, my abiding gratitude for the scholarship that brought me to Toronto to obtain my graduate degrees in English literature and afforded me the opportunity to see, to love and to adopt this bountiful, four-seasoned land for my home.

Hamilton, June 7, 2005

* * *

Credit

An excerpt from *The Jasmine Garden*—Nadia's earliest dream in search of a home with her two young sons—was published in *Kairos*, No. 5 (edited by Robert Megan and Royston Tester, Hamilton, Ontario, 1993) under a working title.

Also by Soraya Erian:

Books of Poems and Drawings
Earth Sphere
The Death of Meleika Erian
The World is Everything I am
I've Been a Fish Before
Ariadne's Thread
In The Eye Of The Sun, a prodigal returns

Book of Poems and Paintings
Were You My Ariel, Song for Samira

MEMBER OF SCABRINI GROUP

Québec, Canada
2005